Going Down

One man wants her heart. The other wants her dead...

Eleanor Owen needs to get out of Chicago and quick. It's
not that she doesn't want to obey the subpoena to testify
against her drug-trafficking ex-boyfriend. It's making it to the
witness stand alive, should a dirty cop make good on his
threats.

Tiny, remote Wyattville, Oregon, looks like the perfect place
to disappear, but it's hard to blend into the woodwork when one
of the town's infamous namesakes sends her heart racing.
Worse, Mr. Tall, Hot and Packing is the town sheriff, which
means she should stay as far away from him as possible.

Tyson Wyatt is positive the sexy new girl in town is hiding
something. Question is, what? He vows to feel out her secrets—
including what she feels like beneath him. Preferably naked.
Until then, he's not buying the story she's selling.

Their chemistry is sheet-melting hot, and Ellie realizes
much too late that the man with the badge is as dangerous to
her heart as her ex is to her life...

*Warning: A city girl on the run, and a small-town sheriff set
to seduce. Explicit sex. Dirty talk. A hint of danger. Oral sex with
a cupcake.*

D1114186

Command and Control

He's afraid of losing his grip. She's about to untie his last knot...

Megan Asher has a thriving career, looks, self-confidence to spare. It all means little without the love of her life. Trevor has returned from deployment in Afghanistan a haunted man, emotionally distant and unwilling to connect—except in bed. Then even that fragile thread snaps. Brokenhearted, she is forced to call off their wedding and, after a few months' separation, try to move on.

With every aspect of his life spinning out of his once-legendary control, Trevor Wyatt convinces himself that Megan is better off—and safer—as far away from his demons as possible. Until he comes back to town for his brother's wedding, and discovers Megan is dating.

Suddenly realizing what he's thrown away, he vows to breach the fortress she's built around her heart. They come together in a cataclysm of rekindled passion that unleashes the very demons he never wanted her to witness.

Back to square one, Megan realizes she must take the ultimate risk to slip past Trevor's defenses. Give him control in the one place she can. The bedroom. The seductive move is one she prays will be the first step in helping heal him and their love.

Warning: This book contains a tormented military hero and the sexy woman he's determined to win back. Mild BDSM and kink, and blow jobs of the beverage and non-beverage kind.

Flash Point

One taste of her lips, and friendship is off the menu.

Kate has always been everybody's friend and the de-facto little sister to the Wyatt brothers. But her feelings for Todd Wyatt, the town's hottest firefighter, run far beyond the sibling variety. Not that he's ever noticed.

After years of nursing her crush, Kate decides it's time to take action. Except she has one awkward little secret: she's still a virgin. She hopes she can seduce Todd without him realizing just how inexperienced she is.

In Todd's mind, Kate's the sweet girl he teases and hits up for free cupcakes. One surprise kiss over the summer, though, and suddenly she's jumped from the platonic side of his brain to the want-her-in-my-bed side. Even though the last thing he wants is to lose her friendship, his resistance to her determined seduction is slipping. Fast.

When malicious attacks on her bakery escalate, it soon becomes clear that for all Kate's friends, she's made at least one big enemy. And if they don't figure it out soon, things could take a deadly turn.

Warning: A sexy firefighter. A virgin bakery owner. A dollop of role playing, kinky costumes, friends becoming lovers, and a little danger along the way.

Look for these titles by
Shelli Stevens

Now Available:

Holding Out for a Hero

Shelli Stevens

SAMHAIN
PUBLISHING

Samhain Publishing, Ltd.
11821 Mason Montgomery Road, 4B
Cincinnati, OH 45249
www.samhainpublishing.com

Holding Out for a Hero
Print ISBN: 978-1-60928-728-3
Going Down Copyright © 2012 by Shelli Stevens
Command and Control Copyright © 2012 by Shelli Stevens
Flash Point Copyright © 2012 by Shelli Stevens

Editing by Tera Kleinfelter
Cover by Scott Carpenter

Going Down, ISBN 978-1-60928-112-0
First Samhain Publishing, Ltd. electronic publication: July 2010
Command and Control, ISBN 978-1-60928-271-4
First Samhain Publishing, Ltd. electronic publication: December 2010
Flash Point, ISBN 978-1-60928-381-0
First Samhain Publishing, Ltd. electronic publication: March 2011
First Samhain Publishing, Ltd. print publication: August 2012

Contents

Going Down

Dedication

Thanks to Becca from the beach and Danielle for your advice on all things legal (and Danielle for being such an awesome beta reader!). To all my family and friends, and of course to my editor, for your support and making me a better writer. And finally a shoutout to the folks I got thrown together with for almost two months, it was great getting to know you and I hope life treats you well.

Chapter One

She had to get out of here. Leave Chicago and find some podunk town where nobody would find her. She needed to disappear. At least until the trial was over.

Eleanor Owens shoved an unsteady hand through her black hair and swallowed against the knot of anxiety in her throat that seemed to have taken up permanent residence since she'd been served the subpoena two days ago to testify against her ex-boyfriend.

Like hell that was going to happen.

Her stomach rolled and she let out a shaky breath. Easy for the court system to just beckon her to the witness stand to testify against James, but she didn't trust their promises to keep her safe. If she'd learned anything from her brutal ex—besides making herself as invisible as possible when he was angry—it was that people couldn't be trusted.

Blinking the sleep from her eyes, she moved the cursor on her laptop over the map of Oregon, scanning the cities. She picked a couple towns and ran a population search for them on a search engine. None felt right.

Too many people... Too few people.

And then she found it, a small town near the Oregon Coast called Wyattville. No towns or cities too close by, and it had a population of just over a couple thousand.

Ellie nibbled her lip and hesitated. She was risking everything. Abandoning her apartment, leaving all her yoga classes without a teacher, emptying her bank account, and essentially disappearing. Everyone would be looking for her, but hopefully wouldn't find her.

Was she really going to do this? Go and hide? When she was a witness who could be really effective in helping put James away...?

An image flickered in her mind. Lionel Maliano, a cop, sitting in his unmarked car across the street from her apartment while she'd been served. She remembered the white curl of his cigarette smoke and the dark expression on his face as he'd watched her.

And then, the moment the woman at her door had left, Lionel had come to her apartment and knocked. She hadn't been stupid enough to answer, but he'd gotten his message through regardless. Calling softly though the door, *"You don't know nothing. Just remember that, bitch."*

An icy shiver of fear slid down her spine at the memory, leaving nausea in its wake. She knew his words were a threat. Knew exactly what her ex-boyfriend and his friends—cops included—were capable of. She bit her lip and printed the map of Oregon.

Maybe leaving town *was* an extreme choice, but it was the only one she had.

Tyson steered the patrol car onto First Avenue and gave a small smile at the familiar scene. Summer was in full swing, with the kids out of school and the tourists trickling into town. Even though it wasn't even noon, a line had already formed at the Coastal Creamery for ice cream.

He cruised down the road, finding no signs of trouble stirring, but then really not expecting any. The sheriff's department in Wyattville was made up of himself and five other deputies. Though the crime rate in town wasn't nearly what it was in the bigger neighboring cities, there were still a handful of calls that came in during the week to keep them busy. Granted most of them were small thefts or trespassing calls.

Scratching the back of his head, Tyson rolled the car to a halt at a stop sign. It was a slow morning. Maybe he should just head back to the station and catch up on some paperwork.

His gaze slid to the left, up the hill toward the residential area of town. Curiosity simmered in his gut and he narrowed his eyes, thinking about the Bakemans' old house that had just been rented out for the summer.

From everything he'd heard around town, the renter was a woman in her mid-twenties.

Maybe he oughtta stop by and introduce himself. Hell, he

pretty much did it whenever somebody new came to stay for a while. And the Bakemans' house wasn't too far from his place, just about a half mile up a dirt road—they were practically neighbors. The area was probably one of the more isolated places in town.

Flipping on the left turn signal, Tyson turned and headed up the hill. No reason why he shouldn't drop on by.

Ellie set the book she was reading down with a sigh and lifted her head to gaze out the window. Beyond the hills and trees, there was the faintest hint of blue. The Pacific Ocean.

Longing twisted inside her and she bit her lip. She was so tempted to say screw it all, leave the house she'd rented and go explore the beach. Or the cute little part of downtown she'd only been to once. Good God, *anything* to get outside.

It wasn't that the house was awful or anything, it was wonderfully quaint and cozy. A small, two-bedroom cottage with a great kitchen and nice view. She knew the house inside and out. Had explored every nook and cranny, knew every spot where the floorboards creaked, had discovered that the hot water had a tendency to scald.

It was like she'd lived here for years. When, really, it had only been five days since she'd gotten off the Greyhound bus in the larger neighboring town and then taken an expensive taxi ride into Wyattville.

Five days since she'd emptied her bank account and fled Chicago. She'd paid cash for everything, having hidden her bank and credit cards before leaving. Fortunately, the couple who'd rented her the house had been more than happy to accept cash as her deposit and two months worth of rent.

Hearing the soft bubble of water from the kitchen, Ellie stood and headed for the kitchen to check on her eggs.

Maybe she could go into town today and buy some more groceries, though she really didn't need any, since she'd bought a ton during her one and only trip to the store.

The whole point of her being here was keeping a low profile, not that there was a chance anyone would figure out who she was. How could they? The trial might have been hot news in Chicago, but she was in a small town in Oregon.

As she peered into the pot of eggs, watching them spin over themselves in the water, her stomach growled. Soft-boiled eggs and toast had always been her favorite. She'd grown up on it. It was good old-fashioned comfort food, and right now she needed the comfort.

Ellie pulled the pot from the burner and was about to reach for a spoon, when the sound of crunching tires hit her ears. She stilled and listened carefully, but there was no mistaking the sound. It was a car, and it seemed to be coming down her little dirt road.

With the pot still in her hand, she rushed to the window.

"Oh my God," she whispered. Her heart slammed against her ribcage and her mouth went dry. "This isn't happening."

But the writing on the side of the approaching white car clearly identified it as a sheriff's vehicle. How in the hell had they found her?

When a tall man unfurled himself from the car, she stumbled away from the window, her empty stomach churning and her hands shaking so badly that the water sloshed over the side of the pot, scalding her hand.

"*Shit.*"

Ellie thrust the pot back onto the stove as her head moved from side to side in denial. There was no way she was going back to Chicago. She couldn't testify. She was as good as dead if she got on that witness stand.

Terror stretched its cold hands through every inch of her body, and when a knock came at the front door, she completely lost it and fled out the back.

"Well, that's funny." Tyson pursed his lips. He could've sworn he heard someone inside.

He walked around the porch to peer in the kitchen window and immediately spotted the pot on the stove. Water boiled over the sides and onto the floor.

His brows drew together as his gut tightened with the instinct that something was off. A second later, a door slammed from the back of the house.

Tyson moved quickly to the end of the porch, just in time to see a blur of black hair and bare legs, before the woman headed for the gathering of trees at the edge of the property.

Without a moment's hesitation, he hopped the porch railing and took off after her.

Was she running from *him*? Why?

He shook his head, reminding himself that he didn't really need to ask himself why. He knew the answer. He was in uniform and driving a marked car. And when a person ran from law enforcement, it was generally because they had something to hide.

"Stop!" he hollered, increasing his pace.

But, if anything, it spooked the woman even more and she disappeared into the woods.

Tyson didn't lose speed. Was this the tenant of the house running? Or had someone else broken in? Either way, he wasn't letting her get away that easily. Not that he thought for a minute she would, the woman was heading right toward the cliffs above the beach, so she was going to have to stop at some point. And when she did, she'd have some explaining to do.

Even as he gained ground, his frustration slipped away and unease replaced it as they began to approach the break in the trees.

She wasn't slowing down. Jesus, didn't she realize there was barely six feet out of the forest before the cliff's ledge?

"Stop!" he screamed again, almost an arm's length behind her now. "Dammit, lady, stop before you kill yourself!"

The woman burst from the trees without decreasing her speed and Tyson's heart tripped with fear.

Her sharp scream reverberated as she finally saw the cliff. Her toes dug into the dirt as she tried to halt her inevitable fall.

Tyson lurched forward, grabbed her around the waist and spun them away from the edge just as her right foot went over.

Her soft body slammed against his, causing him to stumble backward and farther away from the edge. He hit the ground first, falling on his ass before she fell on top of him. His hands slid to cup the roundness of her bottom, while her soft chest pressed against his face as her arms flailed to the ground beneath them for purchase.

Jesus. Tyson let out a strangled groan as his body instantly responded to their intimate position.

Her frightened whimper and trembling body reminded him how close she'd been to going over the cliff.

"Are you okay?" he asked gruffly, rolling them so she fell back onto the dirt and then knelt above her.

Wide hazel eyes stared up at him even as she made the tiniest nod.

He grunted and slid his gaze over her slight frame, taking in her flawless pale skin. Breasts that were small, but looked like they could still fill his hand, pushed against her thin pink tank top. Her stomach was toned and her hips flared just a bit under tiny denim shorts. Her feet were dirty from running bare through the forest, even as her dainty toes shone with a glittery pink polish.

Damn but she was a sexy little thing...and she was also terrified. Whether of him, or nearly running over a cliff, who knew.

But the fear in her eyes reminded him to stop thinking with his dick, and get back into sheriff mode.

"You could've been killed if you'd fallen off that cliff, do you realize that?" he said tersely.

Again, a tiny nod.

He narrowed his gaze. "Good. Now would you please explain why you were running from me, ma'am?"

Chapter Two

Why she was running from him? Ellie licked her lips, trying to slow the furious pounding of her heart and the trembling in her body.

Did he seriously not know? Or was this one of those cop mind tricks where he just wanted her to confess first? She stared up at him, her mind spinning with what to say.

She could barely even think, let alone talk, after nearly running full throttle off the edge of the cliff. How had she not noticed it was *a cliff*? She'd been aware of the ocean from the window of the house but assumed the land would have a gradual incline down to the beach. Not a freaking cliff!

He asked you a question, Eleanor, now think.

It didn't help that the sheriff was ridiculously hot. Blond hair and blue eyes, with laugh lines around his eyes that made her guess the scowl on his face right now was abnormal.

And when he'd pulled her back from the cliff and she'd fallen on top of him...his face had been right against her breasts, and his breath a hot caress against her skin. The memory sent another shiver through her, but this one had little to do with fear. Her cheeks flushed with warm color, even as the heat spread to other areas of her body, creating a soft ache low in her belly and making her all too aware of her own femininity.

"Ma'am?" the sheriff's tone sharpened.

He was still waiting for an answer. Then again, he was still leaning over her, keeping her firmly between his solid-looking chest and the hard ground. Shouldn't he have pulled her up and handcuffed her or something?

"I don't like law enforcement," she blurted, the only response she could think of that wouldn't give her away.

"You don't like law enforcement?" he repeated, his eyes crinkling with amusement as a smile swept across his face.

The smile transformed him, made him even sexier. Her breath caught and her pulse quickened. She shifted beneath him and averted her gaze.

"No, I don't," she whispered.

"Really? Would you like to tell me why?"

"I don't trust them." She shrugged, knowing it was a safe answer, because it really wasn't that far from the truth. "I saw you coming up the porch and just panicked."

"So you *are* the tenant at the Bakemans' place?"

"Yes."

"All right." He arched a brow. "A lot of people don't trust law enforcement, that doesn't mean they're going to run like hell when they see one."

He finally stood up, as if he'd just realized that almost straddling the woman you'd been chasing down wasn't entirely appropriate.

When he stretched to his full height her mouth went dry and her heart tripped. Jeez, he was tall. And so strong. Not to mention sexy...

Stop thinking about how damn sexy he is!

Her gaze slid to his uniform, where the name Wyatt was sewn across the front. Wyatt? As in the town of Wyattville? Whoa. That *had* to be a coincidence.

"No answer?" he prodded and held out a hand to her.

She grudgingly took it, inhaling sharply at the slight tingle that raced up her arm as she allowed him to help her to her feet. Even standing next to him, she barely reached his shoulders, and she wouldn't classify herself as short.

"Okay," he said quietly, not releasing her hand. "Well then, why don't you give me your name?"

He wanted her name? Did that mean he *didn't* know who she was? Her heart thudded furiously and she silently cursed herself for panicking and fleeing the house. Of course she'd made him suspicious. Running from the police was like waving a red flag at a bull.

Maybe even more so here, being that he lived and worked in a small town. The most excitement he likely saw was responding to cow-tipping incidents. Still, she hesitated to give him her real name. Even if he *didn't* know who she was, the moment she gave him her real name, it would be all too easy to find out.

Knowing it was her only option, she went for the backup plan.

"Elinamifia Owens." She hoped her cousin Mimi would forgive her. But, it was the perfect solution. They were close in age, and she could answer any questions if he actually ran the name.

"Eli..." His brows drew together.

"Namifia."

"That's...a, ugh, great name."

"Thank you."

She tried not to let her lips quirk, because it was a bitch of a name and her cousin had threatened to have it legally changed more than once while growing up. They'd spent more than a few slumber parties mourning their parents' penchants for nineteenth-century names.

"Where are you from originally?" he asked.

"Brooklyn."

"And how old are you?"

"Does this matter really?"

"Could you just answer the question, Elin—Ms. Owens."

Ellie ground her teeth together before answering. "Twenty-four. And why are you still holding my hand?"

He grinned again. "Maybe because I like holding your hand."

"What?" Was he for real? She tried to tug free, but his grip tightened and his smile faded as he stared down at where their hands were joined.

"Did you cut yourself?"

"I don't think so." But she looked down and sure enough her palm was scraped and red with almost dry blood. "Oh...I didn't even feel it."

"We should go clean that up. Come on Elin—dammit, do you have a nickname or something?"

First he flirted and now he was swearing? Jeez, the cops in this town were a little...different.

"A nickname?" she hesitated, and thought about it for a second before saying, "My family calls me Ellie."

Which was actually a perfect compromise. It was the nickname she went by instead of Eleanor, and it could work well with her cousin's name.

"All right, Ellie. Let's get you back to the house and clean that up."

She followed him back through the trees with a scowl, trying not to notice whether his butt looked good beneath the uniform. Unfortunately, she did notice, and it indeed looked pretty nice.

"So, Ellie," he began conversationally as he held the door to her house open. "If I go run your name right now, what am I going to find?"

Her stomach rolled and she tried to keep her expression neutral as she stepped past him.

"A twenty-four-year-old chick from Brooklyn with no record."

Ellie bit her lip. *At least, you'd better still be keeping your nose clean, Mimi.*

"Great. If you wouldn't mind spelling out your name for me?"

She turned and found him behind her with a pen and small notebook in hand.

"Of course." Forcing a smile, she rattled off the spelling then turned away again.

Eleanor made a beeline for the bathroom, grabbing a small towel and running it under the water. Before she could tend to the scratch, the sheriff was right behind her. He took the towel from her hand.

"Let me," he said softly and caught her wrist, lifting her palm upward so he could dab it with the cloth.

Her pulse fluttered again as she watched him gently cleanse the small wound, his face crinkled with concentration.

She was way too attracted to him, Ellie realized with unease. Oh, this guy was trouble and in a big way. For the briefest second, she thought about packing up and fleeing town the moment he left—*if* he left and was convinced that she was some criminal.

But packing up and leaving just wasn't an option, or would have to be a worst-case scenario one. She'd already paid rent for two months on this place. Cash. And she didn't have bottomless funds.

"How's that feel?"

She blinked out of her thoughts to discover he was watching her closely again instead of her wound.

"It's fine," she managed to reply huskily. "Thank you."

He stepped closer, leaning forward to drop the washcloth in the sink, but not moving away after. Their chests almost touched and his face was just inches from hers.

Ellie's body stirred with awareness at his proximity, her nipples tightening beneath her tank top. She licked her lips, acutely aware of the thin cotton covering her bare breasts.

"How long do you plan on being in town?" he asked softly, his gaze on her mouth.

Her heart thumped wildly and she had the craziest urge to lean forward and press her mouth against his.

"Probably just a couple of months. Getting out of the city for the summer..."

"Well then, Ellie," he murmured. "I have a feeling we'll be seeing each other again real soon. So you'd better get over that distrust of law enforcement bit."

Her knees almost buckled when he stepped away without touching her. Disappointment swept through her. *You're an idiot. Being disappointed that a cop you don't know didn't kiss you?*

"I'll, um, work on it." She cleared her throat. "Was there a reason you dropped by in the first place?"

"Just wanted to welcome you to Wyattville and introduce myself." He laughed and shook his head. "Damn, guess I forgot to do both of those, now didn't I? The name's Tyson Wyatt and welcome to town."

She followed him as he headed toward the front door. "So that Wyatt part. Umm, you're not like named after the town or something, are you?"

"Descended from the original founders," he called out as he stepped onto the porch. When he reached his squad car, he turned and glanced back up at her. "And there's a good handful of us Wyatts, Ellie. Just to warn you."

With a wink, he climbed into his car and backed away.

Ellie stood on the porch for a moment, wondering what the hell had just happened and what kind of crazy-ass town this was anyway.

Tyson steered his patrol car back onto Main Street, his brows once again drawn together in consternation.

Well, one thing was blatantly clear. Elina-however-the-hell-you-said-it was one desirable woman. But she was also hiding something, and he sure planned on getting to the bottom of just what that something was. Already he had a call in to Julianne at dispatch to do a check on her.

He hit the brakes as a familiar teenager darted into the empty road and came running up to the driver's window of his vehicle.

He lowered the window and called, "How you doing, Amie?"

"I got into Stanford, Sheriff Wyatt! I'm not sure if you heard already, but I'm totally excited."

"That's great, Amie." He patted her hand, genuinely happy for the shy and smart girl he'd watched grow up over the years. "I knew you'd get in. Congratulations."

Amie's smile widened. "Thanks! And, hey, your brothers are stirring up trouble down at Kate's Cakes, you should totally go check on them."

"I'll drop by." He reached for the wheel again and winked. "Congrats again on Stanford, Amie. Say hi to your folks."

"Will do."

A minute later, he parked the patrol car next to Kate's shop, smiling fondly. God he loved this town. Sure, some of the folks had the urge to leave at some point, like Amie. Whether it was for school, to seek out a more exciting life, or whatever oats needed sowing, but most of them eventually came back. He was the perfect example.

After climbing out of the patrol car, Tyson headed to the shop and then ducked slightly to get his tall frame under the pink overhang that was supposed to resemble the frosting on a cupcake. He entered just in time to hear his brother begging for food.

"Come on, Kate, just one chocolate cupcake," Todd pleaded with his most charming grin. "Besides, have you supported your local firefighter today?"

Tyson rolled his eyes and approached the counter, wondering how many times his brother had used that line to get free food from Kate. Although, it probably didn't help that Kate had been nursing a crush on the youngest Wyatt brother for years now.

And Kate's scowl wasn't convincing, because her cheeks were flushed as she muttered, "I *support my local firefighter* every day of the week! If I give you cupcakes all the time, Todd, I swear to God, I'll be working for free." Still, a moment later, she reached for one of the frosted treats.

"I'll support the firefighters today," Tyson intervened with a grimace. "Just put it on my tab, Kate."

"Ty, when did you get here?" Todd turned away from the counter, cupcake in hand and flirting with Kate forgotten.

"Just dropping in for a few," Tyson murmured, feeling a twinge of sympathy for Kate when disappointment flashed in her gaze. But then she lowered her head and busied herself with something behind the counter.

"Coming in for breakfast?" Trevor, the oldest Wyatt brother, called out from where he sat by the window, reading the paper. He'd driven down for the weekend from Fort Lewis in Washington State, where he was currently stationed in the Army.

"I would, but some of us work for a living." Tyson grinned and scratched the back of his neck. "Got a question for you guys, though. Anyone know anything about the new gal renting the Bakemans' place?"

Trevor shrugged, but didn't lift his gaze from the paper. "Heard she's hot."

"Wait, what's this about a new hot chick in town?" Todd asked, pulling out a chair at the table.

Annoyance had Tyson's smile tightening. Usually the fact that Todd flirted with anyone with breasts amused him, but thinking about his younger brother dropping by Ellie's place wasn't quite as funny this time.

"Don't know much about her. But I'm planning on remedying that," Tyson admitted.

Trevor lowered his coffee mug as his brows rose. "Interesting. I do believe our brother just staked claim on the new chick."

"Suck it, Trevor. I'm just saying—"

"That you think she's hot and we should back the hell off. We got it, bro," Todd inserted before taking a huge bite of his cupcake.

Tyson stared at them in disbelief, heat stealing up his neck. Staking his claim on Ellie? Hell, he didn't even know her. All he knew was she was a stranger in town who ran from law enforcement. Which was *not* a good sign.

"Shit, you guys are impossible," he grumbled. "Let me know if you hear anything about her."

Then he turned to leave the shop and head back to his patrol car to see what dispatch had discovered.

Chapter Three

Ellie sat at the small table in the kitchen while waiting for her steaks to broil. She offered another mutinous glare at the computer in the corner and kicked her foot against a chair leg.

"You can't tempt me," she muttered. "You're probably dial-up Internet anyway."

But dammit, the computer *did* tempt her. She was addicted to her email—could barely go a few hours without refreshing it. And it had now been *how many days* since she'd last checked her inbox?

It was just too risky, though. She'd watched enough thriller films to be slightly paranoid about that kind of thing. The police knew she was missing now and might be checking her email and cell phone activity. Which was why she'd left her Blackberry in her apartment too—she simply couldn't trust herself not to give into the temptation to use it.

Oh, God, her Blackberry... Her fingers flexed, itching with the familiar urge to send a text. A groan of self-pity built in her throat as she stood up to check on the steaks.

"Oh, sweet, sweet, Blackberry, someday we'll be reunited," she muttered and then nodded at the steaks.

Medium rare. Perfect. One for dinner, and she'd keep the other for lunch tomorrow, saving her from having to cook again. Although, cooking had somewhat become her source of entertainment.

She grabbed a potholder and pulled the steaks from the oven. As she began to set them down a sharp rap came at the door.

Jumping with a curse, she dropped the pan fully onto the stove and placed a hand over her pounding heart.

Really? Again?

She moved toward the window, experiencing a sense of déjà

vu, which only doubled when she spotted the sheriff's car outside.

"Oh you've got to be kidding me." She shoved a strand of hair from her eyes, ignoring the way her pulse quickened.

And she knew it wasn't just from the possibility that he'd discovered she wasn't who she claimed to be.

She considered putting on a sweater, since she was still in the thin tank top and pants she'd worn to do yoga in. But then another knock came and she muttered under her breath, moving to answer it.

"Sheriff Wyatt." She forced a pleasant expression as she swung the door open. "Something I can help you with?"

Tyson leaned against the doorjamb, a disarming smile on his face and a bottle of wine in his hand.

"Thought I'd drop by and see if you wanted to have dinner."

Ellie blinked, opening her mouth to reply, but then closed it again. Was the sheriff hitting on her?

"Oh, well, I just cooked some steaks..." she protested lamely.

"Great. Steaks. Plural. As in enough for two?" His smile widened as he straightened and stepped through the doorway. "Now there's an offer I can't refuse."

It hadn't been an offer, dammit! She bit back the words and gave an uneasy laugh. "Umm—"

"I promise to return the favor, Ellie," he murmured with a wink, shutting the door and taking a step toward her. "Tomorrow you can come to my place and I'll cook. I make a mean lasagna."

Oh, yeah, he was definitely hitting on her.

Ellie unconsciously backed away from him, completely thrown off balance by his directness. Her butt bumped against the floor-to-ceiling bookshelf and she came to an abrupt halt.

Tyson took another step forward, until his hips brushed hers, pressing her back against the wooden shelf. The smell of soap and woodsy cologne immediately tickled her senses. He'd changed out of his uniform and through his jeans she could feel the thickness of his cock and the heat of his hard body.

Her mind screamed at how absolutely bizarre this was. She didn't trust him—didn't trust any law enforcement officer right now. And yet, having the sheriff's muscled body pressed up against hers sent awareness sizzling through her. Tightening her nipples and creating a throbbing ache between her thighs.

What was it about him that made her want to do all kinds of raunchy, naughty things that would probably have gotten her kicked out of Catholic school eight years ago?

"You know, Ellie, we're neighbors."

"Are we?" And *why* did her voice squeak?

"Yeah. I'm just a couple minutes up the road." His gaze met hers, the pupils in his clear blue eyes dilated. "So if you need to borrow a cup of sugar, or...something, all you need to do is ask."

Ellie swallowed hard and gave a quick nod. "I-I'll remember that."

"You do that." He set down the bottle of wine on the shelf, his face drawing even nearer to hers. "You know what else?"

Mutely, she shook her head, not even about to guess what he was going to say next. Her mouth watered and it had nothing to do with the steaks in the kitchen.

It had been months since she'd had sex, and right now she was on the verge of grabbing the back of his head and kissing the hell out of the slightly loony—or maybe just drunk—sheriff.

He lowered his head, until his mouth was just a breath's away from hers. "I had your name run."

And just like that, her arousal vanished. Drying up as fear closed off her throat. She couldn't reply, even if she'd wanted to. Just lifted one brow and made a small gurgle of sound as she exhaled.

"You were right. Twenty-four-year old from Brooklyn," he murmured, tracing her jaw with the backs of two fingers. "But you weren't entirely truthful, were you, sweetheart?"

Her knees buckled, threatening to give out. *Oh no. He'd figured it out.*

Caught by his hypnotic blue gaze, she found her head moving back and forth.

"I didn't think so," he said, as his thumb made a slow glide over her bottom lip. "But I can see why didn't want to tell me."

"You don't understand." The words erupted from her in a husky plea.

"Oh, no, I do, Ellie." He gave a soft laugh. "An indecent exposure charge is probably something you don't want to brag about."

Ellie blinked, her heart thundering in her chest.

"Indecent exposure," she repeated, relief slamming through her. He hadn't figured it out. "Right."

"I mean, I suppose I can understand. It was Mardi Gras and you probably didn't realize that bus was full of senior citizens when you flashed them."

Holy crap, what had her cousin been smoking?

"Yeah...something like that," she muttered.

"You're a fascinating gal, Ellie." He pulled away and grinned, grabbing the bottle of wine again and heading toward the kitchen. "Do you need some help with dinner?"

Ellie wanted nothing more than to slide down to the floor and bury her head in her hands. Instead she settled on silent scream and face scrunching, since his back was facing her.

"No, it's pretty much ready," she finally answered, her voice surprisingly steady as she moved after him.

When she entered the kitchen, Tyson was already grabbing two plates from the cupboard.

She pulled a drawer open to retrieve silverware. Casting him a sideways look, she couldn't resist muttering, "You're a very...forward guy. Do you realize that?"

"I do." He cast her a wry look over his shoulder. "My whole family seems to have the habit. Sorry if it offends."

Shrugging, she set the table. "I didn't say it offended. It's just different. I don't think I even know my neighbors' names in Chicago. I mean, having the sheriff of town just dropping by for dinner—"

"You mean Brooklyn?"

Ellie froze in the midst of laying down the forks next to the plate.

Fuck.

"Right," she said slowly. "Brooklyn. Sorry. I grew up in Chicago and sometimes I just mix them up in conversation."

"Understandable."

His reply was said lightly, so she hoped he hadn't been too concerned with her mistake. Still, her pulse quickened. She'd let her guard down for one moment, got a little too comfortable, and then slipped.

Forcing a smile, she gestured toward the wine. "Is that a

white or red?"

"Red. Do you have an opener?"

"I do. And I think there's even some wine glasses around here some place."

"There should be. The Bakemans are wine people."

Ellie hurried back to the cupboard, swinging it open. She spotted the wine glasses on the top shelf and scowled, stretching on her tiptoes to reach them.

Tyson watched her for a moment, before he decided to help her.

"Here let me." He stepped forward and reached past her, grabbing them easily.

"Thanks."

He watched the flush of pink in her cheeks and his gut twisted with disappointment. She was definitely hiding something.

Hell, after getting the reports this afternoon, he'd been relieved to discover she'd been telling the truth about who she was.

Because in a town the size of Wyattville, Ellie was uncharted territory. She was a new body. *And damn, what a body it was.* She was like a brand new toy. And he couldn't wait to figure out what wound her up and what got her gears moving.

Ever since he'd been home, none of the girls in town had managed to catch his interest very long. That wasn't to say he hadn't dated a bunch of them in the past—hell, of course he had. He'd been your average horny teen, lusting after any girl with a pretty smile. His brothers had been the same way.

Fortunately, he and Trevor had grown up a bit. Now Todd, on the other hand, was another story.

He'd come here tonight hell bent on seduction. Her record was clean—well, almost, but it could've been far worse than *indecent exposure*—and he hadn't missed the arousal in her eyes earlier today in the bathroom.

But now, seeing the tension in her sexy little body and the way she averted her gaze, he knew this little bombshell wasn't telling the whole story. Something just wasn't right. And his gut told him that her little Chicago/Brooklyn slip up was at the heart of it.

He located the corkscrew and then opened the bottle, pouring them both a glass of wine while watching her load up their plates with food.

"Do you like steak sauce?" she asked, a little too brightly.

"No, thanks. Just a little salt and pepper will do me fine." He sat down at the table next to one of the settings.

"Great, because those I have. Steak sauce, not so much." She leaned over him, setting a plate down.

For a moment, the smell of steak mingled with roses, and Tyson got a glimpse of the pale curves of her breasts above the neckline of her tank. She wasn't wearing a bra.

A breath slid silently from between his clenched teeth as his cock twitched beneath his jeans.

Damn. He might not trust her fully, but he sure as hell wanted her.

Ellie had changed out of her denim shorts and tank top, and was now wearing what seemed to be some kind of workout outfit. Though she didn't seem the least bit concerned by her attire, even if he found it was surprisingly sexy.

The loose-fitting black bottoms fell over the slight curve of her hips, and the skin-tight tank top with thin straps was almost the exact shade of green as the flecks in her hazel eyes.

She moved to sit across from him, reaching to take a sip of wine. "So, Sheriff Wyatt, do you make it a habit of inviting yourself to dinner with all the new ladies in town?"

"I'm out of uniform," he said with a small smile, and picked up his knife and fork, cutting into the steak. "Feel free to call me Tyson."

She set her wine glass down and nodded. "All right. Tyson it is."

"And only the pretty single ones." His smile faded. "Actually, no. To be honest, this is...a first for me."

Ellie watched him for a moment and in her gaze he saw a flicker of awareness, watched her breasts rise and fall a bit quicker.

"So, tell me more about your family. You've mentioned them a couple times." Her request was overly bright and an obvious diversion tactic.

"My family. Well, I've got two brothers."

"Older? Younger? Maybe you're a twin?"

He laughed and shook his head, spearing a piece of steak. "Not a twin, sorry. I'm the middle."

"Ah, you're the middle? I guess I'm not surprised." She took a bite of rice and then asked, "What do they do? Police stuff as well?"

"No. Todd, the youngest, is a firefighter. Trevor, the oldest, has been in the army for fifteen years now."

Her fork stilled as she stared at him, her lips parting slightly. "Seriously?"

He finished chewing his bite of steak and cast her a puzzled glance. "Yeah. Why?"

"It's just..." She cleared her throat and dropped her gaze. "Never mind."

"No, now you've got me curious. What were you going to say?"

"I...well, just that that you're all in careers that are notably sexy and attractive to women." She gave a nonchalant shrug, but the slight pink in her cheeks belied her indifference. "And if they look as sexy as you, I'm guessing the Wyatt brothers are pretty popular in town."

Chapter Four

So she thought he was sexy?

Tyson's brows lifted with surprise at the confirmation, even as his blood heated and his desire for Ellie stabbed sudden and sharp.

His abdomen clenched and he drew in a slow breath, lowering his gaze to her small, berry-colored lips that had just closed around a piece of meat.

"No more than any of the other guys around, I'm sure," he replied vaguely, his voice gruff.

"Hmm." She rolled her eyes and lifted her glass of wine. "Forget I said anything. I think it was the wine talking."

She'd barely drunk a quarter of her glass. And there was no way in hell he was going to let her back down from that comment.

He turned his attention back to his dinner, eager to have it gone and out of the way. Eager to not have a table between them.

"How about you, Ellie? Any siblings?" he asked, trying to distract himself.

She was quiet for a moment, before she said, "Umm. I have a brother."

"What does he do?"

"He's...a teacher."

Funny, but she didn't sound totally confident on that.

"And what do you do?" He lifted his gaze to her face again, just in time to watch the emotionless shield slide down over her expression.

"I'm a waitress."

A waitress who could afford to rent a summer home on the Oregon coast?

"Are you? Where at?"

"It's in Brooklyn, I doubt you know the place."

"Try me."

"Look, I'd rather not," she finally said, pushing her half-eaten plate away. "We don't really know each other, and there're some things I'd just like to keep private."

Interesting. She completely shut down when he probed too far into her personal life.

"Sure, no problem." To disarm her again, he set down his fork and gave her an easy smile. "Have you seen much of Wyattville? I'd love to show you around."

Her mouth tightened as she looked around the room—everywhere but at him.

Finally, "I'm not sure that's a good idea."

"Why not?"

She moved away from the table, her chair scraping on the tiled floor as she scrambled to her feet.

"Listen, I'm just out of a really bad relationship and I'm not really looking for anything right now."

Tyson cocked his head and slowly slid his chair back as well. "And you think I'm looking for something?"

She swallowed hard and gave a sharp laugh. "Well, you did invite yourself to dinner."

"Being neighborly."

"You said you'd never done it before," she said, obviously flustered as he approached her. Then she blurted, "And you called me pretty."

He backed her up against the sink, until his hips brushed against hers.

"You called me sexy."

Her eyes narrowed. "A tiny confession that I had *no* intention of admitting aloud—until you pretty much forced me to."

"Define force."

"Okay, you need to stop cornering me like this," she said breathlessly.

He slid his gaze over her, took in the hardened points of her breasts beneath the tank top, and her uneven breathing.

"I think you like it when I do, Ellie."

Instead of replying, her tongue darted out to trace over the mouth that was tempting the hell out of him.

His blood pounded harder and he knew he wouldn't be able to stop himself.

"You do like it. Don't you?" his voice dropped an octave as he curled his fingers around the swell of her hips.

"Tyson." His name on her lips was a breathy combination of plea and protest.

But when he lowered his head, there was no protest in her wide eyes. And before his lips could touch hers, her lashes fluttered down in submission as she leaned into him.

A wave of need washed through him, primal and potent. With a low groan, he closed that last distance, taking her mouth.

Her lips, pillowy soft and pliant, moved against his. The warmth of her breath teased him, ripped at his self-control.

He nipped her bottom lip with his teeth, using her gasp of surprise to thrust his tongue inside the hot cavern of her mouth.

He moved his hands around her hips and grabbed the firm roundness of her ass, squeezing, and then lifting her onto the counter.

Jesus. He was going to lose it. So much for being professional. But screw it, just like he'd told her earlier, he was off duty. And right now, his only duty was to see how far she'd let him take this.

And if he played his cards right, maybe all the way to the bedroom.

You need to stop him.

Ellie ruthlessly silenced the voice of reason in her head and moaned as Tyson pushed her legs wide to step between them. The only thing that mattered now was pleasure, and following the thread of temptation that Tyson had so carefully laid out for her.

The edge of the counter bit into her bottom, the angle and pressure adding to the intensity and spontaneity of the moment.

His tongue danced with hers, rubbing and sucking. Their mouths separated for just a second, giving them both enough time to gasp in air, before once again he claimed her lips.

His hands, confident and knowing, moved to her waist, gathering the tank top she wore and pushing it upward.

Cool air brushed her belly and her pulse quickened. *If you're going to stop him, now would be the time.*

Then it was too late, and she really didn't give a damn as the fabric lifted over her breasts and her nipples tightened.

His head lifted from hers again, and she refused to open her eyes, because she knew he was looking at her body.

"Oh, yeah, sweetheart," he muttered thickly. "You like it."

Wet friction rasped over her bare nipple and she groaned, pleasure rocking through her as she finally let her lashes flutter up.

The vision of Tyson's head bent over her breast sent heat exploding in her belly and a rush of moisture between her legs.

His tongue moved against the tip, teasing and exploring her, making her nipple lengthen and tighten for his touch.

With a soft laugh, he parted his lips and drew her into his mouth, suckling lightly.

So good. It felt so damn good. How could she possibly stop him when this moment was so exquisite? She was only going to be in Wyattville for a couple months...why not indulge in a little harmless sex?

Ellie squirmed on the counter, her breath quickening as she tunneled her fingers into his short, blond hair, holding him against her. Wanting him to suck harder, to use his teeth.

His free hand came up to cover the other breast, squeezing and massaging the flesh. Then he caught the nipple between two fingers and pinched lightly.

She jerked against him, crying out. More, she wanted so much more. Wanted his fingers buried deep inside her, and then his tongue, before finally, his cock.

The image of it skittered through her head, robbing her ability to breathe, making her wetter.

Tyson switched his mouth to the other nipple, sucking fiercely as he eased his hand down her belly. His teeth grazed over the tip over her breast, before he lifted his head.

"I want to touch you here," he muttered thickly, just before he cupped between her thighs. "Feel how hot your pussy is right now."

Shelli Stevens

"Tyson," she moaned, her sex clenching at his erotic words. Jesus, it was like he'd known her thoughts.

"I bet you're nice and slick, sweetheart." He licked her nipple, moving his hand back up to her stomach. "Aren't you?"

Yes. Her heart pounded and her body wept for release. This man, almost a stranger, had aroused her more than any man she'd ever dated before. And more than anything, she wanted him to follow up and touch her like he'd just said.

She issued a husky, "Why don't you check for yourself?"

He lifted his head, possessiveness and desire flaring in his eyes. "No games. I like that."

Without breaking eye contact, he maneuvered his hand beneath the waist of her pants and thong. The brush of his strong fingers at the top of her mound had her biting her lip to hold back a groan.

"No games," she repeated and caught his wrist, pushing his hand lower. "No teasing either."

"Ah, but teasing is so much fun, Ellie," he muttered, before his palm cupped her sex completely. A second later, he curled one finger deep inside her sheath and Ellie's world went spinning.

With one finger in Ellie's hot, wet, pussy, Tyson's throat dried out and his cock jerked against his jeans.

She was so fucking sexy. With just a small tuft of curls above a satiny smooth mound.

Shit. He wanted her. Wanted to pull down her pants and the tiny panties she wore and tongue the hell out of her slit. Suck on her clit and bury his tongue in her pussy, tasting the slippery juices that right now coated his finger.

First though, he wanted to see how fast she'd go over the edge.

He moved his finger, slick with her arousal, up to her clit and rubbed the firm little button slowly.

She let out a low groan and clutched his shoulders, her pink-painted nails digging into his skin beneath his T-shirt.

Tyson lowered his head to her breast again, capturing the tip that was puckered for his mouth. God, she had the sexiest tits. Small and perky, with succulent berry-stained nipples that were the size of half-dollars.

36

He pressed harder against her clit, using the pressure of her fingers on his shoulders as a guide to how soft or hard to rub her.

Her hips rocked against his hand, as her breathing quickened and grew more erratic.

Tyson caught her nipple with his teeth and tugged gently, while rubbing her clit even faster.

Ellie let out a choked gasp, and then her thighs tightened around his hips and her head fell back.

His nostrils flared with triumph and he thrust his finger deep into her channel again to feel her muscles contract and the rush of her orgasm.

Hell, yeah.

Her face twisted and her lips parted to let out breathy cries. Ellie's body trembled and he had to slide his free hand up her back to keep her from falling back against the cupboard.

Her lashes fluttered up, and her hazel gaze, disoriented from her release, locked on his face.

"Whoa," she whispered, dragging in a ragged breath that made her tits lift again. "I...whoa."

"My thoughts exactly." He pulled his finger from her still-shaking body and brought it to his mouth.

Watching her reaction, he licked the shiny juices clean. A primal rumble escaped his throat at the musky and sweet taste of her.

Ellie's gaze darkened and she let out a strangled moan. He wanted to taste her completely. Reaching for the waist of her pants, he started to pull them down when his cell rang.

"You've gotta be fucking kidding me," he muttered thickly, leaning forward to press his forehead against hers.

Ellie's hands smoothed down his back, holding him against her. "Can't you just let it go?"

"It's work. They don't call when I'm off unless it important." He sighed and pulled away from her.

"Seriously? What, did someone forget to return a library book or something?" she mumbled, her expression grouchy.

Tyson's gaze narrowed on her as he reached into his pocket to grab his phone.

"This is Ty."

He dealt with the call and hung up a few minutes later,

pocketing his phone again. Still standing between Ellie's spread thighs, he was torn between his irritation with her, and the need to fuck her senseless—or maybe just fuck some sense into her.

"We may not be a big city, Ellie, but we're honest, good people who aren't immune to bad things happening," he said quietly. "And as sheriff of this town, it's my job to take care of them when they do."

Her cheeks flushed and she lowered her gaze. "You're right. I'm sorry. That was a *really* lame thing for me to say."

Tyson placed a finger under her chin and lifted her head to look into her eyes again.

"You just need to get out more. See the town and get to know the people here."

She swallowed visibly and the smile she gave him was strained. "I should, yeah."

"Great." He pressed a light kiss against her mouth and then stepped away from her. "So then I'll pick you up at ten tomorrow."

"Okay—wait, what? Pick me up?"

"I've got the day off, so we should get started on that showing you around bit."

Ellie trailed after him. "Oh, but I—"

"No buts." Tyson grabbed the handle of the door and turned, giving her one last, lazy smile. "You're getting out of the house, Ellie. And I'm a damn good tour guide, so consider yourself lucky."

"Lucky. Right."

Because there was unease in her eyes, and her cheeks were still flushed from her orgasm, he couldn't resist lowering his head for another kiss.

She gripped his shirt, swaying toward him and parting her lips to accept the demands of his mouth.

He nibbled and sucked, wanting to leave her weak in the knees and dreaming of nothing but him when she slept tonight.

When he lifted his head, Ellie's body was pressed snug against his and her eyes were once again closed.

"Save that thought, sweetheart. And next time, I'll make sure there's no interruptions."

With a wink, he turned and left her house, wishing like hell his dick wasn't rock hard.

Tomorrow morning couldn't get here soon enough.

Chapter Five

Pacing the living room, Ellie plucked at the fabric of the black and white sundress she wore. Why the hell she was dressing up to tour Wyattville was beyond her.

Then again, how she'd let Tyson Wyatt—*Sheriff of Wyattville*—talk her into going out in the first place was also a mystery.

Stupid, stupid, stupid. So much for keeping a low profile, Ms. Smarty Pants.

She glanced at the clock. Fifteen minutes to ten. Maybe he wouldn't show, or would change his mind about today.

Disappointment had her stomach sinking and she blinked in dismay at the realization.

She wanted to go. Being inside day in and out was driving her crazy. The idea of wandering around Wyattville, enjoying fresh air and the summer sunshine was like being offered a trip to the Bahamas right now.

Her gaze slid to the clock again. Thirteen minutes to ten. Walking to the antique mirror on the wall, she checked her appearance.

A scowl slid across her face as she pinched her cheeks to bring color into them. Why hadn't she packed any makeup?

Because this is not a vacation where you're out bar-hopping to meet guys. You're here to hide.

Well, at least she'd had some lip-gloss to apply. Though that almost didn't count as makeup in her book.

Sighing, she walked into the kitchen and glanced at the computer. She'd caved and turned it on early this morning, but had just barely stopped herself from logging into her email or any social networks.

Still, it was up and chugging along—she'd been right about it being dial-up—and sitting on some recipe site.

She pursed her lips as curiosity kicked in her gut. Maybe she could check out the *Chicago Tribune* online and see if there was any information about the trial.

Jerking the chair away from the computer desk, she slid in and quickly typed in the website. The little browser spun in circles while the computer made little chugging noises as it struggled to change pages.

Damn dial-up. She glanced at the clock. Shit, it was already seven minutes until ten.

The website slowly popped up and she scrolled the mouse down over the headlines. Lower, lower. There it was.

Her gut clenched and fear slammed into her, dampening her palms and drying out her mouth.

She clicked on the link and waited for the article to open. Her gaze slid to the clock again. *Five minutes.*

The article blinked onto the screen and she quickly scanned the content. One week until the trial...and shit, they mentioned a key witness was missing. Her. Though, thank God they didn't give her name.

Guilt twisted in her gut. What if by some chance James went free?

Tap. Tap. Tap.

Ellie jumped in the chair, her heart rising to her throat. Tyson was early.

"Just a minute," she yelled hoarsely as she fumbled to shut down the computer, but the damn browser kept freezing.

With a curse, she turned off just the monitor, not wanting to risk hurting the computer by powering off the hard drive.

Drawing in a deep breath, she grabbed her purse and went into the front room, opening the door.

Tyson stood on the porch, thumbs hooked in the loops of his jeans as he smiled that impossibly sexy grin.

Her stomach flipped and her pulse kicked up a notch. Good lord, she'd almost forgotten how sexy he was. But unfortunately she *hadn't* forgotten how that mouth had felt on her breasts, or how those talented hands had brought her the best orgasm ever last night.

Oh, wow, suddenly a trip to the bedroom sounded almost more appealing than a trip into town.

She lifted her gaze back to Tyson's face and found his smile had faded. Instead his gaze smoldered with heat as it slid over her body.

"You look mighty sexy in that dress, sweetheart."

Her cheeks warmed with the compliment, and she gave a small smile, far more pleased than she should've been at what he thought of her appearance.

"Thank you."

Tyson cleared his throat and scratched the back of his neck. "Maybe we should get out of here? Because if I step inside the house, we're not going to be leaving anytime soon."

Ellie bit her lip and gave him a slow smile. So they were on the same wavelength. "Hmm. I suppose we can always come back afterward."

"I like how you think." He grinned again and took her hand, pulling her through the doorway.

Closing the door behind her, Ellie tried to smother the ache of arousal, wondering if maybe she should've tried a little harder to convince him to stay.

Chapter Six

"Did you eat breakfast?" Tyson asked when they were in the car a few minutes later.

"Yeah. I've been up since six."

"Morning person, huh? I like that in a girl."

He slung an arm over her seat and turned to glance over his shoulder as he backed down the drive.

"Yes, well, it's more out of habit. I'm up doing yoga at seven a.m. every morning."

"Ah. So you must work afternoons? Evenings?"

Both. Whenever they'd needed her to teach. But that was teaching yoga classes, not waitressing like she'd told him.

"Right. I'm the swing shift."

"Italian?"

Her lips curved in amusement. "Why are you so determined to figure out where I work?"

"It's my nature, sweetheart."

"I guess it must go with the job." She hesitated, and then figured if she told him, it might tide him over for a bit. "Yes. Italian."

He grinned and cast her a sideways glance. "Nice. I love me some Spaghetti Carbonara."

"Tell me about it. It's my parents' favorite, actually."

Which was another truth. She smiled wistfully, thinking back on her parents' penchant for good wine and Italian food.

Her smile faded and her stomach clenched. God, they must be worried sick. By now, they probably suspected she'd fled town, versus being the victim of foul play.

Though, if she'd stayed in Chicago, her chances of the latter would have gone up... Even though it was warm in the car, a cold shiver racked her body.

"You look like someone just walked over your grave," Tyson said softly.

She blinked rapidly, trying to dispel the unease as she forced a small smile.

"Sorry. Just a bad thought mixing with the good ones for a moment," she admitted honestly, and it felt good.

It felt good not to lie, and it felt good to admit there were dark, terrifying thoughts running through her head. Though it would have been nicer to confess to the full extent. To be able to confide in *someone.*

But, for the last year, there'd been no one. No one who knew just how much she'd gone through with James. The mental and physical abuse she'd suffered at his hands.

Unconsciously, she reached up and touched the small, faded scar on her left cheek. The night James had given it to her would probably be forever branded in her mind.

Tyson caught her hand and smoothed his thumb over the inside of her palm. "Do you want to talk about it, Ellie?"

Talk about what?

James's red face, twisted with fury, flashed through her head. Him storming toward her.

"I told you to mind your fucking business, bitch."

And then his fist had slammed into her cheek. The bruise had faded, but the money clip he'd been clenching had forever left its mark.

Ellie shook her head, her throat tight with emotion, as once again she found herself lying. "It's nothing. Really."

Tyson didn't buy it for a second. Whatever had been going through her head hadn't been *nothing.* Her expression had been taut with whatever demons she was silently fighting.

He finally had to drag his gaze away from her to watch the road, turning the car onto Main Street a few minutes later.

Ellie let out a small gasp. "Oh, wow, it's so pretty and picturesque. Like something out of a painting..."

Tyson let his gaze slide over the street, trying to let himself see it through her eyes. Most of the buildings spanning the street were over a hundred years old. Though many had been remodeled and recently painted white.

At the end of the street was Sage Park, where the trail led

down to the beach. Wyattville was centered around an inlet of the Pacific Ocean, so you had to hike a half mile to get directly to the beach. But, this time of year, the call of the ocean seemed to be in everyone's hearts.

He braked to let Mrs. Avery and her toddler cross the street. All over town, people were out socializing and enjoying the summer.

"Yeah, this town is really something," he murmured. "Careful now, 'cause it'll grow on you."

She gave a soft laugh. "I'll be sure to remember that."

Tyson pulled his truck into an open spot and climbed out, hurrying around to open Ellie's door. She already had it half open and one leg out when he got there.

"Oh, wow, sorry." Her cheeks tinged pink and her eyebrows rose. "I've never had a guy actually do that before...you know, open my door for me."

He scowled and took her hand, helping her down from his truck. "You've been hanging out with the wrong kind of guys, sweetheart."

Her fingers clenched around his for a moment, before she gave a strained laugh. "Apparently. I'll try to do better."

Not caring that anyone walking by would see them—and no doubt be curious who the sheriff was flirting with—Tyson pulled her to him and caught her chin, lifting it so she met his gaze.

"While you're here, I'll personally see to it that you do, sweetheart."

He brushed his lips against hers, making the gesture soft and unthreatening. Keeping his control rigidly in check, even as her lips parted on a shaky breath.

When he lifted his head, her eyes almost seemed to have a gleam of tears, then she blinked and it was gone.

Tyson's gut kicked with tenderness and an unfamiliar protectiveness for this woman.

"Let's go walk around town," he said softly and caught her hand, giving it a small squeeze.

She nodded and her hand even seemed to tighten around his as they stepped onto the sidewalk and moved down the street.

"These buildings are so quaint. Like little old houses people put shops in," she said, shaking her head. "How old are they anyway?"

"Late nineteenth century. They've had good upkeep though. 'Bout every five to ten years they get a fresh paint job." He gestured to the store they were passing. "Mrs. Carty owns the Yarn Barn here, she's been around almost as long as these buildings."

Ellie gave an amused laugh and glanced up at him. "And I'm sure she'd love being referred to as over a century old."

Tyson gave a playful scowl. "Give her another twelve years and she'll be a century."

"Wow. And she still can run a business?"

"Her granddaughter mostly runs the shop now, but Mrs. Carty still comes in a few days a week to make sure things are in order."

"That's incredible." Ellie sighed. "I can't knit. Or sew. Or anything along those lines."

"But you can cook. That steak last night was pretty darn amazing." Tyson rubbed his belly as it growled. "Getting hungry just thinking about it."

"Thank you. Didn't you grab breakfast?"

"Course I did. But I'm always hungry. Which is why our first stop is going to be Kate's Cakes."

"Cake? For breakfast?"

"They got more than cake."

Tyson steered them to the side as a younger man carrying a couple of grocery bags walked by.

"Morning, Sheriff."

"Morning, Chip. Wife at home?"

Chip stopped walking and shifted his bags, grinning. "No, Sally ditched me with the grocery list, and went to a scrapbooking party with friends."

"Nice of her." Tyson grinned and glanced at Ellie, pulling her forward. "This here is Elin—well, just call her Ellie. She's staying at—"

"The Bakemans' house. Right. Welcome, Ellie. I'd shake your hand but my arms are a bit tied up. I'm Chip."

Ellie gave a small smile and nodded. "No problem. Nice to meet you, Chip."

"Will I see you at poker tonight, Ty?"

Tyson hesitated, his thumb sliding over the softness of

Ellie's inner wrist. Poker on Saturday night was a tradition, and even though he and Ellie didn't have any official plans, he intended to remedy that.

His plans tonight had nothing to do with getting lucky in cards, and everything to do with getting lucky in bed.

"Don't think I'll be able to make it tonight," he said lightly. "But say hi to the boys."

Chip's grin turned knowing. "Will do, Sheriff. Well, I'd best get these groceries home. You two have a good day."

"Chip and Sally are newlyweds," Tyson explained as they continued down the sidewalk.

"That's sweet."

"Yeah. I hope you don't mind if I just introduce you as Ellie for now. Unless you want me to try the Eli—"

"Ellie is perfect. I know my full name can tend to tie the tongue in knots." She cleared her throat. "So, does everyone pretty much know everyone in town?"

"For the most part, especially if you live here long enough. Though, there's always some folks who prefer to be left alone."

"That sounds kind of nice. The knowing your neighbors bit..."

When he glanced down at her, he caught the amazement and wistfulness fading from her expression.

"Though I suppose it's harder to just fade into obscurity in a small town."

Fade into obscurity? Tyson's brows drew together at her interesting choice in words. He kept his gaze straight ahead and decided not to reply to her comment, since she seemed a bit lost in her own world.

"There's Kate's Cakes," he said instead, pulling her toward Kate's shop.

"Where? Oh! *Look* at that. It's like...pink frosting melting over the doorway. This place is so original."

"Wait until you try her stuff. Prepare for a sugar orgasm."

She looked up at him, her lips curving into a tempting smile as her eyes flashed with heated challenge.

"A sugar orgasm, hmm? I wonder how that compares with a regular one."

Tyson's cock twitched and his blood thundered through his veins. He tugged on her hand, stopping her before she could step into the shop.

"Well, you had one last night," he drawled softly. "After you try a cupcake here, you can let me know."

She licked her lips and placed one pink fingernail on his T-shirt, tracing it over his chest.

"And what if I needed a reminder of last night's orgasm? You know, in case I forgot and want to compare?"

Tyson drew in a ragged breath as every muscle in his body strained to jerk her against him and let her feel exactly what her question had done to his cock.

"I think a reminder can be arranged." He caught her finger and traced it with his thumb. "Especially since I'll be at your place tonight."

Her brow arched. "Hmm. It seems you were so entirely confident on that fact, that you bailed on poker tonight."

"Pretty confident." His mouth curved into a half smile. "More so now that you've requested a reminder."

She moistened her lips with her tongue. "Will that be a hardship for you?"

"Oh, it'll be hard, Ellie. You don't need to worry about that."

A tremble racked her body and she seemed at a loss for words after their seductive verbal sparring.

"Come on, before curiosity gets the better of Kate and she comes outside to get us."

He reached for the door handle, but before he could grab it, the door swung inward and a woman stepped out.

"Tyson!"

She watched as Tyson bit back a sigh and pasted a wide smile onto his face, before drawing the woman into his arms for a hug.

"Hey there, Mom."

Chapter Seven

Mom? *Mom?*

Ellie's cheeks burned scarlet and she knew her eyes had to be the size of half dollars.

Jesus, how much had she seen? They hadn't done anything too scandalous had they?

She took a second to look over Tyson's mom. The woman appeared early-forties, though must have been at least close to sixty, going by what Tyson had told her. And she was still absolutely beautiful.

Dark hair was pulled back in a loose ponytail, and familiar blue eyes watched her with open curiosity. She was tall, probably five ten at least, and thin.

The woman pulled away from Tyson and glanced curiously at Ellie.

"Forgive me for being so rude, I'm Sharon Wyatt, Tyson's mother. You must be the new girl in town. It's nice to finally meet you."

Finally meet her? She hadn't even been in town a week and had only known Tyson the past two days.

"Mom, this is Ellie. We were just stopping by Kate's to grab something to eat."

"It's nice to meet you, Mrs. Wyatt," Ellie replied and reached out to shake the other woman's hand.

"Oh, we're not real formal here in town, honey. Give me a hug." Sharon scoffed and then drew Ellie into a tight embrace "Aren't you lovely. I can see why Tyson's keeping you to himself."

Ellie's heart skipped a beat, before she pushed aside the initial warmth and happiness the comment it had evoked.

"Now, I heard you go by Ellie, but how do you pronounce

your full name?"

Eleanor. She bit back her instinctive response, even as guilt pricked that she had to lie. Again.

"Elinamifia."

"Well, that's a...lovely name." Sharon glanced between the two of them and frowned. "I was just picking up some cupcakes for dessert at the barbeque this afternoon. You're coming, aren't you, Tyson?"

Barbeque? Ellie's stomach flipped and she shot Tyson a narrowed look. He wouldn't have tried to blow off a family barbeque for her, would he?

"Actually, Mom, I probably won't make it today."

Shit! He had!

"What?" His mother's face fell as he she looked between the two of them. "You both have other things to do?"

Oh, the hell was she getting blamed for this!

"Actually, no," Ellie said quickly. "Tyson just volunteered to show me around town, but I really should get back to the house soon anyway. I've got some work—"

"Nonsense." Sharon adjusted the box of cupcakes in her hand. "Go see the town, Ellie. And then why don't you both swing by the barbeque later? It's not for a few hours yet. Your brothers will be there, Tyson, and your dad is looking forward to seeing you."

Panic shot through Ellie and she felt her brows lifting. Going into town alone with Tyson was one thing, meeting all of his family was another.

"Oh, no, I..." *Decline politely.* How the hell could was she going to pull this off? "I don't... I wouldn't want to intrude on family time."

"Not intruding at all, dear. We'd love to have you. Unless you don't want to come, of course."

Going from bad to worse here. "Oh, no...we'd love to come."

Tyson cleared his throat. "Mom, we—"

"Great, then we'll see you both at two." Sharon grinned and kissed Tyson on the cheek, before waving and continuing on her way.

"I can't believe you did that," Ellie hissed. "You tried to blow off your family barbeque off for me!"

"Ah, hell, I was going to call her later. I didn't mind

skipping it, Ellie." He sighed. "Look, I can still call her in a bit and let her know you're not comfortable. We don't have to go."

"Oh no. You're not making me the bad guy here. We'll go to the barbeque."

"Lovely. I'm sure my brothers put her up to this."

"Your brothers?" she repeated. "How could they have anything to do with this?"

"You're the talk of the town, sweetheart. And since they know I'm with you this morning, they probably told Mom to invite you. I'm guessing we would've gotten a phone call, even if we hadn't run into her. Everyone wants to meet you."

Ellie shook her head and glanced back into the cake shop. "Oh. Well, thanks for the warning."

"That and my brothers want to check you out."

Ellie nearly choked and shot him a look of disbelief.

"Just a little joke." He winked and opened the door to the coffee shop, muttering not quite under his breath, "Sort of."

Great. So she not only had to lie to Tyson, but his family as well. At this rate, she may as well have stayed in Chicago and just lied on the witness stand.

Tyson gestured for her to enter first and she did, giving him another quick glare. Her frustration faded, however, the moment she inhaled.

The shop smelled heavenly. Vanilla, sugar, and cinnamon all tickled her nose, and Ellie's mouth started to water.

"Hey, guys! Good morning!" A perky voice called out. "Or, oops, probably close to afternoon now, huh?"

Ellie discovered the shop owner standing behind the counter. The pretty, plump blonde watched them with blue eyes full of inquisitiveness.

"Probably is closer to afternoon." Tyson grinned and stepped to the counter. "How are ya today, Kate?"

"Doing good, Tyson. Thanks."

"Glad to hear it. Kate, I'd like you to meet Ellie, she's staying up at the Bakemans' house. And Ellie, this is Kate, the owner of this place."

"Nice to meet you, Ellie." Kate's smile widened as she reached over the counter to shake her hand. "You're the talk of the town."

"I am? Really?" Ellie struggled to keep her voice even. She'd

51

thought Tyson had been kidding earlier.

"Well, you know how it goes. New girl in town. Pretty. All the boys are curious." Kate's cheeks turned red and she gave a nervous laugh. "Anyway, what can I tempt you both with?"

All the guys? Talk of the town? Maybe picking a smaller town wasn't the best idea...

Ellie kept her smile pinned on as she lowered her gaze to the case of sweets. And then her thoughts did a one-eighty.

"Oh God..." she said fervently. "Umm...I'm going to need a minute."

"Sure, just let me know when you're ready."

Carbs. Lots and lots of carbs. Cupcakes, large and small round cakes, cinnamon rolls, doughnuts... God, when was the last time she'd indulged in something so sinfully decadent?

Back in Chicago, she'd always avoided the hell out of sugar. Eating as healthy as possible and teaching her hot yoga classes at least five times a week.

In Wyattville, she still managed to practice yoga, though instead of a sweltering studio, it was on a cold floor in a quiet house early in the morning.

"Live a little," Tyson murmured against her ear. "The cream puffs may just make you cream your panties."

Ellie choked, her cheeks burning even as her pulse quickened. Her gaze darted up to see if Kate had heard, but the other woman had walked to the other end of the counter and was scribbling on a pad.

"You're terrible," she muttered, elbowing him in the stomach and mock scowling up at him. "What if she'd heard you?"

Tyson grinned. "Kate grew up with us. She's more than used to the Wyatt brothers by now, sweetheart."

"Are your brothers as depraved as you are?"

"More so. Well, at least Todd is." His smile faded a bit. "Trevor is just a little...darker."

Ellie bit back a groan. The Wyatt boys sounded like trouble all around—and she'd only met one of them so far.

"So, anything look good to you guys?" Kate called out, setting down her pen and walking back their way.

"Anything? Try *everything*," Ellie said and then groaned. "Oh...why don't I try one of the chocolate éclairs."

"Good choice. They're pretty popular."

"Definitely good choice," Tyson echoed and leaned forward again. "That custard filli—"

Ellie jammed her elbow into his stomach again and held her bright smile for Kate. This time the other woman's eyes did widen a bit and her lips quirked.

"And how about you, Tyson? What'll it be?"

"I'll have the vanilla bean cupcake, Kate."

"All right. I'll get those ready for you both. Here or to go?"

"To go," he answered.

When Kate went to fill their order, Ellie couldn't resist turning her body toward his and whispering, "You're a vanilla kind of guy, huh? I have to say I'm a little disappointed, Sheriff."

He arched a brow over dancing eyes. "Somehow I don't think you're referring to cupcakes anymore?"

She made a non-committal murmur and bit back a giggle.

His head dipped and his lips brushed her ear. "I'll have you know I go from vanilla to red velvet in under ten seconds."

Her amusement died as all kinds of images flickered in her head. Being tied to the bed. Spankings. Handcuffs...

Oooh, that's right, the sheriff probably has a nice pair of handcuffs.

"Here you go, guys. Thanks for coming by." Kate came holding out a plain white paper bag. "It was nice to meet you, Ellie. Have fun while you're in town, and hopefully I'll see you again."

"I'm sure you will," Ellie replied, ruthlessly shoving aside any images of Tyson and just how *not* vanilla he might be.

Tyson winked at Kate, before turning away from the counter. "She'll be back. I'll see to it."

"Don't you have a reputation or something to uphold?" Ellie grumbled, stealing the bag from his hand. "What if she tells everyone how perverted you were in there?"

"Nah, Kate's not a gossip. If it had been Lisa Thompson, I might be a little worried."

"Still. I mean, as sheriff, aren't you supposed to set an example, Tyson? Not run around making lewd comments to the new girl in town."

He laughed softly. "Was that lewd?"

"Totally." Pulling her éclair from the bag, she lifted it to her lips and took a bite.

Oh. My. God.

"Sugar orgasm, huh?"

She nodded and licked a tiny bit of chocolate from the corner of her lip.

Tyson's gaze followed the movement. "You know, I think you might like lewd."

She swallowed the bite and glanced up at him. "You know...you're probably right."

He held her gaze as he pulled out his cupcake, then ran his tongue over the fluffy white curves of the frosting.

Ellie couldn't drag her gaze away from his mouth, from what his tongue was doing to that damn cupcake. And then he thrust his tongue straight into the middle of the frosting. When he pulled it free again, white cream clung to the tip.

God, it was like he'd just gone down on a cupcake. It's what she'd wanted him to do to her last night. What she was hoping he'd do tonight.

Her pussy clenched as his tongue disappeared back into his mouth and his gaze flickered with pleasure.

"Sugar orgasm?" she choked out, mimicking his question from a minute ago.

"Definitely," he said quietly, his voice a bit raspy now. "Sweet and moist. But not quite as decadent as that taste of your pussy I sucked off my finger last night."

Holy hell! Had he really just said that? Ellie's knees wobbled and her panties grew damp. The way he spoke to her was so damn erotic. So shocking. And she loved every minute of it. Loved it so much she wished they weren't in the middle of the damned street in a small town.

But two could play at this game. She caught his wrist and pulled it forward, dipping her head to swipe her tongue over the swirl of frosting on his cupcake. Dragging the sweetness off with her teeth and closing her eyes and moaning.

"Ellie," he growled.

She laughed and opened her eyes again, meeting his smoldering narrowed stare. "You started it."

Tyson scowled. "You're right. And now I'm going to end it before I do something on Main Street that'll have me arresting myself." He caught her hand with his free one and started them walking again. "Come on, let me show you the beach."

Another giggle escaped her throat as they walked toward the end of the street.

Giggling. It was such a weird concept—she'd never been the type to giggle with boys. Definitely not with James.

Though, James had made her pulse race too. He'd given her the butterflies in her stomach. But they were nothing like what she experienced with Tyson.

And, after the fact—or even late into her relationship with James—she knew any pulse racing and butterflies had been more fear based.

She'd been drawn to James because he was the ultimate bad boy. She just didn't realize *how* bad until later.

"You've gone miles away, Ellie."

"What do you mean? I'm walking right beside you," she said lightly, and took another bite of the amazing éclair.

"You know what I mean."

"Guess my mind went off into left field. It does that sometimes."

"What was in left field?"

For a moment, just a split second, she had the craziest urge to tell him everything. The impulse hit so hard that she had to bite down on her tongue to keep herself from blurting it out.

And then it was gone again, replaced with the realization that Tyson was first and foremost an officer of the law. Once he heard her story...

"Nothing important," she finally answered and pulled her hand away. Giving herself a bit of emotional, as well as physical distance to try to give herself a better perspective of the situation.

Tyson bit back a curse as he watched her do it again. Watched Ellie bring down the shutters on whatever she was hiding. But she couldn't quite mask the unease in her eyes.

His gut twisted and he bit back a sigh. Dammit, for a while there he'd forgotten he didn't completely trust her. She'd just been an intriguing woman with whom he could be himself and have fun. And who he just happened to want to fuck until her eyes crossed.

He didn't want it to be more complex than that. Why the hell did it have to be? But his cop instinct told him it was, and that whatever she was hiding made *her* not trust *him* much either.

They stepped onto the trail that curved around a small inlet that would ultimately drop them on the beach.

"You know," she said suddenly. "I've never actually seen the ocean before."

Tyson's gaze jerked to her, his brows shooting up. "Never? You serious?"

"Yeah, kind of crazy. But...until Wyattville, I never really traveled anywhere that was close to the ocean."

"How far is it from Brooklyn to the Atlantic? Surely not that long of a drive."

Her lips parted and something that looked an awful lot like disbelief flashed in her eyes, before her lips flattened into a tight smile.

"Well...no, it's not too long of a drive." She hesitated and then seemed to relax a bit. "There was this one time, when my cousin and I had just turned twenty-one, we got in her Mustang to head to Atlantic City. Her back tire blew out not even a quarter of the way there. It was late at night anyway, so we took it as a sign that it just wasn't meant to be and headed back to Brooklyn."

"And you never tried again?"

"I...my cousin, moved around a lot. I didn't see her all that often and she was always the adventurous one." She offered a stiff shrug.

Again Tyson had to wonder how many half-truths were in the story she'd just told. Her body language clearly indicated she was lying about something. But it was a conversation about the *ocean*, why the hell would she have to lie about that?

"It's so pretty here." Ellie gestured to the pool of water that flowed in from the Pacific to form the small inlet. "Do people swim in it?"

"Yeah. It's real popular this time of year. The inlet is a little calmer than the ocean, with all the waves, so lots of parents bring the little kids," he replied. "In fact, the place will probably be packed by noon."

"I'll bet. Well, we got here just in time then."

A few minutes later, the trail emptied onto the soft sand of the beach, and beyond that lay the blue sprawl of the ocean. He tossed their empty bakery bag into a garbage can and slowed down as Ellie paused.

He heard her catch her breath and then let it out a moment later on a soft sigh.

"Oh my God. It's more amazing than anything you see on television." Her voice trembled a bit. "Sorry, but I have to."

Tyson was still trying to figure out what she was apologizing for, when she grabbed the bottom of her dress and took off running down the beach. Straight toward the ocean.

Chapter Eight

His mouth curved into a wide smile and his chest bounced with laughter as he watched her. She squealed and then laughed, as she waded out into the water.

"It's cold!" she yelled, turning to look at him. "And it feels amazing."

Tyson didn't reply, just started after her again, making his way down the slippery slopes of sand to the ocean's edge.

"Come in!" she cried, playfully kicking a spray of water toward him. "Take off your shoes and come in."

For the moment, he was content to just watch her. Watch Ellie tilt her head back and suck in a breath of sea air as she stumbled through the shallow waves.

She was beautiful. He traced her body with his gaze. Starting with her pale shapely calves sparkling with water, to the thrust of her breasts against her dress, and the huge smile of delight on her face.

He wanted her at this moment more than he had since they'd met. Because this was the real Ellie. No pretenses. Real. Honest. Uninhibited.

It didn't matter that he had on his leather sandals or was wearing jeans, he wanted to share the moment with her. Her never having seen the ocean was obviously one thing she hadn't lied about.

A moment later, with his sandals off and his jeans rolled up, he took his first steps into the water. He let the coolness swirl around his feet as he breathed in the salty ocean air. He felt what she felt. Smelled what she smelled.

Ellie's eyes opened again and her hazel gaze, alight with wonder and happiness, fell on him.

"I love it," she said softly. "Can you feel the power of the ocean? The energy and life? The way it sucks the sand between your toes as it pulls back out."

Hearing her words and watching the joy in Ellie's face, it was as if he were experiencing the ocean for the first time too.

"I feel it," he murmured, wading closer to her.

Her smile faded a bit and awareness flickered in her eyes. She'd figured out he wasn't referring to the water anymore.

He cupped her cheek and gave her a gentle smile. "You're incredibly beautiful. Do you realize that, Ellie?"

She ran her tongue over her lips, while she shook her head in a tiny gesture of denial. Of his words, or of this moment, who knew.

"I can't stop touching you. Watching you," he confessed. "You've captivated me, Ellie. Whoever the hell you are."

Guilt slid over her expression. "Tyson..."

"Tell me."

"I can't."

The two words were barely audible, but they were the admission he'd been waiting to hear.

She might not have been able to say more than that right now, but it was a start.

"You will," he said quietly, but firmly. "When you're ready. You can trust me, Ellie. You know you can."

Her lashes fluttered down, hiding the trace of fear that had flickered in her gaze.

He cupped her other cheek, so that he was cradling her face and they stood just inches a part. "But for now..."

Lowering his head, he allowed his lips to catch whatever response she'd been about to make. Her mouth opened on a breathy sigh as she leaned into him.

Hunger built inside him, burning his gut and racing through his blood. It took all his restraint to keep the kiss light, and not let the intensity of the moment rip away his control.

The beach was already scattered with a handful of town folk and there were some kids wading not too far away. The last thing he wanted to do was give the people even more to talk about. As it was, taking Ellie around today would already make them a juicy topic.

With a sigh of regret, he lifted his lips and pressed his forehead against hers. "I probably shouldn't have done that."

"I don't know, felt pretty nice to me."

"Me too. A little too nice." He glanced over her shoulder, wincing as his hypersensitive cock pressed against her hip. "I'm tempted to take a few steps farther out and dive under the water...cool myself off a bit."

She laughed softly. "It might be a bit cumbersome swimming in jeans though, don't you think?"

"You're probably right." He lifted his head again. "Why don't we walk a bit on the beach before we head out to my parents'."

"That sounds great."

He took her hand again, threading his fingers through hers in a gesture that he hoped implied he had no intention of letting her back away emotionally again.

But Ellie made no effort to free herself, instead her smaller fingers tightened around his and she gave a soft sigh as they headed out of the shallow waves and back to the beach.

He'd gain her trust. No matter what it took. He needed to convince Ellie that he wasn't the bad guy. Whoever that might be in her life...

Each minute they spent driving to Tyson's parents' house, Ellie got a little more nervous. She sat staring out the window at the cute houses they passed. Some literally had white-picket fences, flower gardens, kids and dogs running free.

This town was surreal. The *people* were surreal. But in a good way that she hadn't known existed outside of the sitcoms.

And now she was going to meet the rest of Tyson's family. It seemed so overwhelming and, well, soon. They weren't even dating—though pretty soon they'd most likely be sleeping together.

"You have nothing to worry about," Tyson said softly, glancing her way with a reassuring smile. "It's just a barbeque, Ellie. Seriously."

"Oh, I'm fine," she said a little too quickly. "Was just thinking maybe we should've brought a potato salad or something."

Damn. Now that she'd mentioned it, she realized they probably should have.

"Nah, mom makes enough food to feed an army."

"Do a lot of people come?"

He hesitated. "Not too many. Depends if the cousins, aunts and uncles show up."

Cousins. She bit her lip and wondered if these cousins were as much trouble as Tyson and his brothers seemed to be.

Her gut clenched. When was the last time she'd met a guy's family? Probably a few years ago, when she'd been in college, and that had been after almost seven months of dating.

What would Tyson's family think of her? What would his parents be like? Or the now infamous brothers she'd heard so much about. And apparently cousins to top it off.

"Here we are."

She blinked as Tyson turned the vehicle onto a dirt road. The property was massive, with an old wooden fence running along the open land.

"Wow, that's a lot of green. Do your parents have horses or something?" she asked.

"A few, actually. We all grew up riding."

"Do you still ride?"

His expression turned reflective. "Not as much as I'd like. Trevor's the big rider in the family. But I do hop on Jimmy every now and then. Riding's a great way to de-stress."

Ellie's lips twitched. "Jimmy?"

"Mom named the horse after Jimmy Buffett. She loves the guy."

Her smile widened. Something told her she was going to like Tyson's mom quite a bit.

A few minutes later, they parked in front of the large, sprawling ranch house. It was painted white with a green trim, and of course had pretty flowers aligning both sides of the front door. It was almost too lovely.

"You grew up here?" she asked softly.

"Sure did." He turned off the engine and opened his door. "My parents have been married for almost forty years."

Wow, that many years was pretty amazing nowadays. Her parents had just hit twenty-seven and she'd always been impressed by how long they'd made it.

Though she sometimes wondered how much her parents really loved each other. They bickered constantly and slept in separate rooms. It had crossed her mind more than once that they both just didn't want to deal with the hassle of a divorce.

Shelli Stevens

"Ready for this?" Tyson asked when he opened her door a moment later.

"As ready as I'll ever be." She gave him what she hoped was a confident smile. "I mean, it's just a barbeque, right?"

"Tyson Gerald Wyatt!" Sharon's voice called out. "Will you stop your stalling and bring your girl in so everyone can meet her already?"

Ellie's brows shot up and a barely audible whimper slipped past her lips.

"Sorry about that," Tyson muttered under his breath as he shook his head. "She gets excited if we bring a girl over."

"Totally a mom thing. I get it." And she did. But still, it didn't make it any easier as they walked up the pathway to where his mother stood in the doorway.

"Nice to see you again, Ellie." Sharon took a step back and waved them inside. "Go on in, everyone's out back."

Ellie stepped over the threshold of the doorway and into the house, one ear still open to hear the greeting between mother and son behind her as they continued to stand outside.

But their friendly exchange faded from her mind as she gave a wistful sigh. What a great house—a comfy layout, with plush furniture and cream-painted walls.

Pictures covered most of those walls. Pictures from twenty years ago, when the brothers were obviously kids, wedding pictures from Tyson's parents, and current photos.

Ellie picked up a framed picture of Sharon and a man she assumed to be Tyson's dad. They were in a fishing boat, arms around each other, smiling, and holding up a salmon they'd caught.

So sweet. Something she'd never had...but, God, wouldn't it be nice to find some day? For a moment, the image of her and Tyson flickered through her mind, but she snuffed it out, her stomach clenching.

"Damn. I can see why Ty staked his claim on you."

She dropped the picture with a startled gasp, then fumbled to pick it up again as she cast a glance over her shoulder.

Another ridiculously hot male stood behind her, arms folded across his wide chest as he glanced her over with an appreciative smile.

One of Tyson's brothers, without a doubt. His T-shirt with

the firefighter logo gave that away. Not to mention he had the same hard, chiseled face and body as Tyson's, but darker coloring. His hair was brown, almost black, and his eyes a rich chocolate.

Oh, yeah. She knew without a doubt by his words and his appearance alone that this guy must have a trail of broken hearts a mile long.

"Have I been claimed?" she asked lightly, turning fully to face him with a smile. "Because that would be news to me. I'm Ellie."

"I've heard. Todd Wyatt."

"Nice to meet you." She held out her hand for him to shake, and then immediately wondered if he would try to hug her like his mom had.

Instead, Todd caught her hand between his two, and lifted it to his lips to brush a kiss across her knuckles.

"I see you've managed to corner the one single woman in the vicinity," Tyson's amused voice drawled from behind her, but there was the faintest hint of warning in his tone.

She felt the heat of Tyson's body just behind her, before his hand settled possessively on her lower back.

Todd's grin widened. "Are you surprised?"

"Not at all." Tyson stepped forward again to hug his brother, pounding him on the back with a closed fist. "I think I've got you pretty much figured out by now."

"Jeez, you boys are going to scare her off." Sharon swept through with an exasperated sigh and caught her arm, pulling her away from the two. "Come on, honey, you've still got two more to meet."

Two more. Well, at least that meant the extended family hadn't shown up today. Ellie gave a small laugh of relief and let Sharon lead her out of the house into the backyard.

Chapter Nine

The smell of wood chips and barbeque hit her first and her stomach growled, even though they'd eaten the treats from Kate's Cakes not too long ago.

With the glare of the sun, Ellie couldn't see much as they stepped out onto the patio. But then a few more steps led them to a shady tree and, once again, the details of the backyard came into perspective—folding chairs, lots of green lawn.

"There they are," Sharon murmured. "The other two men in my life."

The two men in question were standing by the grill, deep in discussion. Everyone was tall, she realized, the entire family.

She approached as they finally glanced up and noticed her.

The older of the two was still quite handsome, with his full head of white hair, twinkling blue eyes, and big smile on his face. He was exactly what Tyson would look like in forty years, she thought.

"You must be Ellie!" he called, coming around the barbeque. "Glad to meet you. I'm Dan."

"Nice to meet you, Dan." And he *did* shake her hand. No hugs, no knuckle kissing.

Not sure what to expect from the last member of the Wyatt's family, she turned her gaze to the man who could only be Tyson's older brother.

He looked similar to Todd, with the dark hair and eyes. But, unlike the rest of the family, his expression wasn't quite as animated. He wasn't scowling, but there definitely wasn't a big welcoming smile. Lifting his bottle of beer, he took a long, hard draw on it while keeping his gaze on her.

His lukewarm demeanor was a bit of a jolt and her smile faltered.

He made no move toward her, but gave a slight nod of his

head. "I'm Trevor. It's good to meet you, Ellie."

Well, his words certainly sounded sincere, and some of the tension slipped away. Besides, hadn't Tyson warned her about him?

"Likewise." She brightened her smile again, then turned her attention away in search of her lifeline, the only person she knew here.

Tyson was just stepping out of the house into the yard. His gaze was on her, the knowing grin on his face a welcome relief.

He came to stand by her, holding a beer in his outstretched hand. "You meet everyone?"

"Thank you. I think so." Ellie took the beer gratefully, even if she rarely drank the stuff. She went to twist the cap off and found he'd already done that for her. "Unless there's more hiding that I haven't seen?"

Tyson watched as she tilted the beer bottle back, wrapping her lips around the rim and taking a sip. Jesus, she looked sexy sucking on a Budweiser.

"No, unfortunately my nephews and nieces couldn't be here today," his mom said, moving next to her husband, who promptly draped an arm around her shoulder. "But they send their love to everyone."

"Now that's too bad. I have a serious hankering for some of Ryan's jambalaya." Tyson rubbed his belly and winked down at Ellie. "My cousin went to college down in Louisiana. He makes a mean jambalaya."

Her eyes light up with amusement. "I swear, you have a hollow leg. You always seem to be thinking about food."

His dad chuckled, brushing a kiss across his wife's forehead. "All the boys are like that. You wouldn't have believed the grocery bill when they were teens."

"I can only imagine," Ellie said. "You have my sympathy."

"Speaking of food, how's that salmon coming, Pops?" Todd asked, crossing the grass toward the barbeque. "I'm starving. Didn't quite wake up in time for breakfast this morning."

Trevor snorted and glanced at Ellie. "That's code for he was sleeping off a wild night at some girl's house."

"Why you jealous bastard," Todd yelled, taking a playful swing at the back of his brother's head.

Trevor ducked and countered with a light jab to Todd's shoulder.

"Are you guys always like this?" Ellie asked in an amused whisper, leaning into him.

"What do you mean?" Tyson caught her hand and stroked the inside of her palm, then couldn't resist teasing, "We're on our best behavior today."

She laughed as her fingers curled around his. "I highly doubt you guys are *ever* on your best behavior."

Tyson smiled at that. She was pretty much dead on.

When he glanced at his parents, he found his mom watching them with a considering expression, her mouth curved into a tiny smile.

Don't get your hopes up, Mom, he warned silently. Ellie wasn't in town for long, and he wasn't thinking beyond a summer fling. Even as the thought flickered through his head, the denials came rushing up behind it.

Well, shit.

"So, Trevor, I hear Megan's back in town," their dad announced suddenly.

All talking and laughter ceased, leaving a silence that was only disturbed by the occasional cries of seagulls.

Tyson's breath held as he took another sip of beer and tried to glance over at his brother inconspicuously.

Trevor's expression was unreadable, his gaze shuttered. But Tyson didn't miss the way his fingers tightened around the bottle in his hand.

"Is that so?" Trevor finally replied in a voice without inflection. "I hadn't heard."

Their mom cleared her throat. "Maybe you should invite her over to join us? She's not far from here—"

"No." The harsh word whipped through the group, snuffing out any hope his parents might have for further discussion.

Even Todd's cheery mood diminished some and he turned to check on the salmon, his smile gone.

Ellie moved closer to Tyson's side and tightened her grip on his hand, obviously sensing the tension.

But then she surprised him, clearing the air with a bright, "That salmon smells wonderful. Do you guys ever go out there and go fishing?" She gestured to the ocean that lay just beyond the fenced line of Wyatt property.

"Hell, yeah, we do," Todd said, his grin returning. "I'm the one who caught the salmon we're grilling right now."

"Bah! I believe I caught this one," their dad corrected. "Yours was barely six pounds."

"Bullshit it was, Pops!"

Any remaining tension from the family dissipated as the two began arguing good-naturedly.

Trevor had turned away from the group, silently staring out at the water.

"Good save," Tyson finally murmured against Ellie's ear. "Thank you for that."

She squeezed his hand and glanced up at him. "No problem. What was that all about anyway?"

He hesitated, but then decided Trevor was too far away to hear.

"Megan was Trevor's fiancée until they broke up last year. He won't admit it, but I think Trevor still has some pretty strong feelings for her."

"Why did they break up then?"

Again, he hesitated. "Trevor's unit in the Army deployed to Afghanistan for a year. When he came back...I don't know. Something changed. Their engagement ended shortly after that."

Sympathy flashed across her face, before Ellie turned to watch Trevor. "I'm really sorry to hear that."

"I need to go throw together the fruit salad," his mom said, passing them on the way to the house. "Ellie, why don't you come help? You can tell me more about yourself."

Ellie's eyes widened and her fingers clenched around his, but she said a bright, "Sure."

Tyson bit back a laugh as he watched her follow his mother inside. He should've seen that coming a mile away. It wasn't every day he brought a girl to the Saturday barbeque...hell, it wasn't ever.

Which made him wonder again how he was going to convince himself this was a summer fling.

With a sigh, Tyson took another swig of his beer and went to check out the salmon that he was pretty sure *he'd* caught.

A few hours later Ellie clutched a croquet mallet and glared down at the yellow ball.

"I've got this," she muttered, which only garnered an amused laugh from Tyson who stood behind her.

"Come on, sweetheart. Take it home and win this one for us," he encouraged.

She grinned, then bit her lip in concentration, trying to block out the sounds of Trevor and Todd, who immediately began yelling and making as much noise as possible.

The afternoon had been incredible. Amazing food, wonderful people, and she couldn't remember the last time she'd laughed so much or had so much fun.

And now, she was going to kick some major Wyatt ass with the help of the middle child.

Raising her mallet, she swung it against the yellow ball and watched as it soared through the last two wickets to smash into the stake in the ground.

"You did it," Tyson yelled, picking her up around the waist and swinging her around in a circle. He glanced at his brothers. "Take that, ya pansies!"

Ellie let out a giddy laugh, clutching his shoulders as she stared down into his smiling eyes. And then he lowered her slowly back to the ground, their bodies passing in a sensual glide that left her tingling and short of breath.

Tyson's gaze locked on hers and she saw his pupils dilate and his nostrils flare.

Her heart tripped and she swallowed hard, knowing he must be able to see the same desire in her eyes.

"How about another beer, guys?" Todd called out. "I'm grabbing one for myself."

"Think we're going to pass," Tyson replied back, not removing his gaze from her. "We've got to head out."

Trevor gave a soft laugh. "Get out of here, already. I'm surprised you lasted this long."

Ellie knew her cheeks were pink as they said their goodbyes to everyone, stopping inside the house to hug his parents farewell and thank them.

By the time they were inside Tyson's truck and driving back to her place, her knees were shaking and her pulse pounding.

"They loved you," Tyson said, breaking the silence.

She was almost glad he wasn't bringing up the wild sex they both knew they were about to have. It was the distraction she needed.

"I had such a wonderful time. You have an amazing family. I wasn't sure Trevor cared for me much at first, but he seemed to warm up."

"He's like that with everyone. Trev's got some demons and doesn't trust easily. But he liked you. I could tell he approved one-hundred-percent."

"And that's a good thing?" she murmured and glanced over at him as the truck bounced down the dirt road of her driveway.

He tore his attention from the drive, and looked at her. "That's a very good thing."

Heat slid through her body, gathering heavy between her thighs at his softly spoken words.

Want. I want this man.

A moment later, Tyson slowed to a stop outside her house, putting on the parking brake.

Her hands shook as she reached for the door handle, tugging it open and climbing out of the truck before Tyson could open the door for her.

He was right behind her though, climbing the steps on her heels as she moved across the porch. But, before she could enter the house, he slid an arm around her ribcage, pulling her back against him so her ass brushed his hardened cock.

"We were almost inside," she whispered, her voice cracking.

"I need to touch you. Now." His lips found the nape of her neck, caressing the skin before he bit gently.

Her ass clenched and she gasped. "Tyson."

"Jesus, Ellie, when you were leaning forward earlier, swinging that mallet...your little sundress rose high on your thighs and I got so damn hard just watching you."

With his free hand, he lifted her dress, rubbing his palm over the backs of her thighs.

"I wanted to pull you off behind the trees, away from the family. Get you alone," he muttered. "I wanted to lift your dress like this, and slip my hand between your legs. Feel how fucking wet you were."

He kicked her legs apart and urged her to lean forward, as

if he were about to frisk her. But then his hand went straight between her parted thighs to cup her sensitized pussy.

Ellie cried out, a shudder racking her body as her palms lay flattened against the door, holding her weight up.

"'Cause you were wet earlier," he went on, his voice hoarse as he massaged her mound. "I know you were. Just about as wet as you are now. Weren't you, sweetheart?"

"Yes."

She didn't bother to deny it. To deny that she'd been thinking about him all day and what was about to happen.

"Good girl. No lies between us, Ellie. No lies."

Closing her eyes, she bit her lip, trying not to let the *no lies* comment drag her back to reality.

And then she didn't have to think, because he slid the hand around her ribcage up to close over her breast through the dress.

"I want your tit in my mouth again, Ellie. And then I want my face between your legs." He ground his pelvis against her, so she felt the press of his hard cock against her ass. "I want you to beg. To scream my name. I want *everything.*"

Her knees trembled, and she couldn't do more than let out a gurgle of a moan.

Tyson maneuvered his hand beneath her thong, and stroked one finger into her soaked cleft.

"But I also want you on your knees, sweetheart. I want to watch you undo my jeans and pull out my cock, then take me between those pretty red lips of yours."

"*Yes.*" The vision swept through her, so hot and powerful, that her thighs clenched around his hand.

"I want to fuck your mouth. Come down your throat." He moved his finger up to rub her clit, slow and steady, while the hand on her breast pinched the nipple. "And you'd swallow me, wouldn't you, Ellie?"

She didn't answer. Couldn't answer, because the pleasure was so intense.

"I know you would, because you're dirty like that. You'd swallow every last drop of my come. Tell me you would, Ellie," he ordered thickly, bringing his finger, soaked with her juices up to her mouth.

He traced her lips and she tasted herself, felt her tongue sliding out to flick over the tip before she knew what she was doing.

He groaned. "Or better yet, show me."

Chapter Ten

Tyson's hands moved to her shoulders, spinning her around and pushing her to her knees in front of him.

The rasp of his zipper sounded and her gaze finally focused on his hand, freeing his cock from his jeans.

Her mouth went dry at the sight of him. Thick and long, with the blue ridges of veins throughout. The head of his shaft was purple and engorged, a tiny pearl of moisture gathered at the small opening.

"Suck me," he commanded huskily. "Taste me."

Hypnotized by his seductive order and the complete change in him, she reached out and curled her fingers around his cock. Hot. Silky. Steel.

Her womb clenched and she licked her lips. The hard wood of the porch bit into her knees and it aroused her further. She knelt in front of him, knowing there was about to be a huge power shift. Her mouth watered for the taste he'd ordered her to take.

She leaned forward and let her tongue flick over his mushroom-shaped tip. Caught the salty drop of semen and savored the taste of him.

"Fuck." He groaned, his fingers sliding into her hair to hold her against him. "Take me inside, sweetheart."

Ellie parted her lips and let him slide deep into her mouth.

"Oh, God. Yeah, Ellie, just like that."

She moved her mouth on him slowly to start. Letting Tyson's cock rub against her tongue as her teeth lightly grazed him. She curled her lips over them to protect him, worried about hurting him.

But he gave a low growl in his throat, his fingers tightening in her hair as he took over.

Ellie closed her eyes, rubbing his balls as she relaxed her jaw and let him take control. Let him fuck her mouth.

She felt him tighten in her hand and then he groaned, long and loud. The first warm burst of his release hit the back of her throat and she sucked his length, milking his climax, wanting more. Wanting it all.

A minute later, Tyson pulled from her mouth and leaned forward above her, his palms against the front door of the house in a perfect imitation of the position he'd had her in moments before.

Ellie licked her lips, savoring the last taste of him, and a little shocked at what had just happened.

"Damn," he muttered. "I am so sorry."

"Sorry? Why?"

"I lost control. I was a jerk—"

"Umm, that was hot as hell," she murmured, coming to her feet and sliding between him and the door. "So don't you dare apologize. Besides, you were right."

His chest rose with each uneven breath he took, and he stroked a thumb over her lower lip.

"Right about...?"

She nipped at his thumb and watched him from beneath her lashes. "You going from vanilla to red velvet in under ten seconds."

He laughed, even as his gaze darkened. "Still, I lost control. Here on the front porch, where anyone could've seen us."

"No one saw us. This house is up a long driveway. Besides, is losing control really such a bad thing?"

"Guess not. Besides, I had an ulterior motive when you were going down on me."

"You have a filthy mouth, Sheriff."

He grinned. "And you like it."

"You're right. Now what was your ulterior motive?"

"Well, sweetheart, I needed the edge taken off." He trailed his thumb down to the pulse in her throat that she knew was beating incredibly fast. "Because once I get you inside this house, I want to take my time enjoying that tight little body of yours."

Her heart thumped so loud, she was certain he could hear it.

"Oh yeah?" Her voice cracked.

"Yeah. I want to touch it," Tyson murmured as he slid his hand down to cup her breast. "Taste it." He pressed his mouth against hers, his tongue sliding inside for a brief moment to flick against hers, before he lifted his head. "And then I'm going to fuck it." His pelvis ground against hers, pressing her into the door. "Every way possible. Again and again. Because we have all night, sweetheart, and I intend to use those hours."

Every nerve in her body went taut with need. Her thong, which had slid into the folds of her pussy, was thoroughly wet.

She wanted to make some seductive reply, or at least try for witty.

Ellie opened her mouth, but the only thing that came out was a strangled, "Please."

Tyson watched her body tremble, saw the glaze of arousal in her eyes, and couldn't wait another second to make good on the statement he'd just made.

He slid his hand down the door, grabbing the handle and turning. Since it wasn't locked, the door swung inward.

Ellie's eyes widened as she started to fall backward. But he caught her, and instead of just steadying her, he swept her up into his arms.

Moving into the house, he kicked the door closed.

"Where's the bedroom?"

"In the back." Her words were unsteady and she clung to him as he strode through the small house.

The bedroom door was open and his gaze immediately landed on the queen-size, perfectly made bed.

He laid her down on the mattress and then quickly disposed of his clothes, grabbing the condom out of his jeans and setting it on the table next to them.

Then he climbed on the bed after her, covered her body with his and let his hand sweep down the length of her body as he took her mouth in a hard kiss.

Ellie moaned, thrusting her hands into his hair as she kissed him back, her tongue sparring with his, her body arching beneath him.

Wedging his hand beneath her, Tyson found the zip at the back of her dress and tugged it down. He quickly realized that the style of the dress would have to be removed by tugging it over her head.

He eased his mouth from hers and then sat up, encouraging her to her knees.

"Take it off, sweetheart," he commanded softly. "I want to see you."

She nodded and reached for the hem of her dress. Her arms crossed in front of her as she lifted the black skirt over her thighs and up her body.

The tiny black thong he'd felt earlier showed more than it covered. The lace front was a small triangle that disappeared into the swollen lips of her pussy.

His cock went just as hard as it had been on the porch, and he groaned, raising his gaze to follow the removal of the dress.

Time seemed to stop as she lifted off her dress inch by inch. Her pale stomach was toned, and a small gem glittered from a piercing at her belly button.

Fuck. That was so damn hot.

Then her small breasts, wrapped in a black strapless bra, appeared, before the dress cleared her head and she tossed it to the floor.

"Now the bra," he ordered, his gaze on her chest, waiting for the hard, red nipples he knew she'd soon expose.

She didn't hesitate, but reached behind her to unfasten the bra. The black strip loosened, before she plucked it free and tossed it aside.

"Damn," he muttered thickly and stroked his cock, which still hung free from his unzipped jeans. "Now you just relax and let me do the rest, sweetheart."

With Ellie still on her knees in front of him, he slid a hand around her back and pulled her forward.

Her perfectly sloped breast dangled in front of his face, and he flicked his tongue over one taut nipple.

She drew in a sharp breath and swayed against him, reaching for his shoulders.

"Like that?" He smiled before closing his lips around the tip and drawing it inside his mouth.

Ellie's breathing grew ragged as he suckled her, and he grabbed her other tit, squeezing it, plucking the nipple as he enjoyed its twin with his mouth.

When he eventually pulled his mouth away, his breathing was a bit irregular too. With a low growl, he pushed her breasts together and buried his face between them, flicking his tongue over each nipple in turn, using his teeth, and alternating which one to suckle.

"Tyson," Ellie whispered, her head tilting back. "Oh God, you're making me so hot."

Though he didn't need her words to know how aroused she was—the scent of arousal grew stronger by the minute—he loved hearing her say it.

Catching the sides of her thong between his fingers, he tugged them down. But with his mouth on her tit, it was like unwrapping a Christmas present without looking.

He lifted his head from her breasts and watched the black thong slide over her hips and down her thighs.

"Jesus," he muttered and rocked back on his heels for a moment, just to take her in.

A tiny triangle of black curls was the only hair that rested above the smooth, pink folds of her pussy. The hint of moisture gleamed between his legs, and lust surged through him, knowing he'd brought her to this point.

Tyson reached out and palmed her mound, groaning at the wetness that met his hand.

"I want to taste you, Ellie," he said, and then slid two fingers deep inside her. So hot and wet. His cock jumped. "I want my tongue where my fingers are right now."

"Then do it," she said raggedly, her pussy clenching around his fingers. "Or are you just all talk, Sheriff?"

He laughed softly, lifting his gaze to hers while he fucked her with his fingers.

"I'll make you eat those words in a minute, sweetheart."

"I'd rather you just eat me."

His laughter grew, as he was genuinely amused by her dirty challenge.

With a gentle shove, he pushed her backward so she fell with her head against the pillow. Then he pushed her thighs wide and smiled down at her.

"I can't wait to hear you beg."

"I don't beg," she replied, her gaze rebellious, even as

watched her ass clench and lift off the mattress.

"Really?" He arched a brow as he moved to lie down, urging her legs over his shoulders. "We'll just have to see about that."

She seemed ready to let the argument die, but with his face not even an inch from her pussy, he wasn't all that surprised.

He took a second to breathe in the spicy scent of her arousal, and rubbed a thumb through her folds. Then he dropped a light kiss on her inner thigh.

Tyson watched her stomach clench and her chest stop rising and falling. *She was holding her breath.* He smiled, knowing Ellie wasn't nearly as composed as she'd want him to believe.

He kissed her other thigh, before turning to lazily nuzzle her warm slit. Her strangled whimper made him bite back a soft laugh.

And then his amusement died when his tongue caught the taste of her essence. Hunger, savage and raw, ripped through him, sending his blood raging through his veins.

With a low growl, he forgot the notion of teasing her and gave in to his primal instinct. Needing to taste her completely and to make her lose control like he knew he was about to.

He slid his tongue through her folds, before making it rigid and plunging deep into her core, burrowing in her musky slickness.

Oh, yeah, he was a goner.

Ellie gasped, any intent she had at keeping calm and controlled when Tyson was going down on her vaporized.

Oh God. Oh God.

Her head spun and her heart pounded as he began to slowly fuck her with his tongue. Her thighs tightened around his head, her heels digging into his upper back.

And then he moved his tongue from the channel, dragging up through her pussy, before honing in on her clit a moment later. At contact, her body jackknifed and she cried out. Pleasure screamed through every inch of her being as a film of sweat broke out on her skin.

He suckled the small bud, making quiet masculine growls of approval. And then his hands slid up her body to massage her breasts, squeezing and kneading the sensitive flesh.

"Tyson," she whispered, clutching blindly at the bedding.

"Oh God..."

His mouth moved over her faster, his tongue flicking and swirling, creating havoc on her mind and body. And then, it was too much, even as she needed more.

"Please," she begged, just as he'd predicted. "Tyson, oh God, please."

Tyson's hands slid from her breasts and she groaned in disappointment. But then he caught her hands in his, weaving their fingers together as he slowed his tormenting tongue to hard licks against the button of flesh.

Her thighs gripped his ears as the release built low in her body. Then it spread to every inch, leaving her tingling and on the edge. She just needed that little...*God!*

He lightly bit her clit and she went flying. Her body shook through the orgasm, gasps of pleasure spilling from her lips.

She was vaguely aware of Tyson shifting, moving to his knees, even as her legs stayed on his shoulders. Then she felt the thick prodding of his cock between her thighs.

"I know I promised you slow, sweetheart," he muttered hoarsely. "But I can't wait another minute to be inside you."

Before she could catch her breath, his grip on her ankles tightened and he thrust deep.

Her body arched and she moaned, the lingering pleasure of her orgasm sparking up again tenfold.

"Tyson," she gasped softly and closed her eyes, letting herself adjust to his quick invasion.

Incredible. It felt so absolutely incredible. Her entire body tingled as he made slow thrusts inside her. Her nipples hardened and her breathing grew strained.

But she wasn't the only one. She opened her eyes again when she heard ragged breaths. His face was pinched, the pleasure so clearly sketched in each line on his forehead and the heat in his eyes.

Tyson must have sensed her watching him. He'd been focused on where they were joined, his thumb rubbing her clit as he fucked her, but then he lifted his head and their gazes collided.

"Ellie," he rasped. "Oh God, you're amazing."

She tried to reply back, "Likewise." But it came out more as a gurgled moan.

And then any ability she had to think vanished when he began thrusting harder into her, rubbing her clit faster. Her breasts jiggled and she pinched the tips, heightening her excitement.

The wave of pleasure bore down on her, demanding her surrender and that she let go completely. And she had no choice. With a ragged moan, she gave herself over, grinding herself frantically into his thrusts, moaning and crying out in abandon.

When the wave crested, she screamed hoarsely, clenching around his cock and milking him into his release.

Tyson groaned, the sound ragged and guttural as he did two more shallow thrusts, before going deep and remaining buried.

It took a while before she could form a thought, and by then Tyson had pulled out of her, disposed of the condom, and was climbing back into bed.

"I need a minute," he muttered, looping an arm around her waist and tugging her to him. "And then we can go again."

She gave a weak laugh and shook her head. "I'll need at least an hour, turbo."

"Deal."

Closing her eyes, she let herself snuggle against him and rest. Just for a while...

Chapter Eleven

"Ellie. Wake up, sweetheart!"

Ellie gasped and snapped her eyes open. Her whole body was rigid with tension and she couldn't figure out where she was.

She blinked, turning to look at Tyson before it sank in where they were and what had happened. Judging by the fading light outside, it was probably after eight p.m.

"Did we fall asleep?" she asked uncertainly.

"Yeah." His gaze, full of concern and questions, searched hers. "You were having a nightmare."

"A nightmare..."

"You don't remember?"

She hesitated and then shook her head. Her stomach swirled as anxiety ripped through her. No, she didn't remember. But she had a pretty good guess what it was about.

Tyson's expression softened. "Come here, sweetheart."

When he pulled her into his arms, she didn't resist. She burrowed her face against his hard chest, smelling the soap on him and faint hint of sweat from their earlier lovemaking.

Lovemaking? Her mouth parted in dismay. When in her life had she ever called sex lovemaking?

"Relax," he murmured, stroking her hair and then her naked back. "I've got you, sweetheart. You're okay."

And she was. Somewhere in the past couple of days, she'd really come to trust Tyson. She closed her eyes, listening to the solid thump of his heartbeat. It eased the tension from her body, brought back the peace and warmth.

"Elinamayfia...whatever it is that's going on, I promise, you can tell me."

And just like that, the serenity of the moment evaporated.

He'd finally *almost* mastered her name...and it sounded beautiful on his lips.

Only it wasn't her name, it was her cousin's. And she and Tyson weren't really together like a normal couple, because everything was built on a lie. *She* was a lie.

Ellie squinted her eyes closed, wanting to shut out the guilt and the frustration. Wanting to forget this cute little town and its wonderful people. She wasn't one of them, and she certainly didn't belong here. She was just *using* them.

"Please, Tyson...just hold me," she whispered. "Make love to me."

There was that phrase again, *making love*, only this time she didn't flinch at it. She couldn't really call it sex, because she'd never had the kind of sex that left almost left her crying with joy and her heart swelling with...no. She was not going to go *there*.

She turned her head to glance at Tyson, because he hadn't replied and she knew he was disappointed to an extent at her lack of confession.

But then he gave a slow smile and reached for her, lifting her so she lay on top of him. His hands slid down to cup her ass.

"Damn it, Ellie, you know I can't say no to that kind of request," he said softly and nuzzled her breasts.

She sighed, heat already rocketing throughout her body again. "I know. That's why I suggested it."

"But afterward, we'll—"

"Cook dinner." Knowing that wasn't at all what he'd been about to say, Ellie gave a flirty smile. "I'm going to work up an appetite."

And then, before he could argue, she lowered her head and covered his mouth with hers. Initiating a hot, thorough kiss.

The distraction worked. Tyson gave a low groan and wrapped his arms around her, pulling her tighter against his hard body and plunged his tongue deep into her mouth.

Ellie tried not to think about how much longer she could keep diverting him, because Tyson obviously wasn't going to let it go. Which meant she might have to consider leaving sooner than expected. The trial was in one week, and she really hated to leave Wyattville. If she could just make it a little bit longer...she'd be in the clear.

When Tyson slipped a hand between her legs, she let out a whimper of pleasure and gave herself over to the rush of passion.

She couldn't think about how she was going to deal with tomorrow. Not right now. Not when they had tonight.

Tyson only drove home briefly to grab a change of clothes, before bunking in at Ellie's for the weekend. They spent most of Sunday being lazy. Only taking a break from the bedroom to eat and go for a quick walk on the beach.

And now they were in bed for the night. He listened to the sound of the waves hitting the beach and Ellie's steady breathing beside him. Darkness had fallen hours ago, but now, approaching midnight, he couldn't seem to get to sleep. His mind wouldn't shut down. Which wasn't good, seeing as he had to be at work in the morning.

He propped himself up on one elbow and stared down at Ellie, waiting to see if she'd stir. But her eyes remained closed and her lips parted just the tiniest bit.

Reaching down, he lightly traced a finger over her satiny cheek. His chest tightened and tenderness like he'd never felt for another woman seeped through him.

"How did you do it," he asked softly. "How did you manage to work yourself into my heart in just a handful of days?"

Ellie didn't move, and there was no flickering of her eyelids. She was solidly out.

With a sigh, Tyson rolled over and off the bed. His bare feet made no sound as he left the bedroom to wander around the house.

The Bakemans tended to be gone more than they were here. At least since Roddy Bakeman had retired. He and his wife had been bitten pretty hard by the travel bug.

Rubbing the back of his neck, he wandered the living room, glancing at the paintings that hung on the wall. As he approached the kitchen, the familiar sound of electronic humming broke the silence in the house.

He walked purposely into the kitchen and toward the computer tucked away in the corner.

Though the monitor was off, it seemed Ellie had forgotten to shut it down. Hmm, maybe he'd check his email since he hadn't all weekend.

Tyson sat down at the computer and pushed the monitor button. It hummed, flickering with light, before the screen came to life.

Jesus, this was an old computer. He moved to type in his email server, when his gaze caught on the page Ellie had left up.

His gaze scanned the headline of the *Chicago Tribune* article that was up.

Trial to begin next week for Chicago man accused of drug trafficking.

Tyson's brows furrowed and he made a small noise of interest. It was always possible that Ellie just liked to keep up on the news from the city she used to live in.

He kept reading. Scanning the article until he'd finished. But then his gut clenched. There was a key witness missing.

Glancing down the hall to where she slept, he couldn't shake the sense that whatever Ellie was hiding also scared the hell out of her.

It was a lead. Probably a false one, but he'd be stupid not to check it out.

Easing out of the chair, he moved silently back into the bedroom, determined to keep her sleeping. He didn't want to risk her overhearing what he was about to do.

He found his jeans on the floor and grabbed his cell phone out of them, before moving stealthily back into the kitchen.

Dialing the station, he waited for the twenty-something working the graveyard shift to answer.

"Hey, Eve," he said quietly when she picked up. "It's Sheriff Wyatt. I need you to check something out for me."

"Hi, Sheriff! You're up late. Sure, no problem. What do you need?"

"I need you to make some phone calls, do some Internet searches on a trial going on in Chicago. Any info on the trial and a missing witness."

"I can do that. It's dead as a doornail this time of night. It'll give me something to do," she said cheerfully. "All right, I've got the computer up. All I need is the details..."

The screaming of the seagulls woke Ellie. Her eyes snapped open and she lay still, letting herself take a few deep breaths as she gained her surroundings again.

A moment later, she rolled over, but her excitement faded as she noted the empty bed beside her. Though a dent remained in the pillow, Tyson was gone.

She pressed her hand against his side of the bed and felt the cool sheets. And apparently he'd left a while ago.

With a sigh, she scampered out of bed and stretched, easing the kinks out of her body. Her gaze fell on the alarm clock and her eyes widened.

Holy crap! Eight in the morning? She never slept this late! Then again, she'd never had an evening like the one she and Tyson had shared last night.

She wandered into the kitchen and found the note on the counter. She grabbed it and scanned it. Ah, he'd had to work this morning, but she'd better be ready to see him tonight. And clothing was discouraged.

Her lips twitched into a smile and she headed to the fridge, pulling it open and staring inside. Her stomach growled as she debated what to eat for breakfast.

As she stared, she became aware of the humming of the computer in the corner. Thoughts hit her at once. She'd left it on. She'd left the article open. What if Tyson had read it?

Shutting the fridge again, Ellie moved slowly over to the computer, her breath held. When she reached it, she drew in a relieved gasp of air to see the monitor was still off. She turned it back on, and stared at the *Chicago Tribune* article that sat exactly as she'd left it.

Chapter Twelve

"I'm *so* glad you came in!"

Ellie smiled up at Kate, who was fixing her an iced Americano, and then licked a bit of cream cheese frosting from her finger.

"This cinnamon roll is to die for. And what can I say? You hooked me with that éclair the other day, Kate. I woke up and my first thoughts were of your shop."

Well, maybe after that whole computer freak out thing. Uneasy that she'd left the website up in the first place, and not wanting to risk Tyson discovering it later, she'd shut down the computer.

Then, after a quick shower and throwing on some clothes, she'd headed into town. Breakfast at Kate's Cakes had sounded like a good distraction to get her through the Monday.

Kate carried the iced Americano to the table and gave a mischievous grin. "Those were really your very first thoughts?"

Accepting the drink, Ellie felt her cheeks warm a bit and she cleared her throat. "All right, maybe they were my second...or third."

"Hmm, thought so." Kate sat down across from her and her smile widened. "I've gotta say, I've *never* seen him like this."

Ellie's pulse quickened and she was pretty sure she knew exactly who Kate was referring to, but still asked, "Who?"

"Sheriff Smiley—I call him that because he's always smiling. And Tyson Wyatt's been smiling even more since you came to town. He's fallen for you, girl. Hook, line and sinker."

If Ellie's pulse had been fast before, it was breaking all kinds of records now.

"I don't think he's fallen for me," she said carefully, though she couldn't say the same for herself. "I think it's just that..."

"The sex is good?"

Okay, now she *knew* her face was red.

"Don't answer that, I was way out of line." Kate grimaced and leaned back in her chair. "So, what have you guys been up to?"

Though part of her wanted to declare just how great the sex had been—to confide in a woman with whom she was already building a friendship, Ellie went with the topic change instead.

"Hung out and relaxed yesterday. Saturday, after stopping by here, we walked around town, explored the beach, and then went to Tyson's parents' house for a barbeque."

"Wait a minute." Kate's eyes widened and she leaned forward. "You got invited to the *Wyatts'* barbeque? Wow, Ellie, I'm so impressed."

Ellie gave a nervous laugh. "It was just a barbeque."

"Oh no. It's not just *a* barbeque. It's the *monthly Wyatts'* barbeque. You've got to have Wyatt blood in your veins or be damn near engaged to a Wyatt to get invited."

Damn near engaged to a Wyatt? Ellie's throat dried out and her head felt light. She lifted her cinnamon roll for another bite, and her hand wasn't as steady now.

"You just don't understand, Ellie," Kate continued earnestly. "The Wyatts are like our town's version of royalty."

Actually, she had gotten that impression a little. But it appeared the town folk took it pretty seriously. How had she not realized getting invited to Tyson's family barbeque was such a big deal? Well, she'd realized it was a big deal because she'd been invited to meet *his family*, but she didn't realize it was like the equivalent to getting into Buckingham Palace.

Kate slapped the table and shook her head. "Seriously, Ellie, there isn't a girl in town who hasn't tried to snag one of the Wyatt men."

"Except for you of course." Ellie couldn't resist teasing, her amusement returning.

But clearly it had been the wrong thing to say when Kate pulled back, her expression clouding over.

"Don't worry," Kate said, her voice quieting as she shifted her gaze. "It's never been Tyson."

Ellie blinked in dismay. *What? Really?*

"Seriously? Todd? Trevor? One of the elusive cousins I've

heard about?"

Kate's lips remained pressed together, her expression a bit sad and reflective. Ellie didn't think she was going to answer and realized she probably shouldn't have even asked.

"Todd."

The quiet confession had Ellie's eyes widening. Todd, the firefighter who was known to have seen more action with women than fires. And that was a direct quote from Tyson.

"Has he...have you guys ever...?"

"No. Oh, God, no." Kate rolled her eyes. "Todd doesn't even know I'm alive that way. If anything, I give him the little sister vibe."

Ellie took another sip of her iced Americano and eyed the other woman curiously. Kate might not be society's definition of sexy or beautiful, but she was cute and curvy, and funny as hell. Probably mid-twenties, if that. She was the kind of girl who slipped under the radar, but who some guy would eventually discover and realize how damn lucky he was.

"Maybe you should ask him out?" Ellie finally suggested.

Kate let out a short laugh, her expression incredulous. "Umm, I'll pass. I can think of plenty of other ways to humiliate myself, thank you very much."

Ellie was trying to think of how she could convince Kate to at least try, when the door opened and another customer came in.

"Be back in a minute, Ellie. You enjoy your breakfast."

Watching Kate go deal with the customer, Ellie's thoughts returned to last night.

Memories of Tyson and their two days of hot lovemaking flickered through her mind. And, just like that, her body was alive with need again. Jeez, just thinking about him could make her nerves all jittery. It was like an addiction withdrawal...only her poison was the town's sheriff.

Sighing, she tore off another piece of cinnamon roll and popped it into her mouth.

Maybe he'd get off work early...

Tyson put the brakes on in his truck, turned off the ignition and exhaled a long breath, staring hard at the

Bakemans' house.

Looking in the window, he could see Ellie doing some yoga positions in the living room.

Since this afternoon, his stomach had felt like there'd been a brick in it. Ever since he'd walked into the station and found Eve's report on his desk.

He closed his eyes, seeing again in his head the report that had detailed the Chicago drug trafficking trial. And, through some web searches and social networks, Eve had also managed to dig up some information on the missing key witness.

Eleanor Owens.

A twenty-six-year-old yoga instructor from Chicago, the ex-girlfriend of the defendant. And currently MIA.

Bitterness sent bile rising into his throat and he shook his head. Damn it, he didn't *want* it to be true. Didn't want to think that the woman he'd slept with last night, the woman who'd crawled into his heart and set up real estate, had been lying to him.

Shit, had *anything* she said been the truth? A fucking waitress in Brooklyn?

Right now, he only had some pretty damning similarities adding up that Ellie was Eleanor, but he'd get the proof.

After reaching for the handle on his door, Tyson pushed it open and stepped out of his truck. He strode up the porch and to the front door, knocking once before opening it.

Ellie, bent over in the most fucking erotic pose he'd ever seen, looked at him from between her legs and smiled.

"Hey there. I'm just finishing up."

"Take your time. I'll just sit down," he said, folding himself onto the sofa, "and enjoy the view."

She gave a soft laugh and slid her body into another weird pose. Hell, he didn't understand the yoga stuff, but knew the chicks seemed to dig it. Some of the local gals even drove an hour away to take a class in the neighboring town.

Watching Ellie with her hands and knees on the floor, her back arched, Tyson's cock jerked. Damn, he wanted her again. Which made no sense. Why he could want a woman who could look him straight in the eye and lie without batting a lash.

"Okay, maybe you'd better not watch me," she muttered. "I can't think. You're getting me all hot staring at me like that."

"You can't see me watching you."

"I can feel it."

"Mmm. All hot, huh?" His blood pounded in a metronome of need. Everything primal rose to the surface inside him. He shouldn't want her, and he could tell himself again and again that he didn't. But damn it, he did. And despite his *don't touch her* buzzer going off at full volume, he suddenly found himself reaching for his belt buckle.

She must've heard the rasp of his belt through the denim of his belt loops, because she twisted her head and glanced at him over her shoulders.

Ellie's eyes widened and he heard the swift breath she caught.

"What do you think you're doing?" she asked unsteadily, and began to move into a new pose.

"*Stop.* Don't move," he ordered and stood up, pushing his jeans and briefs to the floor after grabbing a condom from the pocket. "I want you just like this."

It was easier if he didn't have to look into her eyes and think about how she'd lied to him. Having her this way meant he could focus on just the moment, and how damn good it would feel to be inside her.

A shudder ripped through her body, but she didn't move. "Tyson, I'm not quite done."

"No, you're not," he murmured and came to kneel behind her. "In fact, you're just starting, sweetheart."

He hooked his fingers into the waistband of her yoga pants and panties, tugging them down, baring her ass as they fell to her knees.

"Damn." His voice turned husky as he caressed one firm globe. "You look so hot like this."

"Tyson," she protested weakly. "I'm all sweaty."

"I like it." He moved his hand lower, to the cleft of her pussy that lay just below her ass, and pushed a finger through her folds to rub her clit.

A tremble rocked her body and she sighed, pushing back against his hand. He rubbed her steadily, thinking about nothing except making her nice and wet, ready to accept his dick.

He plunged a finger into her channel a minute later and

found it creamy and welcoming.

"I want you now," he muttered.

"Yes."

"Fast."

"*Yes.*"

He sheathed himself with the condom, gripped her hips and then plunged into her from behind.

"Jesus." He gasped as her walls clenched around his cock, so hot and wet.

"Tyson. Oh, God. Oh, God. *Yes.*"

Blinded by lust and lingering anger from her lies, Tyson tightened his grip on her hips and pounded into her. Hard. Fast. Letting his turbulent emotions show through in the way that he fucked her relentlessly.

Ellie's moans turned guttural and she pressed backward to meet his thrusts, bringing him deeper with each penetration.

Knowing he wasn't going to last very long, but wanting her to explode with him, he reached around to find her clit again. He pinched and rubbed, heard her cry of pleasure right before she clamped around him. Clenching and unclenching.

Her hoarse cry of his name sent him over the edge. His mind exploded with light and his knees trembled as he came hard. The roar that left his chest sounded almost animalistic.

She fell forward, lying on her folded arms with her ass still in the air and him buried deep inside her.

When his mind cleared, Tyson slid from her and closed his eyes. Disbelief and anger slid through him again. Jesus. He'd lost all control. Not an ounce had remained as he'd taken her.

He'd come here with a purpose to find out the truth, but then he'd walked in the door and his priorities had changed.

His jaw clenched and he shook his head. Well, now that he was done thinking with his dick, he would get the answers he'd come for.

"I should shower," Ellie said weakly, her heart still pounding and her body sweaty from yoga and making love. Though, this time, their joining had been hard, fast, almost angry. Even still, it had been incredible.

She tried to wiggle out from under Tyson, but gasped in shock as he flipped her onto her back. The breath rushed from her chest as he moved to kneel over her, straddling her waist.

"You're ready for more...?" she started to joke, but then saw the hard line of his jaw and the anger in his eyes. A frisson of unease slid through her, premonition tickling in her gut. "Tyson?"

"Tell me your name again."

Chapter Thirteen

Her name? Oh God. Why was he asking, unless...

"Elinamifia Owens."

His flinty gaze narrowed. "Try again."

Her throat went tight and her heart smashed into her ribcage. She ran her tongue over her bottom lip and drew in an unsteady breath.

"What do you mean? That's my name—"

"Then let's go find your purse, Ellie, seeing that I never checked your ID that first day we met." He was off her in an instant, and striding across the room.

Ellie was on her feet, fumbling to pull up her pants as she stumbled after him, her chest tight with fear.

"Tyson, wait—"

But by the time she entered the kitchen, he was already swinging her satchel purse around two fingers.

She went to snatch it, but he lifted it above her head.

"*Your name*," he ground out, his gaze flashing with irritation. "And don't even think of lying to me this time."

It was right there in her purse, in her wallet. The driver's license that would confirm what he already knew. For a moment, she contemplated turning and running like hell out of the house. Try to disappear again, and just hide for the next week.

"You already know my name," she finally whispered.

"I want to hear you say it."

"Eleanor Owens."

"And Elinamifia is just some person's identity you stole?"

"Elinamifia is my cousin!" she shouted, her cheeks heating with frustration. "You don't understand, Tyson—"

"I understand there's a bench warrant out for your arrest."

Ellie's hands fell to her sides and the blood rushed from her head. She reached for the counter when her knees threatened to buckle. "What did you say?"

"You heard me, Ellie." He shook his head and thrust a hand through his hair. "Instead of screwing you the minute I walked in the door, I should've been arresting your ass."

A few heartbeats went by. "And are you going to arrest me now?"

She watched Tyson, saw the tic in his jaw as he stared down at her.

"I asked you to trust me, Ellie. Multiple times."

"I know."

"And you didn't." Accusation shone in his gaze now.

"I *couldn't*. I can't trust anyone. You still don't understand, Tyson." Tears flooded her eyes and she cursed herself. She was not the type to cry, not even when James had beaten her.

"Damn it, I do understand, Ellie." And then the tone of his voice shifted, gentled. "I haven't always been a small-town sheriff, sweetheart. I was a cop in Seattle for a while, too. I've testified in numerous trials, myself. I've seen the kind of fear that can make a witness walk around puking for days before taking the stand."

"You...you worked in Seattle?"

He sighed and took a step toward her, setting down her purse as he moved to cup her shoulders. She blinked the tears from her eyes, the tension in her body dissipating at the massaging of Tyson's hands.

"For five years. I was young, eager for action and adventure. I got it in spades." He shrugged. "But then I realized what I'd given up. How much I loved and missed Wyattville and its people. I came home two years ago, deciding it was time to put down some roots for good, find a girl and start a family."

"Two years ago? And you're still not married," she said, and then her lips twitched. "Unless there's something you'd like to tell me?"

"No, I'm not married," he said with a soft laugh. "I just never met anyone I could fall in love with." His gaze lifted to hers. "Until recently."

Ellie's heart tripped and then sped up, her body tingled and her head grew light. Was he saying...?

"I want to help you, Ellie. I'm *going* to help you."

Her mind slipped away from romantic, happy thoughts, and right back to her current situation, and how utterly hopeless it was. "I don't see how you possibly can."

"Let me deal with that. Go take your shower and when you get out, things might look a little brighter."

She bit back a humorless laugh and tried to pull away, but Tyson's grip tightened on her shoulders.

"And don't do anything stupid, Ellie," he warned softly, rubbing his thumb over her collarbone. "'Cause if you run, I'll follow you. And then I'll have no choice but to arrest you."

How the hell *could* she run? She didn't even have a car here—she'd taken a taxi into town.

"I won't run," she said flatly, a bit numb now.

"Do you trust me, Ellie?"

She started to nod automatically and then hesitated. She didn't want there to be any more lies. When she answered his question, it would be the truth.

Ellie lifted her head to look at him again, searching his face and her heart for the answer. Some of the heaviness lifted as she replied, "Yes, Tyson. I do."

"Good." Relief flickered in his gaze and then he lowered his head, before brushing a light kiss across her lips. "Go get that shower, sweetheart."

With a sigh, she nodded and headed to the bathroom.

Tyson stared out the window of the Bakemans' house and his pulse jumped when he saw the red convertible pull up the drive.

She was here.

Striding from the kitchen, he went to open the front door, walking onto the porch to greet Megan as she climbed out of her car, carrying her laptop case.

"Megan," he called out in greeting, and grinned as he strode down the steps to meet her.

The tall redhead looked gorgeous as usual, as she smiled back and slid into his embrace.

"How've you been, Tyson?" she asked quietly.

He kissed her cheek and stepped back. "Been pretty good."

"That's what I'm hearing. You fell in love or something? It's about time, Sheriff."

He laughed, holding nothing but affection for the woman who had almost become his sister-in-law. Again, he had to wonder what had happened between Trevor and Megan to make things end so abruptly.

"So, where is she?" Megan asked, taking a step back and smoothing down the silk tank top she wore over her slender frame.

"In the shower. I owe you, Meg. Whatever the cost, I'll cover it."

"We'll see, Tyson, it may be pro bono. This could be your future wife we're talking about."

He laughed, even as his blood quickened. "Easy, Megan, it's only been a few days."

"Sometimes that's all it takes to know when you've found the one." Her smile remained, but he didn't miss the sadness that flickered in her eyes. "Anyway, invite me in already, I'm dying for a cup of coffee."

"Let's hope she has some. Ellie's kind of a health nut." He pushed open the door and waved Megan inside.

Fortunately, he found some coffee in the freezer and soon had a pot brewing.

By the time Ellie walked into the kitchen, hair still damp, and dressed in another sundress, he and Megan were deep in discussion at the table.

"Oh." Ellie's eyes widened and she stumbled to a halt.

Tyson pushed back his chair and came to his feet. "Ellie, I want you to meet Megan Asher. Megan's a family friend and an attorney who's going to be able to advise you. Megan, this is Eleanor Owens."

Megan stretched a hand across the table and shook Ellie's hand. "Nice to meet you, Eleanor."

"Please, call me Ellie," Ellie replied and sat down at another empty chair at the table. "I...thank you for coming over. I don't..."

"Ellie, I'm only here to help you. But to do that, I'm going to need you to fill me in on everything that's going on and then we'll see what can be done," Megan said gently.

"Okay. I'll...try." Ellie cast Tyson a furtive glance. "Can you grab me a cup of coffee, too? I think I'm going to need it."

"Sure. Cream or sugar?"

"Black."

Tyson nodded and pushed to his feet, rubbing her back encouragingly as he passed her on his way to the coffee pot. Damn, he really hoped Ellie opened up to Megan. They needed to find out how much trouble she was in and what could be done to avoid it.

"So, Tyson told me a bit about what's going on, but I'd love you to elaborate. You were called to testify in a trial in Chicago?" Megan began and flipped open her laptop.

"Yes. I was sent a subpoena last week." Ellie was silent for a moment before she nodded. "My ex-boyfriend is being charged with drug trafficking. The prosecution tracked me down and they want me to testify."

Megan nodded and began typing. "And since you're...*vacationing* in Wyattville, I'm guessing you weren't thrilled with the notion of testifying?"

"I can't do it," Ellie's voice dropped in volume, fear lacing her words.

Tyson, returning with a mug of coffee, caught Megan's gaze above Ellie's head. He guessed she suspected the same thing she did, that Ellie was running scared.

He set the coffee down on the table and then pulled his chair closer to hers.

"Are you afraid to testify, Ellie?" Megan asked.

"Of course." Ellie gave a sharp laugh as she reached for her coffee. "I'd be stupid not to be."

Tyson placed a hand on her leg. "What makes you say that?"

Ellie's hand trembled as she took a sip of coffee and then set the mug down. "Because it's all true. James was dealing heroin. And he had some pretty high-profile clients."

"And you can prove this?" Megan prodded.

"We were together for a year," she said distantly, her fingers drifting up to touch the small scar on her cheek he'd been wondering about. "He thought I was his soul mate—even if he smacked me around a bit. And though he didn't usually talk business in front of me, sometimes it was like I was invisible, and he'd do it."

The muscles in Tyson's body went rigid, fury exploding

from his gut and spreading with his pounding blood. "He hit you, Ellie? And you stayed?"

Ellie glanced over at him, genuine surprise on her face. "Of course I stayed."

"Why?" Now it was his turn to be stunned.

"Because it was easier to stay than to try to leave him." She shook her head, looking past him now and out the kitchen window. "It was only when he got arrested eight months ago that I was essentially freed. And, yes, I realize how ridiculous that sounds."

"It doesn't sound ridiculous. And I'm so sorry, Ellie," Megan said, her tone and expression sympathetic. "What happened to you isn't uncommon. Many women don't leave an unhealthy relationship because they're afraid of the reprisal."

"Thank you." Ellie gave a weak smile, but seemed to really appreciate Megan's comments.

Tyson stood up and paced the room, telling himself to calm down. That it was pretty much impossible to go beat the shit out a guy who was already in jail.

"Tyson," Megan said suddenly and glanced up at him, giving him a warning glance. "Why don't you go grab us some lunch? We're probably going to be here for a good portion of the day."

He hesitated, but realized Megan was probably right. Besides, Ellie might feel more comfortable with Megan if he wasn't standing over her looking like he was going to put his fist through the wall.

"All right," he muttered. "What do you gals want to eat?"

"Anything easy," Megan replied. "Pizza works."

Ellie didn't reply, and he knew food was the last thing on her mind.

"Pizza it is." He dropped a kiss on the top of Ellie's head. "You're doing great, sweetheart. Be back soon."

When Tyson walked out the door, Ellie let out the breath she'd been holding. While part of her wanted to beg him to come back, to hold her hand through this, another part of her was relieved he'd gone. Relieved he wouldn't have to hear any more details about her sketchy past with James Mahoney. It was bad enough that he'd learned what a damn coward she was.

"Ellie," Megan began again. "Besides hearing James talk about the drug trafficking, did you ever see anything that could implicate him?"

"I've seen him in action."

Megan nodded, seeming completely unfazed as she typed away. "Did you see money exchange hands? Drugs?"

"Both. He was pretty discreet about it, but I started to suspect things early on. When I confronted him about it...he hit me." Fear lanced down her spine and she shuddered. "I learned to keep my mouth shut after that. I was too scared."

"Did you ever have thoughts about going to the police?"

"Of course. Until I realized they were working with him."

Megan glanced up sharply, her mouth thinning. "You have proof of this?"

"Yes. Well, there's only one I'm aware of. But I've seen him talking to James on multiple occasions. And, after I got subpoenaed, he threatened me."

"A Chicago police officer threatened you?" Megan repeated and then shook her head, fingers flying across her laptop. "Jesus, girl, no wonder you ran."

"So, what happens now?"

Megan pushed her chair back and crossed one leg over another. "Now I request permission from the court to see if I can appear as your attorney." She hesitated. "Look, Ellie, I don't live in Chicago, I'm not licensed to practice in that jurisdiction, but I can make a motion for *admission pro hac vice* that would allow me to get around this. So, if we get that motion granted, I'll see what can be done about your warrant."

Just the word warrant had the ability to make Ellie's knees shake. "Right...God, I feel like such a criminal."

"You were scared and you ran. We're going to fix it. With what you've just told me about being threatened by a dirty cop and your understandable fear, hopefully we'll be able to arrange for you to turn yourself in without being arrested."

Ellie swallowed hard. "Would I still have to testify?"

Megan stared at her for a moment, compassion in her gaze. "Of course, Ellie, you're a key witness in this trial. If you don't testify, James could walk. And now you're likely going to be testifying against this officer as well."

"Of course. You're right. You're totally right." Ellie nodded and stood up, suddenly nauseous. "Sorry. I've just never let myself face the possibility of *actually testifying.*"

"I understand. Look, let me make some phone calls. Go relax and try not to think about it too much."

Ellie gave a wan smile and left the kitchen, her immediate plans not to think about it, but to get sick.

Chapter Fourteen

Ellie walked into their hotel room, her heart pounding a mile a minute. But then, it had been that way since they'd landed at O'Hare over an hour ago.

"How are you holding up?" Tyson asked, closing the door behind them.

"Exhausted. Mentally, at least. I think I want to just eat and then pass out," she said, glancing around the room they'd be holed up in until tomorrow.

The past couple of days had been a blur of activity. Megan getting the motion granted to serve as her attorney and having the arrest warrant removed in exchange for Ellie agreeing to testify. Then Tyson buying airline tickets and getting them all on a flight to Chicago two days later.

After traveling all morning, they had finally arrived in Chicago. Only after dropping by to meet briefly with the prosecutor had they checked into a hotel. Megan had a room down the hall, and she and Tyson were sharing one. They'd agreed to hang out in the hotel, to keep a low profile, until after her testimony.

Tyson set down their bags and crossed the floor to where she stood, cupping her shoulders and pulling her close.

"Why don't I order us some room service and then we can have some time in bed watching television?"

"I'd like that," she finally murmured and wrapped her arms around his waist, pressing her face to his shoulder. "Or maybe you could just hold me after dinner."

He kissed the top of her head and murmured, "You know I will, sweetheart. Now, what do you want to eat?"

"Something light. I'm not sure I can hold down much...too nervous."

"All right." He set her aside and moved to the desk in the

corner, picking up the binder on top. "Let's see what they've got room service wise."

Still half out of it with exhaustion, Ellie walked to the bed and pulled back the covers, climbing in and collapsing against the pillows.

"How about a chicken Caesar salad? And we split some garlic bread?"

Face still buried against the pillow, she mumbled, "Sure. Sounds good."

Tyson laughed softly and then she heard him pick up the phone and order their food. A moment later, the bed dipped as he sat down.

When he smoothed a hand down her back, she sighed and rolled over to face him. He lay beside her, his elbow on the bed and his head propped up on his hand.

"You're amazing, you know that?" she asked softly. "You. Megan. Your family. You didn't have to help me. And yet you've all joined in to help me through this. I'm completely blown away. Humbled."

"We couldn't walk away. For me, it wasn't even an option." He pushed a strand of hair off her head. "And Megan is just an incredible chick."

"Is Megan the same Megan your mom was referring to at the barbeque? Trevor's ex?"

"Yeah. She is."

"Wow. That's sad. She's pretty awesome, and your brother seems great...if a bit haunted."

"Hmm. Interesting word choice for Trevor, but it kind of fits." Tyson frowned and then sighed, glancing toward the bathroom. "I'm going to take a shower before the food gets here."

"All right."

Tyson leaned down and pressed a soft, lingering kiss to her mouth, before climbing off the bed.

"Don't fall asleep. You'll need to answer the door when the food comes if I'm not out."

"Not going to fall asleep," she mumbled, but closed her eyes the moment he shut the bathroom door.

She must've drifted, because she jerked upright when a knock came at the door and someone called out from the other side. Hearing Tyson still in the shower, she scrambled off the bed, blinking away her disorientation and rushed to the door.

"Hang on."

She unlocked the door and then began to pull it open. Wait, the person had yelled *housekeeping,* not *room service.*

The door shoved inward and she stumbled back from the sheer force. Her stomach hit the floor as she realized the man who stepped inside the room was definitely not a hotel employee.

"Thought I warned you keep your mouth shut," Officer Maliano muttered quietly and withdrew a gun from the waist of his pants.

She wanted to scream for Tyson, but her gaze was locked on the gun and her throat had gone tight.

The dirty cop strode toward her and wrapped his fingers around her neck, shoving her hard against the wall. She clawed at his hand, her ability to breathe completely gone.

"You trying to be all brave and honorable, Eleanor?" he sneered. "Going to testify tomorrow? I don't think so. James wouldn't like that. I don't like that. You show up in that courtroom and you're a dead bitch."

He pressed the gun to her head and she closed her eyes, her body shaking violently as she grew dizzy from lack of oxygen.

"Got that? You're *dead.* There are plenty of people who will do it. And you'll suffer first. Maybe I'll bring in some friends to take turns with you. You'll be so goddamn horrified, you'll beg me to kill you."

Stars danced behind her closed lids and her effort to pry his hand away grew weaker as her fingers went numb.

She heard the shower turn off and Lionel glanced toward the bathroom, eyes narrowing.

His attention snapped back to her, as he demanded softly, "Do you *fucking understand me?*"

She nodded, anything to make him her go. And then he did. She dropped to the floor in a dead weight, sucking in air greedily.

His retreating footsteps sounded, followed by the soft click of the door shutting.

Officer Maliano had gone as quickly as he came.

Tyson had just pulled on his boxer shorts when he heard a thud. The hairs on the back of his neck rose and unease shot down his spine.

He jerked open the bathroom door and immediately spotted Ellie on the ground, clutching her neck. Fear and rage exploded in him as he strode into the room, helping her to her feet.

"The cop," she croaked and pointed to the door.

"Call 9-1-1," Tyson snarled, grabbing his gun out of the suitcase that sat open on the bed.

Then he tore out of the room and immediately spotted the man he assumed to be Ellie's attacker pressing the elevator button down the hall.

The man heard Tyson coming and glanced his way. Any pretense at casualness disappeared as the man sprinted past the elevator toward the stairs.

Tyson pushed himself faster, his bare feet flying over the thin carpet of the halls. Shit, anyone who spotted them would think he was nuts. Running down the hall wearing nothing but boxer shorts, gun in his hand.

The cop ahead of him pushed open the stairwell and burst through, but Tyson was just seconds behind him now.

Tyson spotted the gun tucked into the man's waistband, and knew he had no intention of using it. If he had, he would've shot Ellie in the room. No, the guy had only shown up to intimidate her into disappearing again—he was stupid, but not stupid enough to kill someone and face a murder charge.

The cop rounded the first sharp turn in the stairwell, and was almost directly parallel to him, but a floor down.

Tyson didn't think, just acted. He grabbed the rail and leapt over it, falling probably six feet before he landed on the man and sent them both sprawling to the concrete steps.

Pain sizzled through Tyson's wrist and the air was knocked violently out of him, but it only kept him down for a second. He staggered to his feet and leveled the gun at the dirty cop.

"Move and I'll shoot," he said.

But the man didn't reply and his eyes were closed. Tyson knelt down, keeping the gun trained on him, and felt for a pulse.

Still there, but it was obvious the guy was out cold.

Probably hit his head on the concrete when Tyson had jumped on him.

The door at the floor above burst open.

"Tyson!" Ellie's scream reverberated in the empty stairwell.

"Down here," he called out, holding his arm just above the wrist. "Did you call for help?"

"Yes! They're on their way." She hurried down the stairs, cast a glance at the cop out cold, and then threw herself into his arms. "Oh God, I'm so glad you're okay. You shouldn't have gone after him."

Tyson pressed a kiss against her forehead, then leaned back to look her over.

"Did he hurt you?"

Her hand fluttered to her neck where he could see red marks that would doubtless turn to bruises.

"Damn it, sweetheart," he muttered fiercely and pulled her against him. "I'm so sorry."

"I wonder how he found us."

"Probably called every hotel in town until he found one of our names. Before I knew about him, I called Chicago P.D. to let them know I had you in custody." He shook his head, angry both with himself and the situation as a whole. "I thought we were being safe checking in tonight under Megan's name, but the asshole must've figured out who your attorney was too. And when a cop calls a hotel, most of the time they give out info."

"I'm just glad you're okay," she whispered, wrapping her arms tighter around his waist.

He moved his hand over her back, reassuring himself that *she* was okay. That she was here. A chill slid down his spine and a sheen of sweat broke out on his forehead.

He'd been in the bathroom when that bastard had come in. What if she'd been seriously hurt? What if the dirty cop had just decided to put a bullet in her head?

His stomach rolled and he closed his eyes briefly.

Another door slammed and the hotel security rushed up the stairs, saving him from the tormenting *what ifs*. He set Ellie aside gently and went to meet them.

The cold wood of the bench pushed against Ellie's thighs.

She suppressed a shiver and listened, her head cocked, to the defense grilling the current witness behind the closed door of the courtroom.

She was next.

"I'm going to run to the bathroom," Megan said, checking her watch. "They're running behind."

The clicking of her heels sounded on the linoleum floor as she disappeared around the corner.

"You doing all right, Ellie?" Tyson asked, ceasing his pacing of the hallway to come sit next to her. "Do you still feel sick?"

"No. I feel...nothing. I think I'm numb." She sighed and slid her hand into his. "I just want this to be done with."

He squeezed his fingers around hers reassuringly. "Me too, sweetheart. Me too."

She glanced at his other hand, his sprained wrist bandaged after his fall. "How's your hand?"

"Fine. Don't even notice it with a few pain killers."

"Good." She drew in a ragged breath. "I'll have testify against Officer Maliano, too, huh?"

"Not for a few months, I'm sure. Don't think about that now. Besides, at least the jerk is in jail now."

"What if there's more like him?" she asked, voicing the fears that she'd tried to snuff out. "More people who were working for James?"

"Law enforcement doesn't look fondly on a cop who goes dirty, Ellie. Trust me. If there are more, they're trying to find them right now. And you can bet your money that Officer Maliano is not enjoying his time behind bars."

She nodded, suddenly wanting to drop the topic. They'd been awake half the night talking to the Chicago P.D. about him, and when she had finally slept, she'd relived the moment when Officer Maliano had come into the hotel room and threatened her.

The door to the courtroom swung open and a uniformed police officer carrying a notebook—he was apparently the prosecution's last witness—came striding out. He winked at her as he passed.

"Miss Owens?"

She glanced back to see the prosecutor, Robert Samuels, striding out of the courtroom. The thin Asian man, with whom she'd met briefly yesterday, clasped his hands in front of himself and smiled.

"You ready?"

Ellie nodded, though trying to force a smile in response wasn't really possible. She took a step forward and then paused.

"Wait. My lawyer is—"

"Right here," Megan called out from the end of the hall.

The prosecutor turned to look at her and Ellie noted the blatant male appreciation in his gaze before he was once again professional. It didn't surprise her anymore, all the men who looked at Megan. She was drop-dead gorgeous.

"All right," Mr. Samuels said, turning to face Ellie again. "Why don't we head in?"

Ellie nodded and followed him, reassured knowing Tyson and Megan were right behind her. She walked to the witness stand, felt every pair of eyes in the courtroom on her as she took her oath.

Her focus turned to James, sitting beside the defense attorney, and for a moment her heart seemed to stop—her whole body went cold. But then she looked beyond him and saw Tyson and Megan sitting in the first row of benches.

Tyson's gaze locked with hers and she heard his silent words of encouragement, saw how much he supported her and the confidence he had in her.

A calmness and a quiet assurance settled over her. Yes. She *would* get through this.

She sat down in the witness chair, smiled at the jury, and waited for the questioning to begin.

"You were amazing," Tyson muttered, shutting the door to their hotel room.

He cupped Ellie's face and brushed his lips over hers, backing her up toward the bed. When she hit the edge, he pushed her back onto it, following with his body.

Tyson's lips trailed kisses down her neck and to the neckline of her blouse.

"I thought I did pretty good," she agreed with a breathy laugh, delving her hands into his hair. "Think it's enough to convict him?"

He lifted his head and stared down at her. "I think you made a pretty good impression on the jury, Ellie. And, from what I understand, there were at least two heavy-hitter witnesses before you."

"It'll probably be a few more days at least before they finish up, the prosecutor said. Before the jury deliberates." She sighed and closed her eyes. "It's going to be hard not to think about it."

"I have some pretty good ideas how to distract you," Tyson murmured, slowly unfastening her buttons on her blouse with his good hand.

Her eyes darkened with anticipation. "Hey, now, that might just work."

He winked at her and then cupped her breasts. Lowering his head, he suckled her nipples through the silky bra and reveled in the cry of pleasure she made. She squirmed beneath him, before her head fell back against the pillow.

Reaching beneath her, he easily removed her bra and plucked it free from her breasts. Then he brought his mouth to her again, licking and nibbling her nipples while unfastening her skirt.

A moment later, he had removed the rest of her clothing and she lay on the bed. Ellie wrapped her leg over his hip, opening her body completely to him. And Tyson wasted no time taking advantage of it, delving his fingers into the slick folds between her thighs to bring her to a higher state of arousal.

Then he moved lower, replacing his fingers with his mouth. Following the rise and fall of her body until she was screaming out his name and clutching his hair.

Tyson put on a condom, and with the orgasm still shuddering through Ellie's body, he eased into her.

His eyes closed and he breathed out an unsteady breath. Jesus, he'd never get over the way being inside her made him feel. Feeling the strain of supporting himself with one hand, he rolled over so Ellie rode him.

Gripping her hip, he thrust up and into her. She moaned and rocked back and forth, until they were moving in unison. Joining together with such ease that made him feel like they'd been doing this with each other forever.

When he reached his release a short while later, Ellie was right there with him. They both cried out as they came.

As the powerfulness of his climax faded, the pounding of his heart corresponded with the pounding of realization in his head. He had them both booked on a return flight to Portland tomorrow, but would Ellie really fly back? Her reason for being in Wyattville no longer existed and she hadn't left anything behind besides a few clothing items. Then she'd just have to pay to fly home again eventually.

Unless...an idea took root in his head, and he wondered if he was crazy for considering it. But he had to ask. If he didn't, he'd always wonder...

Chapter Fifteen

Ellie snuggled against him, her eyes still closed and her heart racing a mile a minute. She couldn't seem to get enough of him. His touch, his scent, being in his arms. She didn't want to move.

It felt so right. When had anything ever felt so right? When had any guy ever made her feel all giddy inside? Who else could make her feel like she could take on the world—

Her eyes snapped back open and she stilled, unable to breathe. Oh sweet Jesus. She was in love with him.

A fear that was almost stronger than that of this morning's rushed through her. How had it happened so fast? How had she *let* it happen?

"So, did you miss it?"

"Miss what?" she asked, trying to keep her voice normal, but it still came out kind of high pitched.

"Chicago."

Relax, Ellie. Just relax. It's a normal question, just focus and answer it. "Uh, well, considering I was only gone a week or so, not really."

"What about your friends? Family?"

See, this wasn't too bad. "My parents live in Michigan now. Most of my friends I'm not really close to anymore. They're married, have children, or they've moved on. Physically and metaphorically speaking."

Tyson smoothed a hand down her back, silent for a moment. And then he asked softly, "Think you'd miss them more if you moved to Wyattville?"

Ellie blinked. Had she heard him wrong? Hope clung in every inch of her being as she looked up at him.

"What are you asking, Tyson?"

His expression flickered between earnest and uncomfortable. "Well, I realize we've only known each other a short time, and you'd probably think I was crazy if I suggested getting married. But maybe you would consider moving out to the west coast? You could teach yoga in town. I know this great place..."

She gave the tiniest shake of her head and whispered, "I wouldn't."

Disappointment flashed across his face and he nodded. "Yeah, I suppose that's a hell of a lot to ask."

"No. I mean wouldn't think you were crazy for suggesting marriage." It was gambling on a comment he'd loosely thrown out there, but right now, it was worth the risk. "I would love to move to Wyattville. I love the people, the town, and most of all... I love you, Tyson."

Tyson's gaze searched hers and then that familiar grin she'd grown to love sprawled across his face. "And how long have you known this, sweetheart?"

"Um, for about two minutes."

He laughed and rolled her under him again, pressing a solid kiss against her mouth.

"Then I forgive you for not telling me earlier," he said and caressed her cheek. "And I claim bragging rights for having realized I'm in love with *you* about three days earlier."

Her heart swelled with love and she blinked away tears. "Seriously?"

His humor faded and he nuzzled her neck. "Seriously, Ellie. You've only been in my life a short time, but I just can't imagine you out of it now."

"You don't have to." She clung to him, not fighting the tears this time. "Because wherever you are, that's where I want to be."

He groaned softly and then kissed her again, and she gave herself over. To the passion. To the possibilities. And to their future...

Megan disconnected her cell phone call and smiled, slipping it back into her purse. Maybe she should've just left a message for Tyson and Ellie, but the idea of delivering the news in person would be more exciting. James Mahoney had just been found guilty by the jury.

And what better way to celebrate than with cupcakes from Kate's Cakes?

The two lovebirds had been busy getting Ellie moved cross country and into Tyson's house and planning a wedding, it sounded like.

Megan's heels clicked on the paved sidewalk of Main Street as she headed back to her car, adjusting the box of cupcakes in her hands.

"Megan?"

She stopped walking and closed her eyes, tension radiating through her body at the sound of his voice. *For fuck's sake.* Would she ever be able to hear it without getting sucked into the past?

Forcing a polite smile onto her face, she opened her eyes and turned to face Trevor.

"Hi, Trevor."

He stood tall and straight, every bit the soldier with the poker face and stiff nod he greeted her with. His eyes, once full of heat and passion for her, were void of any emotion.

"I just wanted to thank you for what you did for Tyson and his fiancée."

It was amazing he didn't follow it up with a *ma'am*. Her heart twisted and she forced herself to swallow the bitterness in her throat.

"No problem. Your family means a lot to me." She had to leave. If she stood here one more minute, she'd do something foolish—like cry. Or throw a cupcake at him. "I don't mean to be rude, but I'm on my way somewhere. It was good to see you again."

She turned away, hoping he'd stop her. But there was nothing but the sound of her footsteps until she reached her car.

You need to move on, Megan. It's obvious he has. Find someone new.

Lifting her head higher, she opened the door to her convertible and climbed in, vowing to do just that.

Pushing Trevor Wyatt from her head, she pulled the car away from the curb.

It was time to go deliver the good news to the soon-to-be newlyweds.

Command and
Control

Dedication

Thank you to my family and friends for your support of my writing, and to those who are my beta readers and critiquers. To my readers, whom I adore and who've picked up my books over the years. To my editor, Tera, for making my books all sparkly goodness. Special thanks to my friend Patricia for sharing your experience with the military and the time you spent in Iraq. And most importantly, for this book, thank you to all the military heroes out there who've given their time, and sometimes theirs lives, for their country. My characters are fiction, but you're the real deal. And you don't get thanked nearly enough.

Chapter One

What the *hell?*

Trevor Wyatt froze, one foot already outside the coffee shop, his mind echoing with what he'd just overheard.

Megan was getting married.

His chest tightened, almost crushing his ability to breathe as the blood pounded harder in his veins. He moved out of the entryway and back into the store, stepping to the creamer station to slowly add three packs of sugar he didn't even want to his coffee.

"Bev, I swear to God I saw it with my own two eyes," Lisa, Wyattsville's most notorious gossip, proclaimed. "Not even five minutes ago Megan was picking out wedding cakes down at Kate's Cakes."

Five minutes ago? That meant she might still be there. Trevor didn't need to hear another word, just strode out the door—coffee forgotten on the counter—and hurried toward Kate's shop. The fact that he needed to be at his parents' house in twenty minutes had just slipped on his priority list.

His fists clenched and his head pounded with sudden tension. How the hell was it even remotely possible that Megan was getting married? Damn it, he hadn't even realized she was seeing anyone.

Maybe if you came back from Fort Lewis on the weekends as much as you used to, you'd have figured it out.

But coming back to Wyattsville meant facing Megan and the fact that he'd failed her. Failed them. Coming back drove a hot poker into another emotional wound he couldn't seem to heal, that'd he'd begun to realize would probably never heal. He was a fucking mess. Megan didn't deserve that. He'd kept telling himself that until he'd finally driven her away.

Right into someone else's arms it seemed.

"Hey, Trevor, didn't know you were back in town!" one of his friend's called out as they passed each other on the sidewalk.

Trevor nodded, unable to form a response to his friend. With each brisk stride he took, familiar faces rushed to move out of his way, their eyes widening, even as more people called out a greeting or welcomed him back.

An image of Megan flitted through his head. The same vision that usually came to mind when he let himself really think about her. An image from two summers ago. She was lying in the grass over on Evergreen Hill, her red hair sprawled out with the wildflowers as she smiled up at him through her lashes. Her blue eyes twinkled with amusement and intimacy, her breasts rising gently with each seductive laugh she made.

Frustration seeped through his pores and into his blood until he let out a snarl of frustration as he spotted the shop with the pink overhang that was supposed to resemble frosting. The shop Megan was hopefully still in.

She was never supposed to marry anyone else. She was supposed to marry *him*.

He shoved open the door to the shop and strode inside, his gaze sweeping the small confines until he found her.

She stood by the display case full of cakes, dressed in a skirt suit that hugged her curves, laughing as she spoke to Kate, the owner of the shop. But the moment he entered the store, her laughter had died and her lush mouth had parted just enough to show her surprise, even as her gaze remained unreadable. She was always so damn good at that. Keeping her emotions under control. They were one in the same that way.

Longing slammed into Trevor's chest, hitting him like a two-by-four, clenching his heart with an almost physical pain and stirring his blood with a hot arousal that had become somewhat a novelty.

Beneath his jeans his cock twitched, recognizing the only woman who could just about make him come in his pants when she gave him *the look*. The only woman who could affect him on such a primal, sexual, male level.

Megan marrying someone else?
Like hell.

Megan's mouth went dry and her heart rocked against her

rib cage, but she kept her features carefully schooled as she stared at the man who'd once captured—and then crushed—her heart.

She hadn't even known Trevor Wyatt was back in town. Had begun to wonder if he'd show up for his own brother's wedding. There'd been a time when the oldest Wyatt brother would return every weekend from Washington State to spend time with his family...with her. But those days were gone. The citizens of Wyattsville—the town named after his ancestor— were lucky to see Trevor once every couple of months nowadays.

But he was obviously back now. He'd stormed into Kate's Cakes, slamming the door behind him, with an expression on his face one that could make most people draw back in alarm. And Kate, the owner of the shop, was no exception, with her rounded eyes and gaping mouth.

Megan turned her attention fully on Trevor again, trying not to let her gaze meander over his tall, solid, soldier's body. Telling herself it was better not to linger on the dark eyes or hard mouth that could reduce her to a puddle. Even if that mouth was taut with anger right now. The question was, what was behind that anger?

"Trevor," she finally managed in a neutral tone that shocked the hell out of her. "Nice to see you back in town."

But it wasn't nice. Not really. Seeing him again had her heart twisting like someone wringing out a towel. It made her stomach bounce around like she was on an amusement-park ride. Seeing Trevor again made her take another step back in her attempts to get over him. And she was trying. Dear God in heaven how she was trying.

Trevor took a step toward her, but Megan held her ground, refusing to retreat any further, even as her pulse jumped with alarm. Was he angry with *her*?

She finally met his accusing gaze and her breath caught as the air seemed to sizzle between them.

"What's this I hear," he began, his voice low and unsteady, "about you getting married?"

Megan's jaw hit the floor. Whatever she'd been expecting, it hadn't been that. Behind the counter, she heard Kate gasp.

"Megan?" Kate squeaked. "You're not seriously marrying *Henry*, are you?"

Trevor's attention swung to Kate. "His name is Henry?"

Megan straightened and sucked in a breath. "Now hold on a min—"

"Oh no." Kate shook her head and stepped back, lifting her hands. "I'm *so* not getting involved in this. In fact, I think I hear the phone ringing." She nearly ran to the office of the shop.

Megan ground her teeth together. *Marrying Henry?* How had Trevor even heard she was dating anyone? Oh wait, that whole small-town thing. She'd only lived in Wyattsville for five years, and sometimes it was easy to forget how quickly news spread. She just hadn't thought it would spread all the way up to the Fort Lewis army base.

"Is it true?" Trevor asked.

"No. I'm not marrying Henry," she finally said, even as resentment rushed through her. Her fists clenched at her side and she lifted her chin, meeting Trevor's steely gaze with one of her own. "Though I don't see how it would be any of your concern if I was."

Only the ticking of the loud cupcake clock on the wall broke the silence. As she watched, Trevor's nostrils flared and a tiny tic began on his jawline.

"Who is he?"

"*He* is none of your concern."

"Maybe he is."

Was Trevor jealous?

Her stomach churned and she had to snuff out the tiny spark of hope that flared in her heart. This happened every time she saw him. The spark threatened to become an obnoxious flame that wouldn't die—that would ensure she was miserable loving the one man who couldn't seem to love her anymore.

"He isn't," she said resolutely. "You lost the right to be concerned about what happens in my life when you walked out of it."

Trevor took another step toward her. "If I recall correctly, you're the one who ended our engagement."

Pain stabbed through her, tightening her throat with tears she couldn't shed. Why was he bringing this up *now*? After months of shutting her out. Abandoning her and his family. After she'd finally tried to move on. Key word, tried.

She opened her mouth to argue. To point out that he'd

ended their relationship way before she'd made it official. But why bother? If she argued that he was a year too late, she'd just end up crying. And she'd sworn she was done shedding tears over Trevor Wyatt. They just didn't help anything.

Self-preservation had Megan closing her mouth again and adjusting the strap of her purse higher up on her shoulder. "I need to go. If Kate returns, please tell her I'll just come back this afternoon."

"Wait," Trevor pleaded, blocking her exit with his large body. A body she was entirely too familiar with, a body capable of giving so much pleasure.

His gaze sought hers, and the mix of frustration, anger and tinge of desperation in his eyes had her throat tightening with emotion.

"*What?*" she choked out.

"If you're not getting married, why are you looking at wedding cakes?"

Megan blinked. Was that where he'd gotten the idea she was getting married? Because she'd been looking at *cakes*? Of all the ridiculous...

"Because—in case you've forgotten, Trevor," she sputtered. "Your brother's getting married in a week. And seeing as I'm the maid of honor to your future sister-in-law, that puts me in charge of the bachelorette party this weekend. And at this kind of party, women like to eat cake. Got it now?"

"Got it. The cake is for Ellie," he muttered, relief flickering in his eyes. He stepped away from the doorway to let her through.

Megan held her breath, moving past him. She was almost out of the shop when he asked, "So then you're not serious about this Henry guy?"

With her back to him, she closed her eyes and drew her bottom lip between her teeth. She thought about being honest. Telling Trevor that Henry was just a guy from the next town who occasionally asked her to dinner. Seriously debated telling Trevor that *he* was the only man she wanted. Would *ever* want.

But she didn't. Instead she walked away from him and got into her car.

Chapter Two

Trevor set the empty shot glass back onto the counter and savored the familiar burn of whiskey down his throat. It always numbed him a bit. His emotions, and the pain in his shoulder that was more phantom than real now. He tried not to drink too often, because he'd seen how alcohol could become a soldier's crutch. And though many times he'd been tempted to just hit the bottle as a way out, he'd found the strength not to.

He reached for a peanut out of the bowl in front of him, snapping open the fragile shell and digging out the nuts inside, before placing them in his mouth. The crunch of him chewing seemed loud enough to echo in the quiet of the bar.

It wasn't quite noon and he and Evan—the bartender—were the only ones inside the dimly lit Oceanside Tavern. The smell of beer and grease lingered in the building.

"Didn't realize you were back in town already, Trevor," Evan said, wiping down one of the beer taps. "Suppose you're helping Tyson get ready for his big day?"

Trevor managed a nod, but that was all. It was the third time Evan had tried to engage him in conversation, and finally he seemed to realize it was hopeless.

"I'll just turn on some music," Evan muttered with a sigh. "We usually don't get folks in this early."

A moment later the twang of a country song came on, and then the bar filled with a soft crooning.

Trevor reached for another peanut. God, he hated country music. He'd always preferred the harder stuff. Give him Metallica any day over the latest Johnny Cash knockoff.

Megan had always been trying to covert him to *the dark side,* as she'd liked to tease.

His gut twisted and he closed his eyes, reaching blindly for the shot glass again. *Megan.* God he missed her. She'd always been the only one who truly understood him.

"Can I get another one of these, Evan?" he rasped.

"I think you've probably had enough, Trev."

Trevor's shoulders went rigid and he opened his eyes, drawing in a slow breath before swiveling on the bar stool to face the newcomer.

"Tyson," he acknowledged with a grunt. "Is that your opinion as the town sheriff, or—"

"That's my opinion as your brother." Tyson gave a brief smile and crossed the bar to sit at the stool next to him.

"Little brother."

"By two years." Tyson grabbed a peanut and snapped the shell in half. "The parents missed you at lunch."

Shit. The air seethed out from between Trevor's teeth and he shook his head. How could he have completely screwed this up? He was staying in their house while he was in town. He'd left briefly for coffee at one of the shops and then forgotten all about the scheduled lunch the moment he'd stepped into Kate's Cakes and spoken with Megan.

"I'll apologize when I return," he said quietly and then lifted his shot glass, gesturing again to Evan for another.

From the corner of his eye, Trevor could see his brother watching him with a frown.

"Everyone's still up at the house, Trev. Nobody's left yet. They sent me looking for you since you're not answering your phone."

"Turned it off. I'm not good company right now." He nodded his thanks to Evan as the man refilled his shot of whiskey.

"Yeah? Well, you haven't been good company for a while now, bro. Think it's fair to keep letting them down?"

He let everyone down. His family. Megan. His soldiers... Trevor's mouth twisted into a bitter smile as he lifted the glass and downed the contents.

"I don't know what the fuck is fair anymore, Tyson," he finally muttered.

Tyson ate the peanut and sighed. "Talk to us, Trevor. We want to help you."

Trevor stood and pulled his wallet from the back of his jeans. He tugged a twenty out and tossed it on the bar counter.

"I'm beyond help. Tell the parents I'm sorry and I'll be back later."

Turning on his heel, he strode from the bar, stepping out into the end-of-summer sunshine that had his eyes blinking to adjust.

The town was small enough that nearly all the businesses were strewn around Main Street. His gaze moved down a few shops to Kate's Cakes, searching the curb next to it, even knowing the red convertible left over a half hour ago.

"I shouldn't have said what I did."

Trevor hadn't heard his brother approach again, but then Tyson had always had a quiet way about him.

"You had every right to." He paused and then glanced at Tyson. "I saw Megan this morning."

Understanding dawned in his brother's blue eyes and he gave a sage nod.

"How'd that go?"

"Not well." Trevor rubbed a hand over the back of his closely shaved head. "She's seeing someone I guess."

"That's the word going round."

The weight in his gut doubled and Trevor's jaw flexed. He didn't want to think of Megan with anyone else, especially some prick named Henry.

"Don't think it's very serious though, Trev," Tyson said quietly. "In fact, I'm wagering she still has feelings for you. Get your shit together, bro, and try and get her back."

Get her back? How many times had he thought about the idea? Told himself to swallow his god damn pride and admit he was a fuck-up. But the truth of it was, as much as he wanted her back, he knew he didn't deserve her. Megan deserved to be put on a pedestal and damn near worshipped. The woman was smart as hell, sexy, determined...any man who'd ever had her would be an idiot to have let her go. So that put him at the top of the idiot list. He'd not only had her, but he'd been months away from making her his wife. And still, he'd let her slip right through his fingers.

"It's too late for us," Trevor said tonelessly. "I messed it all up."

"Why not try? You have a week and a half, Trevor. Ten days to try and make things right before your leave is up and Uncle Sam gets you back. If you can return to Fort Lewis and not regret not trying to fight for Megan, then by all means, walk away."

Walk away. His stomach knotted and he bit back a sigh. He'd already let Megan do that a year ago when he'd pretty much pushed her into calling off the engagement.

It should have been him and Megan getting married right now; instead it was his little brother and the woman he'd proposed to after knowing her only a couple of weeks. A twinge of jealousy slid through him at the undeniable love and happiness Tyson and Ellie shared.

But not everyone was guaranteed happiness in life. It certainly wasn't in *his* destiny. It should've been enough that he was alive. There were a lot of people who weren't as blessed...

"Think about what I said, and let me drive you back to our parents' place, Trev," Tyson offered, pulling his keys from his jean pocket. "We need you. And whether you want to admit it or not, you need us."

Trevor glanced away, looking out at the Pacific Ocean peeking between the buildings at the end of the road. He rubbed his shoulder unconsciously. Part of him wanted to just walk away and be alone, but then another part of him—smaller, yet determined—knew he'd already been alone far too long.

With a short nod, Trevor followed his little brother back to his car.

Megan refilled her coffee cup with hands that weren't quite steady and cursed Trevor Wyatt for the fifth time that morning.

It was his fault she'd tossed and turned all night, so it was his fault there were dark circles under her eyes and her head felt like it was full of cotton. Fortunately a little cover-up helped the eyes, and the two pots of coffee were almost keeping her awake.

She sighed and crossed the floor of her office to peek out the window. Main Street was just a few blocks to the right and up the hill to the left was the road that led to the Wyatts' home.

Her pulse quickened and she bit her lower lip, shaking her head. She needed to get over this. Get used to being around Trevor again—at least for the next week. Because he was going to be very much involved with all the little details of the wedding, seeing as Tyson had made him best man and she was the maid of honor.

Shelli Stevens

"Shit." Her hands clenched around the mug in her hand and she pressed her lips tightly together to try and stop the flood of emotions threatening.

He hadn't touched her yesterday, but when he'd stood so close, staring down at her, the need and possessiveness in his gaze had ripped her ability to breathe away.

It had been all she could do not to want to press herself up against him and wind her arms around his neck. To lift her mouth to his for the kiss her body and heart craved.

But sex with Trevor was a bad idea. Maybe if she wasn't in love with the man and she could look at it as *just sex* it would be okay. But this wasn't some random guy she'd dated for a few months; this was Trevor, the man she should have married.

The office phone rang, snapping her thoughts back to work. She returned to her desk and lifted the receiver.

"This is Megan Asher."

"Meg, how are you?"

Henry. She bit back a sigh, recognizing the man she'd been dating for almost a month now.

"Hello, Henry. I'm all right. How are you?"

"Great. Was just checking to see if we were still on for dinner tonight?"

The bell above the office door jingled as someone entered the building.

"Dinner? I—"

Her mind went blank as Trevor closed the door behind him and crossed the room in a couple easy strides, before furling his tall body into the chair in front of her desk.

"Meg? You still there?"

"I'm...yes," she said huskily, her gaze locked with Trevor's darker one. "Dinner."

"So that's a yes?" Henry asked, confusion entering his tone.

Trevor's mouth curved into a slight smile, but there was no humor in his eyes.

"Henry, let me call you back in a few minutes." She replaced the receiver before he could answer.

Leaning back in her chair, Megan crossed one leg over another and watched Trevor calmly. Even if her heart was racing a mile a minute, she prided herself on her control. Her ability not to react. Having the upper hand was not just a

124

benefit for her, it was a requirement.

"Trevor," she finally greeted cordially. "How can I help you?"

"Now there's a loaded question, angel," he said softly as his gaze slid over her, lingering on the silk camisole beneath her open blazer that hugged her breasts. "I've got a few ideas on just exactly how you could help me."

Chapter Three

Megan's breath hitched at his not-so-subtle implication. Her breasts swelled beneath his gaze and a liquid heat seared through her body and gathered heavy between her legs.

Keep the control, Megan. You can't let him see how much he affects you still.

"Perhaps you could be more specific?" She arched a brow. "And if this is legal advice, you realize I have a fee."

He laughed, the deep, sexy sound sending a wave of shivers down her back.

"I'm not here for legal advice, Megan."

"No? Then what are you here for? Because, in case you haven't noticed, Trevor, I'm working. And I can't spend my time—"

"Planning dates with a guy named Henry?"

So he'd heard that? A flush worked its way up her neck, but she kept her expression impassive.

"Why are you here, Trevor?" she asked again.

"You'll have to tell him no."

Megan stilled. "Excuse me?"

"Henry boy. You'll have to tell him that you can't have dinner with him tonight."

This time she let out a slow, throaty laugh that had his eyes darkening further.

"And why is that?" she asked.

"Because you're having dinner with me."

The hell she was. Megan let the smile on her face become a bit sympathetic.

"I find it best not to go to dinner with my exes," she murmured and pushed back her chair to stand. "Now if you'll excuse me—"

"Because there's so many of them? Exes?" Trevor asked, standing as well and blocking her escape from where she'd been about to slip past him. "We were together for two years and before that, I remember you saying there was no one serious."

Annoyance sparked in her belly and it pricked her to realize she probably wasn't hiding it from her eyes now. "This is all a bit irrelevant, Trevor. I'm not having dinner with you."

He slowly made his way around her desk, and she took a few steps backward, her pulse quickening and her mouth going dry.

"Come on, angel, just admit it," he said softly, advancing upon her. "The idea of dinner with Henry does nothing for you."

"Henry happens to be a very nice man," she said quickly, her back literally against the wall now.

Oh God, if he came any closer—and there, damn it he did! Their knees were nearly bumping now. She drew in a sharp breath, but it only filled her head with the scent of him. His shampoo and soap that was painfully familiar. The faint hint of his cologne. Megan had the urge to nuzzle his neck, to flick her tongue and see if he still tasted the same.

You're crazy, Megan, get it together.

"Tell me about this Henry guy," he commanded softly, his gaze sliding over her face, searching her eyes. "Does he wear starched suits and bowties?"

"Actually, he doesn't." They were just regular ties.

Her heart thumped wildly against her rib cage and the proximity of his body to hers had every tiny hair on the back of her neck lifting up in awareness. Why oh why didn't she share an office with anyone? Most of her days were spent on the phone with clients, answering e-mails or doing paperwork, but very rarely did anyone come in.

She was alone with Trevor unless she forced him to leave. And right now—though her brain was screaming at her to throw him out on his cocky ass—her body was begging him to stay. To stop just looking at her and to touch her. Because she missed him so much. She missed being held in his arms and kissing him. Touching him. Talking...though the talking had ended long before the kissing had.

Every muscle in her body was coiled with tension. With need.

"I've always loved you like this, Megan." He reached out

and traced the lapel of her blazer. "But you know that, don't you? All prim and proper in your trim little suits."

"Trevor—"

"Nobody could possibly know by looking at you just what a little animal you are in bed," he muttered thickly, his fingers gliding back up her lapel and then inward, to trace the neckline of her silk camisole. "How when you come hard you can scar up a man's back with those claws of yours."

His words had her biting back a throaty moan. Even as her nipples tightened and dampness gathered in her panties. She could see it in her head. Could almost feel his cock pounding into her again as the weight of his body pinned hers to the bed.

No, sex won't fix anything.

"Remember that time when we first started dating, when I fucked you in this office?" he asked. "When I bent you over that desk right over there, lifted your skirt, pushed those tiny panties you love to wear aside and just took you?"

Her sex clenched with an ache to be filled, because she did remember. But she shook her head, trying to make him stop verbalizing such a sensual memory.

"Remember how you begged me, angel?" He smiled. "'Cause I sure do."

"Please..."

"Does Henry make you feel like this? Does he know that kissing the small of your back makes you whimper like a bitch in heat?" His voice dropped an octave as his finger dipped under the neckline of her top to caress the swell of her breasts.

Push him away. Tell him to stop. But she couldn't. Didn't want to.

"Or when he's sucking on your tits, are you biting your tongue not to call out my name?"

"Trevor," she pleaded huskily, arching into his touch.

"Yeah. Just like that." And then his head descended, his mouth slanting across hers.

Megan couldn't have resisted even if she'd wanted to. She cried out as his lips plundered her, as his tongue thrust fiercely against hers as if to remind her just who was kissing her. As if she could ever, ever forget.

Trevor gathered her close, his hands sliding up her back to

jerk her hard against him. Jesus, he'd missed this. Missed her. The feel of Megan in his arms. Her breasts pressed hard against him and the throaty moans coming from the back of her throat. It'd been over a year since he'd touched her like this. An entire fucking year.

Her hands slid up the back of his neck, over his closely shaved head and triumph surged through him. He wanted to wipe out any thought of another man from her mind, shake the visual from his own head of anyone but him touching her.

Damn it, Megan was his. How had he ever been stupid enough to let her walk away? To give up on this? To give up on them?

With a growl low in his throat, he deepened the kiss, tasting her thoroughly. Unable to get enough of her, Trevor slid his hands over her hips and pulled them flush together, loving the softness of her belly against his cock.

And then it wasn't enough. He needed to touch her everywhere. Feel the most intimate part of her that couldn't lie about how much she wanted him.

Trevor moved his hands lower again, catching the edge of her suit skirt and dragging it up to her hips. He slid his hand between her legs, finding the soaked lace covering her pussy.

The whimper Megan let out was the exact one he'd been waiting to hear. Too long.

He tugged aside the silky panties she wore and brushed his knuckles over the wet, swollen folds of her pussy. His cock lurched against his jeans and he hissed out a breath between clenched teeth, trying to keep himself from just taking her here and now. She deserved more than that.

Megan's mouth slid from his, her head falling back as she gasped, and her hips thrusting into his touch.

Trevor's gaze slid to the pulse in her throat that pounded with arousal. The furious beating mimicked the blood raging through his veins. With a groan, he lowered his head to the curve of her neck and shoulders and flicked his tongue over her, tasting her sweet flesh.

Megan, Megan, Megan.

He pressed a finger slowly into her heat, felt the wet grip of her pussy around him and just about came on the spot.

Megan did come. She let out a choked scream, her nails dragging down the back of his neck as her body jerked against him.

Trevor's mouth curved in a small smile of dismay as he buried his face into the curve of her breasts above her top, breathing in her perfume and perspiration as she continued to tremble.

She'd always been so damn responsive, but she'd never come that fast. Usually she needed her clit played with, liked lots of foreplay before she climaxed.

Part of him hoped like hell she'd been saving it all up for him. That the tension had been building and not just anybody could've made her orgasm like this.

But what were the chances she hadn't slept with anyone in a year? He cursed himself again for ever letting her go in the first place.

Trevor gradually became aware of the tension that seeped into Megan's body. She wasn't clinging to him anymore, but it almost seemed like she was trying to sink through the wall behind her.

Lifting his head, he stared down at her and his heart clenched at the dismay and regret in her eyes. Then her thick, black lashes swept down, shielding her gaze.

"Could you please move off me," she asked tightly, her tone void of expression.

Fuck. She hid it well, but Megan's emotional retreat was as methodical and rapid as any unit backing out of an ambush.

Trevor bit back a sigh and pulled her panties back into place, lowering her skirt again. Disappointment clogged thick in his throat as his cock throbbed against the denim of his jeans.

He wouldn't be sleeping with Megan. Not today anyway. But he would have her again. The way she'd melted into him just a few moments ago lit a small spark of hope in his heart. Fragile, but strong enough that he knew he had to fight like hell to get her back.

Stepping away from her, he shook his head. "I didn't mean for it to get that out of hand, angel."

Her lashes swept up, the anger in them brilliant. "The hell you didn't. You knew exactly what you intended the moment you walked in here, Trevor Wyatt."

Maybe he had. But he hadn't let himself hope for one moment she'd be that responsive.

"I won't apologize, Megan," he said quietly. "I can't. Not for something that's so right."

"It's not right anymore, Trevor. Don't you get that?" she almost shouted, frustration causing her brows to draw together. "You don't have a right to touch me. I stopped being your fiancée last year."

"Maybe I want you back."

Megan went rigid, the shock in her eyes twice what it had been a minute ago.

"Get out," she whispered. "Get the hell out of my office and don't come back."

Trevor's jaw clenched. What the fuck had made him make that declaration aloud, without any finesse or plan in his head? Megan had every right to be livid.

"I should go," he agreed with a nod and headed toward the door. "I'll see you tonight at dinner."

"I am not having dinner with you!"

"Yes, Megan, you are. With me and with the rest of my family. So you'd better call that Henry guy back and tell him your date is off." He stopped at the entrance and turned to give her a tight smile. "Ellie asked me to drop by and remind you. She thought you might've forgotten. Guess it's a good thing I stopped by. For more reasons than one."

"Oh, you son of a—"

Trevor slipped out the door, shutting it again before he could hear the rest of her curse. Amusement slid through him, and for the first time in a while he felt a genuine smile slip across his face. Megan had always been sexy as hell when she got pissed.

He strode past the window, feeling her glare on him until he disappeared to where his car was parked on the corner.

He climbed into his truck and slammed the door, let his head fall back against the headrest. His dick was hard as a rock, but he felt better than he had all year.

Tyson was right. He needed to try and get Megan back. Because a lifetime was just too long to live with the regrets if he didn't.

Chapter Four

Megan stepped out of the shower and grabbed the towel folded neatly on the toilet.

She'd been in there for almost a half hour, trying to scrub away the smoldering encounter with Trevor this afternoon. Good God, how had she lost all control around him? How was it that he simply had to decide *he* wanted her again and she was a puddle at his feet?

It was like Pavlov's dog. Only she wasn't a dog and there was no damn bell. Just a sexy soldier who would always have her heart.

Which made her wonder how she was going to ever get through this week. Having to finalize the details of Tyson and Ellie's wedding with Trevor standing by? But she had to get through. Had to keep her head on straight and not get involved with Trevor again. It had been over a year since they'd broken up, and she was finally making steps to get over him.

Tears stung her eyes as she brutally scrubbed her body dry with the towel.

She wanted Trevor to be happy, really she did. She'd been praying for his heart, mind and body to heal since that day she'd received that horrific call from Afghanistan that he'd been hurt.

Just thinking about it now had the ability to make her stomach contents roll and her head spin with terror. She dropped the towel and gripped the counter, shaking her head as she sucked in a great big lungful of air.

Trevor's body had eventually healed, but his heart and mind had never seemed to fully recover. They'd never kept secrets from each other before. But when he'd returned, everything about him had been different. There'd been nothing *but* secrets. And even though the sex between them had still been incredible, she'd always felt like he was holding back. That he was fighting demons while making love to her.

She'd begged him to open up. Begged him to get help. Because they hadn't been a couple anymore, they'd become two people who only came together to have sex. But he'd refused to seek help, to even talk about it. He'd even stopped any planning of their wedding. Retreating more into himself until that chasm between them became so great that not even amazing sex could bridge it. And that's when she'd left. Because staying would've only destroyed her and the love she'd always hold for him.

Megan crossed the bathroom that was still full of steam, and reached for her dress hanging on the door. She slipped into it and then her heels, then made quick time drying her hair and putting on makeup.

When she finally climbed into the convertible, there wasn't enough time to appreciate the summer sun beating down. How the hell had she forgotten about dinner tonight? She'd promised Ellie last week she'd be there.

It was Trevor. He'd returned to town and thrown her entire life for a loop. She wasn't stupid, she knew why he'd tried to seduce her today. The phenomenal sex and chemistry between them had always offered him that brief distraction, moments of happiness where he could just forget. But the price to her heart and own sanity was just too expensive…

By the time she arrived at the local Italian restaurant, the Wyatt clan was already there.

Megan strode to the back of the dim restaurant, inhaling the delicious smell of garlic and olive oil. She kept her head high and avoided looking at Trevor, who sat with the small group of people at the table. Though she knew exactly where his muscled frame was furled into a chair in the back corner.

"Megan," Ellie called out and rushed to her feet. "I thought you might've forgotten. So good to see you."

"You too." Megan embraced the other woman briefly then gave a small smile. "Don't you just look fabulous? Must be that pre-newlywed glow."

She really did look great, Megan thought, taking her seat. Ellie's eyes were full of love and laughter, so unlike the woman Megan had first met over a month ago when Ellie had come to Wyattsville to disappear from a trial she was subpoenaed to testify on.

"Thank you. We're so excited," Ellie said sitting back down and sipping a glass of wine. "And we can't thank all of you enough for helping out and arranging your schedules to be here. Especially you, Trevor. I know the army doesn't just let you run off any time you want."

Tension slid through Megan's muscles and she couldn't help herself from lifting her gaze to the other end of the table. Trevor was already watching her. Their gazes locked and Megan felt the air leave the room.

"No worries," Trevor replied to Ellie without looking away. "I already had the two week leave scheduled for my vacation. So you and Tyson picked a fine weekend to have the wedding. Glad to be here to help."

Megan wanted to look away from him, knew everyone was watching them with open curiosity, but it was impossible.

"Well I'm so glad you said that, Trevor," Ellie went on cheerfully. "Because I'm putting you and Megan in charge of food."

"*What?*" Megan snapped her gaze back to Ellie and Tyson, whose arm was draped around her. She felt the blood draining from her face. "You want—"

"Well, we're divvying up all the areas that need tending to," Tyson explained lightly. "Since we're keeping this a simple, small wedding with just the big barbeque for the reception. We were hoping to trust you and Trevor to plan an easy menu and then make a Costco run a few days before."

"They put me in charge of the alcohol." Todd, the youngest Wyatt brother, grinned from where he sat in the middle of the table and lifted his beer. "Hell *yeah.*"

Megan's teeth snapped together. Costco was like two hours away! Spending that much time alone with Trevor in a car? Planning the menu with him?

She let her gaze slide around all the people at the table. Tyson and Ellie were doing their best to look innocent enough, but she didn't miss the spark of mischief in Tyson's eyes.

Sharon and Dan Wyatt, the brothers' parents, were avoiding looking at her. Instead they studied the restaurant's menu as if this was the first time they'd seen it. Which was ridiculous seeing as they ate here at least once a week.

And then there was Kate, not family, but going to be a bridesmaid in the wedding. She was making no attempt to appear unconcerned, but kept shifting her wide gaze back and forth between Trevor and Megan like they were in some tennis death match.

"I have no problem with that," Trevor said finally, his tone casual.

Right. And if I say I do have a problem with it, I'll be written off as a hard bitch. Though with her reputation in the legal field, it wouldn't be the first time.

"No problem at all," Megan agreed with a forced smile. "Seriously, anything we can do to make this easier on you guys. I'm just surprised you wouldn't want to pick out your own food for the reception."

Ellie waved her hand and laughed. "This is all going to be so casual. I'm sure whatever normal type of barbeque foods you choose will be fine. Besides, I picked the only thing I care about. *Cake.*"

"Nice." Todd ripped a slice of bread off the loaf in the middle of the table, grinning over at Kate. "Kate's of course?"

Kate laughed and rolled her eyes. "Umm, I'd have to hurt someone if they didn't go through me."

"As if there's anybody else I'd choose," Ellie scoffed. "You make *the best* baked goods. You hooked me with those damn cinnamon rolls."

Kate tucked a strand of blonde hair behind her ear and smiled. "Thank you. Those do seem to sell pretty well, too. And the cupcakes. Though my cakes are still what keep me in business."

"I'd come to your place for cupcakes any day of the week, baby." Todd winked and took another swig of beer.

Megan watched as Kate's cheeks filled with color and she resisted the urge to kick Todd under the table. Poor Kate had been nursing a crush on the youngest Wyatt brother for years. Everyone seemed to know *but* Todd. And it didn't help that Todd flirted with every female within fifty miles of Wyattsville.

With a sigh, Megan shifted her gaze and cursed when it connected with Trevor's again. He lifted his beer in a salute and then gave her a slow smile. Probably making a little toast to their unwanted partnership.

Her stomach danced with butterflies and she resisted the urge to press her hand against it to ease the sensation.

Damn Ellie and Tyson for their matchmaking. Didn't they

realize how much this was going to just about kill her?

Tyson cleared his throat. "Now as for dinner tonight, what are you all getting? And remember, Ellie and I are paying. It's the least we can do to thank you all."

There were a few token protests, but Tyson waved them away.

Megan glanced down at her menu, knowing she had to keep her wits about her. Now more than ever.

Trevor ate his dinner in silence, speaking when needed, but happy to remain more of a silent observer on the planning of the upcoming wedding and reception.

It was pretty much what he was used to now, though. Lingering back in the shadows, trying to disappear and be alone with his thoughts.

By the time dinner had arrived everyone had been assigned their tasks, and most of the wedding and reception details had been finalized. It really was a small wedding, which was exactly what Tyson and Ellie had wanted. And Trevor couldn't blame them. It's what he and Megan had once wanted too. Though their dream had always been a quiet ceremony on a beach.

Trevor drew in a painful breath, his fingers clenching around the fork in his hand.

The fact that Tyson and Ellie had paired him up on a project with Megan really didn't surprise him much either. And maybe a week ago it would've pissed him off, but now...now he needed all the help he could get convincing her to give them another chance.

Trevor hadn't even realized how badly he wanted that second chance until he'd thought Megan was about to marry someone else. The memory of this afternoon, what had happened in her office, was still sharp in his mind. Hell, his cock was probably still blue from wanting her so badly.

But then he kind of enjoyed the feeling of being aroused again. Of the need to fuck so badly it felt like he could hammer nails into a board with his dick. He hadn't felt like this since before she'd left him.

He glanced over at Megan, who was seated nearly as far away from him as possible. She also seemed to be avoiding conversation, and instead was focusing on her spaghetti. Sucking a long noodle from her fork and then licking the trace of sauce from her full lips.

She reached for her wine, and her gaze slipped over to him almost stealthily. But he'd been watching, waiting, and he saw it.

Her fingers tightened around the stem of her glass and color stained her cheeks slightly before she jerked her gaze away again.

And just like that he remembered how it felt to have his finger deep inside her body. To feel her squeezing tightly as she trembled through an orgasm.

Trevor took another drink of wine, his gaze sliding over her face. God, he wanted to watch her come again. Watch her lose all control when she climaxed. He'd always loved that. Megan was a confident woman in bed who wasn't afraid to ask for what she wanted.

He remembered one time when she'd shown up at the base just in time for the weekend. She'd been dressed in a familiar tan trench coat, but surprised him by wearing nothing but a g-string underneath. They'd barely made it off base before she'd told him to pull over and fuck her in a small wooded area.

He watched Megan now, the way she shifted in her seat, a sign of her awareness that he was watching her. And Trevor was all too familiar with the way she would trace her fingers low over her neck when she was aroused. Just like she was now.

Her gaze lifted again and then dropped immediately. He watched her mouth move in a silent curse.

Biting back a laugh he turned his attention to his food once more to give her a little peace.

When the dinner was finally over and everyone was saying their goodbyes, he made his way over to Megan, who was edging toward the door.

"Let me walk you out?" he asked softly.

Her mouth tightened and for a moment he thought she would refuse, then she gave a slight nod.

"Megan, I'll see you tomorrow," Ellie called out. "The bachelorette party, baby!"

"Oh, right." Megan nodded and Trevor stifled a laugh at her tight smile. "I'll be there."

He knew she hated the party scene and rarely drank. Though when she did get a few in her...look out world. Because anything went.

Tyson had tried to refuse a bachelor party, but Todd had convinced him to at least hang out at his place tomorrow night with the guys to watch the baseball game, grill some brats and have a few beers. Trevor figured Ellie wouldn't do anything too much crazier with the girls tomorrow.

When they stepped outside a few minutes later, the night air was significantly cooler and Megan shivered, wrapping her arms around her.

Out of habit, Trevor started to shrug out of his light jacket to offer it to her, but she shook her head and stepped back, her expression pinched as she looked him over.

"Let's just be clear about this," Megan said. "I'm not really happy being buddied up with you, Trevor. I'll do it because I care about your family and this wedding, but don't be getting any ideas about us."

Had she been practicing that little speech in her head all through dinner? He arched an eyebrow. "Ideas, angel?"

"Don't call me angel anymore. And yes, ideas. What happened this afternoon was a complete mistake. A fluke." She turned on her heel and started toward her car.

"You coming on my finger wasn't a fluke, Megan."

She spun around in an instant, her palm arcing toward his face. He caught her wrist before it connected, barely blinking at her sudden attack.

Beneath the streetlamp he saw the anger and humiliation blazing in her eyes.

"Whether your mind is ready to acknowledge it or not," he continued softly. "Your body still wants me."

"Yes, well my body would also love to eat a half dozen cupcakes a day, Trevor. Fortunately, I have a brain to overrule its bad instincts."

His lips twitched. "Hmm. Guess it wasn't working this afternoon?"

Megan let out a growl and tugged her hand free. "My original point was—and still is—I'm not sleeping with you again."

"Why not? Would it really be so bad?"

"For one, I'm dating Henry."

He shook his head and called her bluff. "Henry means

nothing to you. You're barely dating him. I bet you haven't even let the guy kiss you."

The way her cheeks went red made him realize he was likely right. A wave of relief and triumph swept through him, easing some of the tension from his muscles that had appeared when she'd thrown Henry in his face.

"Regardless of what I've done with Henry, I *am* still seeing him."

Something about the way she kept throwing the other guy up as a barrier made his blood pressure kick up a notch.

"So call it off," his suggested tersely.

She stared at him. Hard. Until Trevor felt heat stealing up the back of his neck now. He knew it was an asinine request.

"Answer me one question, Trevor," she finally said, her gaze searching his face. "Are you getting help?"

Trevor's abs clenched as if she'd just kicked him. All the emotional doors slammed shut inside him and his expression become flat. Stoic. He went to that place in his head, where everything was automatic and disciplined. It was easier just to be in soldier mode.

"I don't need any help."

He couldn't tell if it was a trick of the light or if her eyes shimmered briefly with tears. Then she blinked and gave a short nod.

"Right. Then a year's gone by, but we're still at an impasse." She turned and unlocked her car door. "I'll contact you soon about us planning a menu for the reception barbeque. Good night, Trevor."

He didn't make any attempt to stop her this time as she climbed into her sports car and revved off into the night.

Chapter Five

Sweat poured down his face as the Humvee rolled across the deserted road. Though it wasn't quite empty, up ahead they could see the burning vehicle of their interpreter.

Trevor's gut twisted as he called out for Burton to stop the Humvee. When the vehicle rolled to a stop, he climbed out, yelling instructions to his soldiers as he crossed to where Housyar lay bloody and motionless. Beyond him, the bodies of three more Afghan men, the acrid smell of flesh and car burned together.

God damn it, not again. Housyar had been with them for three months. Had risked so much, including his family, to travel with them.

Trevor adjusted his M16 and turned back to his soldiers, mouth open to call out more instructions. No. He stilled, and the hairs on the back of his neck rose.

"Get back!" he screamed, rushing away from the car and bodies.

Everything exploded. Metal, dirt and bodies flew in all directions. Trevor landed hard, his helmeted head smashing into the ground as a fist-sized shrapnel slapped into his upper arm. Pain ripped through him, making him see stars as he struggled to sit up.

Dazed, he became aware of the sound of small arms fire. He heard the pings of rounds hitting the Humvee and knew they were in deep shit.

There was no time for fear, no time to hope that his soldiers were still alive. Trevor crawled on his belly over the dirt road toward the Humvee, seeing body parts and car pieces littered everywhere.

He spotted the uniform of one of his men lying ominously still a few feet away. Nausea threatened, but he shoved it aside as he spotted Washington and Foster defending themselves.

"IED. The bodies were boobie-trapped," Trevor screamed. "Don't think Burton made it."

"Bastards. Fucking, bastards!" Foster shook his head, still firing off rounds.

"Call for backup, Washington," Trevor ordered tersely to the younger soldier. "You tell them we're being ambushed and to get their asses in here now."

"Yes, sir!" Washington yelled and climbed back into the Humvee.

Trevor used the door to the Humvee for cover, drew in a deep breath, then lined up his assault rifle and started returning fire. Aiming for muzzle flashes he spotted from the buildings around them, Trevor kept firing, adrenaline rushing through him.

The familiar whistle of an RPG sounded over their head, the only warning, before it hit far to their right.

Damn it, they were going to die out here. He prayed like hell Washington was getting in that call for help.

Another whistle of an incoming RPG sounded, closer now.

"Get back!" He jerked Foster away from the Humvee, just as the second RPG slammed into the front of the vehicle.

Trevor heard the roar, felt the flash of heat, and then everything went black.

Trevor jerked upright in bed, reaching for the weapon he wasn't holding as his unfocused gaze swept the room for an enemy who wasn't there. Sweat pooled from his forehead as he dragged in a lungful air.

The choking, acrid smells in his dream were gone, instead replaced with the salty sea air from his window being open.

His heart slammed around in his chest and he kicked the sheets off his body, pushing himself out of bed.

He went straight to the bathroom and turned on the sink, cupping his hand full of icy water to splash on his face. Each douse rinsed away a little bit more of the nightmare. Brought him back to reality. Or at least the current reality. Until he stared at himself in the mirror and only the haunted look in his eyes gave away the hell he'd just relived in his sleep.

He gripped the counter of the sink and lowered his head, his shoulders quaking with the shuddering breath he let out. *Damn.*

The dreams had become less frequent in the past year, but they still came.

Trevor turned off the water and walked back into his room, letting his alert gaze slip around it. It was the room he'd grown up in; his parents hadn't changed it when he'd left for the army at eighteen. Since he was often being relocated to different bases, or sent overseas, it was the one thing that was constant in his life. The one place he could always count on to return to.

Getting stationed at Fort Lewis had been a stroke of luck, being just a few hundred miles away from Wyattsville. It made it possible to come back and be with his family. To ultimately meet and fall in love with Megan, who'd moved to Oregon from Los Angeles five years earlier.

She'd been planning to relocate to Washington after their wedding, they'd even been looking at houses, and then everything had fallen apart. Or *he'd* fallen apart. He'd held it together for a bit after returning from Afghanistan. But like a loose thread on a shirt, he'd slowly unraveled a little bit at a time...

Trevor slapped his palm against the wall. Damn it. He could fix this. Stitch his life back up. He was a fighter, it was the reason he'd joined the army. He wasn't afraid to face adversity. And he just needed to remember that. At least if he was going to have a chance in hell at getting Megan back.

Grabbing a change of clothes, Trevor went to hit the shower and start the day.

Bachelorette parties. Geez, she usually tried like hell to avoid them. Megan cringed and followed the stream of ladies into The Oceanside Tavern. Ellie led the pack, giving a woot of excitement as the penis antennas on the headband she wore bobbed up and down with her bouncy steps.

They were taking over the tavern. Word had gotten around town about Ellie's bachelorette party and people had cleared out, ready to let the ladies rule the roost tonight. But there were a few guys, mostly in their early twenties, who'd showed up probably hoping for some action from the girls as the alcohol flowed and the inhibitions loosened.

Megan followed the near dozen girls to the counter and lined up with them.

"Round of blow jobs, Evan!" Ellie hollered.

Megan shook her head. "Oh, uhm, no blow job for me, Evan. I'll just have an orange juice, please."

Ellie swiveled to look at her, her eyes wide. "Orange juice? At my *bachelorette* party? No way, Megan! I still owe you drinks—if not my firstborn child—for representing me in court last month."

Clearly Ellie had already been given a drink or two before the party started. "Oh, it's just, I'm getting over a cold. And the citrus—"

Ellie snorted. "You're so creative when you lie. I love it." She turned to face Evan and slapped the counter. "Give her a blow job."

The other girls cheered and patted Megan on the back, hollering out things like *loosen up* and *have some fun!*

And here she'd thought she'd been loosening up by wearing a short flirty dress—because that's one thing Kate had encouraged her to do this morning when she'd swung by the bakery. After all, Kate had reminded her, one had to show up looking sexy as sin to these bachelorette parties. Who knew when the opportunity to flirt would come up?

Not like she had any intention of flirting with any of the boys in town, Megan reminded herself. And it wasn't like Henry would be there. Or Trevor.

Biting back a sigh, Megan accepted her shot when it came. But, unlike Ellie, she didn't take it with her hands behind her back and using only her lips to hold the glass.

She pinched the shot glass between her fingers and tossed it back. Hmm. That hadn't been all too bad. She licked her lips, enjoying the lingering taste of Bailey's and Kahlua.

"God, that was awesome," Kate said fervently. "I'm totally going to have to make a cupcake along these lines."

"I'd buy a dozen of those, Kate," another girl called out. "Can I have another one of those shots, Evan?"

"Me too." Megan blinked in dismay, realizing the request had come from her. She bit her lip, ready to retract her request and then sighed.

Screw it. It *was* Ellie's bachelorette party after all. What could a few drinks hurt?

"You mean you've never tried handcuffs?" Ellie asked, wide-eyed as she leaned forward on the bar stool.

Megan took another sip of her chocolate martini and then shook her head. Half the girls were out on the floor dancing and just her, Kate and Ellie were gathered around the bar chatting.

Everything felt kind of light and fluffy right now. She was on her third drink. Or was it fourth? There'd been at least two blow job shots...

"Never?" Ellie asked again. "Not even when you were with Trevor?"

Megan shifted on the stool and lowered her gaze, ignoring the pang in her heart. That familiar sense of loss she had when someone brought up Trevor.

"No, we never did handcuffs." She tried to sound casual.

"How about being submissive? That whole being-dominated thing?" Kate asked with a sly smile. "I hear that's awesome. Either of you ever do it? Give up control to a guy?"

"Not really my thing." Ellie wrinkled her nose. "How about you, Meg?"

"No." Megan's mouth curved with amusement. "In fact if anything I tend to be the one in charge. Come on, you know me. I'm a control freak."

"Oh my God, you so are." Kate snorted and her gaze turned impish as she glanced toward the door. "What about with Henry? Does that therapist get your bells a ringing? Maybe fix up more than just your mind?"

"Ugh, no." Megan snorted, the alcohol making her a little more honest. "And he's not *my* therapist. I see his partner for that. You know, I don't think I'll ever be able to sleep with Henry. He's just a little too—"

"Umm, Megan." Kate's face turned red and she shook her head.

"Boring? I don't know," Megan went on. "There's just no chemistry. And I'm still all emotionally wrapped up with Trevor. I should probably just tell Henry, huh?" Megan finally recognized the distress on Kate's face and how Ellie's mouth was hanging open. "What? What is it?"

"You don't need to tell me. I heard it all fine myself," a voice clipped from behind her.

Oh shit. Shit, shit, shit!

Megan's eyes rounded as she spun the bar stool around. Yes, Henry was really right behind her. Standing stiffly in his suit and tie, the light in the bar reflecting off his receding brown hairline.

Her smile felt so tight now, her face nearly split.

"Well, of all the people I expected to show up at Ellie's bachelorette party, you're not exactly at the top of the list," she tried to joke.

"No. I suppose not." His brows drew together in disapproval as he took in the scene. "I've been trying to call you, but you haven't been answering your phone. You never called back about dinner last night. I finally dropped by your house tonight. Fortunately, or unfortunately, your neighbor noticed me and told me where I could find you."

"Dinner. Oh, I did forget to call you, didn't I? I'm so sorry—"

"Don't apologize, Megan." He gave a slight smile. "I don't suppose it really matters anymore, does it? Seeing that there's no chemistry and you're still in love with your ex-fiancé."

How did he know that? Or had she just admitted it? This was just weird going on weirder. And her buzz wasn't helping her at all, because she had the sudden urge to giggle.

"Listen, how about I give you a call tomorrow," she said, trying to sound professional. But Henry wasn't a client, so why couldn't she just talk to him—

"No, don't call." He waved a hand dismissively. "It's why I wanted to talk anyway. I think it's pretty much been laid on the table at this point. We're better off not seeing each other anymore. Have a good evening, Megan."

Megan watched him leave the tavern again, her mouth gaping open in dismay.

"Okay, did that just happen?" Kate asked on a wheezing laugh. She leaned forward and shook her head. "Did he just break up with you at Ellie's bachelorette party?"

"He totally did!" Ellie guffawed and then lifted her glass of wine and nodded solemnly. "What a douche."

Kate joined in the nodding. "He really is. Are you upset, Megan?"

"No. Not at all," Megan replied, realizing she didn't even need to think about the question.

In fact it was almost a relief it had been so easy. Maybe

tomorrow, when the alcohol wore off, she'd feel a little guilty, but right now it was just liberating. She never should've started dating Henry in the first place, it was just that her therapist— his business partner—had kept telling her she needed to move on from her past relationship. When Henry had asked, it had seemed like the perfect solution. Hmm. Maybe the whole thing had been a setup?

"Seriously," Kate patted her hand. "You could do so much better than him."

Ellie waggled her eyebrows. "Yeah. You could do Trevor."

Her chest grew tight and another wave of despondency swept over her.

"That boat has sailed," she replied softly.

"Then flag it down and make it come back. Seriously, anything is possible," Kate said earnestly. "You and Trevor are so right for each other. I think the entire town mourned when you guys split."

She didn't want to hear this. Megan's fingers tightened around the stem of her drink. Oh God, she didn't want to be told how awful it was that she and Trevor weren't together anymore; she already *knew* this.

Taking another sip of wine, Ellie nodded. "I have to back Kate here. Though I never knew you guys when you were together, whatever you had is still there. You guys get together and the air just shimmers with electricity."

"Look, the past has passed," Megan said over-brightly and changed the subject. "I want to hear more about these other things, like handcuffs during sex? So Ellie's the expert?"

Ellie spun on her stool and lifted a brow, her smile secretive. "Well, I *am* marrying the town sheriff. I'll leave it up to your imagination."

They all let out another round of laughs, and Megan glanced at Kate.

"How about you? You ever try handcuffs during sex?" Megan asked.

Kate's face turned bright red and then she downed the rest of her drink and shook her head.

"No handcuffs?" Ellie asked. "I'm telling you, you guys need to try it."

"No. Just no sex." Kate lifted her shoulders into a big

shrug. "I'm still a virgin."

Megan had to snap her jaw shut when it just about hit the bar. She glanced at Ellie, who was making no such attempt to keep her shock hidden.

"Shut the hell up!" Ellie finally cried.

"Are you...serious?" Megan asked carefully. Kate had to be close to twenty-five at least.

"I'm dead serious. And I'm only admitting it because y'all got me drunk." Kate wrinkled her nose and took another sip of her drink. "But if either of you ever tell anyone I *swear* I'll ban you from ever buying a cupcake from me again."

Ellie mimed zipping her lips. "My lips are sealed. Don't even try and blacklist me from your shop."

"Ditto," Megan replied, nodding. "But I think I've found my new purpose in life. To get you laid."

Kate snorted and rolled her eyes. "You let me worry about that. Which, speaking of..." She glanced toward the door. "Here he is."

"Who?" Ellie and Megan asked at once.

"The stripper I hired." Kate grinned and hopped down from her bar stool, her curvy frame striding toward the man at the door.

"I don't believe it," Ellie muttered in awe. "The virgin hired me a stripper."

Megan nudged her in the side and giggled. "Not so loud."

Another woman joined them at the bar and ordered a beer. "That's not just any stripper, that's Pete Haggerty. I used to babysit him and his little brother when Pete was ten. He didn't look like this a decade ago...oh my God, I feel so dirty."

Ellie let out a loud hiccup and grinned. "Maybe the boy needs college money." She stood and whistled. "Come on, baby, take it off!"

Some of the men, the ones who weren't dancing with the bachelorette crowd, made a hasty escape when they noticed the male stripper.

Oh, God. Megan shook her head and smothered another giggle. She really should be discouraging this. But after three drinks—or was it four?—it was kind of hard to care anymore. She downed the rest of her martini, spun on the stool and propped her elbows back on the bar to watch the excitement.

And it wasn't long before things got really out of control. Megan watched in fascination as chaos ensued, finally feeling the first prickle of unease when one of the girls climbed onto the bar and started dancing.

"Charlotte, you really should get down," she hollered as the woman began to sway in her heels. "Any second you're going to fall and break—"

Charlotte yelped as her ankle went to the right and her body fell to the left.

"Something," Megan finished on a sigh as the other woman began to scream in pain. "I really should have seen this coming."

She slid from the chair and went to figure out the damage.

Chapter Six

"Can I get anyone another beer?" Todd asked, standing from the couch and stretching. "This game is kind of slow."

Trevor shook his head at the suggestion to another beer. This baseball game wasn't doing shit to distract him from his thoughts, which alternated between luscious ideas of what he wanted to do to Megan and darker memories of Afghanistan. Alcohol wouldn't help his state of mind either way.

There were less than ten of them here at Todd's house, watching the game and drinking beer. The Wyatt brothers, a cousin and a couple close friends. Not much of a bachelor party, but it's all Tyson had wanted.

Trevor glanced over at Tyson and bit back a smile. His middle brother sat at the far end of the couch, his fingers clenching and unclenching around his beer. He'd look at his watch occasionally, then shift in his seat.

"You really should've had a bachelor party," Todd muttered, returning from the kitchen with a beer. "You're just sitting here thinking about Ellie all night anyway."

Wincing, Trevor shook his head, thinking his little brother shouldn't have brought up the reminder that Ellie was at a bachelorette party.

"I'm sure they're just hanging out, Ty." Trevor kept his voice casual as he gave Tyson a brief smile. "Probably just having lots of sugar from Kate's place, some wine and gossiping."

Tyson grunted. "They took over The Oceanside Tavern. I have a feeling it's more than cupcakes and chatting."

The tavern? Really? Trevor scowled and shifted on the couch. Hell...maybe it wasn't quite so innocent.

The front door burst open and a man hurled himself inside, out of breath and wide-eyed.

Tyson came to his feet. "Jimmy? What's going on?"

The just-out-of-college kid pulled his hat off and twisted it in his hands. "Sheriff, I just came from the tavern and it's getting a little rough. A stripper just arrived, think it might even be the younger Haggerty brother. And I think one of the girls just busted her ankle."

"Jesus." Trevor joined his brother on his feet, hoping he didn't sound too excited as he suggested, "Maybe we oughtta go calm things down?"

Tyson's jaw flexed and he nodded. "Someone get me my keys."

Trevor rode shotgun in Tyson's SUV, while Todd sat in the back. The three of them were silent as they made the two-minute drive down to Main Street where the tavern was located.

When they pulled up in front of The Oceanside Tavern the sound of music and women yelling could clearly be heard.

"Shit," Tyson muttered. "I'm surprised nobody called the station yet."

"No kidding." Trevor agreed and opened his door, stepping down from the vehicle.

Todd came around beside him and grinned. "I don't know, this could be fun. Lots of buzzed women, no men. Maybe I'll stick around for a while."

Trevor slapped his youngest brother on the back of the head and bit back a curse. Though the women of Wyattsville would likely love having the town's most notorious flirt—who'd also been labeled sexiest firefighter in Wyattsville—staying to hang out.

"Well," Tyson sighed and placed his hands on his hips, staring at the door to the tavern. "I guess we'd better do this."

Todd nodded, wiping the smile from his face, even though his eyes still danced with amusement. "Let's do this. Time to reel in the fiancée, bro."

Trevor fell back, let Tyson stride in first and do what he needed to do. He and Todd walked in a moment later to join the chaos.

"Holy shit balls," Todd muttered in dismay.

Trevor silently echoed the sentiment as he took in the scene. Jesus, he almost preferred hand-to-hand combat than having to face breaking up this.

All around them women were dancing and slamming back alcohol. Some were even dancing on the bar. In fact one gal, probably the one rumored to have busted an ankle, was sitting on the bar with a fat ice pack on her foot. Poor Evan and whoever else was on duty were standing far back behind the counter, watching with wide eyes as if they contemplated abandoning ship.

Trevor stepped farther into the tavern and slid his trained gaze over the crowd. Searching for any sign of real problems, but mostly searching for Megan.

He caught sight of the stripper—fortunately he wasn't quite naked—with half a dozen gals circled around him hooting and hollering. Ellie being one of them.

No Megan though. He slid his gaze beyond the group to the corner of the bar. Bingo. She was there, facing the crowd, leaning back with her elbows on the bar. Her breasts peeking over the neckline of the clingy blue dress she wore.

And she was watching him. Her blue gaze met his solidly over the madness inside the tavern. Trevor couldn't look away, almost like an invisible laser connected them. Even across the room he could see something had changed. He didn't sense resentment or anger in her eyes. Instead it was something else that gave him a hell of a lot of hope. His breath caught, the muscles in his body coiled, and his dick leapt to attention against the denim of his jeans.

Not breaking her gaze, he pushed through the crowd of people toward her. Dimly aware of Tyson and Todd shouting out instructions for the stripper to put his clothes back on and the women to calm down.

Trevor reached the counter and sat on the empty stool next to Megan. Close up he searched her face, trying to tell if she was drunk or not. Her cheeks were slightly flushed, but her eyes lacked that intoxicated glaze. Instead they sparkled with heat. With need.

He arched a brow and took the almost full cocktail from her hand, setting it on the counter.

"You girls having fun?"

"You could say that." She ran her tongue over her mouth and smiled slightly. "Though I suppose you boys will put an end to that?"

"I suppose so." He tried, and failed, not to let his gaze slip from hers to explore her body. But the way she sat, her breasts thrusting against the clingy blue dress, made it impossible not to.

Megan was sexy as sin tonight, not just the dress, but the darker makeup and fuck-me heels. Her long red hair fell uncommonly loose in waves around her shoulders, so silky-looking and seductive. The question was, who had she been trying to impress? It was a bachelorette party full of women. Or had been.

He tore his focus from her to glance around the tavern. Already the women were dispersing and calling it a night. Tyson had wasted no time with Ellie, who was now cradled in his arms as he carried her out the door of the tavern. She wasn't fighting too hard, instead snuggled against him looking half-asleep. Or maybe passed out.

"Todd, you're spoiling all our fun!"

Hearing Kate's sullen protest, Trevor glanced to where his other brother was shooing the stripper out the door.

"Fun's over," Todd growled.

"Well then you'd better give me some money, because I paid a lot of money for that guy."

Trevor's brows rose. Kate had hired the stripper? *Kate?* No way.

Todd seemed to share his shock, because he let out a few choice words as he pushed Pete—who fortunately was the older Haggerty brother—all the way out the door.

Trevor turned away and shook his head. "I can't believe Kate's behind the stripper."

"There's a lot of things about Kate that you wouldn't believe," Megan muttered almost under her breath.

"What was that?"

"Nothing." She slid off the bar stool and grabbed her purse. "I suppose I should head out too. It's getting late."

"Did you drive here?" he asked, knowing full well she had, because her convertible was out front.

She nodded, digging through her purse for her keys. When she retrieved them, he effortlessly plucked them from her hand.

"I'll be driving you home."

He expected her to argue, but instead she stared up at him

through her lashes, her expression contemplative, before she gave a slight dip of her head.

"That might be a good idea. But I promised Kate a ride home."

The minute the words were out, Megan wondered if she'd lost her mind. Having Trevor drive her home could only be trouble. But right now, trouble was just a little too tempting.

"Hang on and I'll ask if Todd can see her home."

She watched as Trevor went over to his brother, who'd sat Kate back down at the bar and seemed to be lecturing her now.

Trevor leaned down, speaking near Todd's ear and a moment later Todd gave a terse nod and waved him off.

Megan bit back a smile and shook her head. Kate certainly didn't look like she was nurturing a crush on the youngest Wyatt brother right now. More like nurturing a grudge that her stripper had been taken away.

"He'll take her home," Trevor said. "Are you ready?"

She gave a nod and turned toward the door, her stomach suddenly full of butterflies. They stepped outside and she welcomed the cooler air. The inside of the tavern had been ridiculously warm.

Trevor unlocked the passenger door to her convertible and she climbed in, sliding onto the buttery soft leather seat.

Leaning her head back against the headrest, she slid her palms over the side of her seat. She loved this car. How fast it was. How the wind felt in her hair when the top was down. How sexy it made her feel when she was in it.

As Trevor slid into the driver's seat, she glanced over at him through her lashes. Amusement simmered with the hot need in her belly. He was too tall for her car and had always bitched about the fact. He fit in it, but just barely. The man loved his truck. All the Wyatt brothers seemed to love their big cars.

The convertible purred to life and Trevor pulled away from the curb a moment later. With the top down, the wind lifted her hair from her neck and she gave a sigh of content, watching Trevor drive from the corner of her eye. Stared at his large hand closed over the gearshift.

Trevor had always been so good with his hands. With his mouth. God, with everything. Her gaze slid over to the thick bulge in his jeans and a heavy ache started between her legs.

A few minutes later he pulled her car into the driveway of her small rambler.

"How will you get back to your car?" she asked softly when he turned off the engine.

They sat in the darkness, only the starlight giving any hint of light. Megan became acutely aware of every breath he took. Every little flex of his hands as he played with the keys now in his lap.

"My car's at my parents' house. Tyson and I drove together down to the tavern. I don't mind walking."

Sucking in a slow breath, Megan shifted fully in her seat to stare at him. He waited a moment, before turning to look at her with an arched brow.

"Or," she began slowly, "I can drive you back to your parents' house in the morning. You could stay here tonight."

Chapter Seven

The keys in his hands ceased their jingling as Trevor stilled.

"Not sure that's such a good idea, angel," he finally said, his words uneven.

Megan licked her lips, wondering if she was nuts but not really caring at this point. Right now she just wanted one thing. Or one person.

"You thought it was a good idea yesterday."

"Yesterday you weren't drinking."

"I may have had a few, Trevor, but any alcohol in my blood has nothing to do with what I want from you right now," she said with quiet determination. "I'm pretty sure I'd be asking even if I was stone-cold sober."

Trevor closed his eyes and she could see him fighting to keep control.

"And what is it exactly you're asking, Meg?"

"For you to make love to me," she whispered, sliding a hand across her seat to touch his thigh. "For you to touch me like you used to once upon a time."

His teeth clenched, even as she watched his cock stir beneath his jeans.

"And what about tomorrow, angel?"

She gave a throaty laugh. "Well tomorrow's going to come whether you fuck me tonight or not, Trevor."

His head fell back against the seat and the air hissed out from between his teeth. "Jesus, Megan, you have no idea what you're doing to me right now."

"I know what I'd like to be doing to you."

He swore under his breath, and then before she could blink he'd reached for her, dragging her out of her seat and placing her on his lap so she faced him, her knees straddling his thighs.

"If I was a better man I wouldn't be taking advantage of you right now, angel," he muttered thickly, cupping her face in one hand, brushing his thumb over her lips as his gaze searched hers.

A pang of sadness flickered through her. And guilt. But she shrugged it away. She needed this way too much to walk away tonight. Needed Trevor.

"You're not taking advantage, soldier," Megan said softly. "I am."

Then before she could let him talk her out of it, she lowered her mouth to his.

Trevor groaned and slid a hand into her hair, holding her head still as their lips met and parted, then his tongue slid deep to rasp against hers.

Heat exploded inside her, rocketing through her blood and making every one of her nerve endings tingle. She kissed him fervently, fumbling to undo the buttons on his shirt.

Tearing his mouth from hers, Trevor said, "We should go inside."

"That would take too long." She leaned down to bury her mouth against his neck. Her tongue flicking out over the pulse, finding the familiar salty taste of his skin she'd been craving for over a year. The taste of Trevor.

She closed her mouth around his flesh and sucked, wanting to leave her mark as if she were a sixteen-year-old girl claiming the quarterback. And maybe the idea of making love in a car was a bit youthful for someone pushing thirty, but right now it was a sensual turn-on.

"Damn, angel, are you sure?" he choked out, sliding his hands down to squeeze her ass.

His hips raised and his denim-clad cock ground against the heat between her legs. Her nipples hardened and moisture gathered in her pussy.

"I'm sure," she gasped, moving her hips against him. "Oh, God, I'm sure."

Trevor let out a low growl and abandoned her ass, immediately moving to pull her stretchy dress off her shoulders and down her breasts. He tugged the satiny cups of her bra down too, baring her to his eyes and touch.

For the briefest moment she wondered if maybe they *should* go inside. They were sitting in her driveway in her convertible with the top down. Anyone could see them. But it was past midnight and the moonless night was dark, so the excitement far outweighed the risk. Or maybe the idea of being seen was a bit titillating, if she let herself admit it.

Trevor's hands moved to cup her breasts and any ability to think period disappeared. His palms, calloused and large, had always brought her so much pleasure, and they didn't fail now.

Goose bumps broke out over her body as his thumbs swept across her sensitive nipples.

"Suck on them," she begged, cupping the back of his shaved head and urging his head down.

Trevor moved his hands to her ass again, lifting her body so her breasts brushed his face. His lips closed around one tip, sucking it deep into his mouth and flicking it with his tongue.

Pleasure sizzled through her and she let out a throaty moan, leaning back against the steering wheel. She stared at Trevor's dark head as he suckled her. The pleasure on his face matched her own.

God, it felt so good to be with him like this again. She'd missed him. Her throat tightened with the emotion of it all.

Maybe she'd wake up tomorrow and realize she'd made a terrible choice when her heart was once again breaking. But right now the only choice *was* Trevor and this moment together.

He was sleeping, and at any moment he was going to wake up. But damn it, if this *was* a dream, then he'd willingly sign the rest of his life over to slumber.

Trevor dug his fingers into the fleshy part of Megan's ass, adjusting her so he could have better access to her breasts. He couldn't get enough of the taste of her and hearing the throaty moans she made.

He wanted more than just her breasts in his mouth, he wanted to kiss and rediscover every square inch of her body.

The sound of a zipper going down followed with Megan's hands sliding into his jeans, finding him and stroking him free from his boxers.

"I can't wait," she pleaded. "I need you inside me."

His cock throbbed almost painfully in her hand and he let

out a choked groan, lifting his head to look up at her.

"Angel, I don't have a condom on me."

"I never went off the pill." She lowered her head, brushing a soft kiss over his mouth. Then she hesitated and said, "And you were right about Henry. I haven't even kissed him. I haven't been with anyone since you."

Possessiveness ripped through him. *Mine.* He trailed his hands up her bare arms, loving the way she trembled. Megan would always be his.

She gave a laugh, but it sounded a bit forced. "So unless you're worried that you might have something."

"I haven't been with anyone either."

Megan stilled, he couldn't even hear her breathing.

"Please don't lie to me, Trevor," she finally said quietly. "It's been a year and we broke up. You're a man, you have—"

"Needs?" he rasped, toying with a silky strand of her red hair, brushing it over one of her erect nipples. "Yeah, I do. I need *you* in my bed. In my arms. I didn't want anyone else, Megan. Any needs I had were taken care of with my right hand while thinking of you."

"Thank you for admitting that," she whispered, her voice cracking. Then she gave an unsteady laugh. "So your right hand, hmm? I thought it felt a little more calloused than usual."

His lips curled into a smile, before he nipped the sensitive curve between her neck and shoulder.

Megan let out a throaty laugh and moved her fingers through his short hair and over his scalp, the gesture almost loving. His chest tightened and he pressed a trail of kisses up over her collarbone, to the rapidly beating pulse in her neck.

Her head fell back, once more an offering of pale flesh. He pressed his lips to her pulse again, while fumbling to push her skirt over her hips.

His cock hardened at the realization of the panties she *wasn't* wearing.

"Fuck me, Megan. What the hell were you thinking?" he breathed, already moving his hand between her legs to cup her hot little pussy. "Not that I'm complaining."

"Mmm, I'm not sure. Maybe I was thinking of this? Subconsciously? Or consciously." She moaned and spread her knees wider. "Please, Trevor, I need you inside me."

"In a moment, angel." He slipped two fingers inside her soaked channel and bit back a groan when she clenched around him. "Just want to make sure you're ready for me."

"I'm ready." She panted, her inner muscles clenching around his fingers. "I've been ready for over a year. Take me, Trevor. I need you."

With her hand still stroking his cock into a granite-like state, he abandoned any attempts to slow down. Wondered why the hell he was even trying.

After pushing his fly open a little wider for comfort, Trevor grasped her hips and eased her down onto his cock.

He watched Megan as she bit her lip, her fingers digging into his shoulders as he slid deep inside her. The hot, wet walls of her pussy gripped him as she sank to the hilt.

Home. God, it was like coming home.

Neither of them moved for a moment. Trevor needed the instant to absorb that this was really happening. To savor the ecstasy of being inside Megan once more. Her breathing came just as erratic as his. In fact the shuddering breath she'd let out when he'd thrust deep hinted that the intensity rocked her to the core as well.

"Incredible," she finally whispered and began a slow glide back and forth. "You feel so incredible."

"Yes," he ground out and gripped her hips, thrusting up into her as she rode him. "Oh fuck yes."

It didn't even take a moment before they found their familiar rhythm. And then they moved together, breathed together, and then entirely too soon—when she kissed him hard again—they came together.

Trevor groaned as he emptied himself into her, again and again as the walls of her sex clenched around him, milking him dry.

Megan let out a choked sob, before she buried her face against his shoulder, her body trembling through the orgasm.

So fast. Jesus, they'd both gone off like lit explosives just moments after he'd entered her.

Trevor closed his eyes and slid his hands up and down her torso, feeling her slender curves, reminding himself what it felt like to have her like this.

"Oh, wow. That was so..." she whispered, the shock in her

voice showing she was just as taken aback as he was. "It's just been so long."

"I know, angel." He brushed a kiss over her forehead and gave a soft laugh. "Next time, I promise we'll slow things down."

Next time. He realized his words were more than a little presumptive, but when she didn't tense or correct him, he figured he was in the clear. And there would be a next time. Many next times.

"We should probably head inside," he suggested lightly. "In case your neighbors start filing out to discover what all that noise was."

Megan slapped him playfully on the back and then adjusted her dress again. "I wasn't that loud."

He laughed, while tucking himself back into his boxers and jeans, before pushing the car door open wide.

Megan slid off his lap and climbed out first, and then he followed after her, shutting the door behind him.

She set off toward the house, her legs trembling like a newborn colt. Smiling, Trevor swept her up into his arms.

"I'm too heavy for you to do this," she murmured, even as her head came to rest against his shoulder.

Trevor snorted. "I've carried weapons heavier than you, Meg."

"Mmm. Well thank you. My thighs are killing me after being in that position. Not that I'm complaining or anything."

When he reached the door, he set her down again to open it. Unlocked. His lips twisted into a slight smile. Some things never changed in a small town.

Megan moved inside and turned on the lights. "I'm going to pass out soon, but I want to shower first." She paused and turned to face him, arching a brow. "Will you be joining me?"

The vision of her naked and water sliding over her body had his cock stirring again.

"Absolutely."

Chapter Eight

In the shower, Megan's heart squeezed with the tenderness Trevor demonstrated with her.

He washed every inch of her gently, brushing off any attempts she made to get him to use her loofah, and instead used his hands.

It was wonderfully sexy. Watching his big, calloused hands sliding over her body, spreading the slippery body wash into her skin. And then he took the shower nozzle and pulled it from its holder, rinsing the suds from her body.

Each patch of skin he cleansed, he brushed a kiss over. Taking his time to swirl his tongue over her nipples and dip into the crater of her belly button.

And then he hung the nozzle back up, falling to his knees and bracketing her hips in his hands.

Megan leaned forward with a sigh, placing her hands on the wall above him as she shifted her feet farther apart. Thick curls of steam swirled around them, the smell of soap heavy in the air.

The damp pressure against her pussy had her gaze dropping and a shuddering breath escaping. And then Trevor's tongue didn't just dance over the folds of her sex, but slid between them.

A moan built low in her throat as she watched him. Trevor had always been so amazingly good at eating pussy. Their first night together had blown her mind, and unlike some of the men she'd dated before him, he seemed to really enjoy it. He'd always seemed to love the foreplay as much as she did. And as their time together had grown longer, that never faded.

He didn't even glance up at her as she watched him. Seemed much too intent on tasting her, on bringing her to pleasure. And dear God was he doing it. Trevor had always seemed to know exactly what she needed.

She let her eyelids flutter closed on a groan as he licked his way up her slit to find the sensitive pearl of flesh.

His mouth closed around her clit, ripping a gasp from her throat. She let go of the wall to clutch the sides of his head. Holding him against her, she rocked her hips against his mouth, needing to find that promised peak.

How had she lived without this for a year? Without Trevor? Living on a vibrator and memories of the man she loved.

The same way you'll get by again when he leaves in a week.

She brutally shoved the voice of reason away, having no place for it when pleasure was so predominant.

He gently bit her clit, and Megan climbed even higher toward that peak. When he slid two fingers inside her, fucked her with them, she exploded.

With her body still trembling, he came to his feet and lifted her, wrapping her legs around his waist. He plunged into her, sinking deep and filling her so magnificently.

Blind with pleasure, her nails dug into his back as her ankles locked around his waist. He backed her up against the wall of the shower stall, slamming into her and taking her mouth in a hard kiss.

Megan kissed him back feverishly, tasting herself on his tongue and thrilling at it. Trevor moved harder, deeper inside her, his fingers digging into her ass cheeks as he fucked her against the wall.

Water sluiced over them, running down her face and in her eyes, but it didn't matter. In fact it heightened the raw sensuality of the moment.

Trevor lifted his mouth from hers and let out a guttural groan, before she felt him spurting warm and thick inside her.

The sensation flung her over the edge again and she let out a ragged cry as she clenched around him. Her nails dug deeper into his back and she clung to him as her world spun.

Finally, reality returned as the water grew cold. She blinked, stunned to realize Trevor had slid to his knees and they were almost on the floor now. He was still imbedded in her, though she could feel him softening.

How long had they been in here? Making love?

She kissed the jagged scar on his shoulder and felt her

throat tighten up. He'd returned from Afghanistan with it, and as of a year ago it had still bothered him a bit. Did it still now?

"I've missed you so much, angel," he muttered raggedly. "I can't tell you how God damn much I've missed you."

Smiling, she bit his shoulder lightly. "You swear too much, soldier."

He gave a soft laugh "I know. Sorry. It's habit from being around my men all the time. I haven't...been spending much time with ladies."

"Mmm. And you consider me a lady?"

"You're a classy as hell lady, Megan. Always have been." He lifted his head to smile at her. "I knew that when I came back to town one day and saw you for the first time. Wanted you like I'd never wanted another woman. I knew I'd have you, but realized it might take a little convincing."

"You were a little rough around the edges," she agreed, her heart quickening. "But you were a Wyatt. The sexiest Wyatt—"

"Damn right. Though don't let my brothers hear you say that," he said smugly.

She gave a throaty laugh. "Anyway, you made me realize pretty quick how hot a rough man can be. One night with you and I didn't want anyone else..."

"Mmm. That's because I made you come twelve times."

Slapping his chest, she rolled her eyes. "Ten. But who's counting?"

"I'm a guy, of course I'm counting." Trevor joined her laughter and reached up to turn off the water. "It's probably two in the morning, angel."

"Good God. Where has the night gone? Thankfully tomorrow is Sunday." She shook her head and yawned.

Maybe just saying the time made her a little sleepy. Or maybe it was getting screwed silly twice in the last hour.

"We should probably get some sleep," he agreed. "Because pretty soon the sun will be rising and we'll have to do some talking."

Her breath caught and she was careful not to look at him. Talking. Did he mean long term? About them? A future? If there was one again? Or was this just a week of hooking up for old time's sake.

The possibility didn't settle well and had a lump forming in her throat. She closed her eyes, thinking of how things had been before she'd left him. That wasn't settling well either.

"We have to plan that menu, after all."

Some of the tension eased from her shoulders and she gave a small nod. Right. The menu. Apparently Trevor wasn't thinking beyond tonight and maybe the wedding. Which was okay...wasn't it?

"Let's go to bed," she said huskily and untangled herself from him. Jesus, her thighs were going to hurt in the morning. "I'm suddenly beyond tired."

Trevor stood and exited the shower, grabbing a towel and then handing her one.

"If you want," he began hesitantly, "I can sleep on the couch."

She froze in the midst of drying herself and glanced up at him. Her pulse quickened and she wondered for a moment if he wanted to sleep on the couch. But once glance at his face showed he was just trying to be respectful. Give her space if she needed it.

Closing the distance between them, she cupped the back of his head and brushed her lips over his. "I'd prefer you sleep in my bed, soldier."

The slow smile that spread across Trevor's face was one that had always made her knees a little weak.

He winked and murmured, "Yes, ma'am," before sweeping her into his arms and carrying her down the hall to her bedroom.

They'd slept in. Megan realized it the moment she opened her eyes and saw the sun coming through the blinds. That was, if Trevor was still here. Her pulse leapt as she sat up and looked at the other side of the bed.

Everything inside her went a little soft at seeing him sleeping next to her. The memories from last night floated to the surface of her mind, sending a warm tingling through her body.

Without the haze of nighttime and a few drinks, she still would've made the same choice and gone to bed with Trevor. And watching him now, she was tempted to do it again. It was as if the year apart hadn't even happened. Waking beside Trevor, making love to him, it was all so natural. So right.

He lay on his back, his brows knit from whatever he was dreaming about. The blankets were off his body, but the sheet still clung to his hip, leaving his upper torso naked.

And, oh yum, what a wonderful torso it was. His chest was smooth, the pectoral and abdominal muscles so defined she had the sudden urge to trace her tongue over the dips and ridges.

With a devious smile, she decided on just exactly how she'd wake Trevor this morning. Scooting down on the mattress, Megan leaned over his body and lowered her head to brush a kiss over his abdomen. He didn't stir and she gave a soft laugh. Well, she'd just have to try harder.

Her long hair fell over his chest as she let her tongue trace one square of muscle on his abs, loving the familiar taste of him as she moved lower.

The air left her lungs as her back slammed into the mattress—the massive arm pinning across her collarbone made it impossible to move and difficult to draw a breath.

Megan gripped Trevor's forearm, her legs kicking on the bed as she tried to throw him off. Drag in air. The eyes that looked down at her were unfocused and almost black with rage. She knew he wasn't seeing her, wasn't really even awake, but the lack of air going to her brain wasn't going to let her rationalize it.

Trevor blinked and just like that he was back. The rage was replaced with shock and horror as he jerked his arm away from her, allowing her the oxygen she'd been deprived.

"Megan?" he rasped and lurched away from her on the bed, thrusting his fingers over his head. "Fuck. Oh my God. *Fuck.*"

Even with her heart still pounding a mile a minute, Megan knew he was more upset than she was. She crawled toward him and reached to touch his shoulder, but he shook her off and climbed out of bed.

"I'm sorry," he ground out, reaching for his jeans and tugging them on, then the rest of his clothes. "Sorry's not even enough. *Shit.*"

She swallowed hard, following him out of bed. "Trevor, wait—"

"No. Not now, Megan. Not now." He shook his head and left her room, heading straight toward the door.

Her heart lurched and she rushed after him, grabbing his

arm before he could leave.

"Don't do this," she pleaded, digging in her feet to stop him. "Don't you dare walk out like this."

He spun around and caught her arms, jerking her against him. His eyes were wild, his face pale.

"Don't you realize I could've fucking killed you?" he asked savagely. "Without even being conscious of it?"

The bite of his fingers against her arms was going to leave bruises, but she didn't protest as she slid her hands up to cup his face.

"You wouldn't have, Trevor. I know you wouldn't have," she whispered. "Please, just talk to me. Tell me—"

"I can't. Jesus, Megan, I *can't*." A shudder ripped through him and he looked down, his gaze taking in where he gripped her. His mouth tightened and he cursed, releasing her immediately.

"You *can*, Trevor. Don't walk out of here right now." She made sure every trace of fear was gone from her face, and she slipped into the woman she was during her day job. "If you walk out of here right now you're risking whatever chance we had at making this work. Is that what you want?"

He shook his head, and opened the door, but she slapped her palm against it.

"Answer me, Trevor," she yelled. "Do you want this to fail before it even has a chance again? Because if you walk out this door, that's *exactly* what's going to happen."

His long fingers circled her wrist, but his grip was gentle this time as he pulled her away from the door.

"The only thing I know anymore, Megan, is that I can't keep hurting you."

After he'd left, Megan closed her eyes and slid down the door to the floor, curling her knees up to her chest and wrapping her arms around them.

She bit her lip fiercely, but it didn't stop the sting of tears in her eyes.

Maybe it had felt natural waking up next to him this morning, and maybe every part of her begged to give them another chance. But with Trevor leaving, he'd just given her the brutal reminder of why she'd left *him* in the first place.

Trevor walked out this morning because he didn't want to hurt her. The only thing he didn't seem to realize was that every time he closed himself off and walked away, a little piece of her died.

Chapter Nine

Sunday on Main Street was quiet, with most of the folks in church or sleeping in. There were only two shops open right now. Kate's Cakes and The Oceanside Tavern. Any other day Trevor would've chosen Kate's Cakes, but today wasn't any other day. Today was the day he'd woken up nearly choking to death the woman he loved. His stomach roiled and his teeth ground together. Sweat broke out on the back of his neck and he shoved open the door to the tavern with unsteady hands.

He strode inside, his unseeing gaze moving over the man sweeping the floor and moving straight to the alcohol behind the counter.

"Morning," the man called out. "Cleaning up after a bit of a wild night. Bachelorette party."

Trevor didn't reply, just gave a slight nod.

"Oh, hey, didn't recognize you at first," the older man said coming around the counter. "Aren't you the oldest Wyatt boy? I heard a lot about you. I'm Sam, new in town. Evan was real nice to give me a job."

The idea of small talk wasn't settling well in the least. Trevor forced a slight semblance of a smile and a gruff, "Welcome to town. And yes, I'm the oldest Wyatt."

"And a soldier, I'm told. Army." Sam gave a hard nod and wiped down the counter. "Me? I'm retired from the Marine Corps. I've got nothing but respect for you, son. What can I get ya?"

"Shot of Jack Daniels."

Sam didn't even blink or comment about the time of day, just grabbed a shot glass and poured the shot, before sliding it across to him.

Trevor lifted the glass and knocked it back, letting the whiskey warm his belly before setting the empty shot down again.

"You been over to Iraq? Afghanistan?" Sam asked quietly.

"Afghanistan." He didn't want to talk about himself or about Afghanistan. Wanting to divert the bartender's attention he asked, "What about you? What kind of combat did you see back in the day?"

"First Gulf War. Somolia." He shook his head and sighed. "I think you boys got it worse though now. Like I said, you've got my respect. And you've got another shot on me if you want it, son."

Trevor thought about it, stared at the bottle on the other side of the counter and the amber liquid inside. Another shot wasn't going to solve anything. Hell, the first one hadn't even helped.

"Thanks, Sam. I'm good for now."

"No problem. Well, then that first one was on me." Sam paused and then said quietly, "Time does help with the healing, son. I promise you. Now I'll leave you in peace, but you holler at me if you need anything."

Trevor nodded as the other man walked away. Staring into his empty glass, he wondered if Sam had come back from combat as fucked up as he was.

The army had offered him counseling when he'd returned from Afghanistan. He hadn't thought he'd needed it, but now, sometimes he wondered if maybe he should've.

Being with Megan last night had been so damn amazing. He'd begun to feel whole again, like everything was finally going to be okay and maybe he'd get the shot at happiness that seemed so damn unattainable. Falling asleep with Megan in his arms, hearing her soft breathing as she'd snuggled against him, he'd had so much hope.

But as he'd fallen asleep, guilt had sliced through any attempt at letting the past go and moving forward. And then he'd woken up from another nightmare to find Megan pinned beneath him, eyes wide with terror, struggling to breathe.

He'd left. Gotten dressed and run like hell. If he was smart, he'd run like hell back to Fort Lewis, stay away from Megan and the potential of causing her any more pain.

The door to the bar swung open, sending blinding light into the dimness and Trevor squinted, glancing away with a scowl.

"Hey, big bro."

For fuck's sake. Really? Trevor bit back a sigh at the sound of Todd's cheerful voice and turned on the stool to face the door.

Only it wasn't just Todd. It was Todd and Tyson. They stood in the doorway, arms folded over their chests, staring at him like they were about to stage an intervention.

"Kind of early to be hitting the bar, don't you think, boys?" he drawled with a slight smile.

"Funny, I was just thinking the same thing," Tyson said, striding across the bar and sitting to the left of him.

Todd took the seat to Trevor's right.

"Megan called us," Todd explained.

Trevor's mouth slipped from the forced smile back into a grim line and his chest tightened with regret. Had she told them about what had happened? That he'd damn near killed her?

"Did she now?"

"She's worried about you. We all are," Tyson said softly.

Trevor gave a short, humorless laugh. "You've got a wedding coming up, Ty, the last thing you need to be worrying about is me."

"Yeah, well I don't have a wedding coming up," Todd said, his mouth curving into that wide smile that had probably charmed half the women in town out of their panties. "In fact I have no intention of *ever* marrying. So that leaves me plenty of free time to worry about my big brother."

"Good to know." Had his brothers always been this determined to drive him nuts?

Tyson leaned forward and grabbed his shot glass, setting it farther away. "You need to cut with the alcohol, Trev. You seem to be seeking out the tavern every time you have a problem."

The hell he did. He hadn't turned into the soldier that turned to the bottle.

Or have you?

Anger and frustration brought a slow flush up his neck. His jaw flexed. "I won't deny it. But I usually stop at a shot or two."

"Even a shot or two isn't the way to deal with whatever the hell's going on in your life," Todd replied, siding with Tyson. "You're better than this, Trevor. You know you are."

"How the fuck do you know I'm better?" Trevor finally snapped, letting all the anger at himself and his life explode. "Either of you? And what gives you the right to walk in here and tell me what I can and cannot do? If I want another shot of whiskey, who the hell's going to stop me?"

"I am." Tyson replied matter-of-factly, cocking his head.

"I'll take that second shot now, Sam," Trevor yelled, but kept his narrowed gaze on his middle brother.

Sam idled over. "Jack Daniels?"

"Actually, he's going to pass," Tyson said calmly. "And, yes, this time I am speaking as the sheriff."

The hell he was. Trevor turned to Sam and repeated his request for another drink.

Sam's gaze slipped between Tyson and Trevor and finally he sighed.

"Sorry, son," he muttered. "But like I said, I'm new in town. Last thing I'm gonna do is piss off the sheriff. Even if he is your brother."

Trevor saw red. Before he could think about what he was doing, he lurched off the chair at his brother, fists swinging. He got in one good punch before Todd jumped in, getting him in a headlock and pulling him off Tyson.

"Fuck you both," Trevor choked out, struggling in his brother's hold. "You have no right. No right to come in here and try and control me. Control my life."

Tyson rubbed his jaw and glared at him. "We're not trying to control your God damn life, Trevor, we're trying to help save it."

"Sorry about this, Sam," Todd called out. "We'll take it outside."

Humiliation warred with the rage as Trevor was dragged outside by his youngest brother. Already he planned on getting in a punch on Todd the moment he let him go.

A few minutes later they stopped on a path that led to the Pacific Ocean. The warm morning sun beat down on them and the only sound came from the waves slamming into the beach.

Todd let him go and took a quick step backward, obviously sensing his intent.

Trevor dragged in a lungful of sea air and glared at the two. They were smart, keeping their distance now. The urge to fight and destroy was ripping through him, and he had to remind himself they were his brothers. They were blood.

He glanced at Tyson, saw the red mark on his jawline and

hoped it wouldn't be a bruise by his wedding day. Guilt pricked at him, not deep enough to make him want to apologize, but enough to make him regret not taking a deep breath before he'd attacked.

"You gotta calm down, Trev. I don't really want to fight you." Todd grinned. "Though, it might be a fairer fight now than when we were younger. Think I'm just about as big as you now."

"Might even be bigger," Tyson murmured.

Trevor muttered curses at them both and turned away to cast his glare at the ocean, anything so he wouldn't have to look at the amusement on their faces. But he saw beneath it, could see the concern lingering, and for some reason that bothered him even more.

"Megan loves you, Trevor," Tyson finally said tersely. "For the past couple of days you've been giving everyone hope that you two might be able to work things out."

"Mom and Dad have been giddy with the idea," Todd agreed with a sigh. "But you're fucking it up. Sure as the sun sets, you're fucking it up, Trev."

Good. He'd been stupid to think for one moment that he could make things work with Megan. What the hell had he been thinking? Sleeping with her had felt so right, so normal, but they could never have normal. Megan sure as hell couldn't if she stayed with him.

"Megan deserves better than me," he said wearily, the anger seeping from him like a tiny pinprick letting the air out of a balloon. "You know this. She knows. I know. Everyone needs to stop pretending that we're meant to be together."

Todd and Tyson both broke into laughter, like he'd just made a hilarious joke. Their amusement grew so loud that nearby seagulls took off into the air with a cry.

A moment later Todd shook his head and grinned. "That was a good one, Trev. Seriously. You and Megan go together like peanut butter and jelly."

Nice. Only Todd, whose main thoughts tended to lean toward either food or women, would compare him and Megan to peanut butter and jelly. His lips twitched with a reluctant smile, and unfortunately his brothers saw it and they beamed, their posture relaxing a little more.

Trevor sighed and rubbed the back of his neck. "You don't

understand. What's between us, it's not what it once was."

"And it'll probably never be. So you start over," Tyson argued, glancing down and kicking a foot in the sand. "You're going to have to do it with someone, why not Megan?"

Trevor didn't reply, didn't have the energy to keep up with an argument his brothers would never win. What was the point? But Tyson seemed to take his silence to mean he was thinking about it.

"You can earn her trust back, Trev," he urged. "I know you can. She loves you. And I'm pretty sure you love her too."

"Oh without a doubt he loves her," Todd agreed.

Glancing out at the dark blue of the Pacific Ocean, Trevor clenched his jaw. The question wasn't whether they loved each other. It had never been about that. Sometimes love just wasn't enough. It was so much more complicated. He had to say something in response to his brothers. They wouldn't leave him alone until he did.

"When the hell did my little brothers get so wise?" He allowed a fleeting smile. "Thanks for the talk, guys, but I'm going to head out. Skipped breakfast this morning."

"Food? Great idea." Todd slapped him on the shoulder. "I'll join you. I'm starving."

"I could go for something to eat, too," Tyson added lightly. "I told Ellie to sleep in and relax and I'd grab something on my own."

Trevor shook his head and gave a soft laugh. He shouldn't have expected anything else. Maybe this was a good thing. Time with his family. If anything it would help keep him grounded.

"All right, guys," he agreed with a nod. "Let's go eat."

Chapter Ten

Megan had just finished pouring herself a cup of coffee when the phone rang. She set her mug back on the counter and rushed over to answer.

"Hey, it's Todd."

She leaned back against the fridge, her fingers gripping the phone as she closed her eyes.

"Did you find him?"

"Yeah, we're with him now at Kate's," he said quietly. "I took a moment to step outside and call you while we wait for our cinnamon rolls. He's doing okay. Thanks for giving us the heads-up."

"No, thank you. You and Tyson both. He needs to be with people right now..." She swallowed hard. "Even if it's not me."

"Don't take it personally, Meg. Trevor's going through some shit. Has been since Afghanistan. I honestly think if anyone can help him through this, it's you."

Her heart twisted and her stomach fell. "I don't know, Todd. I just don't know if I can go through this again. It about killed me the first time."

"I know. Maybe we can figure out something. Find a way for you guys to spend a few days together alone. At least try and work things out. If I could arrange it, would you be up for it?"

Spend a few days with Trevor? Alone? Part of her thrilled at the idea. Images swirled in her head and her pulse quickened. But then the realistic side of her knew it could possibly end badly. She'd invest more of her heart over the few days, only to have it crushed again.

"I'm not sure," she hedged. "It's something I'll really need to think about. Every time I reach out to Trevor, I inevitably get hurt in the end."

"I know. And it kills me to see you hurt. But I've gotta say, he's hurting too. Something fierce." Todd sighed. "I want this to work out for you guys, Megan. I really do."

Megan gave a sad little smile and glanced down at the mug in her hand, staring at the cooling coffee inside. Over the years she'd been with Trevor, his family had become like hers. They'd almost adopted her after her aunt died—the woman who'd been her last living relative, and the reason she'd moved to Wyattsville.

And Todd was a few years younger than her, but he'd always seemed too wise. All the Wyatt men did. There was a reason their ancestor was the namesake for Wyattsville.

"Ah, shit, gotta go, Meg. Trevor's coming my way. Think about what I said though."

"I will. I promise."

Megan hung up the phone a moment later and went to add a little more coffee to her mug for a warm up. She took a sip and walked back across her kitchen to glance out the window, which had a view of the small town below.

She could see the roof of Kate's Cakes, knew the Wyatt brothers were in there right now eating breakfast. Her throat tightened and she closed her eyes. After Trevor had left, she'd been tempted to go back to bed and pull the covers over her head and not come out until she absolutely had to. But she'd been there and done that. And until a few days ago, she'd thought she'd moved on from that point in her life.

And now here she was again, the morning after having gone to bed with Trevor and everything was once more completely complicated.

Which left her at a crossroads. Either she decided last night was a mistake and shot down any possibility of a future with Trevor, which meant definitely not sleeping with him again. Or...she threw everything and the kitchen sink into making their relationship work this time.

Hear heart fought for dominance in the final decision, even if it was the one her mind rebelled against.

"Thank you for driving." Megan fidgeted with her thumbs, casting a sideways glance at Trevor, who'd been uncomfortably silent since picking her up.

"No problem." He didn't smile, or glance her way, just

replied flatly as he drove down the highway toward Costco.

"I don't think my car would've held all the food we need or I would've driven."

Again no comment, just a slight nod.

Megan bit back a sigh and stared straight ahead out the windshield. The sound of Metallica playing on his stereo at one time would have irritated her a bit, but right now it was a warm reminder of who Trevor was and all the good times they'd spent together.

"Whether you like it or not, Trevor, you did sleep with me last night. And not talking about it, or what happened this morning, isn't going to change that fact."

When he didn't reply her stomach sank and she bit her lip, sneaking a glance at him out of the corner of her eye. His fingers had tightened around the steering wheel, his knuckles white from the grip.

"Trevor?" she prodded gently.

"Ribs."

She blinked. "Excuse me?"

"I was thinking we could buy a bunch of ribs for the barbeque. Maybe some chicken." His fingers flexed around the wheel. "Of course, if there's some vegetarians at the—"

"Stop it!" she yelled, anger exploding hot in her belly. "We are *not* discussing food right now, we're discussing us. Remember that part where you fucked me in my car? In the shower?"

"I remember, god damn it!" he shouted back tersely. "And I remember waking up nearly choking you. It shouldn't have happened."

The air rushed from her lungs, but she already knew the answer before she asked, "Which part?"

He shook his head. "Any of it."

Megan stared at him, her jaw flexing as she fought the urge to get sick. "You've fought in a *war zone*. Maybe killed people and have seen people killed. You're not a coward, Trevor, so stop acting like one now."

She had to grab the *oh-shit* handle on his truck as he swerved to the side of the road and slammed to a halt. He grabbed her, hauling her across the seat so she was just inches from him.

"I *have* seen people killed. I *have* killed," he raged, his eyes wild. "I hate that I don't have control over anything anymore. What I am is a fucking mess, but I am *not* a coward."

Tears sprung to her eyes, and she hated herself for hurting him, for prodding at his unhealed wounds. Hearing him confirm her fears only made the miserable ache in her stomach grow. But she couldn't stop the honesty now that she'd broken the seal.

"But you're being one when it comes to us, Trevor. I don't even know how to talk to you anymore," she said thickly, letting the tears roll down her cheeks. "I don't know what to do. To say. Damn it, I don't *know*. I'm not a therapist."

Trevor stared at her and she saw the regret and pain flicker in his eyes, before his gaze hardened once more. "Yeah, well your boyfriend is. Maybe you should've spoken with him last night instead of sleeping with me."

She flinched, but then looked away, out the window and into the mass of trees on the side of the road. "He's not my boyfriend anymore. I'm not sure he ever was."

"When?" he rasped. "When did it end?"

"During the bachelorette party. He showed up at the tavern."

Strong fingers cupped her cheek, turning her head so she had to look at him.

"Good." His head lowered and he kissed the tears that still lingered on her cheeks. "I hate the idea of you with anyone else, Megan," he said raggedly, before his lips moved inward to brush tenderly over her mouth. A moment later he lifted his head and groaned. "But as much as I want you to stay with me—to choose me over any other schmuck out there, I can't give you the life you want or be the husband you deserve."

His words should've made her more despondent, killed any hope at them ever having a chance in hell at making it. But they didn't. Her pulse was fluttering and optimism roared to life inside her. His words shed a bit of light on part of what had gone wrong with them.

I don't have any control over anything anymore. Her mind swirled a mile a minute with possibilities and she knew she needed to choose her words carefully.

Finally, keeping her expression unreadable, she settled on, "Ribs and chicken sound great."

Trevor blinked and his brows drew together, his lips parting slightly. His eyes showed confusion and maybe disappointment. For a moment it looked like he was going to say something, but then he pressed his mouth tightly together and released her.

Letting her go, he turned forward once more, then shifted the gears and pulled off the side of the road.

Already making plans in her head, Megan closed her eyes and hoped like hell she could get through the next few hours without tipping her hand.

"Can I get you anything to eat, Trevor honey?"

Even though he was thirty-three years old and had been out on his own since he'd joined the army at eighteen, some things never changed. Trevor lifted his attention from the television and gave his mom a small smile.

"Thanks, I'm all right."

"You're sure? You barely ate breakfast, and you went to bed without dinner..." His mother sighed and sat on the couch next to him. "You're worrying me, Trevor. Me and your father."

He tried to stave off the irritation that threatened, because he knew his parents meant well. But, shit, maybe he should've just rented a room at the Wyattsville Inn for the time he was back. It was hard putting on a happy face day after day.

"I'm fine, Mom," he promised and wrapped an arm around her shoulders, brushing a kiss across her forehead. "You guys worry too much. Where is Dad anyway?"

"Out fishing. You know that man during the summer. Can't keep him out of the boat." She laughed softly and gestured to the television. "What are you watching there?"

Hell if he knew. He'd been staring at the screen for the last half hour, but hadn't seen shit. A knock at the door saved him from having to pull an answer out of his ass.

"Hmm. Wonder who that could be." His mother stood. "Be back in a minute."

Trevor scratched the back of his head and brainstormed ways he could get out of the house for a few hours. Ever since returning from the mini road-trip yesterday with Megan, he hadn't wanted to do much but sit around and keep company with his misery.

From the moment in the car when he'd told her he could never be the man she needed, she'd closed off. Oh, she'd spoken to him throughout their trip, polite and to the point, almost like they were just acquaintances. Two people who hadn't spent the night before screwing each other silly.

Deep down, he'd foolishly hoped she'd argue with him, do everything in her power to convince him that they were right for one another.

This was a good thing, he reminded himself harshly. It meant Megan was still the intelligent, practical woman he'd always known her to be. She'd probably regretted sleeping with him the moment the alcohol from the bachelorette party had worn off.

"Well, look who's here," his mother said brightly from behind him. "Megan dropped by."

Chapter Eleven

Megan what? Trevor blinked at the television before turning slowly to glance over his shoulder.

Sure enough, the woman who'd just been occupying his thoughts for the past twelve hours stood behind the couch with his mother.

Megan looked meticulous and sexy at the same time, wearing khaki pants that hugged her hips and ass so amazingly and ended at her calves, and a silky blue blouse that fell lightly over the curve of her breasts.

Thoughts of her riding his cock in the car the other night flitted through his head, and his jeans tightened as his flesh stirred to life.

"Good morning, Trevor," Megan said brightly, a wide smile on her face and a playful twinkle in her eye. "Or is it afternoon?"

"I don't have—" *any fucking idea what time it even is,* he'd been about to say, before remembering his mother was in the room. "I'm not sure honestly. What are you doing here?"

Her smile tightened and she gave a slight laugh. "Oh, now, don't tell me you've forgotten about our little outing?"

Outing? Was she serious? There hadn't been any little outing planned. Or had there? He scanned his memory, trying to figure out if it was something from before they'd slept together. Before—

"Well, come on, lazy butt. Get up." She strolled around the couch and grabbed his hand, tugging him to his feet. "I'll help you pack."

He tightened his fingers around her wrist, narrowing his gaze on her. "Pack?"

A slight flush stole up her neck and her gaze turned beseeching, before she glanced at his mom and gave an amused laugh.

"Must've had a wild time at that bachelor party the other night," she teased. "In one ear and out the other. Come on, Trevor."

Curious to see what the hell Megan was up to, he allowed her to lead him off to the bedroom he'd grown up in.

Megan released his hand immediately and began rummaging through his drawers, tossing a few items into his bag that sat next to it. When she bent over, her pants clung to her sweet heart-shaped ass and he bit back a groan.

Folding his arms across his chest so he wouldn't reach out and touch her, he demanded, "What's going on, Meg?"

"Oh, we're going to make a run down to your cousin's cabin over in Canyon Beach." She straightened from zipping up the bag and gave him a small smile. "I figure we can get some lunch there, swim and beach walk. So beautiful down there."

He shook his head. "Why are we going to my cousin's?"

She gave a slight shrug and licked her lips. "Because he asked if we could use your truck to haul back a couple extra barbeques for Tyson and Ellie's reception on Saturday. His car isn't big enough."

Taking a slow step toward her, he arched a brow. "And you didn't think to call me? Ask me if it would be okay?"

Megan lifted her chin and met his gaze head-on. "I knew you might try and get out of it. Or at least insist that I *didn't* come."

"Maybe you shouldn't."

She glared at him. "You're driving. I'm coming. Deal with it. Now we should probably head out since I said we'd be there at two."

"Hell," he muttered. "What the hell time is it?"

"Twelve thirty."

He found himself glaring back at her. They'd always been like this, each one struggling for power.

"Good thing I already showered," he finally said gruffly. "Let me use the bathroom and get my keys."

Triumph flickered in her eyes and she gave a smug smile. "Great. I'll go chat with Sally while you do that."

Twenty minutes later they were in his truck, driving down 101 toward Canyon Beach. Neither of them had said a word,

Shelli Stevens

and after a while he got tired of listening to music even, so he'd shut off the stereo.

He cast a sideways glance Megan's way. The oversized sunglasses she wore shielded her gaze, but her mouth was curved into a slight smile. She looked pretty damn proud of herself for some reason.

The sunlight filtering in through his truck windows made her hair seem even redder, shinier. So damn sexy as it curled over her shoulders and teased one breast. She'd unfastened the top button on her blouse after complaining it was too hot.

He jerked his gaze away from the curve of her tit, but it was too late to avoid the blood that rushed to his cock.

When he finally pulled up outside his cousin's house, it was a relief to get out of the truck. To escape the sensual smell of her perfume, and to keep resisting the urge to smooth a hand down her thigh...maybe trace his fingers inward to find out if she was overheated there too.

"Come on, Trevor." She winked at him and opened her door, grabbing their bags. "Time's a wastin'."

He swore under his breath. Why the hell was she so cheerful? She'd certainly gotten over the fact that he'd told her to move on to another guy fast enough.

Walking up the path to his cousin's house, his brows drew together.

"Hey, I don't see Ryan's truck here."

"Hmm. Yeah I guess it's not," she murmured and reached into her purse, pulling out a set of keys.

When she put it in the door and unlocked it, Trevor froze.

"Where the hell did you get those?" he demanded as she pushed open the door.

Before she could walk inside—and she'd been about to—he caught her wrist.

"Just what the hell is going on, Megan?"

She licked her lips and gave him a slow smile. "Todd gave them to me. Let's go inside and we'll talk."

He didn't release her or move. "*Todd* gave them to you? Where's Ryan?"

"Inside first."

His teeth snapped together, but he stepped over the threshold with a growl.

182

"Now, Megan, you need to tell me exactly what the deal is."

She followed him inside and then shut the door behind them, leaning back against it and watching him from beneath her lashes.

"The deal is we have this place to ourselves for the next few days," she said calmly. "You said you don't feel like you have any control anymore, Trevor. When you admitted that, you opened up to me. Even if it was just a little bit, it was enough."

"Listen, Megan—"

"No. Right now, you listen." She pulled away from the door and approached him, her heels clicking on the linoleum of the entryway. "I want you to open up more. Talk to me about everything. What happened in Afghanistan and why you won't let yourself be happy."

Trevor froze, felt all the emotional doors slamming automatically inside him as he started to shut down. He caught her wrists and pushed her away, shaking his head.

"I've already told you, Megan. I can't do that. So if this was all just a ruse to get me alone so you can play therapist, you'll have to find someone else to play with."

"Yes, about these games, Trevor? I haven't even told you the fun part." She tugged her wrist toward her, dragging his hand with it. Catching his palm, she turned it over and pressed a kiss in the center, watching him through sooty lashes. "*I* want you to open up to me and *you* want control. How about a fair trade?"

What the hell was she trying to say? It was hard to think with the little circles her tongue was tracing on his hand now. The thump, thump of his heart quickened, grew louder, until he was sure she could hear it.

"Maybe you'd better elaborate," he said thickly.

"You open up, and for three days, Trevor, I'm yours to command. Yours to control," she said in a seductive, breathless tone. "Whatever you want. Whatever you say. I'll do it."

Shock hit, but it was nothing compared to the lust that surged through him, making his cock rock hard and his blood heat.

What she asked for was impossible. For him to open and up and talk about things he wouldn't even talk to an Army therapist about. But the vision of her—of Megan, the woman who loved to be in control—being submissive kept flicking in his mind. It was an adult man's fucking wet dream. But it was also a trade he couldn't make. Would never be able to make. Megan asked the impossible.

He opened his mouth to tell her to pick their bags back up and march that cute ass of hers out to the truck again.

"Anything I want?" he rasped instead.

Her lashes swept up, revealing blue eyes full of arousal and excitement.

"Anything, soldier," she said softly.

Trevor's jaw flexed and his grip on her wrist eased as he moved his hand up her arm to cup her slender shoulder. He knew he'd have a devil of a time keeping his end of the bargain, but it didn't matter as he pushed Megan to her knees in front of him.

"Well, angel," he said softly. "You've got yourself a deal. Now why don't you be a good girl and make it official by sucking my dick."

Chapter Twelve

Megan's heart slammed against her rib cage and her mouth dried out. What on earth had she just gotten herself into?

Her knees bit hard into the cool linoleum floor and she shifted for comfort, swallowing with difficulty. She lifted her gaze from the unmistakable bulge now at eye level, to Trevor's eyes. His narrowed gaze was full of heated desire.

"Well, Megan?" he taunted. "Still think this is a good idea?"

Never, ever in her life would she have guessed that she could be the type to do this kind of thing. To *want* to be submissive to any man. But she trusted Trevor not to abuse the power she'd just given him. The expectation in his tone had a rush of excitement coursing through her veins and her nipples tightening, her body tingling, and moisture gathering between her legs.

She licked her lips and gave a slight nod to confirm her commitment, not trusting herself to speak.

The zip of his fly going down sounded in the quietness of the house and her pulse skyrocketed.

Though Trevor unzipped his jeans, he made no effort to do anything else. He was waiting for her. With hands that weren't quite steady, she reached out to pull the fly wider apart, then tugged his jeans down over his hips.

Beneath his briefs the thick curl of his cock strained to be free and her mouth watered with the realization that in a few seconds it would be in her mouth.

She curled her fingers under the elastic waistband of his briefs, brushing the coarse curls over his lower abdomen. A groan slipped from her throat as she gave a tug and he popped free, his erection waving proudly in the air just inches from her mouth.

Calloused fingers traced over her cheek gently, before

Trevor slid his hand into her hair and maintained a firm grip.

"Show me, angel," he coaxed roughly. "Show me what a good little submissive you can be."

He pushed her head forward, but her lips were already parted, ready to accept him. The thick head of his cock slid into her mouth, moving deep in a commanding stroke to the back of her throat.

Megan's eyes widened, but she relaxed her jaw around him and released a soft moan of pleasure. Reaching up to cup his balls in her palm, she let her tongue flick across the underside of his erection. The musky and salty taste of his skin was so familiar, such a potent aphrodisiac that her pussy wept with need.

She slid her mouth back over the thick length of him, to the bulbous head, taking a moment to swirl her tongue over him. When she heard the air hiss out of his mouth, she knew Trevor had no complaints.

With a murmur of victory, she took him deep into her mouth again, and then established a rhythm. Though Trevor seemed interested in helping her with the pace. The fingers in her hair tightened, pushing her head up and down, as his cock explored every inch of her mouth.

She listened to the sound of his breathing become more ragged, felt the tightening of his balls in her hand and knew he was close.

"I want you to swallow this time," he commanded, his words almost guttural.

Her stomach twisted with nerves and she closed her eyes. She'd never swallowed before, had always assumed it would be too unpleasant. Usually Trevor would pull out before he came.

You made a deal. This was your idea.

Even while most of her was nervous to do it, a small part of her wanted to try. Loved that she'd taken any choice out of the matter by making the bargain. Though even still she knew that if she really didn't want to try it, Trevor wouldn't have forced her to do anything she didn't want.

She relaxed her mouth around him, let him take control as he climbed toward his climax. Her heart thudded loudly in her chest and she let out a murmur of pleasure.

"Fuck," he muttered. "I'm coming."

He thrust deep, to the back of her mouth and then held.

She barely noticed the first warm spurt of him sliding down her throat. Making no attempt to pull away, she instead kept sucking on him. Milking him to release it all. The salty taste of him finally registered, but it wasn't unpleasant. If anything it just heightened her excitement.

Opening her eyes, she stared up at him. Watched his expression that seemed almost like he was in agony, but the shudders that ripped through his body, and the low groan he made clearly indicated otherwise.

He continued making slow thrusts in her mouth, caressing the back of her scalp gently now instead of holding her still, until she finally felt his erection lessening. And then Trevor slid his cock past her lips, watching her through hooded eyes as he tucked himself back into his pants.

"That was amazing," he said softly. "I can't believe you let me do that."

Seeing the amazement and gratification in his eyes sent a thrill of excitement through her. Showing her that even when playing by his rules, letting him be in control, there was still so much pleasure to be had.

Megan arched a brow and ran her tongue over her lips, still on her knees as she stared up at him. "I made a promise. Anything, Trevor. I'm yours, however you want to use me, whatever you want to do."

His gaze heated once more and he reached out a hand to help her to her feet. When she stood in front of him, she reached out to play with the fabric of his black T-shirt, nibbling her lip.

"Just remember your side of the bargain, soldier." She'd tried to make it sound playful, but she bit back a groan as Trevor's hand tightened around hers and his expression became shuttered.

"You want to hear it right now?" he asked flatly.

She hesitated, uncertain how to go about this. She didn't want the information to be pulled from him like she was extracting teeth. She wanted it to be more organic. And beyond that, right now, the last thing she was thinking about was a deep discussion. Her body was strung taut with the need for release. But if he wanted to talk now, of course she wouldn't turn that offer away.

Finally, she went back to her bargain, and put him in the

driver's seat. "Whatever you want, then I want. These days together are about you, Trevor. You have control. Not only over me, but when and how you want to confide in me." She drew her bottom lip between her teeth. "As long as you promise you *will* confide."

He watched her quietly for so long, the air around them grew heavy. Her heart quickened and she bit down harder on her lip. *Oh God. He wasn't going to be able to do—*

"I promise."

Relief swept through her, weakening her knees and bringing a wide smile to her face.

"Thank you."

"But for right now," he continued, his gaze still unreadable as he pulled her toward him. "I want to watch you come."

Her breath caught and heat stole through her body. The fine hairs on her arms lifted as he stroked the inside of her wrist with his thumb.

"Take off all your clothes, Megan."

As she shed her clothes she watched him, saw the self-assurance back in his eyes that hadn't seemed as constant lately. It confirmed that in its weird way, giving him control this way had been a good decision. When she stood before him in her thong and bra, he shook his head.

"Everything."

Drawing in a sharp breath, she reached behind her and unfastened her bra, tugging it off of her breasts and letting it fall to the ground. Then, hooking her fingers on each side of her white lace thong, she shimmied it down her thighs and off her legs.

Her nipples tightened in the cool air of the entryway and she glanced beyond Trevor to the living room where couches and chair sprawled about. But she didn't say anything, waited instead for instructions as her body hummed with need.

"What's in the bag?"

Megan jerked her attention back to Trevor. "Pardon?"

"That bag next to mine that you brought in? The smaller one." He jerked his head toward the doorway and where their bags still sat.

Her stomach did a little flip and she swallowed hard. "Things."

Trevor arched a brow, his lips quirking. "Things, angel? Bring it to me."

She turned to do what he said and jerked with a cry when his hand slapped across her ass. Eyes widening, she glanced at him over her shoulder, rubbing her burning bottom. *That* hadn't been expected!

"What—"

"When I ask you a question, I expect a proper response. No ambiguity." Amusement danced in his eyes and he gave her another quick swat to the other cheek.

Trevor bit back a laugh when he heard Megan mutter under her breath. So far she was doing pretty fucking amazing with this submissive thing. But the defiant, power-hungry woman he loved was still lingering beneath the surface.

Before she could move to grab the bag, he strode forward and slid an arm around her waist, jerking her naked body back against him.

"How much did you like that, Megan?" he murmured, nuzzling her neck and inhaling the scent of her expensive floral perfume.

"L-like what?" Her head fell back against his shoulder and he watched as her breasts rose as she jerked in a ragged breath.

"Did you like me commanding you to give me head?" He slid his hand lower on her stomach and felt it clench beneath his touch.

"I loved it," she whispered.

A thrill raced through him at their little power change. Not that either of them had ever really claimed that much more than the other, but seeing as he would have complete power for the next three days... He still couldn't believe she was doing it. And it was a bit of a relief. A sexy and fun distraction. A way to have some control again. Even—or especially—if it was in the bedroom.

His mouth curved into a smile. "You know, angel, my soldiers call me Sir. Why don't you give it a try?"

She was quiet for a moment, before obediently murmuring, "I loved it, *Sir.*"

Trevor smiled against her neck and slid his hand lower to cup her pussy.

"I know you did." He pushed a finger into her sheath and found her soaked. "Seems you liked it quite a bit."

He fingered her clit, felt her body clench beneath his hand, and then set her away.

"Go get that bag, angel."

She pulled away with a purr. "Yes, Sir."

When she bent to grab the bag, his cock stirred to life again at the image she made. The angle showed her spectacular ass givi.   ʌ to the folds of her pussy. Her long, smooth legs had it..ʌ :s ʌ. him fucking her in the shower racing through his mind. How it had felt to have those slender thighs gripping his w..· ʌ·.vhen he'd plunged mindlessly into her.

Megan straightened again, breaking the seductive vision, ʌnd turned around to return to him. The front side of her was j st as spectacular.

Her breasts, always a good handful, rode high on her body and her waist was narrow. Her pussy had always made him wild. Totally bare. Everywhere.

She'd loved to call him during the week, when they still had days before they could see each other, and tell him all about the Brazilian wax she'd just received. It would always make him so damn hard that when she showed up on base Friday evening, they usually wouldn't even make it home before they were fucking.

"Open it," he instructed when she stood before him with the bag.

He watched the muscles in her throat work and her cheeks turn slightly red. But she obeyed, unzipping the bag and handing it to him.

Trevor took it, holding her smoldering gaze for a moment before turning his attention to look inside the bag.

Holy shit.

Chapter Thirteen

Trevor's cock jerked as he sorted through the sex toys, creams, oils, lingerie and various restraints and handcuffs.

"Jesus," he muttered thickly and pulled an object out. "You really did mean anything, didn't you, Meg?"

She let out a husky laugh. "Yes, Sir."

He ran his gaze around the inside of Ryan's house, though he already knew the layout pretty well. Finally he spotted what he wanted and gave a slight nod.

"Over there. Go sit down in the recliner." When she went to move he caught her arm and halted her. "Actually wait here a moment."

He disappeared down the hall to the bathroom and snagged a towel from beneath his cousin's sink. When he returned Megan stood next to the recliner, running her fingers over the leather.

Trevor spread the towel down on the seat and turned back to face her, a slow smile curving his lips.

"Have a seat."

Megan lifted her chin and climbed into the chair, leaning back and placing her hands on the armrests.

"Let me help you get a bit more comfortable." He walked around the chair and took her hands, placing them above her and then reached for her feet.

"What—"

"Trust me."

He quickly arranged her legs so that each one draped over the armrest and her body was spread wide for him, so vulnerable, then stepped back to admire his handiwork.

Between slender thighs, the pink folds of her pussy were blatantly exposed. Cream shimmered in the shadows and he bit back a groan at the wonderfully seductive sight. He barely resisted the temptation to just unzip his fly and take her like that.

But the toys he'd pulled out of the bag were also a temptation, and one he didn't want to dismiss. He'd meant it when he said he wanted to watch her come. And this time, it would be without the focus of his pleasure to distract him.

He reached for the first one, something that looked a bit like a finger puppet, only it was a vibrator.

"You're going to make yourself come, angel," he murmured and handed it to her. "And I'm going to watch."

Megan's eyes widened, but she still accepted the small toy, sliding it onto her middle finger. She twisted it this way and that, before pressing a button on the side. A soft buzzing filled the air.

"Now play with that sweet little clit of yours," he commanded through hooded eyes.

With her legs splayed over the chair, Megan leaned back and closed her eyes, running her tongue over her bottom lip as she brought the tiny vibrator between her legs.

As he watched, her ass clenched and she sucked in a breath, her lower body undulating against her finger.

Damn, she was sexy as hell. Trevor's breath caught and his cock strained against his jeans. Walking in front of the chair, he sat on the edge of the coffee table. "Use your other hand and start fingering yourself."

Megan drew her bottom lip between her teeth, but obediently slid her hand down and pushed a finger into her pussy. Her brows knit together and she shook her head.

"How does that feel, angel?"

"It's not enough... Sir."

Trevor stood again, circling around the chair and leaning down to pinch one of her stiff nipples. She let out a ragged moan and her hips bucked.

"What's not enough?"

"My finger," she pleaded. "It can't go as deep as I need it."

He tweaked her other nipple and smiled when her head twisted against the chair.

"Hmm. Let me see what I can do about that."

Moving away from her again, Trevor found the toy bag and

began digging through it. A long velvet bag drew his attention and he picked it up, pulling the drawstring top open to peer inside.

Well, well, well, wouldn't this be fun?

He pulled the glass dildo from the bag and turned back to Megan. She watched him through heavy-lidded eyes, the pleasure and frustration on her face so fucking sexy. Her gaze slipped to the object in his hands and her breasts rose sharply with the breath she drew in.

Trevor knelt down beside the recliner and leaned over her, pulling her fingers away from her pussy. Unable to resist, he lifted her hand to his mouth and licked her fingers, still shiny with her juices.

"Oh, God, Trevor..." she whispered, a shudder running through her and her eyes darkening to a stormy blue.

He didn't bother to scold her for not saying Sir, the sound of his name on her lips was too damn sweet. Almost as sweet as the taste of her pussy. He caught himself as he was about to lean down and fill her opening with his tongue.

No, this time was about the toys. There would be plenty of time later to go down on her.

Instead, he placed the tip of the glass against her moist opening and then slid it slowly inside.

Megan jerked against the chair with a gasp, her body clenched around the dildo so hard he could barely push it farther in.

"Relax, angel," he murmured. "Just keep rubbing your clit with that vibrator and let me fuck you with this."

Her muscles immediately went lax, and when he glanced at her again she was watching him. Her blue eyes shiny with arousal and trust. And then her lashes fluttered down as she began to rub herself once more. He smiled, his blood pumping a little harder as he pushed the dildo farther inside her body.

Watching the clear glass with purple swirls disappear between the wet folds of her pussy, he clenched his jaw, focusing only on her, not the reaction of his body.

As he began to slowly fuck her with the dildo, her stomach clenched and she let out a low keening moan. Still, she never stopped rubbing her clit with the vibrator.

"There you go, angel. Make yourself come."

Megan rubbed faster, her breaths coming out in ragged puffs as she grew closer to her climax.

"Yeah...just like that," he encouraged softly, moving the dildo in and out of her more rapidly now.

"Oh God!" she screamed, her head falling back against the recliner and her ass lifted.

Trevor struggled to keep penetrating her with the glass as her body clenched around it and she trembled through her orgasm.

When she finally went limp in the chair, her head lolling to the side as she dragged in a shuddering breath, he pulled the dildo from her and removed the vibrator from her finger.

He eased her legs back over the armrests and brushed a kiss across her forehead, then stood and went to clean the toys in the sink.

When he returned a few minutes later she was watching him, curled up in the recliner now, her blue eyes shiny with satisfaction.

"Thank you, Sir," she murmured, as he sat on the arm's edge.

"Mmm. Thank you for the little show. And the toys." He shook his head and ran his finger over the smooth glass dildo. "Tell me what it was like having this inside you."

Megan let out a little snort and then laughed. "It was freezing at first, and completely unyielding. It was nothing like having you inside me," she admitted on a sigh. "I mean it wasn't bad...but... Hmm. Put it this way. Having that glass dildo inside me was probably what it feels like to fuck Edward Cullen."

Trevor stilled, pushing back the flare of jealousy. "And who the fuck is Edward Cullen?"

Megan laughed even louder. "You don't even want to know. But he's not real."

His mouth curled into a smile as he leaned down to scoop her up. "You worry me sometimes, Megan."

"As well I should," she nearly purred, rubbing her cheek against his chest. "Where are we going?"

"To the shower," he replied. "I want you again, angel. I haven't been able to get the other night out of my head, and I want a repeat performance."

Megan kissed his shoulder. "That sounds like a damn fine

plan to me. Lead on, soldier. Err... Sir."

Trevor let out a soft laugh of his own. God, this woman was amazing. She'd kept up her end of the bargain and he knew she was waiting for him to follow up on his. But she wasn't pushing. And that's what made her so incredible.

His jaw flexed and his stomach roiled at the idea of talking about it. Of exposing Megan to the horrors of his past. But he'd made a promise and at some point, he'd have to fulfill it.

But for now he was only thinking about slick bodies under the shower and being buried deep inside Megan again. Adjusting his grip on her, he made his way to the bathroom.

Megan poured a little olive oil into the frying pan and then went to the fridge to pull out the chicken, setting it on the counter.

Every muscle in her body ached at least a little bit, if not a lot. But it was a delicious, wonderful feeling. Her thighs fell into the seriously aching category, and remembering what Trevor had done to her in that recliner this afternoon had the ability to make her legs tremble. And then the wonderfully amazing slow sex in the shower.

"I'm starving."

She glanced up as Trevor entered the kitchen. His hair was still damp and he hadn't put a shirt on, the only thing he wore was a pair of black board shorts.

Just seeing his naked chest and his languid stride had her pulse quickening and her tongue going thick in her mouth.

"I'm cooking up some chicken with pasta," she said with a brief smile. "Your cousin left us a stocked fridge. And seeing as it's about dinner time and we didn't eat lunch..."

Trevor crossed the floor and brushed the back of his fingers across her cheek.

"I thought I gave you a snack earlier."

His wicked smile had her cheeks heating with the reminder of her being on her knees in the entryway.

She turned her head and nipped at his fingers. "You're so bad, Trevor. But don't worry, that's part of why I love you."

He didn't step away or laugh with her, and she faltered at the sudden seriousness in his gaze.

"Trevor?"

"We were ambushed," he said quietly. "In Afghanistan."

Megan blinked in shock. It was happening, he was finally confiding in her. A lump formed in her throat and her heart began a steady thumping. She turned off the stove, pulled the pan from the burner, but didn't say anything, just waited for him to continue.

"Our translator had gone missing and when he finally called for help, we didn't arrive in time. He was dead. I let my soldiers get out of the Humvee, realizing too late it was an ambush."

He cleared his throat and then leaned back against the counter, staring straight ahead.

"The body of our translator and the men who'd been in the car with him were on the road. They were rigged as an IED."

Improvised explosive device. Loving a military man who'd been in a war zone, especially Iraq or Afghanistan, she'd learned really quick what dangers were out there for them. IED's were one of the biggest ones.

Her heart tripped and she felt the sting of tears in her eyes.

"Knocked me out cold. When I came to I found one of my soldiers almost dead, and two others trying to defend themselves against a small arms attack from insurgents."

Megan clenched her fists, wanting to throw herself into his arms, reaffirm that he'd made it out alive. He was standing here today—he'd survived, but hearing the harrowing story made her realize how close she'd been to losing him.

She resisted the urge to touch him, though, knowing if she did he might stop talking. Might shut down like he'd done every other time.

"We fought back, shooting at anything that moved. All I wanted was to keep my men alive," he said stoically. "It was my fault, I should've realized it was a trap and never let my soldiers get out." He was quiet for a moment. "I'd just sent one soldier back into the Humvee to call for help when the bastards started shooting rocket-propelled grenades."

"Trevor..." she whispered, unable to keep silent anymore or maintain her distance. She stepped in front of him and took his hand, squeezing it gently. "I'm so sorry."

He shook his head, his gaze haunted, and he kept swallowing, like he was trying not to get sick.

"One of my soldiers lost his leg that day, another lost his life."

Her heart pinched and she pressed her lips together to stifle her cry of pain for him. Lifting her hands, she cupped his cheeks and brushed her mouth against his.

"I'm sorry," she whispered. "I'm so sorry, Trevor."

He closed his eyes and nodded. "I think...this fulfills part of my side of the bargain."

Megan froze, disappointment sinking through her as she watched him close himself off again, and then literally step away from her.

"I'm going to get dressed and take a walk alone," he said quietly. "I'll be back in time for dinner."

She watched him leave and a wave of sadness swept through her, leaving a heavy feeling in her body, and her mind exhausted.

It was a start, she told herself. He'd opened up a little, and now probably needed some time alone. Though she'd known he'd been hurt in an attack, she'd never known the details.

Now she did, and they were horrific. How had he lived, keeping that locked inside him? She sniffed and blinked the tears from her eyes, and then dragged in a deep breath.

Cook dinner.

Needing the distraction, to not think about the tortured look in Trevor's eyes, she flipped the stove back on and turned her attention to something she could control for the time being.

Chapter Fourteen

Megan brushed her teeth in the bathroom and her stomach roiled with nerves. Who knew what the rest of the night would hold? Earlier today she would've expected some more fun with the toys she'd brought.

But Trevor had been too quiet since he'd confided in her. He'd returned from his walk emotionally distanced, he'd barely spoken and he had made no effort to touch her.

She'd watched him as they ate, seen the rigidity in his muscles and tightness in his jaw. He'd been so uncommonly tense and quiet, she got the distinct impression he was angry. Maybe resented her for making him promise to have the conversation.

She set her toothbrush back in her plastic travel bag and sighed, grabbing her hairbrush before she looked up at herself in the mirror. Her face was pale—but then that was genetics, even the sun failed to help with that. She'd left her hair down more often lately, because she knew how much Trevor loved it that way. He'd always claimed fascination with the red strands.

Megan drew the brush over her hair, brushing it until it crackled with life and shined its brilliant color. She winced. God how she'd used to hate it as a kid. But growing up had made her realize how it was actually kind of cool to have the unique color and not have it come from a bottle.

Setting the hairbrush back down, she pulled a silky green negligee from her bag. She grimaced and tugged it on. It had seemed like a good idea at the time, but who knew what she'd find when she left the bathroom. Maybe Trevor would insist on sleeping on the couch.

The idea made her gut twist and her throat tighten. Oh well, no more putting it off.

Grabbing the door handle, she turned it and pulled the

door open, stepping into the bedroom.

Her steps faltered and her mouth fell open. The slow thump of her heart turned to a fast gallop as she stared at Trevor sitting naked on the edge of the bed.

He dangled a pair of pink fur-lined handcuffs from his index finger and in his other hand held the small flogger she'd bought.

Oh sweet Jesus. The handcuffs had seemed like a good idea, especially after that conversation with the girls during the bachelorette party. But the flogger she'd just kind of thrown into her basket randomly. Not for one moment had she expected Trevor to use it. It was more just to complete the kinkiness of the bag.

Clearing her throat, she tried not to look at the toys and gave him a brief smile. "Hey."

He didn't reply, just used the same finger that was dangling the cuffs to beckon her over.

Shit. Shit, shit, shit. Why had she come up with this anything-you-want submissive thing again?

She drew in an unsteady breath and approached him. "Trevor, about—"

"Sir," he reminded her through hooded eyes. "And no talking unless I tell you to."

Game on.

He stood and she inhaled sharply as her gaze landed on his hardened cock, just inches from her hip. "Take off your nightgown and underwear. You won't be needing them."

Heat slid through her body and her pussy clenched as cream gathered in it. *This was why you agreed, because it's such a turn-on.*

Megan pulled off her negligee and slid out of her panties, then stood naked and unabashed as she waited for his next request.

His nostrils flared and his gaze darkened. "Climb onto the bed and lie down on your stomach."

Her pulse jumped and she licked her lips as she moved to obey. The coverlet had been removed and so she crawled across the sheets on her hands and knees toward the pillows. She lay down, folding her arms and resting her forehead on them.

Firm hands gripped her ankles, pulling them apart and

spreading her legs wide. The air in the room brushed between her legs, making the sensitive flesh tingle and her folds dampen further.

What would he do now? She only had the handcuffs, it wasn't like—oh! Something silky wrapped around her ankle. There was a small tug and when she instinctively jerked back, she found she couldn't close her legs.

The crack sounded before she felt the burn of his hand that smacked across her bottom.

"Stay still, angel," he warned with amusement. "Unless I tell you that you can move."

Megan bit back a groan, her ass still smarted from his reprimanding swat, and she knew it was only the beginning. She stayed as immobile as possible as he secured her other foot to the opposite side of the bed frame. Again she realized how much she trusted him, because being tied up wasn't something she'd do for just any guy. But her love for Trevor pretty much meant she'd try anything. Do anything. At least once.

"Nice," he muttered and then the mattress dipped as he sat. "Very nice."

His palm closed over the cheek he'd just swatted, and squeezed the flesh.

"I like this position. I can see how wet your pussy if for me." His hand slid inward and then he cupped her, sliding two fingers into her aching slit. "Oh yeah. Drenched."

There was more movement and then she felt the leather of the small flogger trace over the back of her thighs. "I'm surprised you bought one of these, Meg. You realize they can sting, right?"

She nodded, without lifting her head from the pillow of her arms. The first wave of unease slid through her. It could very well hurt like crazy. And she'd just allowed Trevor to tie her down, while giving him permission to do whatever he wanted.

"I've never done this kind of thing," he admitted, his tone curious. "But I think we're supposed to establish some kind of safe word. How about marshmallow."

Marshmallow? What were they, sitting around a campfire? Her lips almost curved into a smile, but she held it back and gave another nod. *Marshmallow it was.*

"Your ass looks really pretty," he murmured. "Flushed from my handprint. I bet it'll look really hot in a minute."

How badly would it hurt? And would she be one of those girls who kind of liked it? Or would she be screaming marshmallow the moment the leather connected with her skin. She braced herself, lips parted to scream the word.

There was no warning before the first crack of the leather slapped across her butt. She gasped in surprise, her eyes widening. Despite the sting, a small tingle of pleasure sizzled through her. *Well this was interesting.* Wanting to see if it would continue to grow, she closed her mouth without protest and waited for the next slap to fall.

"You okay, angel?" His gentle question, showing his concern even through the play, had her heart squeezing with her love for him.

She gave a small nod and closed her eyes, almost embarrassed to admit how much she'd actually *liked* it.

"Good to hear." His voice thickened, just before the next slap came.

The leather strips flicked across the same buttock. Once, and then twice. Harder the second time.

Her pussy grew wetter and her nipples stabbed into the mattress. The intense pleasure combined with the amount of trust she had in Trevor had tears glazing her eyes.

"Shit," he whispered raggedly, before his fingers slipped inside her body again. "You really like this, angel."

He slapped her other buttock with the flogger, lightly and then harder as he continued to finger her aching channel.

A guttural moan ripped through the air and it took a moment for Megan to realize it came from her.

When his fingers left her she cried out in protest. But then, a second later, the leather flashed oh so lightly across her pussy.

"Oh God," she cried out. "More. Please, Sir."

Trevor groaned, before the leather hit harder against her sex.

The sting of pain mixed with the building pleasure. Her legs instinctively tried to close, but whatever he'd tied them with prevented her from shutting them. Her legs and thighs were spread wide for the unremitting slaps.

Her eyes crossed from the sensation and she couldn't hold back the throaty moans and pleas spilling from her lips.

Shelli Stevens

Something thick pressed against her opening and she gasped as it pushed inside her. It was the handle of the flogger, she realized a moment later, as Trevor began to fuck her with it.

"I love looking at your body like this, angel. Hearing your cries and seeing your body all flushed."

His hand slapped against her ass, alternating cheeks as he thrust the handle in and out of her body.

Pleasure had her entire body throbbing and she climbed the peak toward climax steadily, moving higher and higher. Her ass and thighs clenched as she fell over. A screamed ripped from her throat as white lights flashed behind her closed eyes. Her pussy clenched around the handle, gripping it as the spasms rocked her body.

A couple of tears leaked down her cheeks and she blinked them away, shocked at the intensity of her orgasm.

"So beautiful, Megan," Trevor said thickly, pulling the handle from her and placing a kiss on her ass cheek. "You all right, angel?"

Again she gave a weak nod and he sighed before she felt his tongue slide between her ass cheeks and rub against her tiny hole. She gasped, but didn't protest.

He lifted his head and murmured, "Good, because we're not done."

She felt the tension that kept her legs spread ease up and then she was free to draw her legs together once more. Her body, still weak, trembled from her climax.

A moment later Trevor closed a large hand over her hip and urged her onto her back. His eyes, full of lust and possessiveness, sent warmth sizzling through her already heated blood.

"Nowhere near through," he murmured again and then leaned down, pulling something black from the bag.

A blindfold. Her pulse quickened as she ran her tongue over her dry lips. Just when she thought it couldn't get more intense, he proved her wrong.

She almost regretted the fact that she wouldn't be able to watch what happened next. He was already such a sexy man and when he made love he never held back the emotions from his eyes.

But she trusted him. Trusted him to bring her pleasure and to never take things further than she was comfortable with.

He winked and slipped the mask over her head, and then everything went black.

"Stretch your hands over your head, Megan."

Trevor watched as she immediately moved to obey and his tongue went thick in his mouth. He almost wondered if Megan had been involved in some kind of kinky relationship in the past, because she was awfully good at this. And the fact that she'd given him so much trust and power still took his breath away. Was the most potent aphrodisiac he'd probably ever experienced.

He looped the fur-lined cuffs around one of the vertical poles in the headboard and then secured each of her wrists in a cuff.

He tugged her hands, testing the restraints and found them good. Turning he went back to refasten her legs to the corner posts.

She didn't protest, but nor did she stop the small moan that came out of her throat. Trevor smiled and stepped back to admire his handiwork.

Her hair spilled over the white pillowcase in a lush red wave, her eyes shielded with the black mask, and her lips parted with anticipation. His gaze slipped down her body. In this position her breasts thrust higher with the pink nipples rock hard. He moved his attention lower to where her legs were forced wide open. Between her slender thighs her pussy was pink and swollen, the dark channel of her entrance creamy with arousal.

His mouth watered to taste her and he swallowed hard. Jesus, she had to be the sexiest woman on the whole fucking planet.

Trevor reached almost blindly into the bag, searching for the object he'd seen earlier. He pulled out the long, thin, pink vibrator and turned it on.

Hearing Megan whimper, he glanced up to find her tongue sweeping over her lips. The black mask that kept her in darkness heightened the eroticism of the moment.

He climbed back onto the bed and settled himself between her thighs, so his face was just inches from her succulent pussy.

Taking the vibrator, he ran the tip over the edge of her pink folds and thrilled in the way her ass lifted off the bed. He circled her opening, again and again. Watched as she grew wetter and her breathing grew more erratic.

Then when she was biting her lip and he could tell she was struggling not to beg, he moved it to her entrance. Pushing it in slowly, he groaned at the sight of her wet flesh greedily sucking in the pink vibrator deeper into her channel.

Using is thumb and forefinger, Trevor parted the folds shielding her clitoris and then lowered his head to take the tender little nub into his mouth.

Megan's hips jerked off the bed as she let out a sharp cry.

The sweet, fresh taste of her arousal drove him to keep suckling her while rotating and pushing the thin vibrator inside her.

She tugged at her arms and tried to close her legs, but the restraints proved to do their job well. His blood pounded faster at the realization that she was completely helpless to do anything but accept the pleasure he gave her.

He flicked his tongue over the hardened nub, faster and then slow, all while her juices spilled onto his hand that fucked her with the vibrator. When her hips and ass moved, he followed, never abandoning her clit from his mouth.

Her whimpers grew higher, morphed into cries, and tears spilled down her cheeks from beneath the blindfold. Her pussy clenched around the vibrator and her ass lifted off the bed and held. When she finally came she was sobbing.

Trevor pulled the vibrator from her and moved himself over her. With his arms braced on either side of her rib cage, he thrust into her still-trembling body.

"Oh, you feel so good," he rasped, sinking deeper into her hot, slick warmth.

She couldn't move her arms or legs, but Megan's hips lifted against his thrusts and she let out a soft moan.

As he stared down at her, into the black mask, irritation slid through him. He didn't want it there. He wanted to see her eyes, shining blue and glazed with desire. He reached down with one hand and plucked the blindfold from her face.

Blinking up at him, Megan's gaze finally lost the disorientation but none of the passion.

With a low growl, he braced his hands on either side of her again and increased the pace of his thrusts. His teeth ground together as he tried to slow his body's urge to explode.

He closed his eyes, reveling in the hot suction of her pussy on his cock. How each time he sank into her he lost a little bit more of his soul.

When Megan's cries grew more fevered and her inner muscles clamped around him, he knew she was about to come.

He slammed into her faster, making her body slide on the mattress as much as the restraints allowed. His balls tightened and when she cried out with her release, he was right beside her.

His biceps locked and sweat rolled down his back as he climaxed, emptying himself and the rest of his energy inside of her.

When the ability to think returned and his arms began to shake, Trevor slid from her body. Guilt hit him that maybe he'd gone too far, and he made quick time untying her and unlocking the cuffs.

Megan sat up and stretched her muscles, her expression a little shaky and unsure, and when she slid from the bed his chest tightened.

"Give me a moment," she murmured and disappeared into the bathroom.

She was gone long enough to have his unease slipping into downright worry, but then she left the bathroom. Her smile was relaxed as she crossed the room and climbed back into bed.

She shook her head and curled up next to him in bed. "I don't even know what to say. That was...incredibly intense."

Trevor slid his arm around her, pulling her close to his heated body and then reached out to turn off the light.

They lay silent in the dark and his eyelids grew heavy. He knew he should stay awake and talk about what they'd done, see how she'd really felt about it, but her breathing was so steady he knew she'd fallen asleep.

And damn it all if he wasn't having a hard time staying awake himself. He let his eyelids drift shut and it wasn't long before he joined her in a deep, exhausted sleep.

When he woke in the morning, with the sunlight pouring in through the gap in the curtains, he knew his fears had been justified.

Megan was gone.

Chapter Fifteen

Megan whipped Trevor's truck into a spot outside Kate's Cakes and rushed out of the vehicle. By the time she pushed open the door to the shop, her pulse was jumping.

Inside Kate sat at a table with Todd, Tyson, another of his deputies and the owner of the hardware shop next to Kate's. When Megan entered, Kate glanced up and relief flickered in her eyes.

"Megan," she said softly and rose to her feet. "You didn't need to come. I shouldn't have even texted you."

"I'm glad you did, sweetie." Megan closed the few steps to one of her closest friends and gave her a big hug. "Are you doing okay?"

"I'm fine. Really."

But Kate's tone belied her words, and for the first time Megan let her gaze slide around the shop. The front window was broken and the brick that had been thrown through it still sat on the floor amongst shards of glass.

"Where's Trevor?" Tyson asked.

"Sleeping. The poor guy was out like a light when I got your message, and I didn't want to wake him. I'll send him a text in a few and just tell him I'm grabbing us some breakfast." Megan sighed and shook her head. "So who do you think did this? Teenagers?"

Tyson and Todd exchanged a long glance before Tyson gave a slight nod and averted his gaze.

"Possibly."

Hmm. She wasn't buying his nonchalant response in the slightest. But Kate didn't seem to notice, instead just went and grabbed a broom to sweep up the broken glass.

Megan crossed to where the men stood huddled like they were plotting defense at a football game.

"Okay, so what do you guys really think?" she asked quietly, folding her arms across her chest.

"Kate's front tire was slashed on her car last week," Todd answered discreetly, his brows drawn together and his expression dark. "Seems a little coincidental to me."

Tyson pursed his lips and shook his head. "Now we don't have any proof it was slashed. Kate said she could've run over some broken glass."

"Hmm." Megan nodded and glanced around the shop one more time.

Kate, who had just gone in the back to dump the glass, returned with a tired smile.

"You guys are all so sweet," she said with a sigh.

"Well, we're worried about you." Walt, the owner of the hardware shop said with a frown. He reached out and gave Kate's arm a light squeeze. "Whoever did this should be held accountable."

Kate gave him a grateful smile.

Megan watched the exchange with curiosity. Hmm. Perhaps Kate should consider dating Walt, he was a young widower in his late thirties, and he seemed awfully friendly with Kate...

"Gosh, Megan," Kate said suddenly. "You really need to get back to Trevor. This is your time with him, don't waste it on me."

"You're hardly a waste, but you're probably right. I should get back," she agreed and then gave them all a slight smile. "Though things are going as well as I hoped. Maybe even better."

"Oh, that's fantastic," Kate cried, her face lighting up. "Breakfast is on me this morning, pick out whatever you want to take with you. After all, this is costing you like an hour roundtrip of driving."

Todd grinned. "Jesus, I hope you're getting through to him. Best news I've heard all day, Meg."

"I'll echo that," Tyson agreed. "Keep us posted."

Megan pulled out her cell phone and nodded, before she sent a quick text to Trevor letting him know where she was.

"Thanks for everything you've done for us," Megan said, sliding her cell back into her purse. "All of you. I'm really hoping this time together has changed things. I owe Ryan big-time for lending us his house."

"I'll pass on your thanks to him," Todd said with a grin. "We're going drinking and wenching tonight."

"Wenching?" Kate repeated, her eyebrows flying high. "Did you really just call it wenching?"

"*Argh*." He threw an arm around her shoulder and squeezed. "Aye, I did, lassie. So batten down your morals and hide your virtue."

Kate's face went bright red and she shot a mortified gaze over to Megan, as if to ask *did you say something*?

Megan shook her head quickly and resisted the urge to kick Todd really, really hard. Was he seriously that clueless on how Kate felt about him? Wait, silly question.

"So, anyway," Kate said over-brightly, untangling herself from Todd's loosely thrown harm. "Megan, what did you say I could get you and Trevor for breakfast?"

Megan set the truck's brake and drew in a nervous breath. During the drive back to Canyon Beach, she'd thought a little about Kate's vandalism, but a whole lot more about Trevor and what had happened last night.

Her stomach flipped at the memory of being tied up and blindfolded and pleasured in a way that had blown her mind. Who could've ever known she would've loved a little kink? The idea still took her breath away.

Trevor hadn't texted back and she wondered if maybe he was still sleeping. She grabbed the white bag from Kate's and breathed in another sigh of delicious danishes before climbing out of the truck and heading for the house.

The house was quiet when she entered, but a few steps inside she drew up short.

Trevor stood in the kitchen, leaning against the counter, and his expression was completely guarded. The tension in his body visible.

Oh, God. No, no, no. Megan swallowed hard and hoped like hell they hadn't just taken three massive steps backward in all the positive advances over the past twenty-four hours.

"Good morning," she said cautiously. "Did you get my text?"

He lifted his cell phone and gave a small nod that he had.

"Kate's shop was vandalized. Not too much damage and nobody was hurt, but I wanted to check it out."

Trevor's brows furrowed. "Was Tyson there?"

"Yeah, and one of his deputies. And Todd."

"I hope they find the punk." He nodded and then looked away again.

"Trevor, what's going on?" she asked and set the bag with their breakfast down on the counter.

"It was too much, wasn't it?"

It took a moment for her to realize what he was even referring to, and when she did relief swept through her, weakening her.

She let a small seductive smile flit across her face as she crossed the floor to him.

"Last night? Not at all," she said softly and wound her arms around his neck. She pressed a light kiss against his mouth. "I loved it. It was incredible, Trevor."

Skepticism flashed in his eyes and maybe a little relief. "Really? You're sure?"

"I'm still kind of shocked how much I *did* love it. Besides, we had a safe word. Even if it was kind of...fluffy," she teased and nipped at his bottom lip.

Trevor growled and slid his arms around her waist, jerking her flush against him.

"Thank God. When I woke up and you were gone...I thought." He kissed her forehead, her cheek, and then finally her mouth, before lifting his head. "Please, angel, don't do that to me again."

"I wo-oh!" she gasped as her feet left the ground and she found herself in his arms. "What are you—"

"I want you again." He strode back toward the bedroom.

"But breakfast...?"

"Can wait."

Megan laughed huskily and wrapped her arms around his neck. Yes. Breakfast could definitely wait.

An hour later, Trevor polished off the last bite of his danish and leaned back in bed. His gaze slid to Megan, who was still nibbling on hers.

Damn, she was just ridiculously sexy sitting naked in the

bed with her hair still tousled from their lovemaking and her knees drawn up to her chest.

"Hmm. Maybe I should've bought you two of those," she teased. "Are you still hungry?"

He shook his head and took another sip of coffee. "I'm fine. Breakfast in bed is awesome."

Megan grinned and finished her danish. "It is, isn't it?"

"Mmm." He gave her another sideways glance. "So what I did to you last night, it really didn't freak you out?"

She gave a soft laugh and kissed his shoulder. "No, I absolutely loved it. I want to try it more often. I mean I'm not saying we should do it every time we have sex, but it's a fun way to mix things up." She glanced up at him, her brow arched and her lips pursed. "Hmm. Maybe you'll even let me try swatting your ass with that flogger thing."

Trevor let loose a laugh from low in his belly at the image. "Not a fucking chance, angel. I like being in charge."

"Mmm. I guess so. Well, I don't mind giving up control every now and then." She poked him in the ribs. "Well, in the bedroom at least."

Trevor grinned and grabbed her, rolling her under him before she could protest. She snuggled eagerly against him, kissing his shoulder and wiggling beneath him. The position was so normal, one he'd missed more than he'd realized over the past year. He couldn't imagine not having Megan in his life again all the time. Everything inside him rebelled at letting her go. But at that thought, his mind wandered down darker paths and his chest tightened with guilt.

"I shouldn't be this happy," Trevor finally muttered, nuzzling her neck. "I shouldn't be thinking about being your husband, and your belly round with my baby."

"You're thinking about that?" she whispered breathlessly. "Because I have been too. You're entitled to happiness, Trevor. Everyone is."

"But you don't understand. Nobody does."

"What don't I understand?" she pleaded softly, pushing on his shoulders so she could look at his face again. "Help me understand, Trevor."

"What it's like. What we go through. I mean, a soldier's death might garner his name and age being flashed on the news for tens seconds," he said harshly. "But people didn't know the man himself--and I use that term loosely because he was only eighteen--like I did."

"Oh, Trevor," she whispered, cupping his cheek. "Tell me who he was."

His heart thumped in his chest and he swallowed with difficulty. The urge to shut down was strangely missing. Instead, he wanted to talk. To explain.

"Darrell Washington," he finally said. "He was one of my soldiers. It was his first deployment to Afghanistan. Hell, his first deployment anywhere." He shook his head. "He loved to play video games and talk shit with the other soldiers. He had a fiancée waiting for him, just like me. We used to talk about you gals. Our women back home."

Megan gave a small smile and cupped his shoulder, massaging lightly.

"A couple of times I mentioned to him that maybe he was too young to be settling down. Christ, he'd only just graduated high school. But he was dedicated to his girl... I'd never seen a guy look so in love, so determined and steadfast about anything. He had the same passion for being in the army."

"What happened?" she asked, almost on a whisper.

"He was the one I sent back into the Humvee to call for help. He was the one killed when an RPG slammed into it."

She was silent for a moment and when he glanced down at her tears shimmered in her eyes. "I'm so sorry."

Bile rose in his throat and his gut twisted. "I survived, Megan. How is it fair that *I* should get to go home, marry my woman, when Private Washington, the soldier I should've kept safe, is dead."

"You're not invincible, Trevor. People die during war. It's not fair, but would it have made it any more right if you had died?" she asked, her voice breaking. "You need to forgive yourself and *stop* feeling guilty that you didn't die. Because you may not have been killed in Afghanistan, but I still lost you."

The air seemed to suck from the room, he couldn't breathe as he stared at the anguish in her eyes and the tears she battled. Something inside of him shifted and the wall he'd kept erected for over a year came crashing down. Reality, crystal clear and unforgiving, blindsided him. He struggled to breathe. To speak. But he couldn't even blink.

Just how much had he lost by doing exactly what Megan

had said—feeling guilty for surviving? How had he ever thought he could handle this on his own? Without seeking help?

"Trevor?" Her fingers tightened around his shoulder, her eyes widening in concern.

"I'm sorry," he muttered dumbly, drawing her into his arms again and burying his face into her hair. "Oh my God, Megan, I'm so sorry. You're right. About everything."

"Trevor, you've been in so much pain..." Her arms wound around him, her grip almost vise-like.

"I love you. More than anything, and maybe I have been in pain, but I've also been so damn blind," he said thickly. "How could I ever have let you go? When I return to Fort Lewis I'll ask for the help I've been too stubborn to accept. I'll talk to someone, Megan, I promise. But, I don't want to lose you, angel. Never again."

"You can't lose me. Not this time. I love you so much, Trevor. I shouldn't have given up on you in the first place." Her voice broke through the tears. "And I blame myself just as much."

Trevor groaned and lowered his head, crushing her lips beneath his and stopping her from pinning the blame on herself. Her arms looped around his neck and her body nearly melded into his.

This was his woman. She'd always believed in him, always loved him. Had always known that he just needed a little extra help to get through the darkness. It was just a damn shame it'd taken him this long to figure it out himself.

He lifted his head and brushed a tender kiss across her forehead. "You will make an excellent soldier's wife, angel. That is, if you still want the position."

Megan's eyes glowed with tears and happiness. "Are you kidding? I'd take out any other bitch that applied. That spot is mine, soldier boy."

An optimism and brightness that he hadn't felt in years rushed through him and Trevor knew this was a new beginning. With Megan's faith and love, the future looked damn bright.

He lowered his head again, claiming her mouth once more in a kiss that sealed their future and their love.

Chapter Sixteen

Kate clutched her glass of champagne and resisted the urge to tug down her dress. What had she been thinking, wearing this flowery tight little thing? She didn't have the same kind of body most of the girls here did, her curves were a little more...well, curvy.

Watching Tyson and Ellie dancing on the lawn of Tyson's parents' house, Kate bit back a wistful sigh. What a beautiful reception, and the wedding had been wonderfully sweet and romantic too.

They looked so happy. So in love. What must that be like? And apparently Tyson wasn't the only one finding love, because Trevor and Megan had just announced they were getting back together. Everyone, of course, had been ecstatic to hear the news that the couple would be marrying within the month in a small ceremony on the beach, before Megan moved up to Fort Lewis to be with Trevor.

Lifting her glass of champagne, Kate took a sip and swung her gaze away from the newlyweds. Unfortunately her attention landed straight on the youngest Wyatt brother.

Todd had brought a date to his brother's wedding. Some skinny, tall, fake-tanned brunette who had an annoying laugh and clung to him like a wet noodle.

She bit her bottom lip, ignoring the hollow ache in her stomach. Her mind flittered back to that moment at Ellie's bachelorette party, when Todd had shown up and thrown out the stripper. Or more so, what had happened *after* that.

Her pulse quickened and her body heated. She closed her eyes and shook her head, downing the rest of her champagne.

When she opened her eyes, she found Todd watching her. Her mouth dried out when he winked and then her heart did a little jump kick in her chest.

She was a fool to have a crush on a man who went through women like she went through flour in her bakery. And she *needed* to remember that Todd Wyatt was nothing but trouble. She could find plenty of other ways to get her heart broken, thank you very much.

There were plenty of other fish in the sea. Like Walt Chapman. The owner of the hardware shop next to hers. He'd taken her out for lunch after her shop had been vandalized, had insisted on paying and had been nothing but supportive and charming.

But he wasn't Todd.

Which is a good thing, she reminded herself. Turning away from his teasing grin, she sought out anyone besides Todd to talk to. Because with the recent vandalism at her shop, she already had her fair share of trouble without adding Todd Wyatt to the mix...

Flash Point

Dedication

Thank you to Andy Finseth from Seattle Fire, Mr. Delilah Marvelle, and Karen Erickson and her dad, for all your fabulous firefighting info. Thanks to my awesome editor, Tera, and to Scott for the great covers in this series! And of course to my readers, because I wouldn't be telling stories without you!

Chapter One

Kate wrapped her pea coat tighter around her curves, slipped from her car and rushed toward the front door of her shop.

The winter wind whipped blonde strands of her hair about her face, and she shoved them aside as she fumbled to unlock the shop door. When the key finally twisted she stepped inside and shut the door, a shiver running through her.

"It's definitely winter," she muttered, flipping on the lights.

With a sigh, she glanced around the shop, taking in the decorations taped to the walls and the small snowflake lights surrounding the bakery display case. Christmas had been over for a few days, but since most of her decorations were more seasonal than holiday, they could stay up for a bit longer.

The smell of sugar, yeast and cinnamon was a familiar scent that never failed to bring a smile to her face. Baking was in her blood—if you cut her open she'd ooze lemon buttercream frosting.

She glanced at the clock on the wall and bit back a yawn. *Five a.m.* The hours, however, were the part of baker's life she wasn't all that crazy about. Some nights she stayed way too late preparing for the morning baked goods.

When she'd opened the shop just over a year ago, she'd been a little worried about whether Kate's Cakes would sink or swim. Especially since she made everything from scratch, the cost of her food was a little more on the pricey side. But during the tourist season business boomed, and fortunately the locals seemed to love her too. In fact it seemed the fresh, high-quality ingredients became her selling point.

With a sigh, she went to start the first batch of cupcakes. A couple of hours later she'd loaded up the display case with a few dozen batches of cupcakes and pastries, when a sharp knock landed on the door.

Her heart leapt in her chest as she tried to see out into the fading darkness. The sun was not quite up and the shop didn't officially open for another hour and a half.

Wiping her hands on her apron, she stepped out from behind the counter and walked toward the door. As she recognized the man outside, the tension eased from her body. Unfortunately tingling heat and sharp awareness replaced it as she let Todd Wyatt inside her shop.

"Well, aren't you up early?" she asked, hoping her voice didn't sound as high pitched to him as it did to her.

Todd grinned, his broad shoulders and tall frame filling the entryway before he closed the door behind him.

Her breath caught and she tried not to think about how handsome he was. He'd always seemed impossibly sexy to her, though. And maybe part of her attraction to the youngest Wyatt brother came from the fact that he'd always been so damn nice to her.

"Just coming off a twenty-four hour shift. Was heading home when I saw your lights on."

"Stalker," she teased and started to fidget, before curling her fingers into fists at her sides. Her heart had yet to slow down, but then, she'd kind of gotten used to it racing when Todd came near.

She cleared her throat. "I'm not even open for business yet. So, what, are you here to mooch some free cupcakes again? Beg me to take pity on my local fireman?"

"You know it." Todd grinned, before his light expression suddenly darkened and he stepped past her and moved around her shop. "And I also wanted to make sure things have been running smoothly around these parts. No more trouble."

Ah, yes. Trouble. Her brows drew together and she worried her bottom lip between her teeth, letting her gaze dart to the window that had been broke a few months ago.

"No. No more trouble. I'm guessing that the brick-thrown-through-the-window thing was just a teenage prank."

"Hmm. Only they never caught the guy, which is unusual in a town this size."

She sighed. "Look, I'm not worried. Besides, I've got Walt next door who's pretty much transformed himself into my own personal guard dog."

Todd scowled and then thrust his hands into his pockets. "I don't like that guy."

Seriously? Kate's mouth parted slightly as she tried to figure out how to respond. What wasn't to like about Walt? The poor young widower was quiet and charming and protective of both her and her shop. But Todd's drawn brows over an irritated gaze clearly indicated he didn't share her appreciation for the hardware shop owner.

"He just rubs me the wrong way."

"Right. Well, I suppose I can buy that." She cleared her throat. "Now, about that cupcake...I can spare one for my local firefighter. I always do."

"You are such a doll." Todd's roguish grin reappeared and her stomach did another summersault as he squeezed her shoulder.

Just a friend, just a friend. He'll never be anything except a friend. She repeated the mantra in her head, keeping a smile on her face as she went to box him up a chocolate cupcake that she knew he loved. Though she needn't have bothered with a box, because he took the treat, sat down at a table and immediately began to devour it.

God, she was such a sucker. Good thing she didn't give away free cupcakes to every hot guy in town or she'd be out of business. Not that there were all that many totally hot guys in Wyattsville...the first ones that came to mind were the Wyatt brothers. Todd was the youngest and the last bachelor standing. To the disappointment of town's female population, the other two brothers, Tyson and Trevor, had recently gotten married.

With a sigh, she went to frost cupcakes again, sneaking the occasional glance at Todd as he ate. Her mouth dried out as his tongue circled the top of the cupcake, licking up buttercream frosting like it was ambrosia.

His mouth was so full and sensual, and the way he worked his tongue...how many women had firsthand knowledge of just how talented Todd Wyatt was with his mouth and tongue? A damn good amount of them, that was for sure. Heat slid low in her body and her hands weren't as steady as she reached for another cupcake to frost.

She should've been repulsed by his womanizer reputation, and yet, it almost fascinated her. Her and the entire town, really. The female sex seemed to know and accept Todd Wyatt for what he was. A charming playboy.

But she knew better than to get *involved* with the one man in town who'd never settle down. Even if she'd been a little more than tempted lately. No matter how good in bed he was supposed to be, or that going to bed with Todd Wyatt seemed to be equivalent to riding a mega roller coaster at least once before you died.

Her nose crinkled as she reached for the bowl of pistachio buttercream frosting so she could frost another dozen cupcakes. Well there was no way she'd give her heart—not to mention her virginity—to a man who wouldn't value either of them. Especially after what had happened during Ellie's bachelorette—

"Have dinner with me tonight."

Kate's fingers clenched around the cupcake she'd been carefully decorating. The top of the cake exploded over the delicate paper wrapping, sending pale green frosting and glittery sugar crystals everywhere.

Her heart thundering in her chest, she set the massacred sweet treat aside and glanced up at Todd again. She had to have heard that wrong. Surely Todd Wyatt had not just asked her to dinner.

Struggling to keep her voice as casual as possible, she still squeaked. "Dinner?"

Todd stood up and crinkled the cupcake wrapper in his hand, before tossing it in the garbage. "Yeah, dinner. If I wasn't going home to crash for the next ten hours, I'd say lunch."

Kate struggled to keep her mouth from flapping. Todd had never asked her to go out with him—not alone, at least. Sure, they'd hung out with friends and his family more often than not, especially with all the weddings lately...but alone? Why? What could possibly be his moti—

"I mean, dinner is the least I can do with you being my cupcake dealer and all."

When he flashed his pearly whites again, her knees trembled a little. She slid her gaze over his face, trying to read his thoughts, but all she could focus on was the dark stubble on his chiseled jaw. She ran her tongue over her mouth and swallowed hard.

Answer him.

"Sure. I'm up for dinner."

"Great. You want me to swing by your place about six?"

"I can meet you somewhere, no need—"

"Come on and embrace your inner tree hugger, Kate. Let's save some carbons and carpool. Or we could even walk."

"It's freezing," she replied automatically. And why was Todd suddenly spouting off like a local environmentalist? "Fine, just pick me up."

"Great. I'm going to head out and hit the sack." He winked and turned toward the door. "See you tonight, doll."

"Okay..." She gave a light laugh. Did it sound as skeptical as it felt? "I'll...see you tonight."

She waited until he'd left the shop to let her laugh turn a bit maniacal. She'd just agreed to have dinner with Todd. It didn't mean anything, how could it? She certainly wasn't his type. And they'd been friends for way too long. But still, dinner with Todd? Just the two of them?

Her stomach flipped and she let out a small groan. How the hell was she going to keep her head on straight for the next ten hours? She shook her head and walked to the back of the shop to start preparing more pastries.

Todd drummed his fingers on the steering wheel as he pulled his truck off Main Street and headed toward the east side of town. Maybe he should've skipped the cupcake—and subsequent sugar rush—when he was going to be heading to bed in a few minutes.

But driving past Kate's shop, seeing the lights on, he'd had the strong compulsion to stop by. Sure, begging for a free cupcake was the usual excuse, and he'd topped it off with the concern of any more vandalism, but there'd been more to it. With his brothers getting married and things dying down a bit, he hadn't seen Kate as much. Hadn't realized how much he missed seeing her.

Which was a little weird. It wasn't like he lacked female companionship by any means. But Kate was the only woman who'd been consistent in his life—the one woman who he'd never let himself imagine what she'd be like in bed. Well, until that night he and his brothers had had to break up Ellie's bachelorette party.

The memory stirred in his mind, almost like it was

yesterday, not almost five months ago. Kate's soft, hesitant lips, pressed against his in what could've only been an impulsive move. A *drunken*, impulsive move. It hadn't meant anything. One minute he'd been lecturing her about hiring a stripper for the bachelorette party, the next she was kissing him to shut him up.

She'd shocked the hell out of him, and for a moment, his dick had taken over. She wasn't Kate, she was a sexy woman kissing him, and he'd almost started to kiss her back. Had almost taken control of the oddly chaste kiss and shown her what a downright dirty one was like. But then he'd remembered who she was. Kate, the girl who'd been a few years behind him in school. The girl who'd grown into a bubbly woman who was everyone's friend. Including his. And like hell he was going to screw with that. So he'd set her aside, paid her tab, and hauled her drunken ass home.

Sure, there'd been times over the years when he'd thought Kate might nurse a bit of a crush on him, but he'd dismissed it. He was a fireman—half the girls in town got wet when they saw a fire truck go by. If she'd had some kind of crush, it was probably some misguided hero worship he wasn't all that worthy of—he certainly wasn't going to take advantage of it.

Still, the kiss with Kate had never really left his mind, and sometimes, when he saw her, it was the first thing he thought of. It bugged him. He didn't want to think about how ripe and pink her mouth had been, delicate like a flower whose petals he wanted to crush with his mouth.

Todd sighed and tightened his fingers around the steering wheel. And yet here he was thinking about it again. So weird. He shook his head to rid the image, firmly placing Kate back in the friend section of his brain. The side where mostly men and sisters-in-law lingered.

Asking her to dinner tonight was just to reaffirm that their friendship was on the level it should be. Just friends. His brows drew together as a thought hit him. Kate had almost seemed panicked when he'd asked her to dinner, what if she'd been thinking he was asking her on a date? Like a real date and not a friend thing.

Shit. No wonder she'd looked like she was ready to faint.

Todd pulled into the driveway of his house and stared out into the fenced backyard and the trees beyond.

Well, he'd just have to put her worries to rest at dinner. The last thing Kate wanted to do was get involved with a guy like him, though she was far too smart for that. Maybe at dinner he'd beg her to share some baking secrets, tell her he wanted some tips on how to charm a girl. Something like that...yeah. That'd put Kate's nerves at ease.

A yawn popped his jaw and he opened his truck door and stepped down. If he was going to even make this da—shit—*dinner* tonight, then he'd better get his ass to bed.

Grabbing his bag, Todd headed inside the house where his bed awaited him.

Chapter Two

Kate locked the door to her shop and checked her watch. Four thirty. That gave her an hour and a half to get ready for her not-a-date. Because no way was she letting herself think that this was anything but dinner with a friend.

She stuffed her keys back into her purse and turned away from her shop, nearly running smack into Walt.

"Oh." She lifted her hands to stop herself from slamming into him, and her fingers brushed against his shoulders. Muscle and bone underneath his denim shirt registered, before she jerked away uncomfortably. "Walt, you crept up on me."

"Sorry about that." He grinned, the lines around his eyes crinkling. "Guess I should've said something, but I thought you saw me approaching."

"No, sorry, my mind was elsewhere." She gave a brief smile and tucked a strand of blonde hair behind her ear. "What's going on?"

"I thought I'd see if you wanted to grab a bite to eat with me after I close at five." He cleared his throat and shifted. "I realize you're heading home, but I could swing by and pick you up."

Whoa. Asked out to dinner, for the same night, by two separate men. Weirdness. Though Walt's offer wasn't all that surprising, seeing as they'd been having dinner together at least once a week lately. He was a nice-looking man, very Northwest with his red goatee and flannel and denim all the time. She just wished she felt...more. But it never seemed more than platonic.

"Walt, I would, but...I have other plans."

Disappointment flashed in his blue eyes, but he nodded. "No problem. Maybe another time. Have a good night, Caitleen."

Kate winced when he turned and walked away. She headed toward her own car. For some reason Walt enjoyed calling her by her full name, had said it was far too lovely not to be used for such a pretty woman. Oh the man oozed charm, and he used it aggressively in his pursuit of her, which overall was a bit of a novelty. Because, well, men generally *didn't* pursue her. And the one time a guy had, well, she really should've known better...

She pushed aside the uncomfortable memory and soon she was cruising up the hill in her old Ford Escort toward her small house.

Once inside, she had a mission. Though it shouldn't have mattered one iota what she wore tonight, it did. And somewhere in her closet, was an outfit that would up her attractiveness, at least a tiny bit.

But after searching for at least ten minutes, she gave up. Apparently, she owned lots of jeans, sweaters and shirts. Nothing suitably *sexy*.

She paused in the midst of her frantic searching and shook her head. "What the hell am I doing? I shouldn't be trying to look all super hot for Todd. I'm *trying* to remind myself we're just friends."

With a new determination, she grabbed a black sweater off a hanger, pulled out a fresh pair of jeans and underwear, and then went to grab a shower.

When Todd rang the doorbell, she probably wouldn't have qualified as sexy, but she definitely looked a little more pulled together.

Before opening the door, she gave herself one quick glance in the mirror. Her hair shined almost white blonde and loose over her shoulders, and the sweater hugged her excess of curves nicely. The V-neck giving just a hint of cleavage— definitely no push-up bra needed there.

Good enough.

Kate jerked her gaze away from the mirror and opened the door.

"Hi," she said brightly.

Todd's answering smile never left her face, didn't drift over the cleavage she'd been more than a little proud of, but she tried not to feel a sting of rejection. This was, after all, exactly what she wanted. Friends.

"So where are we off to?" she asked.

"You up for Mexican? I'm craving some fajitas."

"I'm always up for fajitas," she said, following him out to his truck. "Just load up the guacamole."

"Amen to that." He opened her door and her heart did a little flip.

It's just manners, Kate, some men still have them.

She braced her hands on the door and the truck frame and climbed into the truck. She'd almost made it in, when she wobbled to the left, brushing up against Todd's arm. Or at least her breast did.

Heat rocketed through her body and she lost the air in her lungs. Her right breast tingled with awareness as the nipple slowly tightened.

Should she apologize? Would he say something? But then she was in the truck and he'd shut the door as if nothing had happened.

Right, you dork, she scolded herself silently. *Todd probably touches breasts at least once a day. He probably didn't even realize yours was all over his arm like icing on cake.*

Even still, she was glad for the darkness of the truck so he couldn't see the pink in her cheeks. God, it was going to be a long night.

The streets of Wyattsville were dark and deserted with most people in for the night. Still, Todd gripped the steering wheel like he expected kids to be darting out in the road any minute.

It was just a breast. Kate's breast. It should've been like bumping into his sister—if he'd had one. But when she'd fell against him, the thoughts in his head sure as hell hadn't been brotherly. Just like that night at the tavern, he'd been thrown into an alternate reality with Kate that left him a bit dazed.

When she'd opened the door, he'd deliberately not let his gaze drop to her breasts peeking out of her sweater. Which was damn hard, because he'd still seen the large swells out of the corner of his eye without glancing down for closer inspection.

She was different than most of the women he'd dated over the years. Her personality earthier and a body that was lush and curvy. She was unique...intriguing in a way he was only just now starting to notice.

Shit. Maybe this was a bad idea. Dinner tonight. What the hell was wrong with him? Was he being naïve to think he could keep looking at Kate as just a friend? Had that silly little impulse kiss she'd given him at the tavern screwed that up entirely?

It was part of the reason he'd stop coming around so much. He'd needed to distance himself from her, from the memory of that kiss.

"Weren't we going to El Gordo's?"

He blinked. "What?"

"I think you just passed the restaurant."

For fuck's sake, really? Todd's jaw clenched with disbelief as he swerved the truck around at the next intersection.

"Good catch. My mind must've been elsewhere." *Like on your tits.*

"No problem, I've been accused more than once for having my head in the clouds," she teased.

He glanced over at her and smiled, but caught another flash of creamy cleavage as they pulled under a street lamp. Her breasts looked soft and pillowy, kind of *like* clouds. Might not be such a bad place to have his hea—*fuck!* Sweat broke out on the back of his neck and he jerked his attention back out the windshield as he parked the truck.

Fuck, fuck, fuck. Dinner had definitely been a bad idea. Definitely. How the hell was going to stop his dick from taking control of his brain the rest of the night? He couldn't be thinking about sleeping with Kate. Could not even *consider* the possibility. He was an asshole, but he wasn't *that* big of one.

His brothers would kick his ass to Portland and back if they were aware what he was thinking. Jesus, he was in trouble.

Todd parked the truck and put on the emergency brake, giving a tight smile.

"So, ready to get your fajitas on?"

"Oh, heck yeah I am." She waggled her eyebrows and licked her bottom lip. "Bring on the cheese, chicken, peppers, tortillas—"

"Corn?" he asked gruffly, trying really hard not to look at her mouth.

"Oh yeah. Can't do the flour, it's just not the same." She gave a soft laugh and then reached for the handle on the door, sliding out before he could remember his manners and open it for her.

Shit. Someone needed to slap him upside the head. And hard. He'd do it himself if Kate hadn't been outside on the sidewalk waiting for him.

Biting back a sigh, he climbed out of the truck and went to start the dinner date that never should've happened.

It was only once they were seated, had ordered, and he nursed a bottle of beer, did some of Todd's tension ease. Kate was talking animatedly about this and that, acting as if everything was life as usual. Which was probably damn easy for her, considering she didn't have the same filthy thoughts running through *her* mind.

But he found if he focused really, really hard on seeing Kate in that friend light, blurred his gaze a bit, it almost worked. Almost. When their food arrived, he was grateful for the distraction. Relieved for a reason to look at something else besides her.

"So I've always been curious," she said between bites. "How on earth do you function working those twenty-four hour shifts? Don't you get tired?"

Back on familiar territory, Todd relaxed a little more as he built another fajita on a tortilla. "Sometimes we catch naps during the shift, but it can be a little abrasive on the body when a call comes in. You get used to it. And really, it's pretty awesome having all those days off I get in exchange."

"Oh I'm sure," she gave a wistful sigh. "So what do you do during such a super long shift? When you're not on a call."

"Well, when Jeremiah and I get there for our shift, we relieve the other guys, get our gear on the rig, check out the equipment, roll call and going over the agenda for the day...then, you know, we keep busy. Sometimes we have inspections, training, drills. Other days are slower. We work out, shop for the firehouse, cook dinner." He grinned. "And, you know, just 'wait for the big one'."

"That's really cool, Todd. Sounds like such an awesome job."

Todd drew back a bit emotionally, when he saw the glint of fascination in her eyes. The pink in her cheeks. It pretty much reaffirmed that even if Kate *was* nursing a mild crush on him, it was more for what he did, than for who he was.

"I really can't imagine such a career. Especially having all those days off!" she continued. "I need to hire more people, because right now I'm only getting Sunday off and that's only because the shop's closed."

About to take a bite, Todd hesitated, his brows drawing together with realization. "Yeah. You really do work a lot. How long are you there each day?"

"Usually six to sometimes after four...however long it takes me to clean up."

Biting back a curse, he muttered, "Kate, you seriously need to hire someone else."

"I have other people. Well, sort of. I mean I had a couple extra employees during the summer, but one returned to college in the fall. Now it's just Bree—who's part time—and I." She sighed and then licked a trace of sour cream off her finger. "But you're right, I need to hire someone else."

And just like that, watching Kate's pink tongue dart out, and Todd was back in unfamiliar territory. His blood heated and something primal sizzled through him.

"I need you to teach me how to bake something," he rasped desperately. "I want to impress a girl."

Chapter Three

He might as well have sucker punched her in the gut. Kate blinked, trying hard not to let the surprise and hurt show on her face.

"Oh, right. Sure."

And there it was. The real reason he'd asked her out tonight. It definitely hadn't been romantic, wasn't really even a friend thing, he just wanted baking lesson to get into some chick's pants.

Her stomach knotted and she swallowed hard. God she was a fool, had been acting like a fool all night. Chatting a mile a minute to try and hide how damn nervous she was, to avoid thinking about his arm against her breast earlier, and how she wanted so much more than an accidental brushing.

"It doesn't even have to be anything exciting," Todd went on quickly. "I mean, maybe just some no-brainer cookie recipe?"

She nodded and took another bite of food, even if her food had lost all flavor and enjoyment.

Silence fell between them, heavy and awkward, and the longer she kept quiet, the more she just wanted to *scream*. She could barely deal with Todd talking to her about the women in his life, seeing them was bad enough, but having to help him with it?

Todd seemed to sense her mood change, because any further attempts at conversation stayed firmly away from the topic of women and dating.

When the check arrived, he handled it despite her insisting that she pay half. The entire ride home, the hot ball of anger in her belly just kept expanding, until her vision was tinted with red and her hands were clenched into fists.

When they pulled up outside her house, she didn't trust herself to say anything more than a terse, "Goodnight."

She climbed out of the truck, slamming the door behind her as she strode toward her front door. She'd just blown any pretense of playing it cool, but so what? She heard the truck door slam again, and she flinched, increasing her pace.

Todd's fingers curled around her elbow, spinning her around and off balance. She reached out to catch herself, just like she'd done earlier today with Walt. Only this time, there was no urge to pull away when her palms flattened against Todd's hard, broad chest. But the fact that she was pissed, not just angry, downright pissed at Todd, had her jerking away regardless.

Todd didn't let her go though, instead slid his hands up her arm to pull her closer to him.

Her heart lurched in her chest and her mouth went dry.

"I'm sorry," he muttered.

She lifted her gaze to his and from the light of her porch saw the regret in his eyes.

"There isn't a woman I'm trying to impress with baking. I made that up."

Kate frowned, stilling in her efforts to free herself. "Why did you say that then?"

"Damn it, to keep *this* from happening." His head blocked out the light as it dipped, and then his mouth crashed down on hers.

Shock ripped through her as his lips masterfully parted hers, his tongue plunging inside to taste her. She couldn't move, couldn't even respond for a moment. Until the tingling began and a liquid heat seeped through her veins, pooling heavily between her thighs.

She was in Todd's arms and he was kissing the hell out of her? How long had she fantasized about this?

Kate kissed him back, pressing her body firmly against his, crushing her breasts against his chest as she gave herself over to the moment. To the power of a chemistry never before acted on. A chemistry that for so long she'd thought would always only be one sided.

He lifted his head, his breathing ragged. His gaze tormented. "Tell me to stop, Kate."

"I can't," she whispered. "I won't."

Todd growled low in his throat and then backed her up,

Shelli Stevens

until she slammed into her front door. His hands that gripped her arms slid up to her wrists, jerking them above her head and pinning them against the wood in one of his hands.

Then his mouth was on hers again, while his free hand covered one of her breasts through her sweater. Her nipple beaded and the spot between her legs throbbed with need. Her mew of pleasure was caught on his tongue as it swept across hers.

Oh God, oh God, oh God.

His strong fingers squeezed her flesh, finding her nipple through the layer of sweater and bra. Her panties dampened as he twisted and pinched the tip, his tongue so far from gentle as it plundered her mouth.

She arched into him, wanting so much more than he was giving. And he seemed to know, because he delved his hand beneath the V of her sweater and under her bra to find her bare breast.

Her eyes almost rolled to the back of her head with pleasure. The feel of his rough, calloused hands against her sensitized flesh kept her mind grounded enough to know she wasn't dreaming.

Todd pinched her nipple and arrows of pleasure shot directly from her breast to between her legs. She adjusted her stance, needing to ease the ache. There was so much more she wanted. Needed.

She tugged to free her hands unconsciously, wanting him to unfasten her jeans and slip a hand inside. Wanted to feel his fingers inside her. She'd never had that before. With any man...

Todd's mouth jerked from hers, a guttural "*Fuck*" spilling from his lips.

Kate's lashes fluttered up and she ran her tongue over her swollen mouth.

Tension had Todd's shoulders rigid, his face twisted into an expression of frustration. She held her breath, waiting for what would happen next, as her heart continued to thunder in her chest.

Don't stop, oh please, please don't stop. No matter how many times she'd told herself it would be foolish to get sexually involved with Todd——having just this quick impassioned taste, it was clear her willpower was obliterated the moment he touched her.

232

"Ah, Kate," he muttered, his finger stroking over the inside of her wrist. "I'm sorry."

He was sorry? For what had just happened? Her heart did a big fat nosedive and her throat tightened.

"I shouldn't have done that," he continued, and released her hands from where they were still pinned above her. He took a step backward and gave a humorless laugh. "I guess we can just say we're even now."

"Even?" she parroted, the one word high-pitched and soft.

"Yeah. From when you stole a drunken kiss that you probably don't even remember—"

"I remember."

Todd's gaze jumped back to hers and his jaw flexed. "You don't want to get involved with me, Kate. I'm not boyfriend material."

She swallowed hard, heat burning her cheeks. How the hell did she respond to that? Seriously. *How?* Say she was just looking to get laid? Because was she? It was a huge leap from virgin to one-night stand.

"I was wrong to say I don't like that hardware store guy, Kate. You *should* be dating someone like that. Someone who'll appreciate you. Respect you..."

In the morning? Who knew if they were the unspoken words to the rest of Todd's sentence, but they fit.

Kate sucked her bottom lip into her mouth and chewed it. Why was it so crushingly disappointing that Todd had slammed the door on the possibility of sex between them?

"Why did you ask me to dinner tonight?" she finally blurted, not really knowing what else to say.

Todd sighed and shook his head. "The hell if I know. But it was a bad idea."

"Ouch. You're not doing much for my confidence right now." Her laugh came out brittle as she dug in her purse for her keys.

"*Damn it.* Again that came out wrong. I'm sorry."

"You know, I'm just going to go inside now, before you say something that makes me give in to the urge to drive my knee into your balls."

"I'm sorry..."

"I think you've said that a few times tonight." Which was

weird, because Todd wasn't the type to apologize profusely. She fumbled to unlock the door and shoved it open, before stepping inside. Turning to face him, she gave a strained smile. "It's best if we just call it a night."

"Yeah, probably." Todd shoved his hands into his pocket and nodded. "Shit, Kate, I really am so—"

She shut the door before he could finish another apology.

He'd fucked up tonight. In a big, fat, no-going-back way. Todd slammed his fists into the steering wheel and cursed a blue streak as he headed home.

What the hell had gotten into him? Kate was not any random woman he could seduce without regret. She was Kate. All wide eyes and a touch of innocence he didn't see with many girls nowadays. Hell, *any* of the girls he'd dated. If you could call what he did dating...

He'd wager Kate had probably only slept with a few men in her life. And the only other guy he could remember her being serious with was some guy on the baseball team back in high school. He'd been away at college, but he'd heard about it, seen them when he'd returned during spring break.

But whatever happened in Kate's love life, she kept it private. She obviously wasn't the type to sleep around.

Todd's mouth twisted derisively. And yet that's all *he* did. Playing musical beds like it was an Olympic event.

His fingers clenched around the steering wheel as he thought about the softness of her full breast spilling over into his hand. Jesus, she was sexy. Had tits that were so big, soft and *real*. Everything about Kate was real and lush. How had he never realized it before? How understated her attractiveness was?

Because tonight he'd wanted to push open her front door and toss her inside, get her onto that big white couch of hers and strip her naked. Then kiss the softness of her inner thighs, before moving between them to taste the sweet-as-candy pussy he'd find. She probably tasted better than anything in her addictive little shop.

Todd bit back a groan and shook his head. His cock was like granite beneath his jeans, pushing against the denim and throbbing something fierce. *Damn it.* He had to stop thinking about Kate this way. Everything had changed that night of the bachelorette party. All because Kate had kissed him while drunk, firmly knocking her ass out of the just-friends box and into the maybe-we-should-fuck box.

Shit. Walking away from a woman was a new thing. Women didn't tell him no, and it wasn't very often he told himself no. He needed an outlet.

Maybe he could call someone... Maybe Rita, who worked down at the bank. They'd hooked up a few times in the past year. He visualized the skinny blonde, tried to get excited, but it wasn't happening. In fact everything inside him rebelled at using another woman when he really only wanted one.

"Fuck," he muttered. What the hell was wrong with him? Pussy was pussy. As long as it was warm and wet, who the hell cared, right?

Something deep tightened inside his chest. Guilt? Shame? And a memory that reminded him he hadn't always been like this. But he snuffed it out, shoving the image back into that corner of mind he didn't visit much. If ever.

His cell phone buzzed to life and he practically dove for it, hoping for some kind of lifeline for the rest of the evening. It came in the form of his brother Tyson.

And just like that the guilt disappeared and he remembered why he'd become the man he was.

"Hey, Ty," he muttered. "What are you up to?"

"Sitting around on my butt, waiting for Ellie to get home from her yoga classes."

"That's right, she opened the studio a few weeks ago. You check it out yet? Go to a class?"

Tyson laughed. "Hell, no. You really think I'm gonna do that body pretzel stuff?"

"No. Can't say that I can see you doing that." Todd's mouth curved into a slow grin and he finally started to relax. "Gun range, yes. Yoga, no way."

"Exactly. So I was calling to see if you wanted to grab a beer. We could meet at the Tavern."

Todd barely hesitated. It beat the hell of his back-up plan of going home to jack off. "Yeah, that sounds good. Meet you there in ten."

It only took him five minutes to get to the bar, and by the time Tyson walked in, Todd was already nursing a beer and shooting some pool.

"Hey there, little bro," Tyson greeted, pulling a pool stick down from the wall. "Did you buy me a pint?"

Todd jerked his head toward the high table next to them where a pint of Budweiser sat with the head still white and foamy.

"Hell, I was kidding, but thanks." Tyson paused beside the table to take a drink. "I've got to say, I'm surprised you're not out with some girl, seeing it's a Friday night and all."

Todd's fingers tightened around his beer and he didn't reply, just made a soft grunt in response.

"Kate wanted an early night?"

Jerking his head up, Todd met his brother's pensive gaze. Tyson had never been one to beat around the bush. Someone must've seen him and Kate out to dinner alone and commented to Tyson. Sure didn't take long for word to travel in a small town.

"It was just dinner," he replied curtly. Not that it was his brother's business at all.

"Yeah, that's what I heard. But it was just the two of you, which seemed kind of unusual."

Todd's chest expanded with the slow breath he drew in and a tic started in his jaw. But he just gave an easy smile and asked, "Something you're trying to imply, bro?"

"Not really. I just know how you are with women... But seeing as this is Kate, I know I don't really have any reason to be worried."

And there was the warning, not quite spoken, but definitely implied. Kate wasn't to be touched. At least not by him.

"Kate's a friend," Todd finally replied and moved to take another shot, sinking the eight ball into the corner pocket. He straightened and chalked his tip. "And that's all she'll ever be to me. So you can just cut with the silent implications, Ty."

Tyson grinned and slapped him on the back, before moving to set the rack for a new game. "Good to hear. I should've known better, I know she's not your type."

Yeah, that's what he'd been trying to tell his dick all night.

"Because Kate's not like other women," Tyson continued, removing the rack and picking his stick back up. "And I know she's got that little crush on you, but you'd have to be a total asshole to take advantage of it."

Crush? How the hell did Tyson know Kate had a crush on him?

Todd took another swig of beer and again didn't comment. If Kate had a crush on anything, it was his career. He'd seen it earlier tonight when they'd talked about his job, the way her eyes had lit up and she'd giggled like a schoolgirl. If he'd been the town dentist, Kate probably wouldn't even glance his way.

Letting his smile fade, Todd gave up the pretense of keeping this conversation light and turned a hard stare on his brother.

"I'll say it again. Kate is nothing more to me than a friend. Now drop it, Ty."

Tyson held his stare for a moment, his gaze searching, and then the critical gleam in his eyes faded into one of trust and acknowledgement. He gave a small nod and then murmured, "Consider it dropped."

Todd blew out a breath from between clenched teeth. Well, he'd managed to convince Tyson that Kate would only ever be a friend.

Now he just needed to convince Todd Jr. of the same thing.

Chapter Four

"I can't do this," Kate muttered, the blood rushing to her head as she struggled to maintain some pose that had the word dog in it.

How the hell had she let Ellie talk her into attending a Sunday afternoon yoga class? Oh yes, the promise of lunch out and a long talk afterward.

She was dying to confide in someone about what had happened last night with Todd, but with Megan now living a state away, that left her with Ellie as one of her closest friends. Which was funny, seeing as they'd only know each other for a few months.

Trying to toss her ponytail back from her face, Kate lifted her head and glared up at Ellie, who crooned out words of encouragement to a class that was surprisingly full. Who the heck would have thought this many women in Wyattsville were into yoga?

Sweat poured down her neck and the muscles in her legs started to scream in protest.

God! Exercise was the devil.

Kate glanced over at the clock on the wall and bit back a moan. Still another forty minutes. She'd never make it. She'd be found unconscious in a twisted, muscle-spasming mess.

But somehow she got through the rest of the hour. When Ellie dismissed the class, Kate collapsed on the floor to pass out, but still caught the glare of one woman leaving.

Penny from Penny's Pies. Kate's only competition in town for sweets. And, judging by Penny's glare, apparently the woman still wasn't pleased with Kate being the new shop in town.

When Ellie finished saying goodbye to the rest of the class, Kate was waiting for her on her mat on the floor. Lying on her back and staring at the ceiling, dreaming of a sexy masseuse and one of her big, fat salted-caramel cupcakes.

"Hey," Ellie said cheerfully, bounding over and sitting down next to her. "You did fabulous. Good job."

"I'm not sure you realize, but I think this type of thing is actually considered torture in some countries," Kate muttered and struggled into sitting position.

Ellie winked and stretched her legs out and grabbing her toes. "Trust me, you'll be begging to come back next week. It's addictive."

"Hmm." Kate watched as the last attendee in the room left the studio.

"Okay, spill it." Ellie lifted a perfectly shaped, dark eyebrow. "What's going on?"

Kate swallowed hard, her cheeks getting hot again—but not from exercise this time. "Todd kissed me last night."

Ellie blinked and her mouth fell open.

"And if you say a word to Tyson about this, I swear—"

"I won't say anything," Ellie promised breathily. "Todd really kissed you? *Todd Wyatt?*"

Kate nodded and looked down, her brows drawing together. Jeez, it sounded as surreal saying it aloud as it did in her head. "Yes."

"That's...wow. I don't know what to say. How did it happen? Were you guys drunk?"

"Um, no," Kate muttered and rolled her eyes. "And thanks for implying I'd have to get him drunk to want to suck face with me."

Ellie touched Kate's arm and winced. "No, no! Sorry, that came out wrong. It's just...wow. I can't...it just seems so left field."

Well, it was sort of. Kate sighed and attempted a stretch of her own. She'd never told anyone about how she'd kissed Todd during Ellie's bachelorette party. In fact, she'd kind of preferred to forget that had ever happened. Especially because he hadn't kissed her back, and had instead just pushed her gently away. Talk about humiliating.

That kiss was something she'd tried to block out. She'd just been staring at his lips, had wanted to stop his scolding about the stripper—which was such a double standard—and bam, had just leaned in and kissed him.

She blamed her lapse in sanity on alcohol.

"So, come on, you can't just leave me hanging here. What happened?" Ellie prodded.

"He invited me to dinner. Alone. And it was kind of all weird and tense. And when I went home, he kissed me." Kate looked down, deciding not to elaborate on what had happened beyond the kiss. "And then he got all weird about it and kind of rambled about how sorry he was and how he shouldn't have done it."

"Well no, he shouldn't have."

Kate glanced up in surprise at Ellie's terse reply.

"But I liked it," Kate protested. "A lot. And I'm not sorry it happened."

Ellie's expression softened and she sighed. "Oh, honey, I'm sure you did. The Wyatt men are very charming, and Todd especially so. He could probably entice a nun out of her habit in two minutes flat."

"Okay, I know you're trying to be encouraging with this conversation, but it's not helping so much," Kate said on a sigh, then wrinkled her nose. "You're making me feel a bit like a first-class idiot."

"I'm sorry and you're totally *not* an idiot." Ellie groaned and redid her dark ponytail. "It's just that, since that conversation at my bachelorette party, I know how inexperienced you are..."

A blush heated Kate's cheeks but she didn't back down. "And?"

"Well, answer me this. Have you ever fooled around with a guy at all, before Todd?"

"Yes. One."

"Okay and how did he make you feel?"

Kate's stomach roiled and her head spun a bit as the memory hit her. She glanced down at her hands and replied quietly, "It was exciting. It felt good."

"And with Todd?"

Heat slid through her blood as she compared what she'd experienced when she was a teenager, to what she'd experienced with Todd last night. "It was like a hundred times more intense. Todd's kiss left my knees shaking. It wasn't just a nice, exciting, touch. It was a forgetting-to-breathe touch."

She glanced up again and found Ellie watching her with resignation.

"Well, shit," Ellie finally muttered. "Definitely must run in the Wyatt family or something. Because Tyson makes me feel the same way."

Kate smiled, though Ellie's words actually made her a little sadder. At least Tyson reciprocated Ellie's feelings.

"So...what if I *wanted* to sleep with Todd? I mean, if I could convince him."

Ellie's gaze turned wary. "Kate, if you were anyone else, I might say go for it. But you're a virgin—"

"Jeez, I wished I'd kept my mouth shut that night."

"And I'm worried about you getting seriously heartbroken. Todd is pretty much a one-ride ticket."

A one-ride ticket. The phrase floated around in her head. "But what a ride it would be." She heard herself saying the words aloud and blushed again. Emboldened now, she pushed on. "Look, Ellie, I seriously, *seriously*, need to lose my virginity soon. It's way overdue. I saw the way you and Megan looked at me when I announced it."

"Okay, so we were shocked, Kate. But, being a virgin is not a bad thing."

"I know it's not, but it's just a word. A status that I want gone. So why not do it with someone I trust? Someone who gets my juices floating? Someone who's going to be pretty darn good at it?"

Ellie pressed her fingers to her temples and shook her head. "But don't you want your first time to be special? With someone you love and who loves you back?"

"Was your first time like that?"

Ellie was silent for a moment. "No. But I wish it had been."

Hmm. But what if you never met that person? Were you really supposed to spend the rest of your life abstinent? Sure, there was love. But there was also lust, and as she was quickly learning, the latter wasn't to be underestimated.

"Here's what I'm thinking," Kate said slowly. "A week ago I never would've guessed Todd could look at me the way he did last night. Look at me like I was a sexy woman he desired. He wanted me last night, as much as I've always wanted him. And I know he won't marry me, but...I think I want one night."

Ellie just stared at her, her expression a mixture of understanding and hesitancy.

"If you had only been offered one night with Tyson, would you have taken it?" Kate asked.

Ellie gave a reluctant nod. "In a heartbeat. In fact when I slept with him, I thought what we had could never last. I was on the run, lying about who I was. Logistically, it never *should've* worked out."

"But it did," Kate said softly. The story of Ellie and Tyson still made her heart flutter at the romance of it all. Ellie had found her own personal hero the last place she'd expected.

"It did," Ellie agreed with a slight smile. "But I was an exception to the rule. Not everyone gets a happily ever after."

"I don't expect one. Not with Todd, at least. So you can't tell me I'm being naïve about this." Kate paused. "Tell me this. If I *wasn't* a virgin, what would you tell me to do?"

Ellie sighed. "I'd tell you to go for it."

"I rest my case."

Ellie was silent for again and then arched a brow. "Okay. If you're *really* sure about this, then I can help. We can find a way to make Todd look beyond the friends thing. But you have to promise not to breathe a word to Tyson about my involvement. Because he'll rip me a new one if he finds out."

Ellie climbed to her feet and held out her hand, helping Kate up too.

"I promise," Kate said breathlessly, heart pounding with realization about what she'd just agreed to.

"Now, you know about Ryan Wyatt's New Year's Eve party coming up Saturday?"

"The costume party?" Kate said excitedly. "Totally! I'm going as a giant cupcake. I've got this sparkly pink hat and a—"

"You're not going."

Kate's stomach sank with disappointment. "Oh. I'm not?"

"Well, at least that's what we're going to tell Todd…"

Chapter Five

Saturday night had come entirely too fast.

Kate paced her room and glanced at the bed again. *That* was the costume that she was supposed to wear tonight? Seriously?

A wave of panic washed over her as she lifted up the Little Red Riding Hood costume that Ellie had helped her overnight order online after class the other day. It was only a few minutes ago that she'd finally had the nerve to take it out of the plastic bag.

This costume was nothing like the Little Red Riding Hood that she'd grown up with. This was like...

Oh, dear God, maybe she couldn't do this. Show up at a party wearing an outfit this sexy—half the town would see her tonight! And what if it just showed off all her imperfections and made her look huge? Though she'd ordered an X-large to give herself some wiggle room, especially knowing things tended to be ultra tight in the boob area. God certainly hadn't skimped on her breasts...not that she was complaining. Though she wouldn't have minded a little off the backside. And thighs. And maybe—

Stop thinking negatively. You're on a mission, she reminded herself. Ellie had promised that if she showed up wearing this outfit and acted the way she'd been coaxed, Todd would be hers before the clock struck midnight. Wrong fairytale, but Kate got the gist.

Tonight Todd would be her first, and hopefully without him realizing it. From all the research she'd done, Kate figured that at her age, any physical barriers inside her body would probably be long gone.

She bit her lip and ran her fingers over the stretchy costume. Someday, yes, she probably *would* end up with a guy like Walt. Someday. But tonight was about finally experiencing passion and pleasure. Tonight was all about losing it.

Virginity. The word that just about made her break out in hives. If it hadn't been for a one-minute phone call eight years ago, she probably would've done the deed during her junior prom.

A bitter smile twisted her lips and her stomach clenched. She closed her eyes, and for a moment the old doubt swept in. Todd was pretty much a sex god. Handsome, charming, amazing in bed—so rumor had it. How could he possibly be attracted to someone like *her?*

No. *No.* Kate ruthlessly shoved aside the doubt and the negative vibes she'd spent years beating down. Straightening her shoulders, she stared at herself in the mirror. She was an attractive woman. Maybe she wasn't a size six, but she'd seen the desire in Todd's eyes. He *wanted* her.

And it was time to finally take that step now that she'd found someone who she didn't *want* to say no to. Someone who tempted her back into sexual waters. It wasn't like she'd been holding out for religious reasons. There'd just never been anybody who'd tempted her out of the I-don't-need-a-man stage.

Which made her think about tonight and what she was about to do. She glanced at the clock and swallowed hard. Time to hop in the shower and get this evening going.

Ryan Wyatt's New Year's Eve party was legendary around the coastal towns of Oregon. Friends came, literally, from hundreds of miles away to partake in the festivities.

It was a night for all kinds of debauchery, masqueraded behind every kind of costume imaginable. And every year Todd looked forward to his cousin's party. He was in his element. Women. Partying. Inhibitions left at the door.

So why the hell was he dragging his feet about going this year?

You know why. Kate won't be there. Todd scowled.

Yesterday Ellie had complained his ear off that Kate was skipping out for a date with Walt—who had no interest in a costume party. Which meant she was missing Ryan's party for the first time since he could remember.

And he wasn't sure why that bugged him so much. Whether it was the fact that she was going to be out with Walt, or that she'd be missing the party. Or both.

But the party tonight wouldn't be the same without Kate. He'd gotten used to teasing her about her unusual costume choices. A milk carton. A nun. A gorilla suit. All stuff a little on the bizarre side, but they fit Kate's bubbly, quirky personality.

Todd slid a glance over his reflection in the mirror while fastening the leopard print loincloth around his briefs. Biting back a groan, he rotated his jaw and shook his head.

Damn. When he'd ordered the Tarzan costume online last month, he'd only been thinking about showing off some muscle and living up to the sexy alpha image he'd created for himself over the years. But looking in the mirror now, he thought he looked...a little ridiculous.

Ridiculous or not, he was going to be more than fashionably late if he didn't get his ass in his truck to make the near half-hour drive to Ryan's house.

He slid into his shoes, grabbed his keys and headed out.

By the time he pulled onto Ryan's street there wasn't much parking left. He settled for a spot a half-block down the road and made the trek up to his cousin's house, hoping like hell no one drove by and saw him half-naked.

Jeez, what the hell had he been thinking? It was freezing out here. His dick was shriveling with every passing second.

The front door swung open before Todd could even knock.

"Get your ass inside, cuz. You're late." Ryan grinned, decked out in a cowboy costume, as he handed him a beer, and slapped him on the back. "And you'll never guess who's here."

Todd's grip tightened on the bottle as he stepped into the house, glancing around, hoping he'd see Kate. But he didn't see anything but lots of creative, sexy, crazy costumes and people dancing and drinking.

And then Trevor and Megan stepped in front of him.

"Trev!" He grinned and pulled his brother in for a quick hug, slapping him on the back. "How the hell are you? Did you drive all the way down here tonight?"

"Yeah, Megan wanted to come. Misses her girls." He grinned at his new wife. "Hell, I miss you guys too. Plus I'm getting deployed again in a few months. Thought I should squeeze in as much family time as possible."

"Damn, bro, you ever stay home?"

"Take it up with Uncle Sam," Megan teased and squeezed her husband's arm. "Though, really, I'm so proud of you and everything you do, baby. You *are* an American hero."

Trevor glanced down and they shared an intimate exchange that Todd was almost uncomfortable watching. Clearing his throat he drawled, "So, what? You guys didn't have time to change into a costume? Come straight from work?"

"What are you talking about?" Megan arched a red brow and gestured to Trevor's uniform. "He came as an Army captain, and I'm an uptight lawyer slash trophy wife."

Todd laughed and shook his head. "You guys are too damn perfect for each other. I'm going to go do a round. I'm glad as hell you both drove down tonight."

He turned away, mixing into the crowd and greeting familiar faces. Women approached and he'd talk to them for a minute before looking for an excuse to slip away again.

A commotion started near the doorway. Some hooting and hollering from the men, as the female whispers started rampant.

Todd glanced toward the foyer, mildly curious at who the newcomer was to be causing such a commotion. When the crowd parted, the first thing he saw was a blur of red. Then milky white tits nearly popping out of the white blouse of the chick's costume.

Todd's dick stirred, waking up for the first time in days. *Finally.* He latched onto the realization. Almost desperate to prove to himself he could still want another woman besides Kate.

He lifted his beer and took a long drink, never taking his eyes off of the woman who seemed to be drawing the men in like a magnet.

It looked like Little Red Riding Hood was searching for trouble, and damned if he wasn't about to become the wolf to give it to her. This was exactly what he needed after a week of no sex. Of falling asleep with his dick in his hand and an image of Kate in his head.

Hell yeah. He was back in the game. A combination of arousal and relief surged through him. He shifted into auto mode, straightening to his full height and drawing in a deep breath that had his chest expanding. He slipped a languid smile on his face that generally made the female population melt and made his approach.

Red had her back to him when he finally sidled up next to her. Which gave him a moment to take in the lush curve of her hips and bottom.

He started at her stiletto-covered feet, lingering on shapely legs wrapped in black fishnet stockings. *Damn, those were going to feel nice wrapped around his waist.*

Then there was the red flared skirt, barely covering her ass. Above that, a waist that looked almost tiny compared the rest of her curves was cinched with a thick black belt that laced up the middle with white strings.

Her breasts were fucking amazing, nearly spilling over the gauzy white low-cut top. Creamy and smooth, one little tug on the fabric would have her popping free.

A red cape covered her hair and shoulders, and though she was turned to the side, he could see one long blonde curl curving over her collarbone.

All he needed was a dark corner, a few minutes, and soon she'd be Little Red Getting Ridden Hood.

Drawing in a slow breath, he took another step, until he was right behind her. He slid a hand over a lush, round hip and lowered his mouth to just above her ear.

"Hey, Red," he murmured quietly enough for only her to hear. "You come here tonight to play with the big bad wolf? Because I might be able to accommodate."

The woman froze, tension radiating through her body in waves, and he swore she stopped breathing. And then in an instant it was gone. The tension, the silence, as she gave a husky laugh and leaned back into him.

"That's some mouth you have on you," she said throatily.

"The better to eat you with." He smiled against her ear and slid his hand over her hips to cover her soft stomach. His dick hardened further as she pressed back against him.

A tremble rocked through her body, before she turned to look him over. "Funny, but for a self-proclaimed wolf, you look like you belong in the jungle, not the forest."

"*Jesus Christ.*"

Chapter Six

Todd jerked his hand away from her, stumbling backward as a roaring sounded in his ears. Kate. Fuck, it was *Kate*.

"What's wrong?" she teased, red, painted mouth curving into a wide smile. "You look like you've seen a ghost."

"What the hell is going on?" he muttered. "Ka—"

"Actually you had it right the first time. Just call me Red." She ran her tongue over her bottom lip.

For a moment, he might've convinced himself it wasn't Kate. That it was just someone who looked a helluva lot like her. But then he saw the quick flash of nerves in her eyes, before she was again poised and confident.

Oh, it was Kate all right. But just what in the hell was she trying to pull off?

He bit back a growl and glanced around the room, curious to see if they had an audience. Sure enough, Ellie stood in the corner, watching them intently. But she spun away the moment she noticed him watching her, looking a little too innocent as she took a swig of her beer.

She was in on it. Whatever *it* was. But whatever game they were playing, he wanted no part of it.

Or maybe he did, which was going to be a big fucking problem.

"Outside," he rasped, grabbing Kate's elbow. "Now."

She struggled to keep up with him in her heels, but murmured a coy, "You sure don't waste any time, do you, jungle man?"

Todd cursed under his breath as he maneuvered them through the throng of people and outside the front door. He kept them moving until they were buried in the shadows of the front yard and then came to a halt.

Kate stumbled into him. It was cold as hell this time of year, but he didn't feel it. Not with Kate's lush, inferno of a body smashed against his bare chest.

"What the hell are you up to, Kate," he demanded harshly, meaning to push her aside. But the moment his hands closed around her bare shoulders beneath the red cape, his fingers curled around the satiny flesh instead.

"Call me Red," she said firmly.

"Why the hell do you want me to call you Red?" he muttered, his ability to think draining by the second as she rubbed herself against him.

Like a fucking cat in heat. Jesus, he needed to get out of here. And quick.

"Because you don't look at Kate this way," she said breathlessly. "And because you'll feel a lot less guilty if you're fucking Red tonight, won't you?"

Lust detonated inside him. Todd's cock pressed hard beneath his black briefs, raising the leopard-print loincloth that barely covered him. He slid his fingers over her collarbone and watched the way her breasts rose against the thin white shirt.

"You're in way over your head," he warned darkly, knowing he should leave, but completely ensnarled in her kinky little game.

This wasn't the Kate he knew, this was some sex kitten who'd possessed the sweet little bakery owner. The Kate he knew would've shown up in a clown costume or something equally nonsexual. Not this slutty little outfit that had him imagining the dirtiest, most vulgar thoughts of what he wanted to do to her. What he *would* do to her if she didn't come to her senses and run.

"Walk away, little Red," he muttered. "Now."

"The only place I'm walking is to your truck, jungle man," she whispered and slid her hands over his chest, her nails dragging against his muscles. "All you have to do is say the word."

His pecs tightened in response and he choked on a groan. In one smooth move he spun her around, looped his arm around her waist and jerked her hard against him. He tugged her hood down, burying his face against her blonde hair and grinding his rock-hard cock against her ass.

"If we do this, there's no going back."

Kate's head fell back against his shoulder and she let out a purr of pleasure. "That's okay...I'm only thinking about going forward right now. Hmm. And maybe down."

"Is that right?" He gave up trying to do the right thing and slid his hand up to cover her breast through the thin top, her gasp of pleasure spurring him on.

He kneaded the softness, before tugging the white fabric down and baring her breast to the night air. *Jesus.* She wasn't wearing a bra.

She whimpered when he caught one tight nipple between his fingers and pulled on it.

"What is it?" he demanded, nuzzling her ear, angry with her and angry with himself for not being able to walk away. "Is it the fireman thing? Does that turn you on? Or do you just want to join the list of women who can claim they've fucked me? See what all the fuss is about?"

She stiffened against him, her fingers closing over his hand that cupped her breast. He thought he'd finally done it, shocked her back into her senses with his crude words. But then she dragged his hand away from her breast, down her stomach and beneath her tiny skirt.

"Does it matter why?" she whispered, pressing his hand between her legs. "I just want you, Todd."

An odd combination of frustration and triumph surged through him. Beneath the thin fishnets and satiny panties, he could feel just how hot she was. Damp. Getting to her pussy was like an obstacle course, but he maneuvered a finger through the barriers until he found the humid flesh of her sex.

He sank a finger shallowly into her channel and groaned at how wet she was. How tightly her flesh gripped him.

Kate was a damn fool to initiate such a high-stakes game with him. He wasn't the good guy she thought him to be, and he'd prove it by not walking away tonight like he should—like she probably expected him to. Instead sweet and bubbly Kate— or *Red*—was going to get fucked until her eyes crossed.

"Last chance to come to your senses, Red," he said, nibbling the soft shell of her ear, while sliding his finger up to rub her hard little clit. "You can walk away now, or you can climb into my truck and know exactly what you're getting into."

She didn't even hesitate, just clenched her thighs around his hand and gasped, "Your truck."

Todd closed his eyes and let the air seethe out from between his teeth. He was officially toast.

He pulled her blouse back up over her breasts, while stroking her clit once more. Finally, he slid his finger out of her sweet pussy and let her skirt fall back into place, but not before he gave her soft round ass a quick squeeze.

"Then go and wait for me," he said gruffly. "I need to run back inside and grab my keys."

She gave a shaky nod and didn't look at him, just stumbled off in those amazing come-fuck-me heels and then climbed into his truck.

Todd finally jerked his gaze away and headed toward the house, his jaw flexing. Everyone inside would know what was about to happen if they'd seen him and Kate go outside. But fuck it, he didn't care right now. Couldn't begin to care. All that mattered was Kate.

He'd just grabbed his keys, thinking he might be getting off easy, when Ellie intercepted him at the door.

"You take her back to your place," she warned, eyes blazing with warning. "And you remember who you're with tonight. She's not like one of your normal girls, Todd."

"Ellie—"

"And don't worry, Tyson will never know we had this conversation."

Todd bit back the urge to snarl a curse at the confirmation that Ellie had been involved with this little seduction plan of Kate's.

"I'll take her home," he replied darkly and shook his head. "Just remember you helped set this in motion."

He saw the wariness in her eyes, maybe regret, before he turned and walked away. He left Ryan's house, relieved that neither of his brothers had spotted him.

Ellie's reminder might've been grating, but it was needed. He'd been damn close to driving a few miles down the road and fucking Kate in the back of his truck.

But he needed to slow things down, because she was Kate, and no matter how much of a fantasy she was trying to present tonight, he damn well needed to remember exactly whom he was going to wake up next to.

Which led to one big glaring question that he wasn't about to analyze.

Just how much he was going to regret this in the morning?

Chapter Seven

Oh God, it had actually worked.

Kate's heart raced a mile a minute as she sat in the darkened truck. Her body tingled with arousal and need, even as her nerves got so bad she thought she might get sick.

She'd done exactly as Ellie instructed. *Be flirty. Be confident. Channel your inner Marilyn. Stay in character so he doesn't think of you as Kate, and he won't be able to say no.*

And somehow, she'd pulled it off. Getting into the character of a sex bomb had been surprisingly easy. Maybe it was the costume, or maybe it was the power she'd realized she had. Not over just Todd, but over many of the men in Ryan's house.

She'd walked in and men had paid attention. It had been exhilarating, shocking. When an arm had slipped around her from behind and a naughty suggestion whispered in her ear, she'd known immediately who the Casanova was. And it had left her breathless.

Any minute Todd would arrive back in the truck and...what? Would he drive off to some dark, deserted road and take her? Sex in a truck couldn't be that bad. And obviously she wouldn't be the first girl to "lose it" in a vehicle. Teenagers probably did it every day. Heck, at this rate, *waiting* much longer sounded like the real pain.

Her body was on fire, ready for Todd's touch again. She closed her eyes. Oh God, when he'd slipped a finger inside her... A tremble rocked her body and she sighed.

Opening her eyes again, she saw Todd step out of the house and jog toward the car. The porch light briefly illuminated his body and everything inside her melted a bit.

He should've looked ridiculous in his barely there Tarzan costume, but it just highlighted every glorious part of him. His broad shoulders, defined chest and abdomen, tapered hips and muscled legs.

The driver's side door swung open and Todd slid inside. She took in his profile, his dark hair and chiseled face. The trademark lazy smile on his mouth was uncommonly absent, replaced by lips that were pressed into a tight line. And his brows were drawn together in a way that indicated he was thinking hard. Maybe too hard. Then the door closed and they were cocooned in the dark again.

Unease had her gut clenching and she bit her lower lip nervously. Oh, God, was he going to back out?

Channel your Marilyn. Channel your Marilyn, damn it!

She slid a hand over to his lap, dangerously close to the erection he couldn't hide beneath his costume. Her fingers shook, but she hoped he didn't notice.

"I missed you, jungle man," she said huskily.

He didn't reply or make any kind of move to start the truck. Her throat tightened and her heart slammed around in her chest. Doubt rocked through her and she started to pull her hand away.

Todd grabbed her wrist, stopping her retreat. He tugged her toward him and lifted her arm toward his mouth, then his lips brushed against the pulse on the inside of her wrist, sending another tremble rocking through her body.

"You can still change your mind," he offered.

"No. I really can't, Todd." Her voice wobbled, sounding a lot less Marilyn and whole lot more Kate.

He sat there for a moment longer and then made a small groan. A moment later he started the truck and put it in drive.

Kate gasped, fumbling for her seatbelt as he pulled away from the curb and sped down the street at breakneck speeds.

Where were they going? He never slowed down, just drove them straight back toward Wyattsville. Though she was beginning to get an idea of his intentions.

Her suspicion of their final destination was confirmed when Todd pulled up in front of his house fifteen minutes later. He climbed out of the truck and had her door open before she could think to move.

Instead of grabbing her hand to help her down, he slid an arm around her waist and pulled her from the seat. Her body slid, all delicious friction, against his before her heeled feet hit the paved driveway.

She teetered to catch her balance, but his arm still held her, kept her from falling. And then his mouth crashed down on hers and her balance went wonky for other reasons.

Kate clutched his shoulders and moaned, parting her lips to his fierce kiss. The smell of his familiar, spicy cologne filled her senses. His tongue explored every inch of her mouth, his hands roving over her body. It was deliberate. A man staking his claim. Every female instinct inside of her could sense it.

Heat and sensation sizzled through her as the ache between her legs grew more intense. Her head spun and she could barely think. She needed so much more. More than hands touching her through clothes. She wanted all of him. Touching her, sucking on her, inside of her... *Oh dear god.*

She jerked her mouth from his with a gasp. "*Please,* Todd."

He gave a low growl and hurried them inside the house. He pushed the door closed and turned to face her, the expression on his face almost predatory.

Kate caught her breath as he plucked the red bow tied around her neck that held her cape on. The red fabric slid free a moment later and pooled onto the floor.

"Red," he said thickly. "You have been a naughty girl tonight, haven't you?"

It didn't really bother her that he kept up the fantasy she'd created. Maybe he needed it to not be reminded of the fact of the huge step they were taking and how it hopefully wouldn't screw up their friendship. *It was just one night,* she reminded herself.

But staying in character put her a little more at ease too, made her almost convince herself that she was experienced at this sex thing.

She smiled, her dimples popping out, as she fingered the neckline of her blouse. "I guess I have. And what are you going to do about it?"

The smile that she loved slid over Todd's face. Sexy. Suggestive. All kinds of wicked.

"I'm going to make you come until you can't tell from up and down."

"Funny," she whispered. "But I think I'm already getting there."

His smile remained, even as the glint in his gaze brightened with desire. Slowly, he reached out and unlaced the white string of the black corset that wrapped around her waist. Once it was undone, he put it aside, and then methodically stripped her out of the rest of her costume.

Soon she stood in front of him in nothing but white lace panties and red stilettos. Her nipples tightened in the chilly air and she tried desperately not to feel so exposed. So vulnerable. No man had seen her like this. Ever.

Her heart thumped so hard in her chest, she thought Todd might even be able to hear it.

"Look at you," he muttered, his expression a combination of amazement and lust. "Jesus, how come it took me so long to see just what a little sex pot you are, doll?"

Kate swallowed hard, his words sending a thrill through her. She closed the distance between them and wrapped her arms around his neck, then pressed her mouth against his. Just as she had that night at the bar. Only this time he didn't shove her away. His arms slid around her waist, jerking her flush against him while his tongue swept deep into her mouth.

Her head spun and she was vaguely aware of him walking her backward. And then the cool wall of the door hit her back. Todd's hands were everywhere on her. Cupping her breasts and teasing her nipples.

He tore his mouth from hers and groaned, staring down at her.

"You've got the most amazing breasts," he muttered, lifting one his palm. It didn't quite fit, spilled over his hands, but he didn't seem to mind.

Her cheeks flushed with awareness and her lips parted in a soft gasp as his head dipped. Then his mouth closed around one aching nipple and she whimpered.

She delved her fingers into his hair, clutching the soft strands and arching into his mouth. Oh God. Pleasure rocketed through her as he suckled her with varying levels of intensity. Soft, then hard.

He slid a large, calloused hand down her hip and maneuvered it beneath her panties. When his fingers grazed her cleft, her knees threatened to give out.

"Easy, Kate," he murmured against her breast, while sinking a finger inside her. "Just enjoy and let me take care of you."

Her body clenched around him and she drew in a sharp breath, holding it. Unable to breathe at the exquisiteness of what he was doing. So intense and lots of pressure.

Todd gently bit her nipple and pushed his finger deeper. "Fuck, you are so tight here. You're going to feel real nice around my cock, doll."

The image his words created had a soft moan spilling from her lips.

"But before I fuck you, I want to make sure you're nice and ready." Todd tugged on her nipple with his teeth, before releasing her.

He fell to his knees and she blinked in dismay, her cheeks going red with what he was about to do. Even still, when he tugged her panties over her hips her face burned with awareness and anticipation.

"Spread your legs," he ordered softly, pushing her ankles apart.

She obeyed, then felt the air caress her exposed folds. Or maybe that was due to him parting her with his fingers. She glanced down at him just as his head lowered and the first wet lick of his tongue slid into her.

Her hips jerked and she cried out, reaching down, almost to push him away. But he had none of it, holding her still as he laughed softly and licked her again, murmuring soft, sexy words.

Oh god, it was almost too much. She couldn't handle it. She'd be a sobbing mess in minutes.

But Todd didn't give her any room to protest. He moved his thumb up inside her, found her clit a moment later and begun to rub slowly.

The room around her seemed to spin as pleasure built inside her. It was so foreign, so exquisite to be reaching a peak by a man's touch and not her own hand.

"Todd," she whispered, digging her nails into his shoulders. Holding him now instead of trying to push him away. "Oh please."

He replaced his thumb with his tongue, and flicked against her sensitive bud of flesh.

Kate's breasts rose and fell with each ragged breath she

drew in. With her eyes closed she could only focus on his mouth on her, the wickedly wonderful things his tongue was doing between her legs, and the steady intensity of pleasure that continued to climb.

Her nipples tightened and she could feel the slick juices of her arousal sliding down her thighs.

Todd lifted his mouth from her long enough to croon, "Just let yourself go, Kate. I want you to come in my mouth. I want to taste you."

His words combined with the way he immediately started to suck her clit, pushed her up and over that peak. Kate couldn't stop the scream that ripped from her throat as her body quaked through the orgasm.

Tears burned the back of her eyes and the intensity of the moment took away any ability to speak. When she finally lifted her lids and glanced down, Todd was still nuzzling her pussy, licking her thighs.

He glanced up and the heat in his eyes sent a tremble rocking through her again.

"I knew you'd taste this good," he muttered thickly and came to his feet. His lips crashed down on hers, teeth and lips bumping, before his tongue slid against hers and she tasted herself in the fierce kiss.

When he lifted his head a minute later, she was wet again, her body aching for more. For him. All of him.

"You're amazing." He kissed her brow. "Go meet me in my room. Lie down on the bed and I'll join you in a moment."

Kate nodded, her head bouncing around almost bobblehead-like. She must look like an idiot, but it wasn't enough to take her out of her passion—out of this moment.

She stepped away from the doorway and made her way to his room. She'd been to his place often enough to know where it was, but never had she ever deluded herself into thinking she'd end up in Todd's bed.

When she entered the room, she stared at the large bed covered in a black comforter. The whole room was so potently male. She ran a hand through her tussled hair, before taking the final few steps to the mattress.

She lay down, closed her eyes and waited, knowing everything was going to change.

Chapter Eight

When the hell had he ever wanted a woman so badly? Todd gripped the foil packet in his hand and entered his bedroom.

His gaze immediately sought out Kate, lying supine on his bed. Her lush curves were pale against the black comforter. Large breasts, crowned by the palest pink nipples, fell slightly to her sides. Her stomach wasn't flat, but instead gently rounded like the rest of her. With her knees bent into the air and her red heels digging into the mattress, she looked like sin come to life.

And fucking Kate tonight would be worth purgatory. He climbed onto the bed and stroked a possessive hand down her body, loving the way her thick lashes fluttered down over her heated gaze. The way she drew her bottom lip between her teeth and nibbled.

"You have got to be the sexiest woman I've ever seen," he murmured, surprised at his own words. Even more so that he meant them.

He knew it probably sounded like a line, especially when her lips curled up almost with derisiveness. She didn't believe him. Well, he'd just have to show her.

Drawing in a slow breath, he tugged off his costume and then the briefs underneath. Her eyes opened again and she took him in, lingering on his cock. For a moment, he thought he saw a flicker of fear in her gaze, but then it was gone and the heat returned. It wasn't an altogether strange reaction, since he fell on the larger, thicker side in the package department.

Todd smiled slightly and drew his hand down her body, from neck to feet, teasing and kneading the curves and hollows in between. By the time he ripped open the foil packet and put on the condom, she was trembling and her pussy shimmered slick with her arousal.

Just looking at her made him remember how she'd tasted. The soft, sensual sounds she'd made when he'd been licking her clit.

He moved over her, covering Kate's body with his own and settled between her splayed thighs. Lowering his mouth to hers, he initiated a slow, deep kiss, while using one hand to guide his cock to her entrance.

She was slick and soaked, and he slid easily past her folds and just inside her channel. But then, damn, was she tight. He reached up to rub her clit to help her relax, to take him.

He caught her low moan with his mouth, as she rotated against his hand and arching off the bed. The tension in her muscles eased, allowing him to slide slowly into her. He groaned as her hot pussy gripped him, seemed to suck him deeper.

And yet, she was so damn tight. Almost too tight. The thought flickered through his head but was gone a moment later as she undulated beneath him, rubbing her tongue against his.

He needed to be buried in her now. *Now.* Todd gripped her hips and with a low groan, thrust deep.

Kate gasped sharply and he lifted his mouth from hers with surprise, staring down at her. Jesus, had he hurt her?

He stilled, hating himself for going too fast. What if she hadn't done this in awhile? With the size he was, he should've slowed the hell down.

She stared up at him, some of the passion gone from her face and a hint of discomfort glinted in her eyes.

"Kate?" he prodded, her name almost a rasp on his lips.

"I'm fine," she whispered, stroking her hands over his shoulders and kissing his neck. "Please, don't stop, Todd."

He hesitated, knowing he should try and help her adjust, maybe stop completely, but the feel of her slick flesh gripping him nearly robbed him of all ability to think.

"Please." She lifted her hips, forcing him deeper and drawing in a shuddering breath, even as pleasure flickered on her face now. "I want you, Todd. *Please.*"

"Jesus, Kate," he whispered, not even trying to call her Red anymore. This was Kate beneath him, and at this moment it seemed nothing *but* right that she was in his bed. "You feel amazing, but I don't want to hurt you."

"You won't," she promised and gave him a slow smile, the sultriness returning.

Need rushed through him, making his blood pound with the need to claim her completely. He rubbed her clit again, slowly and deliberately, until the walls of her pussy softened and accommodated him.

He waited until her lashes fluttered shut and she moaned. Waited for the telltale sign of her creaming around his dick again. With her channel slicker now, he started to move in a slow rhythm in and out of her.

Fuck, she felt so damn good.

And then instinct took over as her hot, tight sheath gripped him like a fist. He moved faster inside her and she struggled to keep up with his pace, making soft moans of pleasure as her nails dug crescents into his back.

He stared down at her, watched her bite her lip and the ecstasy on her face. Watched the way her breasts bounced with each thrust into her.

The way she moved and the wondrous expression on her face had a certain innocence that made the hairs on the back of his neck lift. A moment's unease hit him, but then was gone when she grabbed the back of his head and jerked his mouth down to hers again.

Their lips brushed together, parted, and hot breaths mingled. She tasted of passion and sex, her tongue curling around his and sucking fervently as her hips moved against him.

Todd drove into her harder, feeling no resistance now, only the welcoming suck of her pussy around him. The sounds of their joining filled the air. The wetness, the slapping, and it was so damn hot he wasn't going to last much longer. His balls tightened and he groaned.

To slow himself down, if just for a moment, he lifted his mouth from hers and then sought her breast. Licking one pink nipple and murmuring in approval when it tightened beneath his tongue. Her cries grew urgent, higher; she was close to coming too. But she'd need that little push over the edge and so once more he sought her clit.

He'd barely touched the swollen nub when she screamed and climaxed, her pussy squeezing his cock so hard he rolled right over the edge with her.

Shelli Stevens

Slowly his consciousness returned and as his senses grew sharper, he became aware of the lushness of her curves pinned beneath him. The softness of her thighs that cradled him between.

He lowered his head to her breasts and nuzzled his lips against their fullness. Kate's hands stroked through his hair, almost lovingly, as small tremors continued to rock her body. She sighed and her lips brushed his forehead.

His brain chose that moment to switch back on, bringing reality into sharp focus. He closed his eyes and drew in a slow and unsteady breath.

He'd just had sex with Kate. And there was no way to undo the fact. Not that he'd want to. His softening cock once again stirred inside her. Shit, that never happened. What the hell...

No more tonight. Guilt clenched his gut as he reminded himself that he'd already probably used her a little too hard already.

Todd eased off her and onto his side, propping his head up on his hand as he stared down at her. Her eyes were closed, but he could tell she wasn't asleep by the stillness in her body. She was too still. Her breaths shallow.

Reaching out, he traced a finger down her cheek and over her mouth that curled into a small smile.

"You okay?" he asked gently.

Her lashes fluttered open and for a moment uncertainty was in her eyes, but then her blue gaze turned intimate, retelling the story of what had just happened between them.

"I'm wonderful." She flicked her tongue out and licked his finger. "That was...incredible. Thank you."

She was thanking *him*? For sex? Another stab of guilt to his gut. Jesus, it wasn't like he'd done her a favor. If anything, he was blown away by her decision to seduce him.

"Come here," he murmured quietly and slid his arm around her, tugging her against him.

Surprise flickered in her eyes, before she laid her head against his shoulder and slid her arm over his waist. He smoothed a hand through her silky hair and brushed a kiss on the top of her head.

An unexpected surge of tenderness raced through him and he closed his eyes with a frown.

262

This was going to get complicated, if it already wasn't. Sex had always been sex with him. So why did he get the feeling nothing would ever be that simple where Kate was involved?

Kate woke the next morning still in the curve of his arms. The smattering of chest hair against her cheek was the physical reminder of what had happened between them.

A flush stole up her body and she squeezed her thighs together, testing how sore she was. She winced slightly. Apparently a little more than she would have expected. But then, everything about last night had been unexpected. She hadn't thought Todd would be so, well, *well endowed*. It hadn't been easy trying to keep her reaction hidden when he'd entered her.

It hadn't been outright painful, but it had hurt a little. But he'd seemed to know exactly what to do, and each time he'd reach down and rub between her legs...oh God. She closed her eyes, feeling herself get wet again just thinking about it.

"You wake up early, doll."

His sleepy drawl had her tensing in his arms. She hadn't realized he was awake. Lifting her head, Kate glanced down at him and found him watching her.

"Is it early?" she asked huskily. "I have no idea."

"Mmm. Probably only seven. Good thing you don't have to work. Happy New Year, by the way. Guess we kind of forgot about that part last night."

Kate gave a nervous laugh. Yes, she'd completely forgotten about ringing in the New Year. Her mind had been a little one track, though.

"Happy New Year," she murmured.

Todd laughed as his arms tightened around her and then in one quick move he flipped her onto her back and hovered above her. Kate's breath locked in her throat and her pulse quickened and the smoldering look of intent in Todd's eyes.

"Well, since you're up...and I'm up. Literally..."

She opened her mouth to protest, wasn't sure she could go another round so soon, but then his head lowered to her breast and his wicked lips closed over one nipple. Heat slid in an arrow from her breast to down between her legs and she could feel her flesh softening, dampening again.

A low groan gathered in her throat as he suckled one breast and massaged the other. And even though having sex one time hardly qualified her as experienced, she knew in that instinctive woman's way, that she would be able to take him again.

Giving up any thought of protest, she closed her eyes as he slid down her body and once again moved his face between her legs. When his tongue flicked out, thought became a novelty.

Later, after he'd made love to her slowly and thoroughly, Kate woke up again from a light slumber. A glance at Todd's alarm clock showed it to be after noon.

She glanced down at him and found him still sleeping, his expression soft and almost vulnerable in sleep. Her heart did a little tug and the urge to curl up next to him hit hard.

But with the light of day also came the harshness of reality. She'd done it. She'd gone into this seduction knowing the stakes and that Todd was not the type to do serious. She'd *known* this could be nothing more than a one-night stand or she'd risk falling in love and getting her heart broken.

God, she was naïve. Kate swallowed hard, tears prickling at the back of her eyes as she stared down at him. Sleeping with Todd Wyatt might have rid her of her virginity in a very delicious way, but unfortunately it has also made her crush on him jump from harmless to lethal.

Biting her bottom lip, she climbed out of bed, grabbed her heels off the floor, and then tiptoed into the living room to collect her clothes. Relief swept through her that Todd hadn't woken as she finished dressing.

She'd just slipped into her heels and was contemplating how much walking back to her house in them was going to suck, when Todd's phone rang.

Shit. Kate's gaze darted to the door and she thought about just running outside and fleeing.

But then she heard the thump of Todd sliding out of bed, and then a groggy, "Kate?"

Folding her arms over her chest, she stood up straight and met his gaze when he came into the living room. He was unabashedly naked as the day he was born, holding his ringing phone.

"Where are you going?"

"Don't you think you should get that?" she asked instead.

"No, it's just...it's no one."

No one being another woman. Her stomach sank at the reminder of who Todd was and what kind of lifestyle he led.

"I...should go," she said quietly.

Todd's brows drew together and he tilted his head. "You're leaving? But it's your day off."

She cleared her throat, her palms dampening. "I know. I just, I have a lot of things to attend to, Todd..."

"Hmm. The kind of things that could wait?" He took a step closer to her, his mouth curving into a seductive smile. "Seeing as we're both off work and it's rainy and cold, it just seems conducive to spend a day inside...maybe in bed. Don't you think?"

As he grew closer, her knees started to weaken along with her resistance.

"I don't know, maybe we should just call it what it was. One night of fun."

She hated that her voice shook. It obliterated any attempt at sounding casual, and her fears were confirmed when Todd caught her wrist, halting her before she could leave the house.

Kate bit her lip as he turned her around, tried to keep her expression nonchalant.

"You're saying that when you seduced me, you only wanted one night?" he repeated carefully. "That's really what you wanted?"

"Well what do *you* want, Todd?" she asked cautiously. "Something more serious? You can't be thinking of a relationship..."

He seemed to blanch and dropped her wrist, retreating quickly. His reaction, whether conscious or subconscious, cut to the quick. Again she'd been caught with her naïve hat on. No, Todd certainly didn't do relationships, and she should probably thank him for the reminder.

Her heart tripped and she swallowed hard, deciding she needed to make a clean break for both of their sakes. End things before they got complicated.

"Let me just be honest, Todd," she forced herself to say.

"Honest about?"

"You were right. I did sleep with you because of the fireman thing. I'd never been with one before."

Todd stilled, then said harshly, "That's complete crap, Kate."

She bit her lip. *Fake it better.* "I'm sorry. It's just...before I settle down with someone and start a family, I figured it was a good opportunity to check that *sleep with a firefighter* fantasy off my list."

He didn't say anything and when she glanced up she could see the doubt and yet potential for belief in his eyes.

"Someone as in Walt?"

She didn't deny it or confirm. Couldn't bring herself to do either. But it certainly helped her case that way.

He gave a slight nod. "I see."

"Maybe I shouldn't have picked you. I'd considered Jeremiah," she whispered a bit numbly. "But with your reputation I honestly thought a one-night thing wouldn't be a problem."

Todd's jaw flexed and he turned away from her with a callous laugh. "Right. No problem at all."

"Anyway...I'll just head out."

"Wait, let me drive you home, Kate," he said tersely.

Though a twenty-minute walk in her heels would kill, sitting beside him for the five-minute drive would hurt even more.

"I'm fine. Thanks." This time when she opened the door, he didn't stop her.

Kate should've been relieved that he'd bought the bedding-a-fireman excuse. Instead she bit her lip to stop from crying. She'd gone into last night with him a virgin, and now Todd probably just thought she was a skanky groupie.

Lovely. What a way to kick off the New Year.

Chapter Nine

Tuesday morning Kate walked into her shop, wishing the emotional hangover from hell would go away. She'd gone home Sunday and called Ellie as she'd promised to do, but tried not to tip her off to the fact that her friend's concerns had been valid. That her heart did get a heck of a lot more involved once she'd had sex. Why concern Ellie with the minor details? So instead she'd kept it to the light stuff. Great sex, no regrets. That much was true...no matter how much it might hurt now.

Because just as she'd predicted, Todd hadn't bothered to call her or drop by in the two days since. He'd moved on from her like he did every other woman he took to bed. She'd expected it. Hoped to prepare for it.

She glanced around her shop and sighed deeply. Her nose wrinkled a moment later as she noticed the strange smell.

What the hell *was* that? Her eyes widened and she pinched her nose between fingers as she moved around trying to locate the source of the odor.

Had she forgotten to take out the garbage...from like a year ago? Whatever it was was not normal.

The smell grew stronger as she approached the heating vent. Her brows drew together and she paused. Yes, whatever was going on was happening in there.

She analyzed the metal grate that covered the vent, tried to figure out how the hell to remove it. Damn, if she tried, she'd probably end up breaking something or gauge a hole in the wall.

She bit her lip and folded her arms across her chest. *Shoot.* Even though the last thing she wanted to do was call for help, this could be a lot more serious than it seemed. Bottom line, she just didn't *know.*

With a sigh, she went back to her office and picked up the

phone.

It had been a quiet night at the fire station, with just a couple of calls coming in. First one, a senior citizen with difficulty breathing. Second, a minor car accident where a teenager had rounded Cougar's Corner too fast in the later hours of the night.

Todd glanced at the clock, confirming there was just an hour or so left of his shift, and then headed into the small gym in the firehouse to squeeze in a bit of exercise. He'd been in a shitty mood since Kate had dropped the it-was-just-a-one-night-stand bombshell, his mood had gone to shit and fast.

Grabbing the handle of a kettle bell, he swung his arm that held the bell back forcibly and then reversed the motion. Grunting at the sweet burn in his muscles that resulted.

It was nice to distract his mind again. Focus on something else besides Kate. How sensual and strange their night together had been. How she'd completely blown his mind. How she could be so damn seductive and then innocent a minute later.

And how it had all been a ruse to get him into bed. How he'd been nothing more than a fantasy in Kate's mind.

Stop thinking about her. One night. You had your one night, she should be out of your system now.

Unfortunately, she wasn't out of his system. Far from it. He wanted *another* night with her. Another chance to explore her body...another chance to hear her scream his name.

Fuck. What the hell was wrong with him?

He'd just done a set of twenty reps on the kettle bell, when the call came in over the loudspeaker.

Suspicious odor coming from a heating vent, caller wasn't sure if it could be a possible gas leak or something else.

Then the dispatcher announced the location of the call and Todd's gut clenched. *Kate's shop.*

Adrenaline slammed into him as he set down the kettle bells and ran to the fire truck in the bay. Jeremiah, the other firefighter on duty, was already gearing up.

They pulled up outside Kate's shop a few minutes later, becoming the first responders on the scene. Beating Tyson—or whoever else might've been on duty at the sheriff's office.

Parking the truck by the curb, Todd kept on the emergency

lights and then hurried into the shop. His concern tinged with a bit of frustration when he found Kate tampering with the heating vent. She stood on her tiptoes and struggled to pry the vent open.

The jeans she wore slung low on her hips, so when her red sweater lifted with her stretching, he spotted the flash of creamy skin. Skin he'd kissed...caressed. His pulse jumped and he flexed his jaw, trying to shove thoughts of sex with Kate from his mind.

"What the hell are you doing?" he demanded tersely, crossing the room to her. "If this is some kind of gas leak, then you should've waited outside."

She jumped and spun around, guilt and shock filling her eyes. "I don't think it's a—"

"Outside, Kate."

She folded her arms across her chest and swallowed hard. Resentment flickered in her gaze now. "Todd, maybe when you say jump, other women do it while batting their eyelashes. But this is *my* shop and I'm not leaving until I know what's going on. And as I told the dispatcher I don't really think it's a gas leak, but she insisted on putting out the call for help anyway."

Todd's slight frustration lurched to full-on irritation as he advanced on her. Despite her little speech, she seemed to realize she'd picked the wrong fight, because her blue eyes widened and she backed up until she hit the edge of the display case.

Her tongue darted across her mouth and her breasts rose and fell beneath her sweater.

"Look, Kate, there's being stubborn, and there's being foolish. And I don't want to see you getting hurt," he growled.

She laughed at him. A little, high-pitched sound of disbelief before she rolled her eyes.

"Hey, Todd," Jeremiah called out from behind him. "I think we're okay here, pretty sure it's not a gas leak."

Todd's jaw snapped shut. Yeah, he'd pretty much figured that out too. That smell wasn't gas, it was the sour smell of something rotting. But Kate couldn't have known that, and the fact she'd stuck around trying to Nancy Drew it out herself sparked a fierce concern for her safety that he hadn't known was possible for him to feel for a person. Someone outside his family, that was.

Turning on his heel, he joined up with Jeremiah near the vent. Together they pried the grate free and tugged it away the wall.

The door to the shop chimed as Todd reached for his flashlight.

"Got some kind of problem I hear, kid?" Todd heard his brother Tyson call out to Kate.

Apparently the sheriff's department had just arrived on the scene.

"Yeah, something's going on in the heating vent," Kate muttered, and then her tone shifted to surprise. "Oh, hello, Walt."

Walt was here now? Todd's jaw clenched against the surge of anger and annoyance that rushed him. He pushed it aside as he shown the flashlight into the vent.

"Good morning, Caitleen," a concerned voice—he could only assume was Walt—said. "What's all the fuss?"

"That's what we're trying to figure out."

Todd moved the beam of light around the interior, until a small, dark shape was reflected.

"What is that?" Jeremiah muttered next to him.

Todd frowned. It wasn't pretty, whatever it was. "Looks like a dead animal."

He reached in and pulled the small creature free. "Possum."

"Oh my god." Kate was at his side in an instant, her hand over her mouth. "How did it end up in there? The poor thing must've gotten stuck. Is it dead?"

"Yeah. It's dead."

And it had probably dead for quite awhile. Todd's gut clenched and his jaw ticked. In fact, it looked like road kill from the side of the road. Which was making him think someone had deliberately placed it in there.

"It's got blood all over it. And his face is all smashed in," Kate whispered suddenly. "How did it—"

"Tyson, take her out of here," Todd said tersely.

"Don't take me outside, tell me what's going on—"

"Come on, Caitleen," Walt said gently, and he heard their retreating footsteps. "This is not something for the eyes of a lady. We should let them handle this."

Tyson came around to observe the situation, then glanced

outside. "You thinking what I'm thinking?"

Anger, hot and potent, gathered in Todd's belly. "If you're thinking that somebody stuffed this little guy in here already dead, then yeah."

"Shit. Who'd Kate piss off?" Jeremiah shook his head and took the dead possum from Todd's hands. "I'll take care of this poor little guy."

Todd watched Jeremiah leave the shop, and then his gaze caught on Kate and Walt. Walt had her in his arms, was stroking a hand down her back and brushing a kiss across her forehead.

Jealousy blindsided him, tightening his throat and coiling every muscle in his body. How the hell could she let another man touch her? After what had just happened between them barely forty-eight hours ago.

"*Todd.*"

He blinked, tearing his gaze away from the couple and meeting Tyson's questioning stare.

"What?"

"I said I don't think this is a random prank."

"No shit," Todd replied tersely and scrubbed a hand down his jaw, forcing his focus back to whoever was targeting Kate. "I've never thought any of them were. The rock through the window. The flat tires."

Tyson nodded. "Time to talk to her."

"Great idea. Let me grab her." The idea of making her leave the circle of Walt's arms was more appealing than he wanted to admit.

Todd moved toward the door and Walt glanced up, spotting his approach. Then, holding Todd's hard stare, Walt caught Kate's chin in his hands before kissing her on the mouth.

The hell he did. Hot anger coiled in Todd's belly as he thrust open the door, barely restraining the low growl rising in his throat.

"Kate," he damn near snarled. "We need to talk."

She jerked away from Walt, her eyes blue pools of surprise and guilt. She nodded and ran her tongue over lips that had just been beneath another man's.

"Umm, I need to go, Walt," she murmured, tucking a strand of blonde hair behind her ear. "I'll catch up with you tonight?"

"That sounds great, Caitleen. See you then."

Todd held the door and Kate scooted in past him, the curve of her hip brushing his thigh. His blood heated and he ground his teeth together, willing his cock not to get the wrong idea.

He shut the door behind her, noting that she didn't meet his gaze and seemed entirely too fidgety as she made her way toward the back.

Curling his fingers into fists, he resisted the urge to catch her arm and halt her. And he bit his tongue to stop himself from revealing just what he thought of seeing that schmuck next door kissing her.

And when Tyson sat her down to begin questioning her, Todd managed—just barely—to turn his thoughts to darker issues. Like who had it out for Kate and her shop...

What the hell was wrong with him? Todd scrubbed his hands over his eyes and wished like hell he could sleep. Instead, he'd spent half the day tossing and turning before finally getting up and taking another shower.

Why did getting kicked to the curb by Kate bug him so much? It should have been *his* damn fantasy. Kate with no strings attached. Hadn't he wanted that for months now?

Instead, his stomach burned with bitterness and jealousy while instinct pricked in the back of his head that something was off.

He sat in his kitchen, sipping a soda and staring out the window at the setting sun.

There had to be more to it. Something else going on, but what? It was there, he just couldn't put his finger on it. Damn if he didn't wish there was someone else to ask. Someone else who might know exactly what was going on in Kate's little head...

Todd's fingers crushed around the soda and he shoved back his chair. *Ellie!* How the hell had he forgotten about his sister-in-law's involvement?

He ran through the house, grabbed his keys and hurried outside to his truck, a resolute smile curving his lips.

Ellie opened the door after the second knock and her

expression showed she'd been reluctant to.

"Todd," she greeted him mildly. "How are you?"

"You need to tell me everything, Ellie. Everything you and Kate plotted."

She winced and glanced behind her into the house, then lowered her voice. "Give me a minute and I'll come out—"

"Sweetheart, is Todd here?"

At the sound of Tyson Wyatt's voice, Ellie scowled and looked about ready to stomp her foot.

"You should have called first," she hissed and stepped back, opening the door. "Yes, Tyson. Your brother's here."

Todd stepped into the house, not really giving a damn about Ellie's desire to keep their talk under wraps.

"Good," Tyson came out of the kitchen, a dishrag slung over his arm. "I've been meaning to talk to you."

Todd should've been on alert at the hard glint in his brother's eyes, but he was too focused on Ellie's guilty expression.

"You slept with Kate, didn't you?" Tyson asked with deceptive softness.

"Umm, I'll let you two talk," Ellie said quickly and tried to slip away.

"Oh no you don't." Todd shook his head. "I bet Ellie has quite a bit to say on this whole Kate thing, don't you?"

"I..."

"There's been talk around town about Todd leaving the party with Kate on Saturday night," Tyson glanced down at his wife, his brows drawing into a scowl. "But, sweetheart, don't tell me you knew about this?"

"She not only knew about it, she helped plan it," Todd said tersely. "I didn't set out to seduce Kate. She seduced me."

"Kate seduced *you*?" Tyson's scowl deepened. "I know you, Todd, and I'm calling bullshit."

Ellie groaned. "No, it's true. It's my fault, Tyson. I should've talked her out of it."

Tyson glared at them both, before lingering on Ellie. "Seriously? Ellie, you helped her do this? Why the hell would you do that? It's like throwing a bunny in the lion's den. She can't handle Todd."

Jesus Christ, they were acting like he was a goddamned

sociopath or something.

"I think Kate can handle a helluva lot more than you guys think," he muttered, thinking of she was all over Walt this afternoon.

But Ellie and Tyson seemed to be in their own conversation now. "Tyson, she was *determined* and she would've done it without my help anyway."

Todd gave a harsh laugh. "Yeah, she would've. She had a goal and she made damn sure she accomplished it."

Ellie's eyes widened. "Wait, what? She *told* you about that?"

I figured it was a good opportunity to check that sleep with a firefighter fantasy off my list. Her words flickered through his head, making something curdle in his stomach.

He gave a small nod. "Yeah. She did."

"Told him what?" Tyson demanded.

Todd hesitated, not really wanting to air the truth aloud. It was offensive enough in his head.

"Ellie," Tyson's voice sharpened. "What did she tell him?"

Ellie groaned and then muttered, "That she was a virgin."

Chapter Ten

Todd heard the words, but it took a second before they sank in. There was a roaring in his ears as every muscle in his body went taut.

What the fuck?

"Say that again?" he said unsteadily, taking a step toward her.

Ellie's eyes went wide. "Shit! You said she told you."

"*That* is not what she told me."

Jesus Christ. Kate had been a virgin? *A fucking virgin?* He turned away, thrusting a hand through his hair as his stomach took a huge nosedive.

"Oh for God's sake, you can't tell me this is a surprise," Tyson snapped. "Damn it, Todd, have you been living under a rock?"

Todd bit his tongue before he snarled at his brother to shove it where the sun didn't shine.

No, he hadn't fucking known. Though apparently he should've. Kate had always seemed a bit innocent, but that night she'd thrown him off balance. Sexy outfit, coming on to him like he was the last guy on earth. All with Ellie's help, no doubt. But it had all been an act. His skilled little seductress had been anything but skilled. *Kate had been a virgin.*

It made sense. How tight she'd been, the slight look of pain in her eyes when he'd entered her. And he'd been a selfish idiot, brushing it off as the size of his dick.

Nausea and self-disgust swept through him.

"Where are you going?" Ellie asked.

Todd wasn't even aware of walking out the door, only driven by the instinct to confront Kate. She'd been a virgin and she hadn't told him. The betrayal stabbed hard in his gut.

Why had she done it? And why would she want a one-night stand for her first time? He sure as hell didn't believe the whole I-only-wanted-to-fuck-a-fireman thing anymore. That had been a wall thrown up to distract him. One he'd be sure to tear down in her face when he found her.

He gripped his keys and climbed back into his truck, backing out of Tyson's driveway faster than he should've.

When he drove by her house and her car wasn't there, he let out a string of curses before heading into town. He spotted her car outside the Italian restaurant and pulled up to the curb and parked.

He was about to make one helluva scene, but right now, he didn't give a flying fuck.

Kate took another sip of wine and forced another smile at Walt. This whole evening had felt forced. Holding his hand, attempting to respond to his flirtations and compliments. But she was trying, because this was her future. A guy like Walt. Not Todd-the-Bed-Hopper Wyatt.

"It's so awful what's been going on with your shop, Caitleen," he said softly, concern in his eyes as he took her hand again. "Do the police have any suspects?"

She hesitated and shook her head. The attacks on her shop had her on the edge. If she wasn't so miserable with the whole Todd situation, she'd probably be freaking out about it a little more.

Another potential suspect had flitted through her head. Or a dozen of them...any of the women who'd dated Todd. Because more than a handful of them had probably seen her leave Ryan's party with him on Saturday night and didn't like the fact.

"They don't know. We have a few ideas...but, I don't know. I just can't see anyone in this town doing these awful things." Her mouth curled downward and she sighed. "You've been so sweet throughout. Thank you, Walt, for always being there to help me through."

"I care about you, Caitleen," he said gently, and she was surprised to see his cheeks redden a little. "More than maybe I should."

The admission only made her uncomfortable. Obviously their feelings were not equal on the emotional scale. But Walt was such a nice guy. It was great to see him moving on after his losing his wife.

She stared at him, saw only kindness and a small hint of desire for her in his gentle blue eyes. He should be everything a girl wanted, so what was wrong with her?

Kate cleared her throat. It wasn't right. She needed to be straight with him. Explain that her heart belonged to—

"*Kate.*"

Her head jerked up and her mouth rounded into an O as Todd crossed the floor of the dim restaurant. Other patrons turned in their seats to see what the commotion was.

"Todd?" She pulled her hand free of Walt's and blinked in dismay. "What are you—"

"We need to talk. Now."

Walt stood up, a frown marring his face now. "Excuse me, Mr. Wyatt, but Caitleen and I—"

"Are done with your dinner," Todd said flatly.

Kate's mouth fell open and her cheeks heated, even as her heart slammed around in her chest.

"Todd, this is not the time," she hissed. "Go away and we'll talk later."

"We leave, or I start talking now," he warned, eyes glittering with intent. "In front of the whole damn town."

Kate's mouth tightened and she slid her gaze around the restaurant. Sure enough, everyone from the local pharmacist to the Winters family was staring at them in rapt fascination. Damn it.

She didn't doubt for one minute he'd make good on his promise. And no way was she going to air her dirty laundry in public. But she *was* going to kill him. Get outside this restaurant and kill the cocky jerk.

"I'm so sorry, Walt," she apologized softly, her gaze pleading with him to understand. "I should deal with him. I'll call you later."

She set her napkin down on the table and stood, trying to show some dignity as she walked out of the restaurant ahead of Todd.

When the cool night air hit her, she was so damn tempted to turn on him and start swinging. But everyone with a window seat in the restaurant still had a pretty good view.

"Let's talk in my truck," he said, gesturing to the passenger door.

"You're being such an asshole, Todd Wyatt." She glared at him and almost refused, but then saw another couple walking down the street arm in arm. Tired of the drama, she complied.

When Todd climbed into the truck after her she seethed, "I'm never going to forgive you for what you just did. Walt doesn't deserve this."

"I don't give a rat's ass what Walt deserves," he said furiously and slammed his door, before turning to face her. Even in the dimness of the truck she saw the glint of anger in his eyes. "Why don't we talk about what *I* deserve? Like maybe being told I was fucking a virgin on Saturday?"

Oh. God. The blood drained from her face and the anger slid away. He'd found out. But...how?

"What was I to you, Kate? The designated cherry popper? A one-night stand to lose your virginity?"

She opened her mouth to deny it, but then guilt twitched in her gut. In a way that's exactly what he'd been. That and so much more...

"Great. Just fucking great," he muttered and then started the truck.

"Why does it even matter? So I was a virgin. Does it really matter? And where are you going?"

"Yeah, it sure as fuck matters, Kate. And I'm taking you back to my place."

She gripped the leather seat, her palms dampening. "I'd rather just go home."

"Fine, we'll go to your house."

"You're not coming over!"

"My place it is then."

She ground her teeth together. This was *ridiculous*. Why wouldn't he listen to her? Why was he so determined to dissect her reasoning for sleeping with him?

Todd drove them through town until he'd pulled his truck into the driveway a few minutes later.

"I don't really think anything else needs to be said." Her tone was quiet as she followed him inside.

"And see, doll, there lies the problem."

Kate shut the door behind them, trying not to think about

what had happened the last time they were here. She wrapped her arms around herself and suppressed a shiver of awareness.

But when he stepped toward her, his gaze blazing with a heat that was becoming all too familiar, her body trembled. She flicked her tongue out over her now-dry lips and tried not to look intimidated. But she was. Oh God how she was.

Todd was so close his body almost brushed hers. He lifted a hand and placed it above her on the door. Opening his body to her gaze in a way that displayed his ripped upper body and broad shoulders.

She remembered how it had felt to hold onto those shoulders while he moved deep inside her. It sent moisture between her legs and softened the anger she was trying to hold onto.

The sound of the icemaker in the fridge crunching broke the silence in the house.

"It was a bad idea," she finally said huskily. "I never should've picked you."

Todd's gaze narrowed and his thumb swept across the lips she'd just licked. "Then why did you, Kate?"

Her mind scurried for an answer. Another lie.

"The truth," he continued. "I want the truth."

Kate bit back a groan and slid her gaze from his. And then she found herself confessing, "Because I trust you. And I knew you would be amazing in bed. And I wanted to learn what it was like and experience things."

And because I've always been half in love with you. She kept that little tidbit to herself. After all, a girl had to have at least a tiny bit of pride leftover.

"You should have told me," he said softly. "I would have gone slower. I would have taken the time to—"

"You wouldn't have touched me, Todd. We both know it."

He was quiet for a moment, then his chin dropped and he looked at his feet, shaking his head.

"No. Damn it, I wouldn't have, Kate. But I shouldn't have touched you whether you were virgin or experienced as a Nevada whore," his voice rose. "Jesus, you're twenty-five. How the hell are you a virgin?"

Heat flared through her cheeks, humiliation making her ears burn.

"Because for the most part I think men are dogs," she ground out. "I haven't wanted to go near a man, let alone have sex with one, since I was seventeen."

The wheels were moving in his head, somewhat, she could see the thought process in his eyes.

"That's right. You dated Andrew back in high school. You guys were pretty serious. And yet...you never slept with him?" Todd shook his head, skepticism in his gaze now.

"No. I sure as hell didn't." Since humiliation seemed to be the emotion du jour, why not lay it all out on the table? "Because that would've meant he won his bet."

Todd went dangerously still, but his nostrils flared. "What bet?"

"You mean you don't know?" Her brows drew together. She'd thought everyone had heard the rumors, but then Todd had been a few years older than her and off at college by then.

Impatience flickered in his dark eyes. "No, I sure as hell don't know, Kate. So why don't you tell me."

She gave a light shrug, even though the bitterness that had eaten at her those first few years was flaring up again.

Her words dripped with sarcasm and bitterness when she finally said, "Andrew had a bet with the captain of the football team." Her smile hardened. "The bet being that he could fuck the fat chick."

Chapter Eleven

Todd stared down at Kate, shock and disgust running through him. He eyes widened with dismay. Part of him denied it could be true. Andrew had seemed like a good kid, and had grown into the man who ran the auto shop down on Second Avenue.

But the redness of Kate's cheeks and mortification in her eyes was proof enough of what she'd endured. His gut tightened with rage and the muscles in his neck strained.

"Jesus, Kate—"

"Please. There's no need to say anything. There's not much you *can* say except to commiserate with me on what an asshole he is. And no one's going to dispute that." She gave a harsh laugh and wrapped her arms around her lush breasts, her gaze not meeting his. "But maybe now you'll understand why I stayed away from men—from sex—for so long." Her lips twisted into a bitter smile. "And why I have my car taken to the next town over if it needs any repairs."

Todd swallowed hard, his throat thick with anger and an utter helplessness to protect her from something that had hurt her seven or eight years ago. He could almost relate to the pain and humiliation she must've felt with the experience he'd had years ago. The experience that had shaped him into the man he was today, just as Kate's experience had done to her.

"I'm sorry," he muttered savagely. "He is an asshole. How did you find out about that bet?"

"Jenny Erickson, a cheerleader, called me up the night of the prom. Her boyfriend was laughing about the bet. She felt bad enough to warn me."

"What a worthless son of a bitch." Todd cupped her face gently and she looked up at him, allowing him to see the combination of vulnerability and confidence in her that overall embodied who Kate was. "But you, Kate. You are a lush, sexy woman that any man with half a brain can appreciate."

She gave a faint smile and looked down again, but not before he saw the flicker of pleasure in her eyes and her cheeks tinged pink.

"I don't mind being the curvy girl who runs a bakery, Todd," she admitted softly. "I'm comfortable with who I am. Now. It took awhile. But I'm there now."

Todd placed his finger beneath her chin and tilted her head up again, and because he needed her to know how damn sexy she was, he brushed his mouth over hers in a light kiss.

But once their lips touched, it wasn't enough. Especially when she sighed and leaned into him, her tongue flickering out to tease into his mouth this time.

His body was tight with need when he lifted his head a moment later. "I want more than the one night we had, Kate."

She swallowed hard. "How many do you want? Because you don't do relationships either."

He didn't even hesitate. "No. I don't. But you said you wanted to learn and experience things. If you trusted me enough to be your first, trust me enough to teach you more," he urged huskily and kissed her forehead. "Let me teach you pleasure and passion. Let me have at least a couple of weeks."

"You want a couple weeks?"

She sounded stunned, and he couldn't blame her, he was a little taken aback at his request too. When was the last time a woman had tempted him beyond a night or two? Very rarely. But he knew—damn it, he just *knew*—one or two nights with Kate wasn't nearly enough.

"You know I do. And you do too, doll," he murmured and nuzzled the soft scented skin of her neck.

She made a soft moan of pleasure and her hands slid to his shoulders, though still he could sense her hesitation. But why?

He wanted to help the budding sensuality in Kate bloom. God, what it would be like to lead her on that journey. And the thought of some other schmuck being the one to do it had something dark and volatile sliding through his blood.

Actually ever since he'd slept with Kate—and especially after learning she'd been so innocent—he'd been surprised at the possessiveness he held for her. The claim, so instinctive and primal, he wanted to make on her. It was a bit overwhelming.

And at times embarrassing, like the way he'd stormed into that restaurant like a man unhinged tonight.

He kissed his way down her neck to the lush cleavage exposed above her silky top, only wanting her assent.

"Todd," she said breathlessly. "I'm just not sure it's such a good idea."

"I'm pretty sure it is," he murmured and licked between the dark and soft swells of her breasts, while cradling the curves of her hips in his hands.

In fact, seducing away any of her inhibitions about letting him into her bed again sounded like a *damn* good idea. Kate's soft whimper and the way she pressed herself against him showed he'd succeeded.

With a triumphant growl, he tugged her top free from her body and unfastened the clasp of her lacy bra. He tossed the turquoise-and-black fabric to the side and immediately cupped her full breasts.

Todd thumbed her pink nipples, watching the way they hardened immediately to his touch. His mouth watered with the urge to suck them. Swooping his head, he took one tip into his mouth.

Kate gasped, her hips pressing hard into his as her fingers slid into his hair.

Damn she tasted of sweet innocence and sensuality. Or maybe that was just him knowing how innocent she was. Todd lifted his head long enough to back her up, until they hit the sofa in his living room.

He sat down first and then pulled her down so she straddled his lap, her skirt pushed up around her waist. And it left her lush breasts at eye level so he could continue to enjoy them.

Knowing this time around how experienced she was, he made sure to slow things down. To let her feel and savor every moment, to give himself that luxury too.

The sound of her moans as he suckled and massaged her breasts had his dick rock hard. He rocked against her, lifting his hips to press himself against the apex of her thighs, still covered by the pink cotton panties he'd spotted earlier. They weren't sexy and lacy, but something about them made his blood heat and fucked with his mind a bit.

Jesus, he wanted her. Had to remind himself to keep going

slow. He slid a hand between her thighs, to rub her gently through the cotton, and the warm dampness of her arousal greeted his fingers.

He tugged the cotton to the side so he could graze his knuckles over her slit.

"You like that? You're so wet for me."

Kate made a mew of pleasure and her head fell back, revealing the creamy length of her neck and lifting her breasts higher.

So fucking sexy. How could anyone not find this woman an absolute goddess?

Todd curled one finger into her heat, sinking just to the first knuckle to test her readiness. Her hot sheath clenched around him, coating him with her slippery arousal.

"Love the way you feel," he murmured and licked the pulse beating like a butterfly's wings in her neck.

Kate's breasts rose with the unsteady breath she drew in, and her body squeezed around his finger. He slipped another finger into her, working in and out of her tightness.

"I want you nice and ready for me. I promise it won't hurt a bit when you take my cock this time, doll."

"Todd," she whispered, running her tongue over her lips as she stared down at him with pleasure-drugged eyes. "Please don't stop."

Her plea and the expression of blatant need on her face sent a wave of possessiveness through him.

Stop? Hell, they were just getting started. He brought his thumb up to her clit and flicked it, watching the sparks of ecstasy flicker in her pretty blue eyes.

"Lovely," he murmured and then lowered his head to her breast again, sucking her nipple while he fingered her tight little pussy.

She gripped his shoulders and rode his hand, her moans growing louder and more abandoned. And then she gasped, the walls of her sex clenching and unclenching around him as she came.

Christ, she was so responsive. To every little touch and kiss. Which made him only want to please her more, to bring her to another climax.

Todd eased her off his lap and onto the cushions of the

couch. She seemed oblivious as her body continued to tremble. He peeled her skirt and panties from her body, leaving her completely naked.

Her gaze once again became lucid as she watched him. Her cheeks were flushed and she licked her lips, looking both a bit seductive and uncertain.

Todd gave her a reassuring smile and sank to his knees on the floor. When he gently eased her legs open, her eyes widened.

"I want you to watch me go down on you, Kate," he murmured and slid his hands beneath her ass to slide her forward. "Watch what the taste of you does to me."

She let out a low groan as he lowered his head to the pretty pink folds of her pussy, still shiny from her release.

He licked around her swollen labia, lapping up her juices, before delving his tongue into her channel. Her hips lifted from the couch and she cried out, so he slid his hands up to cup her hips and hold her still.

God, this was heaven. The taste of her, musky and sweet, so slick on his tongue. And when she started those sexy little cries, he knew she would come hard again.

He flicked his tongue over her clit, nimble and light, before moving back to bury his tongue deep inside her sheath. Making love to her with his mouth.

Lifting his gaze, he watched her expression. Saw the heavy slant of her eyelids and the way her sultry mouth was parted to allow the soft pants she made.

His blood quickened and he groaned, burying his face deeper against her. Kissing and playing with her pussy until Kate was sobbing and crying out his name.

Triumph surged through him when she came again, knowing that she was here with him. Letting him go down on her, make love to her, instead of being at dinner with that schmuck Walt.

And then she screamed his name, her thighs tightening around his ears and her fingers tugging in his hair. He smoothed his hands down Kate's thighs as he eased her through the release, loving the taste of her that slid over his tongue.

When she went slack and her fingers slid from his hair, he lifted his head. Her eyes were closed and her breasts rose and fell with each erratic breath she drew in.

Lovely.

Todd brushed the trimmed curls around her mound and placed another kiss on her swollen clit. She jumped and hissed, before letting out a soft moan.

A smile crossed his face as he kissed his way back up her body to claim her mouth again, letting her taste herself on his tongue.

Her arms wound around his neck and she kissed him back fiercely, making soft noises in the back of her throat that had his cock jerking against his jeans.

Todd lifted his head and issued a ragged, "I need you, Kate."

"Yes," she whispered and parted her thighs further so he slid between them. "I want you inside me."

He gave a slow smile and moved off her. "Let me grab a condom. And I'll be right back. I want to show you a new way to do this."

A new way? Kate's pulse fluttered again and she ran her tongue over her mouth. She stretched her muscles, which were languid and well used from her climax. Or two climaxes.

God, they had been so powerful. So beautifully intense.

She watched as Todd reentered the room, a silver packet in his hand and still fully dressed. But he set the condom on the couch, so easily, like he'd done this a hundred times before, and peeled off his shirt.

A prick of jealousy stabbed in her chest as she admired his defined, muscled torso. She knew better though, than to let the emotion take any large hold of her. Todd was Todd. He made no pretenses about being the stable, one-woman kind of man. And for tonight—and however many nights she let him make love to her—she'd just have to remember that.

When his jeans hit the floor and his boxers followed, her mouth dried at the sight of his thick, long cock straining in the air.

"I want to taste you." The words were out before she could rethink them. "To please you. Like you did for me, Todd."

He stilled in his movements to open the condom, his gaze darkening.

"You ever done that before, doll?"

Her cheeks heated and she knew he read her inexperience without her confirmation.

"How hard can it be?" she said huskily.

A slow smile slid across his face, before he moved directly in front of her.

He closed his hand around his cock and murmured, "Oh, Kate, it can be pretty damn hard."

Kate's stomach flipped as a shiver of anticipation ran through her. Raising an eyebrow, she nudged his hand aside and replaced it with her own.

Todd's let out a hiss as she moved her fingers up and down the hot steely length of him. So hard and yet silky soft on the outside.

Leaning forward, her hair falling in a curtain around her face, she let her tongue flick out over his swollen head. Todd groaned in response and she watched the muscles in his thighs tighten.

Her pulse quickened and she repeated the gesture, before curling her tongue around his girth and then sliding down his length.

"Take me in your mouth," he pleaded, threading his fingers into her hair.

Swallowing the tiny bit of nerves, she parted her lips and let him slide into her mouth. He tasted clean and just a tiny bit salty. So potently male it had the flesh between her legs dampening again.

"Oh, God," he muttered thickly. "Yes, just like that."

A thrill of power raced through her as she moved her mouth up and down his length.

"Ah—watch the teeth, doll," he hissed. "Wrap your lips around them—oh God, yeah, you're amazing at this."

Kate let her eyes flutter closed as she found her own rhythm, using her tongue and letting him slide deep. But he never went too deep.

Then, just when she was starting to really get into it, he pulled away. Her eyes fluttered open in surprise.

"Todd?"

"I want to be inside you, Kate." He brushed his thumb over her bottom lip. "We can go for the full effect another time, and

I'll come in that sweet mouth of yours. But for now I need you."

He moved onto the couch and sat down, then reached for her, pulling her astride his lap again as they'd been earlier. She straddled him and watched as he quickly placed the condom on his erection.

"I want you to ride me this time," he said softly, settling his hands on her hips. "See how you like this position."

Kate nibbled her lip, her cheeks flushing. Ride him. Oh how casually he could make the suggestion. But he was an excellent teacher, clasping her hips in his large hands and easing her down onto his cock.

She caught her breath as he stretched her, filled her, and only when he was buried to the hilt did she let out her throaty moan. A tremble racked her body and she refused to move for a moment, just leaned forward and pressed her face against his shoulder.

"Jesus, Kate, you feel incredible," he choked out and then pressed a kiss against her forehead. "Take your time. This is all you, doll."

She bit her lip and squeezed her inner muscles around him, just to see how he'd react. The groan he let out and the way his fingers tightened on her hips showed he approved.

Drawing in a slow breath, she began to rock back and forth on him. Small, gentle movements that helped her become used to him inside her, until it wasn't enough and she wanted more.

She experimented with moving hard and fast, slow and gentle. Lifting up and down. Following the sounds of Todd's groans as a guide and the way her own body responded. It didn't matter, though. No matter what she did the sensation was pretty much fantastic.

And then Todd slid his hands down to her ass and he cupped her hard as he began to thrust up into her, stealing the control he'd promised without apology. She gave it over without a fight, grateful to just cling to his shoulders and *feel*. Be thoroughly taken.

The hot, out-of-control sensation grew low in her belly again, spreading throughout her body and swirling in her mind. It was so intense tears filled her eyes as she dug her nails into Todd's shoulders, her moans mingling with his.

Even without him directly touching her clit, she was so close to coming because of the angle. She ground down on him, pressing just the right spot, and sent herself into another orgasm.

Todd pounded up into her, again and again as she trembled through her climax. Then he let out a cry, holding still, before making a couple shallow thrusts and finally staying deep.

"Oh God," she whispered raggedly, blinking away the tears. She sensed Todd had also experienced the power and emotional impact behind what had just happened between them.

She tried to lighten the thickness in the air, by saying, "I'm not going to be able to walk for days."

Todd gave an unsteady laugh. "Staying in bed could be fun."

"Except you need to work tomorrow and so do I."

He lifted his head and tucked a strand of hair behind her ear. "Stay the night anyway. We can get up early."

Her heart skipped a beat and she glanced down, running her tongue over her lips. Stay another night in bed with Todd. There might even be cuddling—which would make it really hard to remember she was only supposed to be thinking about sex here.

"Please, Kate."

With his soft plea, she gave a small nod. She didn't really want to go home anyway.

"Great." And then he stood up, to her shock, and wrapped her legs around his waist as he moved them to the bedroom.

It was sexy as hell, but she was really hoping he didn't throw his back out carrying her. *Fireman, Kate, he works out.*

And when she was cuddled up next to him awhile later, falling asleep, she could admit that these two weeks would be worth the risk to her heart.

Chapter Twelve

Friday came and Todd was itching to get off work and see Kate. She'd been at his house every night this week. It was like the time they spent apart nursed a lit fuse, and when they came together the need and passion just exploded.

When neither worked, they spent every moment together. And when one of them *was* working, he couldn't stop thinking about her. He was pretty sure Kate felt the same by the sweet or sexy text messages she'd send him.

It had never been like this. Where a week into being with a woman, he still had no desire to run. Well, he couldn't say never. Once before.

But Kate was different. There was no urge to move on. Sexually she was amazing. Always so excited to try new things in bed, and it blew his mind with the trust she placed in him. Her eagerness and innocence so completely refreshing.

It wasn't exactly a relationship, but...it went beyond sex, he thought as he drove home from the fire station. Yes, they were good in bed. But they were good out of it too. They'd spent time outside the house, bundled up in their winter coats and walking the beach. Going to dinner, not caring who saw them. And he knew people saw them and were talking. But it didn't matter. This was between him and Kate, and to hell with whoever had a problem with it. Including his brothers...

Tonight Todd was already planning on charming her with a cedar-planked salmon and wild rice dinner, maybe an action movie after, followed by a little action of their own. It didn't really matter what they did, he loved every minute he spent with Kate.

Before he could swing by Kate's shop though, a text came in from Tyson. Todd checked it and scowled. His brother had asked him to drop by for a few minutes to talk about the attacks on Kate's bakery.

Todd hesitated, but since he was about twenty minutes early picking up Kate, he made the turn toward his brother's house.

He parked his truck a few minutes later in his brother's driveway and climbed out. The door swung open on the second knock.

"Come on in," Tyson drawled. "Can I get you a beer?"

"Thanks, but I'm meeting Kate—"

"Have a beer, Todd. I called Kate and let her know you'd be late."

Todd's jaw flexed. "You don't say."

Tyson gave a hard smile. "It's been a week, Todd. Shouldn't you be moving on to the next vagina by now?"

Instinct had Todd's fist flying, and Tyson just barely blocked the punch to the face. In the next instant Todd found himself pinned against the wall, his older brother glowering at him. The verbal attack had thrown him off guard, but he shouldn't have been surprised.

"Ah, now you know violence isn't the answer, little brother," Tyson teased. Then his tone hardened, "Look, I don't know if your male-whore stage is because of Anne, but you need to let that shit go. You can't hurt Kate like this."

"Fuck you," Todd growled and threw his brother off him easily. Heat stole up his neck as Tyson's works sunk in.

As an unspoken rule they didn't talk about Anne. Had barely discussed it all those years ago, and now here Tyson was resurrecting it in his face.

Todd turned and headed for the door. "I'm outta here."

"Hang on," Tyson said placidly. "I've said my piece about Kate, and I'll back off now. But I really did want to talk to you about the attacks on her shop."

His anger faded, instead tension swept through Todd's body and he paused, before turning to face his brother again. He'd been ready to walk out, but this had to do with Kate's safety and that was his top priority.

"And? You find out who's doing it?"

"No. Penny might be a crotchety chick with a grudge toward Kate's shop, but she seems to have an alibi for all the events."

Todd drew in a slow breath and shook his head. His conversation earlier in the week with Kate flitted through his head. "And what about Andrew Lewis?"

Tyson cocked his head and stroked his jaw. "The guy she dated in high school?"

Dated? Hah. The scumbag had been using her to win a bet. Todd's lips curled with derision. "Yeah."

"Hmm. I can check into it, but he's kept a pretty low profile lately. Keeps to himself and runs the garage."

"Do that." Todd nodded and narrowed his gaze. "And while you're at it, why don't you do some digging into Walt Chapman too."

Tyson folded his arms across his chest and smiled. "Looking for a reason to rule out the competition, Todd?"

"What competition? Kate would pick me over any guy hands down."

The smile faded from his brother's face. "And you don't see a problem with that? Kate loving the one man who will never want more than a brief fling?"

His chest tightening, Todd said firmly, "She doesn't love me."

"Doesn't she?"

Holding his brother's hard stare, and hoping like hell Tyson was wrong, Todd gave a small shake of his head.

"Kate's not stupid. Virgin or not, she knew exactly what she was getting when she seduced me."

Disappointment flickered across Tyson's face, before he looked away and shoved his hands into his jeans. "I hope you're right, Todd. I really do."

Todd tried not to show the wave of unease that swept through him.

He hoped he was right too.

Kate finished prepping the dough for tomorrow's danishes and slid it into the fridge. After checking her watch, assuring herself she had at least another ten minutes before Todd arrived, she went to the bathroom for some primping.

A little perfume, lip gloss and she was about as good as she would get.

Pulse racing, Kate stepped out of the bathroom, then yelped in surprise.

"Sorry," Walt said quickly. "I didn't mean to startle you. The door was open and I came in."

Right. She'd left the door open for Todd.

"Oh right," she said a bit lamely. What was he doing here? She'd...oh, God. Dinner. It had been kind of routine for the past few months. They'd been doing dinner on Fridays.

Shoot. She really should've called him and let him know things were definitely off...though shouldn't he have figured it out by now? It wasn't a hardly a secret about her and Todd.

Time to step up and be a woman. She cleared her throat. "Walt, about us—"

"Don't worry, Kate. I'm not here to take you to dinner." He gave a small smile that held more sadness than humor. "I realize you most likely have...other plans."

"Yes," she said softly, guilt twisting in her gut. "I'm sorry. I should have told you earlier."

He lifted a hand and caressed the side of her face. "I told myself I wouldn't say anything, but I can't help it. You're too good for him, Caitleen."

Her throat tightened and she lowered her gaze. Damn, she really wished people would stop pointing out how bad Todd was for her.

"But that's not why I dropped by," Walt said quickly. "I just wanted to mention that I saw something a little out of place the other day. Penny was snooping around after hours, peering in your shop, and scurrying off when I came out to see what was going on."

"Penny?" Kate's brows drew together as she thought of the owner of the local pie shop. "Snooping around? Are you sure?"

Walt grinned. "Can't mistake hair like that. Anyway, just thought I'd mention it. I know nothing's happened in awhile, but it never hurts to be careful." He paused and slowly traced his finger down her jawline. "And you *should* be careful, Caitleen."

She knew he was referring to more than her business but refused to acknowledge the underlying hint that Todd was bad news.

The sound of the door opening had her gaze swinging to the

doorway.

"Todd." Her face flushed with a guilt that was completely unnecessary as she stepped away from Walt. "Hey."

"I should be going." Walt cleared his throat and then moved toward the door.

When he passed Todd, Kate didn't miss the challenging look the men exchanged.

Her throat tightened and she folded her arms across her chest. The door opened and then shut with Walt's exit.

"Hi," she said softly. "I was just closing shop."

Todd nodded, his expression unreadable. "Let's head out."

In his truck Todd didn't say much, and her unease grew. He seemed distant, a little angry. But why? Because of Walt? That would make no sense.

With the heat blaring on her face she grew uncomfortably warm and shifted, tugging loose her scarf.

"What was Chapman sniffing around for?"

Something in her gut started to simmer, annoyed and a little angry at his curt and sudden question.

"He came by to mention he saw Penny snooping around my shop," she said stiffly. "We used to have dinner on Fridays, but he figured out those probably wouldn't be happening for awhile."

"Awhile?"

The simmering turned into a boil. Her mouth tightened. "Where are you going with this? What would it even matter if I kept seeing Walt?"

"It would matter because you're sleeping with me," he said tightly.

Her sharp response back died on her lips as he turned the truck abruptly down a small road that led to the beach. The road was generally deserted this time of year, and especially this time of night.

"What are we doing here?" she asked unevenly.

His gaze glittered as he turned in his seat and snagged her scarf, unwinding it from her neck.

"I want you."

Her heart threatened to gallop out of her chest and her sex clenched with excitement. But her mind wasn't ready to give up without a fight.

"You can't avoid our discussion by deciding you want to fuck me," she said crudely.

"Can't I?" He arched a brow as he unfastened her seatbelt, his expression so cocky she wanted to slap it off his face.

He climbed out of the driver's seat and over to the passenger side. He reached down beside her and pulled something that had her seat sliding back and reclining.

"Todd—"

"Then push me away," he challenged, deftly unzipping her jacket and sliding a hand beneath her shirt to find her breast. "Tell me to leave you alone, Kate."

He kneaded her flesh and she cried out despite herself, her nipple tightening into his palm. Damn him, he knew her too well. Was taking advantage of the fact that she couldn't deny him.

"Yeah, I didn't think so."

His mouth crushed down on hers and she gave up trying to fight him. She didn't want to anymore, because she wanted this moment as much as he did. And she hated herself for it.

The slide of her zipper going down was the only warning she got before Todd pulled her jeans and panties from her body. Then his hand was back between her legs, his finger plunging inside her slick channel.

Pleasure rocketed through her and her hips arched off the leather seat.

Todd's mouth commandeered hers, while he brought her to a quick, intense orgasm with knowing fingers. Her body still trembled when he reached into the glove compartment for a condom.

He unzipped his jeans and pulled himself free from his boxers, sheathing himself with the condom all in probably under a minute.

Kate's heart slammed in her chest and her body ached for him inside her. Todd leaned over her, his knees braced against the seat, one hand gripping the leather seat while the other guided his cock inside her.

She moaned, her head falling back against the seat as he buried himself to the hilt. She clung to the Gore-tex jacket that he hadn't bothered to remove, while he pounded into her.

"Who's inside you, Kate?" he demanded raggedly.

She shook her head, wanting to salvage a little of her pride. But then he reached between them and rubbed her clit, his mouth slanting over hers again.

When he lifted his head a moment later she was dazed and shaking with pleasure.

"Say my name, Kate."

"Todd," she choked out.

"Damn right."

And then his mouth was on hers again. He was almost rough. Mindless, taking her in a way he'd never done before— not even that first night. It thrilled her and yet also left a seed of unease inside in her belly.

Sensation built inside her as he rubbed her clit faster and moved harder inside of her. And then she was there, cresting that climax peak and crying out her release, just as Todd had his.

He fell heavily on her, burying his face against her neck. Kate slowly fell back to reality, aware of her heart slamming around in her chest and the seatbelt receptacle biting into her hip.

And then it realization slammed into her. What had just happened, what she'd let happen. Humiliation had her cheeks burning and her hands—which had been clutching him— thrusting him away.

Todd stiffened and cursed, lifting his head.

"Oh my God," he muttered and eased off her. "Kate, I don't know what came—"

Her palm glanced across his face before she could stop it. She stared at him in the fading light, saw his jaw flex and the shock in his gaze. Watched the red marks of her fingers appear on his cheek.

Nausea swelled in her stomach and she bit her lip, tears burning at the back of her eyes.

"I don't deserve to be treated like this," she said quietly, struggling to keep her voice even. "Yes, Todd, what *did* come over you?"

He closed his eyes and thrust a hand through his hair, looking heartbreakingly handsome and conflicted.

"I don't know, Kate."

"Yes, you do. You acted like I was your possession." She

gave a short laugh, feeling ridiculously exposed and vulnerable being half-naked with her jeans and panties sitting on the floor of the truck. "An object for you just to use whenever you had the whim to. You get like that when I'm with Walt."

"You're right. I'm jealous," he finally admitted quietly and moved back into the driver's seat.

"Yes, you are. Though I'm surprised you would admit it. Why are you jealous, Todd?" she pressed on, not caring that she was tearing apart their unspoken agreement of casual sex for a couple weeks. "You don't want to be exclusive with me. And you don't do relationships. So why are you jealous?"

Todd shook his head and then sighed. "I don't like the idea of you with anybody else."

The tears that had threatened flooded her eyes. She couldn't do this anymore. Couldn't deny what was in her heart and pretend that just sex for a couple of weeks would be enough. That she could walk out unscathed.

She grabbed her discarded clothes and slid back into them.

"Well, likewise, Todd," she said miserably. "I don't like the idea of you with anybody else. I don't like walking around town and wondering what women you've slept with and who will be next after me."

His face tightened with distress. "Kate—"

"I shouldn't even *want* someone like you, Todd. That's the irony of it. Not after what happened with Andrew."

"You can't compare me to him. I'm *nothing* like that asshole," he said savagely.

"You're not. You're caring, funny and charming. And most of the time a wonderfully attentive lover." A whimsical smile flitted across her face. "You have so much love to give, Todd. But you won't let yourself. And I'm done trying to figure out why. Hoping deep down that maybe I can be the one to change you."

"You don't want my love, Kate."

"Why wouldn't I? When a girl loves someone, she generally wants that love to be reciprocated."

She should've regretted the words, especially when he paled and seemed to scoot further away from her in his seat.

"You're not in love with me, Kate. You're confused because I was your first."

"That's bull crap. I would've *never* let you take me like you just did—like some whore getting paid by the hour—if I didn't love you, Todd." Her voice trembled and tears slid down her cheek. "But I can't do it anymore. I can't go on for another week, a month, or however long until you tire of me."

Panic flickered in Todd's eyes and he reached for her, but she shook her head and moved away until the door handle bit into her lower back. Grabbing her purse off the truck floor, she clutched it in her hand.

"You're just upset right now, Kate," he said desperately. "Please, we can work this out—"

"I don't want to work out *sex*. I want you to love me."

He flinched. "I can't."

"Can't, or won't? What or who made you into a guy who jumps from bed to bed, afraid to commit to any woman?"

"Let's just say you weren't the only one traumatized by your first relationship, all right?" he said thickly.

Kate had reached for the door handle but paused, her pulse quickening at this gleam of new information. "How so?"

Todd didn't answer right away. "I fell in love when I was eighteen. I was ready to give up college to stay in Wyattsville and marry her."

Kate frowned, trying to remember if Todd had ever been serious about anyone. But then when he'd been eighteen she'd only been fourteen or fifteen and completely oblivious to his social life.

"And what happened?"

Todd looked straight ahead as he murmured, "She never wanted me. She'd been sleeping with me, using me to get closer to Trevor."

Kate winced. She knew how that must have affected him. The betrayal, shock, and deep burning anger. It wasn't unlike what had happened to her. And it had taken her how long before she'd been ready to move on? To trust a man again?

She tried not to get too excited by the spark of hope that lit inside her. That maybe, just maybe, there was hope for Todd.

Touching his arm gently, she murmured, "Oh, God, I'm sorry, Todd. Really, I know how that must've torn you up. But can't you see what you're doing? You're channeling your bitterness at her on every woman you sleep—"

"Goddamn it, don't try to analyze me, Kate," he said tersely, shrugging off her touch. "My dating habits have nothing to do with that bitch. And you knew what you were getting into when you went to bed with me."

"Dating habits? Try sex habits. You don't date, Todd. You jump from bed to bed, thinking any chick would be happy to screw you because you're a fireman." Her nose wrinkled with scorn and her stomach clenched. "And thank you for the poignant reminder on why I need to walk away now. Yes, I knew what I was getting into, and now I know why I need to get out."

She pulled on the door handle and jumped down before he could stop her. She took off, plunging down the darkened road and toward the trail that led to her house not too far away. The truck couldn't drive down the trail, which meant Todd couldn't follow after her unless he was on foot. But she heard nothing, which meant she was safe.

Alone in the darkness, she let out a sob and allowed the rest of the tears to fall.

Chapter Thirteen

He couldn't sleep. Again. Todd stared at the empty side of the bed and closed his eyes before getting up. He hadn't been able to kick the tightness in his chest and overwhelming sense of despondency since Kate had run from him last night.

Her words kept pounding home, relentless and unforgiving. Her statements mixed with Tyson's and together they left a pretty damning image of him. But it wasn't undeserved.

How had he never seen it before? Just how much of an asshole he'd turned into. All because he'd let himself fall in love so many years ago.

Or so he'd always thought he'd been in love. It was only tonight, after Kate had left the truck, had he faced the reality that he'd probably never loved Anne. Losing Anne had hurt, but it was nothing like losing Kate. And he *had* lost her. He'd seen it in the sad but determined glint in her eyes as she'd slipped from his truck.

Kate had held a mirror to his life tonight, showing the good, the bad and the ugly.

The ugly? The man he'd become over the years. The good? Being with Kate made him happy. Completed him a way he hadn't realized he wanted. Needed. And the bad...how horribly he'd hurt her tonight.

Shame lanced through him as he paced his bedroom. Kate had been right, she hadn't deserved what he'd done tonight. It had been deplorable. Never had he taken a woman like that. He'd been angry and jealous and...fucking *stupid*.

It was better that Kate had ended things. She deserved so much better than him.

His cell phone rang and he glanced down at in surprise. Maybe it was her. Not able to sleep. Wanting to talk and try and work things out... It was the fire station.

Swallowing the disappointment, Todd answered the call. A few minutes later he hung up and headed for the shower. Bruce had a mild case of food poisoning and they wanted him to start his shift early.

And why shouldn't he? He sure as hell wasn't going to spend the rest of the night sleeping.

By the time he got to the station, it was a relief to be awake and distracted. Working. Though a couple of the guys gave him sidelong glances and seemed to keep a wide girth, obviously sensing his dark mood.

An hour passed and after a hard workout in the gym, Todd glanced at his cell phone by habit to see if anyone called.

A message from Tyson reflected in the window, and Todd frowned, noting the time from late last night.

He clicked open the message, scanned it, and everything inside him went cold with fear.

Fresh blueberry muffins. Who wouldn't appreciate them? Especially since she was coming in three hours before opening to make them.

But after tossing and turning all night, coming into work sounded like a mighty fine idea. It wasn't the first time she'd done it. Baking had always been her way to ease stress and distract herself. Fortunately she now capitalized on it.

She hadn't stopped thinking about Todd all night. Wondering if she'd made a huge mistake. Because this past week had literally been the best of her life. And who knows, maybe Todd would've come around. Maybe he'd... Oh God, who was she kidding? Todd was Todd. He would forever be the town's Casanova.

After she left her car and arrived outside her bakery, she fumbled to unlock her shop, her fingers growing numb with cold. It was still dark, but then, it was barely three in the morning.

When the key connected with the lock, she gave a small moan of relief and pushed open the door a minute later. She stepped inside and shut the door behind her, a shiver racking through her body.

The sounds of metal hitting the ground tore a scream from her throat.

Kate spun around, heart pounding, and scanned the darkened shop. The lights were right beside her, but she almost too terrified to hit the switch.

She finally did and the shop lit up, illuminating a man who had relief slipping through her.

"Walt," she said in exasperation. "What are you doing here? You nearly scared me to death."

When he didn't answer her, just looked at her, her relief faded. She remembered that it was basically the middle of the night and there was absolutely no logical reason for Walt to be in her shop. Or holding a container of lighter fluid.

Fear washed in cold waves down her back and she cast a quick glance at the door behind her.

"I wouldn't try it," he warned, then, "You're just like her, you know."

"Like who?"

"My wife. She was a lying slut, leaving me for another man. I couldn't let her do it." He shook his head, his gaze narrowing. "I couldn't let her make a fool of me."

His wife? His wife was dead. Oh God. Had died in a fire. Her gaze slid to the bottle of lighter fluid in his hands again. Her fear tripled and her throat locked. And when she took a deep breath in to calm herself, she smelled the smoke.

She took what she hoped was an inconspicuous step backward.

"I had such high hopes for you, Caitleen. You were so innocent. It seemed all my little incidents were bringing us together just as I'd planned. Anytime something happened to your shop, you turned to me for comfort. It was so perfect." He scowled. "Until that stupid Wyatt boy got a hold of you. Turned you into his little sex toy, didn't he?"

Walt strode forward and wrapped his arm around her neck, dragging her away from the door as he turned off the lights at the same time, plunging them into darkness once more.

She struggled to breathe with the crook of his elbow cutting off her air. Clawing at his forearm, terror overran her. The realization that Walt had been behind everything. Not Penny. Not one of Todd's exes.

"You weren't supposed to *be* here tonight, Caitleen. I was just going to teach you a lesson. Have you watch your precious bakery burn down while your stupid boyfriend attempted to put it out."

Kate's body started to tingle and she grew dangerously lightheaded.

"But you are here and it's going to cost you. Just like it cost my wife. I probably could've saved her. She was always leaving her silly candles burning at night. But it was just such an easy solution. If she was dead, she could hardly leave me, now could she?"

His hold on her tightened, cutting off the little air she was getting.

"Sorry, Caitleen, I was really hoping you were different. But you're just a slut like the rest of them."

She struggled, dug her nails deep enough to draw blood. But her energy was fading.

Then it was too late.

Chapter Fourteen

Todd disconnected the call and swore beneath his breath. Okay maybe it was the middle of the night and she hated his guts, but Kate should damn well be picking up the phone.

He regretted volunteering to come in tonight, or he'd be on his way over to her house right now to warn her about Walt Chapman.

Todd had called his brother, waking him out of bed, after receiving the cryptic text about Walt. Had gotten the full scoop on the record Mr. Chapman had—apparently under a different name and almost fifteen years ago.

Stalking. Domestic violence. Destruction of property. The list went on and contained just about everything besides murder. Which right now, Todd was really itching to look back into that file about the house fire his wife had died in.

A call came in over the loudspeaker, tearing him from his frustration and unease. Once he heard the location and the nature of the call, he sprinted to gear up, adrenaline and rage running through him.

There was a possible fire at Kate's shop and he had no doubt who was behind it. The only thing he was grateful for was the bastard had struck while she was asleep and not while she'd been at work.

When the engine pulled to a stop outside her shop a few minutes later, he could see smoke inside and the hint of flames coming from the back of the shop.

They quickly read the situation, and Tony called out, "Doesn't look too bad yet. Whoever called it in must've spotted it early."

Todd nodded, moving to grab the booster line off the truck. Regardless, the smoke damage inside would still mean Kate could be closed down for a bit. Insurance claims filed. His gut clenched with regret for the struggle ahead for her. Had she heard about the fire yet? Was she on her way in?

He glanced up as a deputy pulled up, sirens wailing, but his attention slid beyond the squad car and focused on the parked Ford Escort in its headlights. His blood chilled and every muscle in his body went taut.

"I'm going in," he shouted, dropping the hose and reaching for his mask. "I think Kate's inside."

The burning in her throat woke her. Kate struggled to pull herself up and coughed as she sucked in a lungful of smoke.

Relief that she was still alive surged through her, followed by panic as she struggled to rise to her feet. The bakery was so thick with smoke she couldn't even tell where the door was.

She tried to hold her breath, her head pounding as she took an uneven step toward where she hoped the doorway was. Dizziness assailed her and she wavered.

Her knees buckled and she swayed on her feet. It had to be a hallucination when what looked like a fireman broke the smoke. But when she started to fall, the arms that caught her were real enough.

Kate was vaguely aware of being slung over her rescuer's shoulder and rushed outside, passing by another fireman who rushed past them with a hose.

Then she was on the ground, coughing hacking breaths of clean air and trying to stop her lungs from burning. A group of people swarmed around her and someone placed a plastic mask of her mouth.

She sucked in the oxygen eagerly, clutching the heavy sleeve of the firefighter's jacket. Even with his mask on, she sensed it was Todd. And then he pulled off the mask and confirmed it.

"You're going to be all right, doll, stay with me. Just keep breathing," he said thickly, his eyes full of concern and fear.

Kate listened to the sounds around them. The sound of water from the hoses hitting the roof of her shop, the footsteps pounding, men yelling.

Suddenly she stiffened and tugged at her mask.

"Walt," she croaked. "It was—"

"We're on it and Tyson's trying to hunt him down right

now." Todd smoothed her hair back off her face. "Try and relax, Kate. Please, baby doll. Everything's going to be fine."

If she wasn't so weak she probably would have started laughing. How could everything possibly be fine?

Sirens sounded and she closed her eyes as she saw an ambulance show up. Somewhere in her head was a happy place and she was going to try like hell to find it.

Kate pushed aside the breakfast a nurse had brought her a half hour ago, giving up on trying to eat. Her throat was still a bit sore from the smoke inhalation, and she wasn't hungry. Couldn't begin to pretend she had the desire to eat.

Though she'd protested, the hospital had decided to keep her overnight for observation. She felt about eighty times better than she had last night. Well, physically.

Her heart twisted and she closed her eyes, twisting the sheet that covered her lap. It was hard to believe how everything had changed in twenty-four hours. She'd gone from having a busy, fabulous bakery and spending her nights with Todd, to having an arsoned bakery and being, once again, alone now that she'd booted the man she loved out of her bed. She wasn't sure which bothered her more.

You made the right decision, she told herself. Todd had told her again and again he didn't do relationships, he couldn't love. So maybe it hurt now, but it would ease. It had to.

She blinked back tears, trying not to let herself drown in self pity and misery, and glanced out the hospital window at the green trees.

"Mind if I come in?"

Whipping her head back around, her lips parted in surprise as she found the very man she'd been pondering standing in the doorway. He held a bouquet of roses in his hand and her heart sped up, hope rising inside her. But just as quickly she tried to push it down.

Todd was always a charmer. He probably brought every sick friend flowers. And that's all she was to him, would ever be.

With that painful reminder, she gave him an attempt at a smile and waved him in.

Todd stepped inside Kate's hospital room and his gut clenched from the emotional punch of seeing her like this. She was entirely too pale, while areas of her hair and along her skull line still had spots of gray soot.

Though fortunately she didn't look as fragile this morning. But watching her hours ago had just about killed him, kneeling over her with the oxygen mask while she lay weak and hurting on the cold cement.

"How are you?" Her hoarse voice made him wince.

"I'm fine, Kate. It's you I'm worried about." He set the vase of flowers down on the table next to her and leaned down to kiss her forehead. "I'm not sure if they told you, but Tyson picked up and arrested Walt as he tried to leave town."

"They told me." She nodded and he saw the flicker of pain in her eyes. Whether from trying to use her voice or thinking about what Walt had done, he wasn't sure.

Before he could stop himself, he pulled her hand into his. Her eyes widened with surprise.

"Your shop's not as bad as it could've been. The fire stayed pretty contained to your office, where Walt started it in the waste bin." He hesitated. "I'm not going to lie, there's some smoke damage, but you should be fine with insurance. Be back on your feet before you know it."

"I sure hope so. This could kill my business." She clutched his fingers, then bit her lip and looked away.

"It won't. We'll arrange a huge grand re-opening. You're already the talk of the town, Kate. Everyone will be lining up to support you."

A wan smile flickered on her mouth.

He cleared his throat, which suddenly felt too tight. "So, I ran into your parents in the hallway. Told them I'd drive you home when the hospital discharges you and take care of you."

"You?" Kate glanced at him in surprise again, her sharp gaze searching his.

"Yeah, they're heading back to Portland now. Said they'd call you tonight."

Her mouth flapped open as she clearly tried to make sense of what he was saying. And since he didn't want there to be any more doubts, and more confusion, it was time to lay it all on the table.

"I'm sorry, Kate," he said quietly. "You were right. About me. About everything. I was bitter, trying to prove I didn't need a woman for more than a few nights. And you were just another woman moving through the revolving door."

Hurt flickered in her eyes and she tried to pull her hand away, but he tightened his grip. His stomach roiled and his muscles were coiled with tension. Even though it was hardly hot in the room, beads of sweat broke out on Todd's forehead.

"But I knew when you left me last night how wrong I was. That no matter how much I didn't want to give a woman that much power, didn't want to fall in love, it was too late."

Shock mingled with hope in her eyes, but he could see her fighting it, not wanting to believe. She shook her head and her mouth tightened.

"And even then, Kate, I was too damn proud to admit it. To tell you." His voice trembled as he relived the fear from last night. "But when I realized you were inside the bakery, saw it burning, it became so clear everything I was about to lose. I've never been so scared in my life."

Todd watched the wall around her crack, saw that she finally believed him and her eyes shimmered blue with sudden tears. He cupped her face, brushing the moisture from the corner of her eyes.

"You have every right to tell me to go to hell, Kate, I deserve it. I thought I knew what love was, but I was wrong. *You* showed me what it meant to be in love. To love someone so much that thought of losing them makes you literally sick to your stomach."

Tears spilled down her cheeks, faster than he could wipe them away, and she began to tremble. He leaned down and brushed his mouth across hers, before kissing her damp cheeks.

"I don't want to take care of you for the next few days, Kate," he admitted softly. "I want to take care of you forever. I want to marry you. Have kids with you. Grow old with you. *I want it all, Kate.*"

"Yes. Oh, yes. I love you, Todd." Kate wrapped her arms around his neck and clung to him, whispering, "And I want it all too."

Todd blinked, surprised to find his eyes misting a bit, as relief raged through him. His chest tightened, swelled with an emotion he'd denied for too long.

He clutched the sexy woman in his arms, never wanting to let her go. Knowing he'd never be stupid enough to again. She was his sweet Kate, whom he'd known his whole life. There was no doubt anymore. No hesitation.

"I love you so much," he murmured again against her hair and sighed when she lifted her mouth to his again for a kiss.

It was damn shame he'd fought destiny for so long, he thought, kissing her deeply. But he had plenty of years to make up for it.

About the Author

Shelli's the author your mother warned you about! She read her first romance novel when she snuck it off her mother's bookshelf when she was eleven. One taste and she was forever hooked on romance novels. It wasn't until many years later that she decided to pursue writing stories of her own. By then she acknowledged the voices in her head didn't make her crazy, they made her a writer. Shelli writes various genres of romance and currently lives in the Pacific Northwest with her young daughter.

Email Shelli: shelli@shellistevens.com

Sign up for her newsletter at: shellistevens.com/contact

Let a terrorist take her?
Not over his dead body and damned soul...

Collateral Damage
© 2010 J.L. Saint
Silent Warrior, Book 1

One thing makes Jack Hunter invaluable to his Delta Force Team. The same trait that makes him suck at relationships. Single-minded focus on his career—and honing his ability to never miss a kill.

After a terrorist missile devastates his team and leaves him with only partial memory of a FUBARed rescue mission, he retains only one clear picture no one believes: the last face in his gunsight belonged to a prestigious American businessman. The man's wife has to know something, but the only way to get to her is go AWOL.

After her husband trades his family to tango with double-Ds, Lauren Collins decides her dogs are better judges of character. She's unaware how far her soon-to-be-ex's web of deceit reaches—until the only thing between her, her sons and a killer is a wounded Delta soldier who activates her sorely neglected X-chromosome like nobody's business.

Their instant attraction is kryptonite to Jack's injury-dulled edge. Thrust into a world of peril, political treachery and treason, Lauren has no choice but to trust Jack with her life. Even if she and her sons survive, she's not sure her heart will...

Warning: Contains a warrior who doesn't hesitate to lay his body on the line, more than one emotional love story to tug at your heart, and chaos at Chuck E. Cheese.

Available now in ebook and print from Samhain Publishing.

SAMHAIN
PUBLISHING

It's all about the story...

Romance

HORROR

www.samhainpublishing.com

WITHDRAWAL

For Every
Individual...

Renew by Phone
269-5222

Renew on the Web
www.imcpl.org

For General Library Information
please call 275-4100

CPSIA information can be obtained at www.ICGtesting.com
Printed in the USA
BVOW071003190712

295672BV00001B/24/P